The Whitechape

A madman on the loose, driven by dark urges and uncontrollable violence.

A hero, lost in the grip of addiction.

The greatest and most desperate criminal investigation in history.

Who will save us from Jack the Ripper?

The most terrifying and realistic Sherlock Holmes story ever told.

A Note about this Edition

The Gentleman's Edition contains the story and events from the original publication, but has been edited to remove all adult content. However, it is not intended for children.

WHITECHAPEL

The FINAL Stand of SHERLOCK HOLMES (Gentleman's Edition)

Bernard Schaffer

Table of Contents

Prologue

ACT I: PRETTY GIRLS MAKE GRAVES

One Two Three Four Five Six Seven Eight Nine

ACT II: COME ARMAGEDDON, COME

Ten Eleven Twelve Thirteen Fourteen Fifteen Sixteen

ACT III: YOU ARE THE QUARRY

Seventeen Eighteen Nineteen Twenty Twenty One Twenty Two Twenty Three Twenty Four

ACT IV: NOVEMBER SPAWNED A MONSTER

Twenty Five Twenty Six Twenty Seven Twenty Eight Twenty Nine Thirty Thirty One

Thirty Two Thirty Three Thirty Four

ACT V: A LIGHT THAT NEVER GOES OUT

Thirty Five Thirty Six Thirty Seven Thirty Eight Thirty Nine

About the Author

Copyright

Prologue

Annie Chapman slumped against the doorway to her landlord's office. "Tim? Ain't got money for me doss just yet. I feel quite ill. Any chance you might spot an ol' bunter?"

Tim Donovan counted the last coins stacked on his desk, jotting down the amount, and swept them into his register. He turned the key and dropped it down his shirt. "You've got money for beer, but none for bed, that it?"

"No. It's not like that, Tim," Annie said, fishing in her pocket. She lifted a torn piece of envelope to show him the pills within, "See? Had to get some medicine at the ward earlier. They took me last bit of change."

"I heard yeh downed a pint with Freddie Stevens just an hour ago. He told me it when he paid his doss. Crossingham's is a house of lodging, not charity, Annie Chapman. No doss money, no doss."

Annie shrugged, putting the pills back in her pocket. "Not a big 'fing. Never mind, then, Tim."

Donovan sighed. "Listen, why don't you go and see Brummy? He fancies you. See if he'll pay your way tonight."

Annie shook her head, "No, don't want to do that. Brummy's angry with me because I told him I'd take care of him if he bought us a pint last week, but I was just trying to get the pint."

"Yeh don't like Brummy?"

"It's not that." Annie lowered her eyes, "Just prefer strangers. People I never have to see again. Hold us a bed, all right?"

"Wait a tick. I was just reading about that girl they found last week. Some poor bird named Polly Nichols. Paper said her throat was cut from ear to ear, an' they found her body right over on Buck's Row. Dangerous out there. Lots of strange people about. I think you should go see Brummy and square with him."

"You're a sweetie for caring, Tim. I am coming back for that room, so don't let it." Annie left Donovan's office, heading down the steps, calling back to him, "I'll soon be back."

Donovan shook his head, frowning as Annie descended the stairs. He opened his ledger and penciled one of the rooms as occupied, leaving the "PAID" space open under Annie's name.

Dorset Street ran from Crispin to Commercial Street, and Crossingham's Lodging House sat in the Spitalfields section of the East End. There were so many flophouses that locals called it "Dosset Street." Annie had stayed for varying lengths of time at the Brittania, the Blue Coat Boy, Commercial Street Chambers, and the Horn of Plenty, but none of them would even let her in the door without money-in-hand. There were other houses, near Flower and Dean Street, but Annie would not venture into that area alone. Even within the whole stinking cesspool of Whitechapel, that particular quarter of a mile was infamous. Annie had heard Polly Nichols, the dead girl in the paper, was from around those parts. Really no surprise there.

No one seemed to be about on Commercial Street at that hour. Annie looked down Little Paternoster Row and continued on. What she needed was a generous drunk she could take care of with a quick rub off. She did not feel up for much more than that. As she turned toward Spitalfields Market, fishing a bit of baked potato from her pocket, she let out a long, slow burp into the cool September air.

The beer provided earlier by Freddie Stevens had cooled her fever, and now she was worried about her stomach. If it took a bad turn, she'd be retching beer, potato, and several small white medicinal pills all over the street. Waste of the money she'd spent at the ward then. She found a bench and sat down, waiting for her belly to settle. The wheels of a hansom cab turned across the cobblestones of Hanbury Street at Brick Lane. The horse's hooves stopped, and the rear of the cab opened. It was too murky to see the man exiting, but as he shut the door behind him, the horse began walking again, leading the carriage away.

Annie munched her potato as the man began making his way toward her up Hanbury. She did not think he saw her yet. The sixth anniversary of her daughter Emily's death had come and gone with Annie refusing to acknowledge it. She had drunk herself stupid and spent the day in a jail cell.

Ah, John, she thought. He was no good for work, no good for anything really, except drinking. Annie begged and begged the landlord to let them stay, crying how Emily's condition would only deteriorate rapidly once they were on the street. The landlord did not care. He sent the police to remove them, and one of them cracked John across the skull with his nightstick when John protested.

The man was coming closer. Almost time to call out to him.

It occurred to Annie that Emily's eighteenth birthday was coming up that September, and it would be time to visit her grave. She would visit John's as well.

It was only a few short weeks after they were kicked out of their flat that Emily pressed up against her mother in the dark alley they had been staying in, shivering, complaining of pain. Annie kissed her child's head, stroking her hair, whispering that it would be all right as long as they stayed together. Emily never woke up.

Annie and John agreed that it would be best if they simply went their separate ways and leave one another in peace. It was only after they parted that John began to reveal the content of his character. He sent Annie an allowance through the post every week, tracking her down wherever she was staying. In 1886 Annie was living with a man in Spitalfields, and even when John found out, he still sent her the money. Good man, Annie thought. Never find another like him. When the money stopped coming that December, Annie assumed it was because John was finally tired of supporting her and her habits. She was wrong, though. John was dead.

Annie blinked, trying to pay attention to the man coming closer through the darkness of Hanbury Street. He was near enough that Annie called out, "Hello, guv'ner!" kicking her legs back and forth on the bench, more excitedly than she felt. "Feeling good natured this evening?"

"I suppose so," the man said.

"Care for any company to while away the time?" she said.

The man looked her up and down. The wide brim of his top hat blocked Annie from seeing much of his face. She could see that he was younger than she, and well-kept. One of the posh West Enders who liked to come down and slum it up with East End bunters, she thought. "I was looking for somewhere that is quiet and dark," he said.

"I know just the place," Annie said, getting up from the bench. "Gladly take you there if you got a thruppence." The man nodded. "Good," Annie said. "For a few extra I'll even kiss it."

"Will you?"

Annie nodded, "Yes, if you've got the coin." She put her hand to his chest, cupping it close, showing the man how it was done. "Put your money right in me palm, like that. There's plenty a robbers about that'd love to knock one a' us on the head while we is settling up. Can't have that happen, now can I? Not to me fine, handsome new friend. But you have nothing to fear, my dear. Ol' Annie will protect you from the things that go bump in the night," she said, bumping her hip against his, and laughing.

"Your name is Ann?" the man said.

"Yes. Well, Annie." Annie held out her hand. He put several coins in her palm. Annie checked the alley behind the Hanbury Street houses, picking a spot next to a fence. She hiked her skirt and moved into the shadow between the fence and the steps leading to the back of the house. "Put it in me this way first," she whispered, putting her hand on the wall and bending forward. "Annie's going to take real good care of you," she said, hiking her skirt up to her waist and poking her bottom toward the man.

He stepped close to her and hesitantly touched her waist. He squeezed the pale white flesh of Annie's meaty bottom. "There you go," Annie said. "That feels nice."

"No," the man said, taking his hands away instantly as if repulsed. "I want you to tell me that you hate it."

Annie smiled in the shadows, burying her face quickly in her arm. He was one of those types, she thought. "All right," Annie sighed. "Don't do it. I hate it. Do you want me to struggle a bit?"

"Call me a beast," he whispered, pressing close against her.

"You are quite a little beastie, dearest," Annie said, covering her mouth to stifle a giggle. Suddenly, the man yanked her hair straight back, snapping her chin into the air, and Annie felt something sharp pierce the soft flesh beneath her jaw.

Act One

PRETTY GIRLS MAKE GRAVES

One

The interior of Twenty-Two One B was dimly lit by the flickering gaslights of Baker Street far below. Their illuminations slipped through narrow gaps in the curtains as wind blew through our poorly shuttered windows, rattling the glass panes. The Great Detective sat across from me wrapped in a worn velvet smoking jacket, sucking his pipe silently. His thin face was gaunter than I'd ever seen it and his eyes drawn to serpentine slits. I cleared my throat, finally summoning the will to say, "Holmes, I have wonderful news. Miss Mary Morstan has agreed to be my wife."

Holmes removed the pipe from his mouth and inspected its contents. He reached into the small pouch on the side-table and gathered several pinches of aromatic tobacco, packing it carefully inside the pipe and relit it. Finally, after a long time he blew out a thick, stream of smoke and said, "I expect you'll be leaving Baker Street then?"

I paused, waiting to see if he was making a joke. "I am utterly serious, Holmes. This is no jest. I am getting married."

"Are you waiting for me to congratulate you?"

"That would be the standard reaction to the announcement of pending nuptials, I suppose."

"Perhaps for those who see such things as occasion to celebrate," he said. "Personally, I cannot fathom why you would want to do something so foolish."

"Foolish?" I scoffed. "How can you say that? Mary is quite a beauty. Also, she is loyal, intelligent, and charming."

"Intelligent, indeed," Holmes sniffed. Suddenly, his face grew quite grave and he leaned forward, "Have you accidentally impregnated this girl? If that's the case, there is no need to do something so foolish. I know of a few doctors who can remedy that quite easily."

"How dare you! That type of talk is beneath even you."

"Fine," he sighed. "Farewell then, Watson. I will be able to find other ways to content myself with you no longer here." Holmes reached above the fireplace for the cocaine bottle upon the mantle, and I snatched it away before he could grab it.

Holmes and I now stood face to face as I held the bottle at my side, away from his reach. "Why is it so hard for you to congratulate me?"

"I congratulate you, Watson," Holmes said, looking hungrily at the bottle. "Does that content you? Hand it over." When I did not move, Holmes seized my arm, trying to wrench the bottle from my hand. "Give me the cocaine, Watson! Run off with your sweetie and be out of my life forever if you want, just hand me the damned bottle!"

I shoved him and Holmes fell backwards into his chair with a cry. Normally I would never have been able to fight him off, but after weeks of heavy usage of his damned cocaine and morphine, he was like a frail old man, and he collapsed like an unstrung puppet. "You do not mean that," I said, catching my breath. "I think your jealousy and this poison have affected your mind."

Holmes snorted, "Jealous? Be serious, Watson. I would rather die than marry some little orphaned rantipole who cannot help but fall for the first handsome man that pays her but a speck of attention. Just give me my bottle and go away."

I slipped the bottle into my pocket, out of his sight. "Perhaps you are not jealous of me, then, but Mary. You are afraid she is stealing me away from you."

"That is quite enough, Watson. I am weary of your foolishness."

"Admit you do not want me to leave."

"Why? Would you stay if I said so?" Holmes said.

"Say it. Admit that you are more than just some damned machine. Be honest, just this one time."

"As God is my witness, Watson, I would like nothing more than for you to get as far and as fast away from me this very instant."

"Fine." I grabbed my coat and hat. "You have made it quite clear that my companionship is of little value to you. Farewell."

Holmes's voice suddenly became soft, "Watson?"

"What?" I said sharply, expecting he'd finally come to his senses and was about to apologize.

"The bottle."

I cursed and threw it at him, striking him in the chest. I slammed the apartment door shut so hard that pictures on the stairwell rattled as I descended toward Mrs. Hudson's apartment. Mrs. Hudson opened her door and poked her head out, "What is all that racket about?"

"Him!" I said, jerking my thumb in the air. Mrs. Hudson peered at me over the tops of her spectacles down the bridge of her nose, looking like a stern nanny who'd just caught her charge snatching a biscuit without permission. I glanced back up at the top of the stairs and sighed. "I apologize for the noise, Mrs. Hudson. I am going to go for a walk in hopes that perhaps in a few hours things will have cooled down."

"For years I have watched all sorts of masked regents and befuddled policemen come through that door, all seeking the help of the Great Detective," she sighed, shaking her head. "Why on earth he was putting his talents to such paltry use, I never understood. I always suspected he was meant for something much greater. But then I realized that he is just biding his time before fate comes calling on him in an hour of desperation. And sometimes I fear for that moment, Dr. Watson. I truly do."

"Why?"

"Because then the world will truly need its Great Detective, Dr. Watson," she said, "but more than that, Sherlock Holmes will need you."

I recalled the day fate came walking through the door of 221 B Baker Street, in the form of Mary Morstan arriving at our doorstep and begging our assistance. Actually, she begged Holmes's assistance, since he had previously worked a case for her employer, Mrs. Cecil Forrester.

As is my custom, once Mary announced her intent to divulge personal details to Holmes, I excused myself and rose to leave. Her skin was so fair that it appeared almost alabaster, and curled wisps of light blonde hair escaped teasingly from her bonnet. "Please, do not leave, sir."

"You do not mind me staying?" I said, accidentally touching her hand. It was warm and delicate.

Holmes cleared his throat, breaking the moment. "Oh, do sit down, Watson. Obviously the young lady feels put at ease by your presence." I felt my cheeks flush with embarrassment, and Mary looked down, stifling a smile. Holmes chuckled, "I must confess that I often feel the same way, Miss Morstan. Doctor Watson is simply essential to my success and sometimes, even, to my very well-being. Have you, by any chance, heard the story of our adventures with the horrific beast haunting the moorlands of Dartmoor?" I looked at Holmes curiously, and he winked at me.

"No," Mary said, shifting in her seat. "It sounds dreadfully exciting."

"We were summoned to Devon on an investigation for a series of terrible murders. During the course of this, we began hearing reports that the killings were the work of a terrifying creature. We set off in search of this beast, expecting it all to be some sort of elaborate ruse concocted to frighten the locals and allow the culprit to steal off with the fortune of the Baskervilles," Holmes said. He lowered his voice and leaned closer to Mary, "But it was not. The beast was horribly real. We came upon it in the moor, face to face with its terrible glowing eyes, and bared fangs spilling with drool as it leapt to rip our very throats out."

"Good heavens! Whatever did you do?"

Holmes clapped me on the back, "My stalwart friend Watson calmly pulled his pistol and shot the wretched thing dead. His hand was as steady as our Mrs. Hudson drawing a morning cup of tea."

"Really?" Mary gasped. "Dr. Watson, you must have been in the military service, to remain so calm under such conditions."

"Well, in fact I did serve in the army."

"He did more than just serve, Miss Morstan," Holmes said. "He was wounded on the Afghan front in battle."

"Then you can be of some help to me," she said. "My father served in the Army of India, and his involvement there lies at the heart my problem. You simply must stay."

"All right, Miss Morstan. But, as I recall, Holmes, you fired your pistol at the same moment I did. And then, as the beast was about to devour poor Sir Henry, pumped five more rounds into its belly and put an end to its misery."

Holmes shook his head, sighing. "The details are but a blur to me, Watson. I was too filled with fright to properly recall. Thank heaven the good doctor is also talented enough to make a written account of our more noteworthy adventures."

"Oh, so you are an author as well as a man of action?"

"I have not published anything yet, but someday I hope to. Just a few short stories about our more interesting adventures, if anyone is interested in reading that sort of thing."

"You must tell me, what is the title for your adventure with this most ferocious beast of Dartmoor?"

"I am calling it '*The Adventure of the Great Detective and the Evil Snarling Beast Which Massacred Most of Devon County.*' What do you think?"

Neither Holmes nor Mary replied. Finally, Holmes cleared his throat, "So, Miss Morstan, what seems to be the trouble?"

Captain Arthur Morstan spent most of his daughter's life serving as an officer in Her Majesty's Indian Army on Andaman Islands. Upon his return to England, Captain Morstan vanished, never to be heard from again. However, on the first anniversary of her father's disappearance, Mary received a small pearl in a box via post with no return address, and no explanation. Another came the next year, and another after that, until she had received six in total. Finally, Mary received a letter asking her to meet with the sender of the pearls at the Lyceum Theater. This letter advised Mary that she could bring two companions with her if she was distrustful, but that they should not be police.

The game, as Holmes likes to say, was afoot. I set quickly to the task of recording the details of the investigation, in part, I confess, to have Mary appear in my writings. I made sure to detail my thoughts on her beauty. Once I'd finished the piece, titled "*The Sign of Four*," I stood by nervously as Mary read every page. It was the first thing I'd ever written that I felt I could be proud of. By the time Mary finished, there were tears in her eyes and she thanked me for giving her father such a noble eulogy. In the heat of the moment, I kneeled on the floor of the visiting room at the Forrester estate and confessed my love, telling her that I wanted nothing more than to spend my life with her. Much to my surprise, she agreed.

For as much as I wanted Mary in my life, I needed to keep her at arm's length from Holmes in his present condition.

Baker Street was covered in filth and trash from the evening commute as I returned home. I called out to the man leaning against the lamp-post across the street, where I needed to go. "You there! Look sharp, lad."

"Yes, sir!" he cried. He rushed out toward me, stepping around the piles of horse manure, hoisting his broom. "Hold on one second, sir," he said.

"How much?"

"A tuppence, sir."

I nodded, and waited for him to get ahead of me, sweeping the cobblestones clear of muck and grime enough so that they were fit for a gentleman to cross. Once he'd cleared a path, I dropped a two-pence coin into his palm. "Thank you, sir!" he said gratefully, as I continued toward the apartment.

"Holmes?" I called out as I made my way up the stairs. "You still awake, man? I want us to sort this out." There was no answer. I turned the lamp on, and as it flickered on, I saw him. His hands were spread across the lid of a box made of dark Moroccan thuya burl wood. The box's sturdy latches were painted bright gold, the kind that made a loud snapping sound when flipped open. Holmes's left sleeve was pulled up his arm, and a leather belt was tied tightly around his bicep. One of his syringes was sunk in the crook of his elbow and blood trickled from the needle, staining his chair. He was slumped over, head hanging down, moaning.

I plucked the needle from his arm and threw it on the floor in disgust, "You are quite a sight, Holmes."

He slowly lifted his head, eyes fluttering as he squinted, trying to focus. "You do not like what you see, Watson?" He fell back against the seat, letting out a great sigh. "Why should I care? You are looking at God's great joke. It is his cruel trick that I was given the tools and means to fight a great evil, but damned if there is one to be found."

Two

Montague Druitt's earliest memory was his sister's body slamming onto the spikes of the wrought iron fence that surrounded their mother's garden. The garden was just behind the Druitt's home and the spikes Georgiana landed on were far below the window of her bedroom, which had been converted from an attic.

Monty, as his family called him, was hiding in the garden playing with dolls he'd stolen from his older sister's room. He was making them do things to one another, delighted by the stiffness of his member as one doll stripped the other and tied it down with vines that grew between the fences. A large shadow passed over him with its arms spread and flapping like a great bird. He looked up, shielding his eyes as he peered into the sky, just as Georgiana landed on the fence.

She was impaled face down, staring directly at him, squirming on the spikes. One was speared through her throat, reducing her voice to hissing, gurgling noises as she sputtered his name.

Another spike stuck out of her side, opening her so that intestines spilled down the length of fence beneath. Cords of her innards uncoiled towards him, spooling all the way to the ground like a slime-ridden ladder.

Georgiana reached for him, fingers wriggling in the air. He ignored her, hesitantly touching the intestines, feeling their warmth and wetness.

Georgiana grabbed him by the collar, shaking him violently. Monty screamed, trying to wrench her hand away. Monty's screams brought his father running, who quickly began screaming on his own.

There was no funeral. Georgiana's body was placed in the wine cellar, covered by a sheet, until William made arrangements for her to be taken away. A carriage came to their home and the body was placed inside. When the carman strapped the horse and the carriage wheels turned down the dirt road leading away from their home, Dr. William Druitt collapsed in a sobbing heap on the front porch.

Ann Druitt's expression did not change as she watched the wagon pull away. She looked down at her weeping husband, then went back into the house and up the stairs without speaking.

For the next week, Monty's father moved about the house in complete silence, as if in a fog. He did not eat or speak to anyone, except for the late nights when he would come into Monty's room and hold the boy, kissing his forehead again and again.

One day, a new carriage arrived, coming down the path and Monty looked out the door in wonder as dust billowed up from the ground.

The carriage stopped and a young man in a British military uniform dismounted and smiled at him. William raced past Monty through the door and grabbed his eldest son excitedly, kissing him on the cheeks, thanking him over and over for coming home. Will waved for Monty to join them, and he regarded the boy for a moment, "You were just a little bloke when I left home, Monty. I cannot believe how much you have grown. I brought you something." Will reached in his pocket and produced a carved ivory elephant, which Monty took from him, eyes glowing.

That evening, the two brothers sat together in the front yard, leaning back on a large oak tree, looking up at the stars. "Do you like it so much in India, Will?" Monty asked, turning the elephant in his hands to see it from all sides. "Is that why you never come home?"

"There are other reasons, but I would rather we discuss them when you are older," Will said, blowing smoke rings from his pipe up toward the sky.

"Is it our mother?" Monty said. "Was she as cruel to you as she is to me and Georgiana?"

Will carefully regarded his younger brother and then played with his hair, "You are a startlingly bright young man, little brother. The worst thing about being in India is that I do not get to see you. Would you like to come visit me?"

"Yes!" Monty said, taking the pipe. "I want to join the Army when I am old enough. I bet everyone thought you were a hero when you went to fight the dirty Indian rebels." He sucked on the pipe eagerly, but retched when the hot bitter smoke filled his mouth, gagging him.

Will laughed while patting Monty on the back. "Well, be prepared for a battle long before you join the army. When I first signed up, the whole family was against the idea. Georgiana told me I was a barbarian for wanting to go slaughter innocent people who only wanted freedom from the oppressive East India Trading Company. That all changed after Cawnpore, though."

"What is Cawnpore?" Monty asked, spitting the pipe's foul taste from his mouth and handing it back to Will.

"Cawnpore was a garrison town for the Company. The British General stationed there was married to an Indian woman. He spoke the local language. When the rebellion started, he was a close friend to many of the high-ranking Indian members of the opposition. Even as the insurgents came closer and closer to Cawnpore, he thought his family and the people he protected would be safe, spared by his many connections to the local community."

"Were they?"

"No," Will said. "The bastards attacked his town, overwhelmed them and forced everyone to surrender to the resistance's leader, Nana Sahib. One hundred and twenty women and children were taken hostage by the Indian forces, imprisoned in the home of a local clerk. Nana Sahib then hired five men to kill every single one of them with hatchets. They say that by the next morning three women and three little boys were found hiding under the mountain of bodies. The women were forced to strip all of the corpses, and throw them into a well at the rear of the property. Once these proper English women had finished this gruesome task, the five men came and pushed them down into the darkness after their compatriots. The little boys were thrown down next."

"Alive?" Monty said.

"Yes, alive. I should not be telling you these things, Monty."

"Why do you say that, Will? I find it amazing!"

"Amazing? What the bloody hell is so amazing about that? You a sickie, Monty? That is what we call the boys in our unit who see something ghastly and think it's exciting, instead of wretched."

"No," Monty quickly added. "I am not a sickie."

"Of course you aren't. Come on then, enough of this nonsense," Will said, getting up. "Do you play cricket?"

"No. It looks too difficult."

"Of course it isn't. Playing that game is simply all we do in India. Starting tomorrow, I will teach you to play."

"India sounds wonderful, Will. Promise you will take me there someday."

Will put his hand on Monty's shoulder and said in a serious tone, "If it is the last thing we ever do together, I promise to take you there."

Will cut his pudding into small sections, sopping up the gravy politely, then smiling and sighing over each bite. "I will tell you this much, it is a sheer delight to eat food that does not have curry in it."

"I will thank you not to discuss that disgusting, foreign culture at my dinner table," Ann said.

Monty lifted his pudding and took a bite, quickly dabbing the gravy from the corners of his mouth before anyone noticed. He did not find the meal nearly as delicious as his brother, and was trying to finish it as quickly as possible.

Will nodded at him, pointing to a bit of gravy he'd missed. "Actually, Mother, at the risk of speaking further about things that disturb your delicate sensibilities, I need to talk to Father about something."

"William," Ann said through gritted teeth, "Do you hear him ruining my Sunday dinner?"

"Now, now, darling," William said, patting her hand. "Let the boy speak. It sounds important. Will, please use the utmost restraint."

"As you wish, father. I wanted to tell you that I am going to finish my service with the Army and return to England."

"Really? What are you planning on doing?" William asked.

"I would like to go to the University," he said, adding quickly, "but not for medicine. I want to pursue legal studies."

William's face darkened at first, but he managed a nod. "Well, I am pleased that I will no longer have to worry about you dodging bullets in India. You have my blessing."

"Thank you, Father."

"I hope you do not intend to stay here," Ann said. "I have my hands full taking care of these two, and will not suffer to be worked like a slave in my own home. Your father refuses to hire on anyone to assist me, as much as I beg him."

William shook his head. "Let us not discuss this now. There is no need for things to become agitated."

Monty recalled the last person who worked in the home, and how Ann had attacked the woman and chased her from the home at point-of-knife. It was one of the few times that he'd seen his father lose his temper and shout that he would never subject another living soul to his mother's insanity. She'd ripped handfuls of hair out of her head and shrieked furiously as William locked her in her bedroom and told her through the door that he would let her out when she collected herself. It took two days.

"I will be leaving for Blackheath in a few weeks," Will said. "There is nothing to fear, mother."

Monty's head whipped toward him, "You're leaving?"

"Just for a little while, Monty," Will patted him on the shoulder. "The time will fly until I return, you'll see. Once I am home, I promise you and I will have grand adventures together. Does that sound all right?"

That night, the two brothers lie in Monty's room. The young boy listened intently to everything his older brother said about the mysterious and faraway places he'd been to. Will talked about interesting foods he'd eaten and unusual instruments that made sounds stranger than anything Monty could imagine. He talked about wild animals that would stalk you in the darkness and slice you open if you did not kill them first.

Every day when Dr. William Druitt finally came home from Portsmouth, Monty would be standing by the front window listening for the sound of the cab's wheels crunching along the country road. The boy smiled brightly when William emerged from the carriage carrying his worn leather medical bag. William always tipped his top hat at the cab's driver as he passed, entering the house.

Sometimes Monty and his father played a game, where William would pretend not to remember where he'd hidden a treat for Monty, and the boy would have to guess which pocket held the taffy, or sometimes a small, wooden toy.

"When can I go with you to work, father? I want to be a doctor like you."

William hugged him tightly. "When you are old enough, if you still want to be one, I will train you to be as I am."

One evening, as father exited the cab he was met by a man and his son. The man introduced himself, and William shook his hand, gesturing for the two of them to enter the house.

"Monty?" William said, opening the door to let the others in. "This is Mr. Jack Reed. He is the new manager of the farm next to us, and his son Clifton is your age. Come say hello so you can make friends."

Clifton was handsome and tanned. Monty smiled and they waved to each other quietly. "Can you play cricket?"

"No," Clifton said.

"Come on and I'll teach you."

Clifton was instantly better at the sport that Monty was. The boy was strong and sure of himself after spending his entire life on one farm or another. He had been helping his father scythe wheat and chop wood since he was old enough to hold the tools. The only consolation Monty could find was that Clifton knew every possible thing about animals that Monty could think to ask, and could describe in intimate detail how cows were butchered and how chickens behaved when beheaded.

Clifton had also seen several cow births, and at Monty's insistence, related the colors of the juices that spilled out of the animal's orifices, and the gelatinous sack the newborn calves slid out in.

One day the two boys were playing in Monty's room, and Clifton was complaining that he was tired of telling the same stories over and over, and no longer wanted to play cricket or any of the other games they knew. "Do you ever want to become lost from everyone around you? To hide yourself so that no one may find you?" Clifton said.

"I have one place," Monty said, "but it is a secret place and you must swear to never tell anyone you were ever there."

Clifton nodded eagerly and Monty took his hand, leading him down the hall toward the staircase. He instructed him on tiptoeing silently around the jars and toiletries. He told him which steps to avoid stepping on and keep them from squeaking.

As soon as they were in the room, Clifton surprised Monty by kissing him on the lips. Monty stepped back and swiped his hand across his mouth in disgust and said, "What did you do that for?"

"It is just for practice, Monty," Clifton said. "So you can do it right when you kiss a woman for the first time."

Monty looked down, feeling his cheeks grow hot. Clifton came closer to him, pressing his chest against Monty's and lifting his chin. Their lips touched again and Monty relaxed, letting Clifton control him. He lost himself in the embrace, not hearing the door open behind them.

"Do you like how you look?"

Tears spilled hot and thick down Monty's face. He could not bear to look in the mirror. Ann snatched him by the back of his neck, shaking him. "Look! Look!" she screamed. She swung the thick belt across his bottom again, stinging one of the open wounds. Monty howled in pain.

Porcelain dolls lined the shelves of the room. Rows and rows of wide-eyed, evil-looking, ceramic children stared at Monty in all his humiliation. None of them had been touched since Georgiana took a running leap past the bed and out of the window.

"Look at yourself, in all your filth," Ann said, grabbing a handful of Monty's hair.

Monty finally looked in the mirror, seeing the bright yellow flower print of Georgiana's dress. For a moment, he thought he saw his dead sister's face, wearing the dress and winced. Georgiana looked as she had the day she died, face swollen and blood-stained. This face, however, was Monty's own, covered and smeared in the makeup his mother had forced him to apply.

"Do you like being a girl?" she demanded, shaking him.

"No," Monty said.

"Do you want to be a girl?" she screamed, bending so that her mouth was directly in his ear.

"No!"

"Do you like wearing your sister's dress, sinner?"

"No!"

Ann whipped him across the back and shoulders, making the boy scream even louder than her own shrieks of "Never, ever do that again! Filthy animal! Filthy, wretched beast!" The leather snapped across his skin, raising welts with each strike. She lost her grip, and the buckle of the belt clipped across the back of his head, cutting it open.

Monty felt the split flesh at the base of his skull and panicked, screaming that he was going to die. Ann grabbed another dress from Georgiana's closet and threw it at him, telling him to press it against the wound.

He spent that night locked in Georgiana's room. The moon was enormous and shined brightly through the wide windows surrounding the bed. With a start, he realized his sister was on the bed at his feet, staring through the window with black hollow eyes. Her belly and throat were split open and the organs spiraled from her like tentacles, glistening in the light of the moon.

Three

Dr. William Druitt was never informed of the incident, but he quickly took notice of his wife's cold behavior toward their youngest son. Whether it was his guilt from losing a child, or his desire to protect the boy from her hostility, he invited Monty to come to work with him. A permanent position was not offered, only a conditional invitation. His continued apprenticeship would depend on his performance and attention to detail.

On his first day, Monty stood impatiently by the front door, waiting for the carriage to arrive. Finally, it was rolling down the road toward their house and Monty passed William his tall, black hat, but insisted on carrying the medical bag. Once inside the carriage, William mopped his forehead and sat back. He clapped his son on the shoulder and smiled gently, "I am proud to be taking you to Portsmouth, Monty. I had originally hoped your brother would be the one making this trip with me, but instead he chose to go gallivanting around India, blowing the place to bits. Now he seems content to be a solicitor for the Western Circuit."

"I am proud as well, Father."

"Excellent. Now, before we get there, I want to tell you something. People in other parts of this country live in a substantially different way than we do. Not everyone is as fortunate as we. Do you understand?"

"Will I get to cut people open?" Monty asked.

"Absolutely not. Did you hear what I said? I will stop the carriage this instant if you are not paying attention to me."

"I understand, father."

"All right. As far as your duties go, you will assist me by cleaning my surgical instruments, and in labeling the preservation jars. When we do not have any patients, I want you to sweep or mop." William turned to Monty, looking at him sternly. "Under no circumstances are you to enter the operating room when I am with a patient, unless I give you specific instructions. You are to stay in the specimen laboratory during those times."

"But—"

"This is not open for discussion."

"Do you not think I am ready to witness your surgeries?"

William put his hand on the boy's head and tussled his hair. "Perhaps you are ready, son. But perhaps it is I who am not. Soon the day will come when you are a man and able to see all of the grim realities this world has to offer. I just prefer it to not be all at once, and not today."

As their carriage pulled into the train station, Monty was impressed by the crowd of well-dressed men and women standing on the platform, surrounded by swirling steam from the engine. He smiled in wonder, studying the train's gigantic mechanical gears as they smoked, banged and hissed. He had never ridden the train before, and was taken by William's understanding of how to acquire tickets and who to present them to. The men on the train assisted the women to their seats and lifted their belongings up onto the overhead track. William tipped his hat to women as they arrived onto the train, and shook hands with several men who greeted him by name. The train hissed, belching a giant gust of smoke that rained ash on Monty's hand through the open window. With a loud whistle and a shake, they began to move. "You might as well try to sleep, Monty. Portsmouth is quite far."

The train rocked back and forth as it sped along, soothing Monty into a light sleep. A whistle blew and William tapped him on the arm, "Get up, Monty. We have to go."

Monty cleared his eyes and looked through the window at a sign that read Portsmouth. Wisps of foul-smelling fog swirled past the train car as Monty leaned forward, trying to see. Buildings blocked his view, one after the other, much taller than any he had ever seen. Everything was grey, carved from concrete and steel, and dripping wet from a brown mist that descended over the entire city.

Even from inside the train car, the sounds of Portsmouth filled Monty with both terror and excitement. Men hawked goods from the train platform, calling out in loud carnival-barker voices. Women screamed, and police blew sharply pitched whistles. Carriages crashed into the pavements when the horses pulling them veered out of each other's ways and the carmen operating the cabs shouted angrily at one another.

Monty gripped his father's hand tightly as they left their seats and began moving toward the exit, scanning the people waiting to board the train. These people were dirty. Their faces were filthy, dripping grey sweat down their necks. William pulled him through the crowd, whispering in a quick, hurried tone, "Do not make eye contact with anyone, Monty. Do not look afraid. Do not look at even the tallest buildings in wonder. Act as if you are in a hurry. Act as if you belong here." They reached the entrance to the train station, and there was a cab waiting for them. William lifted Monty into it, and shut the door tightly behind them.

"Good morning, Dr. Druitt," the carman said. "Made it again, eh? How was your trip?"

"Excellent. This is my son, Montague."

"Montague?" the driver said. "That's a big name for such a small lad."

William smiled, putting his hand his son's shoulder. "I wanted to name him Jack, but his mother insisted on naming him after her father. He will grow into it though. Today was his first time on the train."

"That right, Mr. Montague? First time in Portsmouth, then?"

"Yes, sir."

"Different here than back home, I reckon," the carman said. "You get used to it. Mind yourself, though. Desperate people do desperate things."

Monty stared in wonder at the swarms of people crowding the streets of Portsmouth. Women leaned against the walls of broken-down buildings and called out to anyone who passed, "Feeling good natured, sir?" Children in ragged clothing coughed and spat black clumps of phlegm into the sewers, looking up at him as the carriage flew past.

"Are these the people we are going to help, father?"

"The ones out there?" William said, laughing. "No, I am afraid not, Monty. Unfortunately, there is no money in that. Those folks cannot afford food, let alone my services. It is already too late for my clients."

"I do not understand," Monty said.

"If I wanted to cut off tumors and spend my day treating tuberculosis, I could work in Dorchester or Weymouth. Multitudes of sailors there are willing to promise payment, but then they ship off to Africa, never to be seen again. A prostitute will try to barter, promising goods that no one in their right mind would take. In medicine, there is only one sure way of receiving money, and that is from the dead."

The horse pulled their cab to the curb, underneath a small grey sign that read "*Medical Offices of William Druitt Sr.*" Monty waved to the carman, as William unlocked the door, telling Monty to come along. "No time to waste, son. Let us see what work the police surgeon has left for us to do today."

Monty followed his father into the operating room and gasped. The stench was unlike anything he had ever experienced, unlike anything he thought possible. He had become accustomed to the smell of dead animals in the woods near their house, and the spoiled food that his mother had forgotten to remove from their stores, but this was quite different. Tears formed in his eyes as the gasses stung them and snot began to drip from his nose down his chin. "Excellent," William said, removing his coat and his hat as he glanced at the corpses laid out in his operating lab.

Three dead bodies lie lined up on racks in the room's center. One of the corpses was a docksman whose skin had turned various shades of blue and black. His fingers were outstretched and his face frozen in a look of shock. The other two were women, and they had been dead longer. Their faces were swollen, with fat, puckered lips and bulging eyes that stared at the ceiling. One of the women had a huge, expanded stomach, as if she'd sucked in more air than she should have and could not let it out. William looked at her and chuckled, "We had better get to her first. She looks ready to pop."

"Pop?" Monty gulped, covering his mouth.

Each body was dressed as it had been when the person died, as if the corpses had walked into William's office and laid themselves down on the rack waiting to be found. Flies buzzed around their bodies, and Monty realized that the smell reminded him of something he could not place. Something familiar.

Georgiana.

"There is only one designated police surgeon for this entire area of England," Dr. Druitt explained. "He is hired by the police departments to investigate deaths that are, for whatever reason, suspicious, or undetermined. Those bodies all get collected by the police and brought here for examination. I conduct an autopsy and record my findings for the surgeon. He signs my reports, as he does for all of the other doctors who contract their services to him in this region. I am paid depending on the number of bodies I examine. Say what you will about Her Majesty's governance, but she pays her bills on time."

Dr. Druitt pointed Monty toward a room in the rear. "I have a set of instruments in the specimen laboratory that need to be cleaned. I'll begin here with the ones in my bag. You can also help prepare my specimen trays. Give me one tray for each body set up and labeled exactly as you see this one, which is already outfitted. Take it with you, and arrange the others precisely the same way."

Monty nodded, carrying the tray into the room. There were rows and rows of shelves holding labeled jars containing every organ imaginable. He passed a large jar of two dozen eyeballs floating in yellow liquid. Severed orbs tailed by stringy rectus muscles that trailed lazily behind the eyeballs. There were hearts of all shapes and sizes, each marked with a name and age. Some appeared healthy and strong. Others looked sickly and discolored. Monty inspected jars that held potato-shaped kidneys, jars packed with winding lengths of intestines, others with appendices, gall bladders, spleens, pancreases, and more. He twirled each jar, watching the organs move within their formaldehyde pools.

William unzipped his medical bag and began setting his tools on an empty tray table. Monty crept to the door and opened it slightly, just enough to watch his father undress one of the women, about to cut her open. William looked up at him, surgical blade still high in the air. "Out, Monty."

"Yes, father," Monty said, backing away from the door.

After two years of working with his father, Monty could properly name and spell all of the organs and muscles shown in the diagrams of his father's medical books without reading the text. Monty squinted, holding the book closer to the candle's flame on his bedside table. He ran his finger over the drawing, tracing the branching arterial lines that travelled from under the jaw all the way to the groin. His prized possession was his father's worn "Grays

Anatomy: Descriptive and Surgical" and he set it down carefully, then snuffed out his candle. A knock at the window startled him. He saw Clifton grinning stupidly at him through the window, clinging to the upper portion of its frame. "Monty! Open it quickly, I'm about to fall!"

Monty stormed to the window and heaved it open, clutching Clifton and yanking him into the bedroom. "What are you doing here? Spying on me? I ought to thrash you."

"I was not spying!" Clifton said. "No one answers the door when I knock."

"People in polite society call that a clue," Monty said. "Mother said she'd kill us both if we ever saw one another again."

"Well, she doesn't have to know now, does she?"

"If she catches you here, she'll have your testes for earrings."

"My what?"

"Your nutmegs!" Monty said.

"Then best we hope that she is a sound sleeper."

Monty paused, listening for the sound of anyone coming. His house was quiet, and the hallway dark save for the moonlight cutting through the shutters. "Come on," Monty said, waving toward the door. "I'll get in less trouble for being outside the house than I will for having you in it." He took off his nightshirt, aware that Clifton was watching. "Hand me those clothes on the floor, but try and walk lightly."

Together, they crept down the hallway, past Ann's room. The door was shut. Monty's heart beat so rapidly that he thought the pounding would wake his mother, and he clearly envisioned her throwing the door open, pale face shining in horror. William's door was open, but he was snoring loudly, his stockinged feet hanging over the sides of the bed. They made their way down the stairs, seeing Will standing at the foot of the steps.

"Christ!" Clifton gasped, nearly turning and running back up the steps.

"Stop!" hissed Monty, grabbing the boy and holding him tight with one hand clamped over his mouth. "It's my brother."

"What the bloody hell are you two doing skulking around the house in the dark?" Will grinned.

"What are you doing here in the middle of the night?" Monty whispered. "Keep your voice down. If mother wakes up we'll be in for it."

Will shrugged, walking away from the steps and into the kitchen. "I came to give you that adventure I promised, but it seems as if you're already about to go on one."

They followed him. "What sort of adventure?" Monty called out.

Will turned, eyes cast low so that his face was covered in shadows. "There is a beast loose in the woods. Some say it is a wolf."

"What? Ridiculous," Clifton said.

"You think," Will said, smiling. He reached into a dirty military knapsack and removed a bottle from within, setting it on the counter. "I'll have you know there have been reports of a wolf nearby, terrorizing the farm animals. I intend to go out and find it tonight."

"You're joking, Will. Father said wolves have been extinct in England for over two hundred years."

"Maybe it is high time they returned then?" he said, uncorking the bottle. He lifted it to his nose and inhaled deeply, moaning as it entered his nostrils. "You boys are not afraid, are you?"

Clifton sniffed, "Of course not. But I live on the farm next door and I've heard no such reports. All of our animals are accounted for."

"Perhaps they did not think the news fit for such young, delicate ears."

"We're nearly thirteen," Monty said.

"Is that right? Hmm. Well, that seems far too young to go off into the woods at night. I think I'll just drink this all by myself and have a look then."

Just as Will lifted the bottle to his mouth and was about to drink, Monty asked, "Is that wine?"

"No, no, no, silly boy," Will said. "It is something much different. Here, smell it." Will held it under both their noses. "There is an ancient text in India called the Vedas, written before Britain existed. Those texts describe a god that disguised itself as a plant, grown in the mountains that Indra and Agni ground into powder and drank. It is said that any mortal who drinks it is flung into divinity."

"Is that it?" Monty whispered, staring at the bottle.

Will drank deeply from it, setting it back on the counter, half-empty. "There is only one way to find out," he said, wiping his mouth. "Off I go, boys. I will see this monster for myself."

Will opened the back door and vanished into the darkness. Clifton and Monty looked at one another silently, then down at the bottle.

The boys stared in wonder at the iridescent trails of modulating light left by the lightning-bugs, connecting them all to one another. Clifton laughed, putting his hand out to grab one of the glowing threads and held his hand up, seeing pure light dripping from his fingers.

Monty realized it was just a spider's web clinging to Clifton's hand but as he tried to pull it away, the web stuck to him as well. Monty found himself bound to Clifton, unable to pull away.

"How strange that I never recognized the song that each cricket was singing. Do you hear them Monty? So many different voices."

Monty nodded, staring up at the tree tops which seemed only a few feet away from the surfaces of the stars. "I am going to climb them," Monty said. "I'll never return."

"Oh don't be silly," Clifton laughed. Suddenly, he went silent. "Did you hear that?"

"Stop trying to scare me."

"Be silent," Clifton said. "I hear something."

A horrible scream rang out in the woods. Both boys dropped to the ground instantly. The voice was like a terrified child or woman. "What the hell was that?" Monty whispered. His hands were shaking uncontrollably, and he felt like he might vomit. The drink had been bitter, tasting of bark and smelling like ivy, scratching his throat as he swallowed. His eyes burned, and he was sweating as if it were a summer day.

"Let's go back," Clifton said, pulling on his shoulder.

"I hear something again." Monty lifted his head in the air, cocking his ear toward the darkness. Branches were creaking and cracking, and something large was being dragged through the woods. "Over there."

Both of the boys bent low, crouching as they approached. Ahead in a cluster of trees, hidden in the shadows, a small calf slammed down onto the leaves and dirt of the wood's floor.

The creature came out of the shadows hunched over, its claws sweeping over the calf. It struggled, as if trying to rise, but the beast struck it back down to the ground with a heavy blow. The calf kicked wildly, but the beast grabbed it by one of its legs and pinned it down, leaning over the bleating animal and ripping it open with one long shining claw. Blood sprayed into the cold air.

Clifton moaned in terror, and Monty felt the back of his leg go warm and wet against him. The beast grabbed the calf by the scruff of its neck, yanking it backwards and sinking its claw into the exposed pale throat.

"Christ, it's Will," Clifton groaned. "It's your brother. He's become a demon! Run, Monty, or the devil will claim us too!" He stumbled out of the thicket and darted through the darkness.

Monty could not move. The beast looked down at him with bright red glowing eyes, and beckoned, offering him the dripping meat of the calf. "Will?" Monty whispered.

The beast's height and shape changed as it stepped into the moonlight, taking its twisted, grinning face. "Come, Monty. Share in the kill. Join me."

"No," Monty gasped, backing away. "No, I can't! Clifton, wait!"

He broke into a sprint, tearing blindly through the thick, thorny brush. By the time he found Clifton, both were wheezing and bloodied from branches whipping them as they escaped. Neither of them spoke, listening to the silence of the woods save for the birds and crickets. "How far did we run?" Clifton huffed.

"I do not know," Monty said, clutching his side. "Hopefully far enough."

"You have a branch stuck in your hair." Clifton laid his hand on Monty's shoulder and unwound the branch from his hair. "Try not to move while I pull it out. There."

"You have thorns stuck in your shirt." Monty pulled Clifton's shirt tight and plucking the thorns out. The two of them were close enough for Monty to feel Clifton's breath on his neck.

Monty pulled him close and the two of them sank down together into the moss, entangling themselves beneath the bare, pale moon.

William left trays for Monty with all of the organs separated and Monty would carry the tray into the specimen laboratory to measure, weigh them, place them in a jar, then label and seal.

"Monty? Bring us a set of instruments," William said.

Monty leaned out the door, "The ones you have are clean, father."

William looked up at the boy, one eyebrow cocked. Monty nodded and collected a tray of tools. He selected a pair of sturdy forceps, several clamps, a variety of bone handled saws and blades, tweezers, several sutures. He carried the tray out, expecting to see a collection of organs and a cadaver on the operating table with a sheet covering its open body, as William always made sure to do before Monty had to enter the room.

Instead, William was seated, rubbing his chest. He was sweating heavily and breathing as if he could not fill his lungs. William waived for Monty to put the tray down. A naked woman lied on the table, untouched. Monty set down the tray and went to William's side. "What is it? Are you all right?"

"Just a damned tightening in my chest," William said, cringing. "No bother. I've been working too hard lately, pushing myself too much. This is the last one. I may-" William had to stop talking, needing to take several breaths before continuing. "I may require your assistance, Monty."

Monty looked at the woman and swallowed. Her milk white skin was marbled with blue veins that ran the length of her body. Her sagging breasts peaked with indented nipples and areolas the size of Monty's palm, hanging sideways against her inner arms. He had never seen a completely naked woman before. It occurred to him that several hours ago, this woman had been living and breathing. Hours ago she might have died of shock to think herself naked and exposed in this manner under his astounded eye.

Her belly was riddled with wrinkled skin. The indentations from the waist of her skirt were etched in her flesh eternally by rigor mortis. Monty stared at the furry black bush of hair between her legs. "What do you need me to do?"

"Help me to my feet," William said. Together, they got William up from his seat and over to the table. "First, we must ascertain that she is dead." Monty laughed sharply. "This is of the utmost seriousness, Monty. You cannot imagine how many people are mistakenly thought dead. I've heard horror stories of careless doctors who do not take the time to conduct the tests. Fetch me a scarificator and three cupping glasses."

Monty brought William's tools from the cupboard. The scarificator was an older model, made of brass with several wicked blades that shot through the edge at the push of a button. William took the device and held it to the woman's bicep, pressing the button and shooting the blades into her flesh. "Write this down, Monty. No blood flow observed on upper limb." He placed the scarificator on the inside of the woman's thigh and pressed the button. When he moved it, Monty could see a dozen slashes in her flesh, but no blood leaking through. Monty documented that as well.

William struck a match and held it inside each of the cupping glasses, placing them onto the woman's belly, breast, and thigh. The skin inside the glass did not rise or change color. "No epidermal response to cupping glasses," William said. "Hand me a needle." William took the ten-inch needle and pierced the sole of the woman's left foot, driving it in above her heel until the tip poked under the skin on the arch of her foot. "No response to that either. I think it is conclusive that she is dead. We may begin."

At William's instruction, Monty did a quick sketch of the woman's body, noting the position of her arms and legs, which had been in the same position as when they arrived at the office. Monty stared in wonder as his father took a knife and slit her forehead from ear to ear, pulling her scalp free with a firm tug on her hair. "Next, we expose the skull and check for injuries."

The skull's crown was pearl white, and at the center was a large circular indentation, chipping the bones around it outward in a spider web. "Here we are. Make a drawing of this, please," William instructed.

Monty quickly sketched the wound while William read through the paperwork underneath the woman's clothes. "Her husband reported that she fell down the stairs after drinking too much brandy. I think that wound looks more like a hammer's blow. I believe it is safe to say that the police will want to speak to this man at length. Give me the saw." William sawed across the scalp line, scattering white bone dust on his clothes and the floor. He went around her entire head with the saw, then twisted and uncapped the woman, revealing her brain. "Get me a bucket," William said. Monty held the bucket underneath the skull as blood and clumps of brain matter leaked into it. William severed the connective nerves of the wet gray mass inspected it between his thumbs over top of the bucket. "Here it is," he grinned, spreading the gelatinous surface of the brain flat with his thumbs. "Do you see the clotted blood where the skull was broken?"

Monty nodded. William told him to fetch a tray for the brain, which was set on the table.

"Help me flip her over," William said. Monty grabbed the woman beneath her cold arms and pulled her toward him, feeling her breasts squash against his chest. "Let her down on her chest." He cut her open down the length of her spine, along either side, exposing the knotted bones of her spinal cord. He inspected each length of the spine, and grunted with satisfaction. "Now flip her back over. Hand me the larger knife." William's hand shook as he wrapped his fingers around the bone handle. "This is why we always sharpen our knives at the end of business on Friday, Monty. We never know which one we will need them that following Monday. Here we are. Help me, I cannot seem to steady my hand."

"Allow me, father," Monty said, putting his hand over William's. With his son steadying him, William made the cuts and reflected the skin flaps under her jaw. "Now we must plunge the knife in and under the symphysis of the jaw."

"Where is that?"

"Where the two mandibular bones meet, right at the center of the jaw directly below her two lower front teeth," William replied. Monty pointed the knife into the woman's gullet as William instructed. He looked down at her calm face, with the large knife's handle sticking out from her chin. "Reach in and grab her tongue, and pull it down and through that opening in her throat."

Monty looked down at the woman's severed skull, splayed front, and tongue poking out of the opening in her throat and exhaled deeply. "Are you all right, son?"

"I am fine. How are you feeling?"

"Better. Take your knife and divide her palate. Can you identify the pharynx, larynx and trachea? Good. Remove them one by one and place them on the tray. Now remove her esophagus. As you examine each organ, do you see any foreign objects in them?"

Monty inspected them carefully and said no. William then instructed Monty on slitting the bronchi and removing it, then cutting the lungs into sections. Once finished, William bent over and wiped his brow. "Just give me a moment, son. I need to collect myself before we perform the abdominal incision."

Monty caught a whiff of scent from the opening at the woman's throat. For a moment, he was back in the garden at his parent's house, staring at Georgiana. This was not the same, but it was close enough.

Monty turned away from his father, adjusting himself.

"I need to rest for a moment." William collapsed into a chair near the operating table. "I will be ready momentarily, my boy."

"May I continue? I have studied this aspect of the operation extensively, father."

William coughed fitfully and nodded. "Thank you," Monty said through gritted teeth, now pressing against the table so hard that he was crushing himself against its metal edges. His grip on the knife's handle was slick, and he had to readjust several times to make sure he held it tightly enough. He touched the blade to the woman's flesh and felt his pulse in his fingers.

"Do it slowly, do not make a mess of it."

"Yes, sir," Monty said. Sweat was dripping from his brow. Monty pushed again, this time with the knife, and it slid inside the woman's gut, little by little, inch by inch.

"Good," William said. "Now draw it downwards and open her up."

He sank into her flesh, grinding the blade against her rib cartilage and sliding it in and out to saw away the ligaments below. He cut down toward the dark curly thatch of hair between her legs and the red and pink organs within her that burst through the opening, onto Monty who squeezed his thighs together and grunted, feeling a warm wetness trickling down his thigh.

Four

Monty soon became so proficient at performing autopsies that William spent his days sitting in the specimen laboratory labeling jars while Monty provided him with trays of organs. Often, they would take the last train home, arriving late in the evening.

One night, as their cab rolled toward the front of their home they heard a door bang shut and saw the shadow of a man leap from the rear steps behind the house, and race into the darkness. Monty gasped in shock as the man turned for a moment into the light of the carriage's lanterns. "Stop the cab!" William shouted. He jumped to the road, ordering Monty to go check on Ann while he gave chase.

"You want me to come with you, young sir?" the cab driver asked.

"No, that is not necessary. My father is ill. Please pull the car to the back in the turnaround." Monty watched the man race into the woods. He walked slowly toward the front door and opened it just as a glass bottle shattered over his head. She stood naked in the living room, fists balled.

"Mother?" Monty said. "What happened to you?"

"Why are you here!" she screamed. "Why do you always have to ruin my life?" She collapsed to the ground, shrieking.

"My God, did that man do this to you?" Monty said, grabbing a blanket from the sofa and throwing it around her.

"Bring him back!" she screamed. "He wants to be with me! Why are you here?"

Understanding dawned on him, and Monty's face twisted in rage. "How could you?"

Ann raced forward, beating Monty with her fists across his chest, "I know about you and that farm boy! Everyone knows! Filth! Sinners!"

Monty seized Ann by the throat, "Be silent, whore." He heard William's voice behind the house, approaching the back stars.

"I wish you were all dead!" Ann hissed back. "Your father knows what I do and does not even have the courage to protest."

Monty slammed his forehead into her face, cracking the bone over her eye. Blood spurted from the wound, and Ann cried out. Monty punched her, opening up her lip. Ann fell backwards, reeling and whimpering. Monty listened for a moment to the voices behind the house, assessing how far away they were and how much time he had. He slapped and pinched her neck and shoulders, hard enough to leave welts and bruises.

He kicked her several times, until Ann whimpered and lifted her legs to her chest to protect herself, sobbing. He knew what needed to be done. Monty headed for the kitchen, eyeing the counters for the sharpest knife he could find.

"Monty? Where are you?" his father called, running to the door. He gasped at Ann's sprawled body.

"I found her like this," Monty said, turning from the kitchen. "I think she was violated! Oh God!" Monty said, throwing his face into his hands.

William and Monty did not leave Dorset for many weeks after that. William cared for Ann, unwilling to leave her side. He lamented being so far away and leaving her vulnerable. Ann seemed calm in those days. She did not leave her bed, but also did not shriek or curse at them. When Monty passed her room, he saw William on a bench by her bed, reading softly to her. Monty grimaced at the affection his father displayed on her, but could not bring himself to tell William the truth about his whoring wife.

He took long, undisturbed walks in the fields, searching for signs of the beast he and Clifton had seen. There were none. He checked the place where they'd seen the calf, but that too was gone. Monty continued through the woods, coming to the edge of the farm and saw a group of men working in the field. Clifton was not among them. They looked at him as he came out from between the trees, stepping into the amber stalks of wheat. He could see that they were talking to one another while looking at him.

Monty walked up to the farmhand's house and knocked on the door. A young woman answered. "May I help you?" she asked.

"Is Clifton here?" Monty said.

She stared at him for a moment. "Are you Montague Druitt?"

Monty's eyebrows raised, "Yes, I am. How did you—"

The door slammed in Monty's face. He could hear words spoken quickly within. Someone was coming to the door. Finally, Clifton opened it and smiled. His teeth were very white and very straight when he smiled, Monty thought, smiling back. "Hello Monty." The men in the field were now all staring at him and laughing. Clifton shut the door behind him, "I am sorry for that."

"It is all right, I suppose. Did you hear about what happened to my mother?"

"I heard a few things."

"It was your father. I know it was. I saw him running from the house."

"That is not true!" There was panic in his voice. Both of them knew any man of their class would be hanged immediately if accused of raping a physician's wife. "He was with me that whole night. I swear it," Clifton said.

Monty looked at Clifton and shook his head, sighing. "As you say. It truly makes no difference to me one way or another."

Clifton took a deep breath. "There is something I need to tell you."

"Let us talk about it while we walk. Want to go looking for that wolf? Maybe down by the creek?" he said softly. He reached out to touch Clifton's hand briefly, so that no one could see.

Clifton looked back at the house for a moment. "I can't go into the woods with you any more, Monty."

"What? Why?"

Clifton looked down at the ground. "I do not do those things anymore."

The front door opened and the young woman came out onto the porch, staring at them both. Monty glared at her, "Who is she?"

"My cousin. Her father owns a small stand at the new rail station in Gillingham," Clifton said. "I am travelling with her in a few days. I'll be going to live with them and work at the stand."

"For how long?"

Clifton shrugged. "My father says that if I marry her, I can take over the stand and become a businessman, Monty."

"Marry? You cannot be serious."

"Yes," Clifton said. He looked down at a patch of grass he'd been kicking with the point of his shoe, seeing that he'd uncovered the dirt completely. "We have to grow up sometime, Monty. Can't go ripping around the woods together forever, you know."

Monty nodded, looking away. "When you are ready to stop joking, let me know."

"Truly, I wasn't joking, Monty."

He looked back at Clifton, feeling his cheeks glowing hot. "If you want to play house with some strumpet, feel free, but do not pretend that it will make you happy."

Clifton's face clouded with anger. "That is enough, Mr. Druitt. Good day, sir."

"It is best that you call me sir, you lowly little farm scum. That is all you are and all you will ever be. You, your whore, and whatever little creatures you two manage to grunt into existence. Scum, the lot of you."

Clifton stopped in his tracks, looking over his shoulder. "I am sorry if I've hurt you, Monty. Some things are beyond our control, though."

"If I showed you what was beyond your control it would be that whore's guts spread across your conjugal bed."

Clifton turned, half-smiling in surprise at the sudden malicious turn in Monty's normally gentle voice. As their eyes met, Clifton's smile turned to a scowl, seeing the naked fury in Monty's face, and he found himself wondering if it had not been a rather serious threat.

"Go away from here and never return, Mr. Druitt. If you come anywhere near me or my loved ones ever again I shall hurt you."

Monty turned and began walking quickly into the woods. By the time he reached the trees he was running, crashing through branches, unable to see.

Dr. William Druitt stopped practicing medicine and devoted his later years to the care of his wife. Ann's condition deteriorated to the point where William kept her confined to her bedroom. She had broken, smashed, and cracked every possible thing within it until nothing remained but a bare room with four walls. William threw a mattress on the floor for her to flop around on in between fits of shrieking. Ann lost the ability to attend to even the most basic bodily functions and William risked his own safety even attempting to bathe her. She had become wild.

One night William's eyes were mere slits as he sat on the couch, clutching his chest. "What is wrong, father?" Monty said.

"I just need to rest a moment," William said. "Your mother has been even more active than usual today."

Monty considered this for a moment and then picked up a blanket and draped it over the old man. "Stay here and relax. I will attend to her."

William thanked him and patted his hand. "Be gentle with her, son. She is a fragile creature and she loves you dearly, even if she is incapable of showing it."

"I will," Monty said.

Ann Druitt was lying on the floor, covered by a thin sheet. Her eyes did not look away from the window when Monty went into her room with a tray of tea and biscuits. "Good evening, mother," Monty said. "I will leave these by your bed in case you would like them. Father will be in later after he has rested."

"Do you ever see her, Monty?"

"See who?"

"Your sister," Ann said. "I do. She comes down from her bed sometimes and whispers things to me. Things about you."

He thought of that night so long ago when the black eyed corpse had stared at him while he slept in her bed. "No," he said. "Never."

Ann turned toward him sharply, "Georgiana could not endure knowing what she was. She was too weak. It is up to you now, Monty."

He set the tray down on the floor and said, "I have no idea what you are talking about, but I will not stand here and listen to the ravings of a lunatic. Goodnight, mother."

"Why do you think you are so in love with that farm boy? It is your natural instinct to be like the women of my family."

Monty pounced on top of her and covered her mouth with his hand as she bit and squirmed under him. "If you utter one more word I will snuff out your life, you wretched, evil creature. I would be doing everyone in this house a favor by putting an end to your misery."

"Monty?" his father called from downstairs. "Is everything all right up there?"

Monty pushed up from the mattress and told her to be silent. She laughed shrilly. "You do not even have the courage to kill a defenseless woman. Filth! Sinner!"

He kicked the tray at her with a clang, sending it crashing against the wall. Tea sprayed Ann and the plate of biscuits went flying, making her screech. William shouted, "Montague! Hang on, son. I'm coming up."

Monty snatched the tray from the ground and said, "No need, father. Mother has decided she is not hungry this evening." He shut the door behind him and went back down the stairs, assuring the old man that everything was fine.

Montague Druitt left Dorset as soon as he was old enough to enroll at New College in Oxford, dismayed at his father's decision to abandon his practice. He begged William to institutionalize Ann so that the two of them could open the medical office they'd always spoken of. William refused, and Druitt moved away. He applied himself ferociously to his studies but found that the medical classes were too far beneath his level of experience and understanding to keep his interest. Druitt chose to focus on a new area of study that seemed to hold as much depth and complexity: Law. In truth, Druitt threw himself into school and work to try to ignore the strange desires welling within. He felt an uncontrollable rage bubbling beneath the surface of his being, threatening to overwhelm the carefully constructed personality he'd crafted during his school years.

Druitt observed the women he passed on the street, thinking of what lovely mysteries lay beneath the curtain of flesh, how he could plunge his hands into any one of them and tear out their insides. At night, he dreamed about the bodies from his father's office. He dreamed about cutting them open, but instead of being cold, stiff corpses, they were warm and wet. Screaming.

Dr. William Druitt died of a heart attack in 1885. His youngest son returned for the funeral, staying just long enough to see the casket lowered into the ground. At the funeral he issued a cheque for the entirety of his inheritance to a local doctor, with the understanding that Ann would be regularly visited and cared for. Druitt provided the Inner Temple's address to the doctor and told him, "Do not contact me until either she is dead or the money runs out."

In early 1888, Druitt settled in Blackheath, a small section of the southeast area of London. Will had been living there for ten years, and both were delighted to live so close to one another. Druitt took up a position at the George Valentine's Boarding School for Boys in Blackheath, residing at the school as Assistant Headmaster. His expertise in cricket, an interest he'd fostered since his brother first taught it to him, gained him the interest of the Morden Cricket Club, and earned him the position of Treasurer and Secretary for the Blackheath Cricket, Gottball, and Lawn Tennis Company.

In July of that year, Druitt received a letter from Dorset. He opened it expectantly, hoping to finally have word of Ann's departure from the world. It was not. The doctor had died, and his widow wrote that there was not enough money in the world for her to continue caring for Ann as her dead husband had.

Druitt contacted the Brooke Asylum in Clapton and arranged for staff members to travel all the way to Dorset and transport Ann over one hundred miles to their facility. "If you do not mind me saying so," Dr. Steward said, "I think it is delightful that you would go to all this expense to bring your mother close to where you are. We will do whatever is in our power to make her trip a pleasant one. But, and I hope you do not mind me saying so, you are aware that there are other facilities closer to where she would be more comfortable?" Dr. Steward asked, puzzled.

"Of course I am," Druitt said.

"But you still want her to come to here?"

"I insist."

That night, as Druitt lay in bed, he pictured Ann struggling against the confines of her straightjacket in the darkness of the storage car of the train that carried her from Dorset. She screamed and thrashed, beating her head against the wooden boards of the car, howling so loud that the other people in the car were awakened. Small children were terrified. The conductors shouted at the men bringing her to the Asylum that she must be silenced or else thrown off the train. That would be perfect, Druitt thought. He imagined them opening the door to her car, wooden clubs raised.

Five

The Brooke House Lunatic Asylum was fewer than ten miles away from Blackheath. It was only one month since Druitt confined his mother to the Asylum, and he visited her at every possible chance.

Carmen sought fares along Greenwich, and Druitt flagged down the nearest one while side-stepping steaming piles of horse dumpings. The carman asked Druitt where he would like to go, cocking an eyebrow as Druitt responded vaguely, "Somewhere near Kenninghall Road, in Upper Clapton. It does not matter where you let me off." The carman snapped his rein and clicked with his mouth, bringing the carriage around to face the opposite direction. "What do you think you're doing?" Druitt said.

"Takin' you where you said, sir."

"Why are you not taking Bow Street through Mile End?"

"We can go that way if you'd like, sir, though it really don't make sense, if you don't mind me saying. Most carmen don't like to go anywheres near Whitechapel, and I expect they been takin' you the long way round. Costs twice as though, dunnit?"

Druitt gritted his teeth in annoyance. "Why do they avoid Whitechapel?"

"You new to these parts, sir?"

"So what if I am?"

"No offense sir. It's just a bit of a shady spot, is all. I knows me way around it like the back o' me own hand though. I can have you in an' out of there in a jiffy, like. Unless you want to go the other way, that is. You're the boss, sir," he said, snapping his reins.

"I care not which way we go." Druitt opened the shade on the cab's window as the carman increased the pace of the horse and the carriage began to rock from side to side as it moved along the uneven streets. Druitt dabbed sweat from his brow and pulled his damp shirt away from his body, fanning his skin with the wet fabric. The large, well maintained homes of Blackheath and Greenwich gave way to smaller, more closely packed together ones the farther they travelled. The men and women in expensive coats, hats, and umbrellas strolling Eliot Place vanished, only to be replaced by a simpler, working-class folk with dour, dirty faces.

Druitt heard a crunch and squeal over the side of the carriage. He leaned out the window to look as a rat's body rolled up toward him on the rear wheel before being ground into the cobblestones below.

"Still all right, sir? Not regretting it, is you?"

"No," Druitt said, scoffing. "I am familiar with Portsmouth. It is a highly depressed area also."

"That right?" the carman said, chuckling. "Portsmouth, you say. Far cry from Whitechapel, I reckon."

Druitt looked ahead, noticing several buildings on the upcoming block had collapsed roofs. The houses beside them were boarded up, and though they were clearly meant to be vacated, people still sat on the front steps talking idly. The wooden planks covering the entranceways had been ripped away and hard eyes peered at Druitt from within their dark confines, watching them pass.

The carriage stopped for traffic at a busy intersection where a woman stood near them on the corner, holding the hand of a small child. The carriage was close enough that Druitt could hear the child singing and her mother murmuring soothing words to her little girl. She caught Druitt looking at her and turned, staring directly at him with a cocked eyebrow.

The carman turned in his seat, smiling with a mouth that was blackened and jotted with bits of broken teeth. "You want I should ask her in for you, sir?"

"What do you mean?"

"She's a working girl...you were looking at her. Never mind, sir. On our way," he said, cracking the rein.

Druitt turned in his seat to see the woman fix her attention on the next cab as it pulled up. The driver of that carriage slowed his horse and stopped. He got down and opened the back door for the woman, who immediately entered, then he scooped up the little girl and sat her down on the seat beside him up front. The last thing Druitt saw before turning around was the driver putting one of the reins in the little girl's hands and telling her to crack it as hard as she could. The man in the back of the cab undid his trousers and grabbed the child's mother by the back of the head and forced it into his lap.

"Has she been like this for long?" Druitt asked. "Why was I not immediately informed of the change in her status?"

Ann Druitt stared blankly back at him. The irises of her eyes had gone milk white. Her mouth hung open, as if someone had unscrewed the hinges of her jaw and strings of drool were spooling from her teeth.

Doctor Steward checked his notes. "It has been three days since she's spoken. Her last reported complaint was that all of the blood in her body had shifted to the left side. She told me that the entire right portion of her body had been replaced with a colorful variety of other fluids. Since your mother's arrival last month, she has regularly complained of similar ailments. On the last night anyone heard her speak, the patient stationed in the bed beside hers reported that Ann began screaming in the middle of the night. Of course, around here that can be quite common. When we checked on her that morning, she was like this. Am I to assume that your father's name is Jack?"

"No, it was not."

"Curious," the doctor said.

Druitt banged his fist on the table, "Enough chatter, I want something done. She needs to be conscious of her surroundings. She needs to know exactly where she is."

The doctor set his notes down, "I am glad that you feel that way, Mr. Druitt. I have been reading about a doctor in Switzerland who has been performing an experimental psychosurgery on his patients. He's met with some success, but is currently looking for more test subjects. I think your mother fits his criteria, and we would certainly be interested in having someone from Brooke House participate in such a prestigious endeavor. Is that something you might consider?"

"No," Druitt said.

"The only cost involved is getting your mother to Switzerland," he said. "Dr. Burckhardt is-"

"No," Druitt said. "I want her near enough that I can see her regularly."

Dr. Steward cleared his throat, and picked his notes back up. "There is another matter I wish to discuss with you, Mr. Druitt. It is noted on your mother's charts that mental aberration runs in your family, and recent research has shown conditions similar to hers can be hereditary. However, given her condition, I want to qualify some of the things she has told us. It is not unusual for our patients to wholly fabricate histories for themselves. Given her condition…"

Druitt ignored him, staring into his mother's eyes.

Dr. Stewart cleared his throat, "She told us her mother committed suicide when she was five years old. Apparently the body was discovered on Christmas morning. After her mother's death, an Aunt moved in to help care for the children, but that woman subsequently slit her wrists in a bathtub two years later. Finally, it says that your older sister committed suicide as a child. Your mother said she leapt out of a window and landed on a wrought-iron fence. Is all of this true?"

Druitt turned on the doctor and suddenly smiled, his voice calm and soothing when he spoke, "All of that is a complete fabrication, Dr. Steward. I would request you do not besmirch my family's good name by recording such nonsense on any official documentation."

"Of course," Dr. Steward said, making notations on the chart. "I will give you a moment alone with her, before I return. Have a good day, Mr. Druitt."

"One moment, Doctor. Why did you ask if my father's name was Jack?"

"She was calling for someone by that name," Dr. Stewart said. "She kept saying she'd been expecting him."

Druitt watched the doctor leave. He looked back at the old woman, who had not moved at all. Only the puddle of drool on the table below had gotten larger. Druitt leaned forward and whispered, "I will not let you slip away so easily."

On August Seventh, Druitt sat in his apartment preparing for the next day's classes, when he found a copy of the Evening Star slid under his door. He sipped a cup of tea, glancing through the paper, when he saw an article that caught his eye.

"A WHITECHAPEL HORROR."

A woman, now lying unidentified at the mortuary, Whitechapel, was ferociously stabbed to death this morning, between two and four o'clock, on the landing of a stone staircase in George's-buildings, Whitechapel.

George's-buildings are tenements occupied by the poor laboring class. A lodger going early to his work found the body. Another lodger says the murder was not committed when he returned home about two o'clock. The woman was stabbed in 20 places. No weapon was found near her, and the murderer has left no trace. She is of middle age and height, has black hair and a large, round face, and apparently belonged to the lowest class.

Druitt read the article several times, picturing the woman's body sprawled on the stairwell, blood leaking from the multitude of wounds. What daring, he thought. None of the tenants in the building had heard a thing.

The next day, Druitt read more articles about the killing. The Star had been wrong. She was actually stabbed thirty-nine times. The official tally of Martha Tabram's destruction was five wounds to the right lung, two to the left lung, five to the liver, two to the spleen, and six more to the stomach. The newspapers could not make sense of the injuries, but he could. Perfectly.

Druitt sifted through the piles of papers again, setting aside the ones that showed artist's renditions of the murder, or the crime scene.

Had the killer lured Tabram into the stairwell with a promise of reward for a quick sexual favor? It was not his pego that he showed her, Druitt thought. It was something stronger, something sharper, and he shoved it into her again and again. Druitt imagined the woman screaming and begging, and he sighed, sitting back in his chair, touching himself.

Over the following three weeks, Druitt followed each detail released about the murder. There were plenty to be had. The newspapers enthusiastically detailed Scotland Yard's utter lack of ability to pursue the investigation in a serious manner. The investigators were pinning all their hopes of identifying the killer on a few local drunken wretches who claimed to have clues for them.

He travelled by train back to Whitechapel and paced Commercial Street, finally finding Wentworth, and then the George's Yard building. "Pleasure for a penny, sir," women called out to him as he passed.

"Oy, come have a go at me ol' lady, mate. She ain't got no diseases," a man said, grabbing him by the arm.

"I haven't eaten in days, m'lord," a woman said, carrying a small dirty child. "Spare a coin? I will earn it."

Drunkards lie scattered in the alleyways as thieves rifled their pockets, kicking the men if nothing was found. Small cringing children cried from the stoops of the buildings. Immigrant shopkeepers stood by their doors with heavy truncheons in their hands, eyeing the people on the street cautiously. Desperate people doing desperate things, Druitt thought, recalling the words his father's cab man had spoken so long ago.

He came to Dorset Street, eyeing the mass of people coming in and out of the bars. He smelled stale urine covering the walls of the alleyways, where shadows moved within, mounting one another and stealing off into the night. A sign hanging outside of a tavern called Blue Coat Boy advertising rooms for rent.

Druitt went inside the pub and up the steps. A man sat at the top of the stairs, behind a small, rickety desk. "This ain't the sort a place for a well-dressed man like yourself, sir. I'd go back downstairs before somebody decides to keep yeh up here."

"I would like to inquire about a room, sir," Druitt said.

"Well then, you came to the right man, sir! We have several rooms available. You do have money on yeh?"

Druitt pulled out several coins. "Is this sufficient?"

"Only for you an' about a dozen other people to stay the week. Gimme two o' them an' you can have a room all to yourself, with sheets an' all."

Druitt handed the money over, and thanked the gentleman as he was shown which room was his. Druitt looked away from the people who stared at him as he passed. He shut the door to his room, feeling his heart beating so rapidly that he had to sit down. The bed's metal springs bit into his skin, but he did not move for hours, fascinated by the sounds of people in the rooms around him, fighting, copulating, and screaming.

He sat, recounting the details of the streets he'd walked; how the alleyways snaked in and out of the tenement buildings. His eyes began to grow heavy, and he closed them.

Druitt was inside a carriage sitting next to his father. His father was the same age as when they had first travelled to Portsmouth, but Druitt was a fully grown man. The carriage was taking them to William's office, which was no longer in Portsmouth. Now they were headed to Commercial Street in the center of Whitechapel. A long line of whores waited outside the door to William's office.

The carriage stopped and they exited the cab. The whores cringed as he stepped onto the sidewalk and opened the door to the office. He left it open behind him and walked into the operating room. It was crowded with onlookers. Police, journalists, royalty, all had crowded into the room to watch him perform.

William brought the first woman in. The crowd gasped as William stripped away her clothing and she walked timidly toward Druitt. Druitt showed her the knife, turning it so that the light reflected from the overhead lanterns on its bright mirrored surface. "Lie down, whore," Druitt commanded.

"Thank you all for coming to bear witness to our little demonstration," William said, wiping his hands on a towel. "My son, Jack, will now begin with the first cut."

Druitt paused, staring at his father.

"I am so sorry, my boy. Jack is what I meant to name you before your mother insisted on giving you that dreadful name. Jack is who you should have been, rather than what you became. These things happen when your mother is filth."

Druitt met Polly Nichols the next night on Buck's Row, one of the narrowest, darkest streets in the northeastern section of Whitechapel. He stood under the streetlamp at the corner of Buck's Row and Baker's Row, watching people stagger along Whitechapel Road. Polly approached him. Her black bonnet was trimmed with velvet, and she moved like her limbs were stiff under the several overcoats she wore. She was shorter than he was, and when she slurred her words through several missing front teeth and he smelled the booze and flop sweat on her breath. "You feeling good natured tonight, guvnah?"

Druitt swallowed hard, his heart hammered and it was all he could do to keep his arms and legs from shaking. "What does that mean?" he said.

Polly smiled gently, "New to this, are you? You are shaking, dear. Let ol' Polly warm you up," she said, pressing close to him. She put her arm through Druitt's and began leading him toward an old stableyard's gateway.

She spoke, but Druitt could not hear her. A roar arose in his ears, like a stern wind, drowning out everything but Druitt's short, sharp breaths. Sweat ran down his armpits, sliding down his sides.

"So? You just need thruppence. If you want me mouth, it is just a tuppence more. If you want to put it anywhere else, it is-"

Druitt was too excited to wait. He grabbed her face before she finished speaking and slashed her across the throat. Polly Nichols crumbled at his feet, thrashing on the pavement like a fish suddenly yanked from the sea, horrified at its new surroundings.

Her twitching body was a revelation, and he gasped as the stream of blood began to slow. Druitt bent, taking her into his arms like a lover. He unbuttoned her coats and dress slowly, taking his time, savoring the moment.

Polly's belly was pale in the dim light, and Druitt withdrew his long, curved blade, taking a moment to pick the exact spot he wanted to put it inside of her. Oh yes, he wanted to put it inside of her, he thought, beginning to breathe quickly. The hour of fate had finally arrived for both of them.

Six

Inspector Gerard Lestrade spat on the ground and muttered, "This is bollocks. We are supposed to be Scotland Yard."

The London Metropolitan Police Department was formed in 1829, when Parliament replaced the disorganized rabble of local town constables with a modern, efficient crime-fighting entity. Headquarters, known as "Scotland Yard" was established in Westminster, and the Police Department quickly evolved from a small force of one thousand, to nearly fifteen thousand constables, sergeants, inspectors, superintendents and commissioners.

Their jurisdiction covered more than a thousand square miles that encompassed Middlesex, portions of the counties of Essex, Hertford, Kent, Surrey and all of London except for one bastardized little square mile known as the City of London. The two sheriff's responsible for "The City" refused to join with the larger force, preferring to maintain their little fiefdom of autonomy. In 1838 London City formed its own police agency, and just to show that it had no intention of being shown-up by the Met, it now had nearly five hundred police constables swarming through that one square mile. Better equipped and paid than we are, by far, Lestrade thought, grimacing.

The Commissioner of the Metropolitan Police Department answered to no one less than a member of the Prime Minister's cabinet. The rest of the world looked to Scotland Yard as the gold standard for municipal policing.

Damn it, Lestrade thought. Now we look like a bunch of gabby cork-brained half-wits.

On April Third Lestrade responded to London Hospital to interview a forty-two year old Whitechapel bunter named Emma Smith. She had reported being beaten, raped, and robbed by four youths on Brick Lane. The doctors kept trying to stitch the old girl back up as Lestrade attempted to interview her, but her responses were too faint for him to make out. The next day, Emma Smith was dead.

Lestrade immediately targeted the Old Nichol gang, a group of thugs constantly out harassing the whores of Whitechapel. Mickey Fitch, their leader, had lost an eye fighting with the Bessarabian Tigers in a street brawl. Rumor had it that one of the Tigers smashed a broken bottle into Mickey's face, and severed the eye's attachments. Mickey supposedly reached up and felt the dangling orb, wrapped his fingers around it and yanked the damned thing free.

That's the East End for you, Lestrade thought. They will make any piece of garbage criminal into a legend.

The Old Nichol gang wanted the whores of Whitechapel to pay them for protection. If the whores did not pay, the protection they needed was from the gang itself. Lestrade worked the Emma Smith case for seventy two hours straight, sleeping at odd intervals in his office at the local Whitechapel police station, chasing various members of the Old Nichol. He threw one into the City Prison and loudly announced to the other prisoners that the bastard had crippled an old woman. "If you lot want to eat anything besides bread and water for the week, this bastard had better have a hard time of it in here!" As he left the prison, the Old Nichol boy was screaming for his mother, and Lestrade smiled the rest of the day.

Lestrade beat another senseless with his baton in Spitalfields, screaming, "Where the hell is Mickey Fitch? Where is that one-eyed bastard!" The bloke's head gave way before his loyalty did, and he collapsed in a bleeding heap on the pavement. The dozen spectators who witnessed the assault were horrorstruck, but did not move to help as Lestrade left him lying there as a message to the rest of the gang.

Not one criminal even admitted to the existence of Mickey Fitch, let alone his involvement in the Smith shakedown and murder. Lestrade was no closer to finding the actual four suspects than when he began, but if truth be told, he was enjoying the work.

On August Seventh, Lestrade was sitting in his office, eyeing the hands of his pocket watch move toward the time he told a local bunter named Louise to meet him outside of the Princess Alice. Louise was easy on the eyes, but she had a bad habit of dragging her little girl with her all over Whitechapel, even when she was working. "Leave the little girl elsewhere," he'd told her. "I do not want to be distracted." He figured he would give her an extra coin or two if she left the little one behind.

One of the young constables came running into his office to report that they needed him immediately at a stairwell in the George Yard Building on Gunthorpe Street. Martha Tabram, an older whore from the neighborhood had been stabbed thirty nine times. The killer was frenzied, puncturing her in the neck, the gut, and twat.

Lestrade looked at the body and scowled, angry at the old bitch for getting herself murdered when he had places to be, and things to do. Anyway, it was obvious how Tabram had gotten herself killed. The only time a person bothered to stab anybody that many times, with that much ferocity, was someone with a serious personal grudge.

Lestrade figured that Tabram had refused to pay her pimp, or maybe tried stealing something from one of her punters. Whatever the case, it had caught up with her on the rodent-infested steps of the George Yard stairwell.

And then, August Thirty-First at three forty in the morning, a forty-three year old prostitute was found on Buck's Row by a carman on his way to work at Pickfords. He saw her lying on the street and called to a friend for assistance. They both checked her and thought she had a heartbeat.

A constable was summoned, and he, in turn, summoned a doctor. Finally, the doctor was able to determine that the life of one Mary Ann "Polly" Nichols had been snuffed out. Lestrade thought, maybe it was the fact that her throat had been completely cut open and her belly slashed several times. The Polly Nichols murder, while daunting, could be worked if Lestrade was given the time and manpower. He knew that people were out in that area all times of night. He knew that someone had seen something. He knew that at some point, an angry housewife would walk into his station and say that her husband was hiding a bloody knife and shirt under the floorboard of their home. An arrest would be made, his name would be in the papers, and he would finally get promoted out of the stinking hole known as Whitechapel.

Enter the mutilated corpse of Annie Chapman.

Lestrade's jaw tightened, picturing the scene of Chapman's murder. He had seen much horror in his time as a police officer in the service of the Metropolitan Police Department, but what found in the rear of Twenty Nine Hanbury Street would haunt his dreams forever.

Lestrade's years of policing, dealing with all the varied aspects of humanity, had stolen both his faith in God and his faith in Good. Looking down at Annie Chapman filled him with only fear.

"Bollocks," Lestrade whispered, seeing John Pizer coming toward him, smiling. The man all the papers and locals called "Leather Apron" was holding up his hands, waving them to show Lestrade how he was no longer handcuffed.

"Bad luck again, eh, Inspector? Told you they was lying."

"Keep moving," Lestrade said without looking at him. Louise had told him about Pizer. She'd been warned by the other girls to keep her distance from him because he was a real bruiser. He always carried a long knife tucked in his apron, and liked to punch up girls if they gave him reason. He liked to punch up girls even if they did not. Pizer had no alibi for the night that Martha Tabram was murdered.

"Just tell me, Inspector," Pizer leaned close to Lestrade, "how many times are we going to do this? How many whores are going to lie to you about me threatening them before you start arresting them, instead of me?"

"I said keep moving."

"I demand an answer!" Pizer shouted, bringing the police station to silence. "The newspapers write about me being a suspect for murder every day to the point I can't leave my own house! Now, I am being held against my will for days at a time on the word of anyone who wants to become famous for pinching Leather Apron!"

Lestrade grabbed Pizer by the front collar of his shirt and yanked him forward so abruptly that Pizer nearly crashed into him. "Listen to me, porker. If I want to, I'll arrest you every day of your sad, putrid little existence until either the killings stop, or you mysteriously end up dead. For the last time, get out of my police station before I lose my patience."

"You do not frighten me," Pizer said.

"That right?" Lestrade doubled Pizer over with a vicious right hand to the gut. "Not frightened, eh?" As Pizer bent forward and groaned, Lestrade slammed a knee up into his teeth, rocking him up into the air and backwards to collapse onto the station floor. Blood spilled from Pizer's nose and mouth as his eyes rolled back in his head.

Sergeant Byfield looked up from his desk at Pizer's sprawled form. He snapped his fingers at two constables. "You two get that bastard out of my police station."

The constables hustled over to Pizer, grabbing him by the ankles and dragged him toward the front door. "Not that way," Lestrade said, catching his breath. "There's a hundred newspapermen out there. Take him out the back."

The constables spun Pizer around and dragged him back across the floor and down the hall. Pizer's head made a satisfying bump with each poorly navigated turn.

"Inspector Lestrade, please sit down," Detective Chief Inspector Herman Brett said.

Lestrade sat, trying to keep his feet and hands steady. He had not yet received any reprimand for the incident with Pizer, but was well aware that any number of officers might have filed a complaint. In the Service, there were many ways to receive promotion. For those who shied away from doing any actual police work, the most assured way to obtain rank was to snitch on another copper.

"Inspector Lestrade, why are your people arresting John Pizer three days after we told the press that we have not a shred of evidence against him?" Chief Inspector Brett did not look up at Lestrade as he spoke, only at the blank piece of paper on his desk. Brett tapped the end of his pen on the paper, waiting for Lestrade to begin.

"First off, I would like to go on record that I do not understand Inspector Helson's logic in releasing that information to the press. Every day I see some new aspect of our investigation appearing in the damn newspaper. We might as well announce to whomever is doing these killings to go ahead and slaughter prostitutes at will," Lestrade said.

Chief Inspector Brett wrote as Lestrade spoke, continuing after Lestrade had finished. Brett paused writing, "Go ahead and slaughter prostitutes?"

"At will, sir."

"Any other persons you'd like to cast blame on to excuse your inability to capture the killer?"

Lestrade nodded, "Well, now that you mention it, I consider Coroner Wynn Baxter responsible for the Annie Chapman killing."

Brett dropped his pen and peered over his glasses, "Excuse me, Inspector?"

Lestrade leaned forward, "I can spell his name if you would like, sir. Might as well jot this down too. In for a penny, in for a pound, as they say."

Chief Inspector sighed and picked up his pen. "I assure you I can spell it, Lestrade. Best not to take that tone with me at this moment. Carry on."

"Sorry, sir. I meant to say that I should like to file a protest with you over the conduct of Coroner Baxter concerning the Polly Nichols inquest. It is the duties of the coroner's court during inquest to determine only the identity of the decedent and the cause of death. Instead, he used the hearing as a way to puff himself up and get into the newspapers. They knew who the girl was and how she died the very first day of the inquest, but it continued for nearly two more weeks. Now, the public has as much information as I do about the murder, if not more, depending how many newspapers they can afford to buy," Lestrade said.

"How does that implicate the Coroner in Annie Chapman's death?"

"For one thing, Baxter made a big production discussing the method in which Nichols was killed, including what kind of knife the killer used. How it enabled him to dispatch her silently with a cut across the throat straight away. Every maniac in the city could have read that and began to formulate their own interesting ways to get themselves into the paper as well. Worst of all, he started blabbing about all of the other murders I am trying to solve, saying how he was drawing connections between each of them. Now the public is stirred up into a frenzy thinking there is some wild roving pack of murderers all over the streets, and Scotland Yard is buggered to anything at all about any of them."

Brett had stopped writing before Lestrade finished speaking. He folded his hands calmly and set them on the desk. "I will be certain to pass along your opinion of Scotland Yard to the Assistant Commissioner."

Lestrade sighed, thinking it was a good time for a little career preservation. "I have been working around the clock on these damn murders, trying to bring you some arrests, sir. I am a little out of sorts. I apologize."

"Working around the clock on the murders, eh?"

"Yes, sir. Why do you say it like that?"

"You are married, correct, Inspector?"

Lestrade shifted in his seat. "Yes, sir. I have two little ones as well. What does that have to do with this?"

"There are some rather unsettling rumors about you, Inspector. Let me just say that it would not be very prudent for any of our Inspectors to be caught in a compromising position with one of the people responsible for bringing this killer into our midst. Do you understand me, Lestrade?"

"Sorry, sir? Who is responsible?"

"The whores of Whitechapel, Gerard! Because they cannot find a more decent existence than bunting, we now have this murderous bastard to contend with. Get me?"

Lestrade looked down for a moment, then nodded. "I understand, sir."

Brett nodded, picking up his pen. "Let us just sum up your feelings about Coroner Baxter and his responsibility in the death of Annie Chapman, shall we?"

"Yes, Chief Inspector. Can we just say that I believe the coroner overstepped his duties, and that by making such a large spectacle of a routine inquest, created a frenzy among the public. During that inquest, the Annie Chapman woman was killed. I would stake my career that she will not be the last."

Chief Inspector Brett turned the paper over, "If you or your officers had cause to arrest Pizer, otherwise known as 'Leather Apron' that was unbeknownst to Inspector Helson when he gave his statement to the press, then why was Pizer released the very next day?"

Lestrade sighed. "Sergeant Thick said he brought Pizer in for his own safety, sir. It had already been in the newspapers that we were looking for 'Leather Apron' in connection to the Tabram killing. Sgt. Thick has known Pizer for quite some time and escorted him in so that we could question him, and protect him from the crowds that were staking out his house."

"And?"

"He could give no account for the night Tabram was murdered, but he was able to give successful alibis for both the Polly Nichols and the Annie Chapman murders. I am of the opinion that he is possibly responsible for killing one woman, but not the others," Lestrade said.

Chief Inspector Brett continued writing. "Is that all?"

"No, Chief Inspector. While he was being questioned, a man from his neighborhood came forward to claim he'd witnessed Pizer fighting with Annie Chapman the night she was murdered, threatening to knife her."

Chief Inspector Brett looked up and smiled, "That sounds promising. What came of it?"

"The damned witness turned out to be a publicity seeking idiot who only wanted to see his name in the paper," Lestrade said. "After all of that, we had to let Pizer go. At this point I still consider him a murder suspect and intend to pursue his arrest as soon as I get the chance to focus on that individual case."

Chief Inspector Brett continued writing. "And how did Mr. Pizer leave the station, Inspector Lestrade?"

Lestrade paused and took a deep breath. "He was assisted in leaving through the rear, sir."

The Princess Alice Pub was less than a mile away, and Lestrade stormed out of the police station toward it, covering the distance quickly as he sputtered curses at the Chief Inspector. He was intending on drinking himself sick when he saw Louise waiting outside the Pub's doors, holding her little girl's hand. "Good evening,

Inspector," Louise said politely as he approached. The little girl watched him silently. "You feeling good natured the evening?"

"Yes, I suppose I am," he said. He looked down, finding himself standing in the stinking pool of someone's sickness, splattered not too long ago onto the entranceway of the Princess Alice. No one had bothered to splash a bucket of hot water on it.

"Might you be interested in getting a bit of drink first, then?" she said eagerly. He knew Louise was keen on her drink. A bit too keen, sometimes, by the look of her.

"Maybe after," he said. "I can't relax just yet."

"You look a bit bound up tonight, Inspector," Louise said, stepping close to him. "Why don't you let Louise take some o' that bad mettle out of yeh?"

"What about her? She going to be all right out here by herself?"

Louise patted the child on the head, "Abbie will be just fine, won't you my love? Stay right here under the light where Mummy can see you. I am going to talk to the nice policeman in the alley for a moment, so do not disturb us."

The little girl nodded silently and watched as Louise pulled him into the shadows. He found himself unable to relax because Abbie was watching them. He tried looking the other way, into the darkness of the alley. "Not right here. Someone might see us."

"Let them," she whispered. "This is Whitechapel, darling. No one gives a toss what happens here."

Seven

I tucked the fresh bouquet of tulips behind my back and rapped on the door. Mary threw it open, smiling brightly. "Miss Mary Amelia Morstan," I said, bringing the flowers around toward her hands in a sweeping, dramatic motion. I bowed deeply, "Doctor John Watson at your service. It is my great privilege to escort you to the ball."

Mary curtseyed, saying, "I believe you should get used to calling me Mrs. John H. Watson."

I laughed, grabbing her close and kissing her quickly on the mouth. Mary allowed me that, but as I tried to press against her, she turned away. I sighed as she went to fetch a vase from the kitchen.

"How is Mr. Holmes?" Mary called out.

"Wretched." I hung my hat and coat by the door. "I've never seen him in such a state."

She returned, setting the flowers on the mantle next to photographs of her father and mother. "These are really quite lovely, John. Thank you. Since I've moved back from the Forrester's, I have not had the chance to do any decorating of my own. The house looks as though its true owner will return at any moment and chase me out onto the street."

"You will have all the time you need, my love, whenever you are ready."

Mary smiled and nodded. "So what pray tell, is ailing the World's Keenest Deductive Mind?"

"Try not to be wicked, darling. I told you he is ill with a rare strain of 'flu. But I must confess, it should have been through his system by now. I am beginning to fear that Holmes's illness is not just of the body."

"Is he seeing a doctor?"

"Why does everyone insist upon asking me that?"

"I meant someone not held in Holmes's thrall. An outside observer."

"Thrall? I am not at all in Holmes's thrall. You think me to be some sort of servant of his?"

"No," Mary shrugged, "But you are admittedly his ever-present assistant. How many years have you been back in London? And all that time you were supposed to be building a medical practice, but instead you've been lurking about in the background as Holmes's self-appointed biographer. And now, when you should be well-established and respected in society and ready for your new life with me, I have to cart you around instead. It is up to me to make the introductions and try to help you drum up business. Yet, even now, you are completely consumed with playing Holmes's nursemaid."

"Mary," I said softly, "Please. I know you are upset with me because I have not been visiting as frequently as I promised. I am sorry, my darling."

Mary shrugged, "Do you think me so bereft of beauty that no other man would be interested? Is that why you treat me in this way?"

"Not at all!" I put my arms around her waist, "You are all I think of, day and night. I swear it. But Holmes is my friend. He needs me."

"He has family, does he not?" Mary said.

"You mean Mycroft? That man is worse than Holmes by a million! If he even took the time to stop calculating how to enslave other nations long enough to remember that he had a brother, it would be a miracle. No, dearest, Sherlock Holmes has no one else but me."

"Do you honestly believe Holmes thinks of you as a friend?" Mary said.

My eyes widened, "Yes. Of course! I believe so, anyway. Don't be ridiculous, of course he does!"

"Well I think of you as my fiancé. One I have barely seen for months," Mary said, taking a deep breath. "I love you, John Watson, but if we are to be married, I need you to act like a man and not a manservant."

I was too stunned to speak. Her words struck at the core of my being. Mary came off of her chair and sat between my legs, cupping my hands in hers. "Swear to me that from now on, you will stand up for yourself."

"All right," I finally whispered. "But can you give me just a little more time to help my friend heal? After that, it will be just you and me forever after."

She nodded and kissed me deeply on the mouth. I tasted her sweet lips and tongue, playing against them with my own. I caressed her neck and shoulders, sliding down the front of her dress, winding my fingers through the twirling ribbons around her neck. I ran my hands over her corseted bosom for one wonderful moment before she swept them away and stood up. Her face was flushed, and she fanned herself with her hand. "That will be quite enough of that, Dr. Watson."

"As a medical professional, I must disagree with you."

"How so?"

"I am a physician, Miss Morstan, and thus feel that it is only proper to conduct an immediate and full examination of your person." I came up behind her, pressing close against her back. My hands wrapped around her hips, fingers tracing her flat stomach. I kissed the back of her neck softly. "It may very well be a matter of life and death."

"But, Dr. Francis is my physician," she teased, tilting her head so that her ear was exposed to me. I kissed it and bit it gently.

"That old quack? Scandalous. Francis is barely a veterinarian. No, darling, what you need is a specialist. Someone qualified to observe the biological changes to your body once your heart rate is elevated, to measure the quantitative amount of sweat dripping down the small of your back during strenuous…physical…exertion."

Mary pushed my hands away, "Stop it, John."

"Did I do something wrong? I apologize."

"No." She took a deep breath, "It is my fault. I let you get too comfortable. We only have to wait a little longer."

"All right," I sighed, sitting back down and straightening my tie. I took measure of the room and its furnishings. Mary was correct about not making any advances in decorating the house since her father had died. Further, I doubted if her father had changed a single thing since Mary's mother had passed on ten years prior to that. It was the house of a dead person who'd lived in the house of a different dead person. What a dreadfully stuffy place for poor Mary to have been raised.

Mary worked for years as governess for the Forrester family, assisting Mrs. Cecil Forrester with duties of the household, and in raising their children into fine young adults. The youngest had been sent off to finish his schooling and prepare for his life at University, but Mary and Mrs. Forrester were so close by then that they were nearly mother and daughter.

I knew that I needed to dedicate myself more directly to expanding my medical practice, and securing my financial future. I wanted to provide the best life possible for Mary, we both wanted children, and more than anything, I wanted to make her proud to call herself "Mrs. John H. Watson." I sat back in Captain Morstan's chair and crossed my legs, suddenly feeling very much at home.

"This will pass, Holmes," I said, patting his knee.

He thrashed in his chair, cursing in protest as I mopped his forehead. "Get away," he groaned, pulling the collar of his gown tightly around his throat. "I need my pipe, Watson. Please get it for me?"

"Fine, if that will settle you." I packed tobacco into the bowl of his pipe and lit it for him. Holmes snatched it, sucking the stem greedily until thick grey smoke filled his mouth and nostrils. "I know you hate to hear this, but I take your condition as a good thing." Holmes snorted in protest. "I am serious. It is almost as if your body is leeching itself of all the damned chemicals you pumped into it."

Holmes sucked on the pipe, folding his legs onto the seat underneath him and covering himself with a blanket. "Why are you still sitting there, Watson?" he said, looking up. "Certainly we have not become so rude as to not ask Mrs. Hudson what she wants?"

"Calm yourself, my good man. There is no one here but you and me. Mrs. Hudson is in her flat downstairs. You are safe here, and no one will—"

"Mrs. Hudson is at the door, Watson! Are you deaf as well as a sadist?" he said, just as there was a faint rap on our door.

"You never cease to amaze me, Holmes."

Mrs. Hudson scowled at me when I opened the door. "Missive for the ill one," she said, holding out a sealed letter. She looked over my shoulder, sniffing in dissatisfaction. "I reckon he needs a doctor."

"He has one, my good lady. I assure you that I am giving him the finest care possible."

"As you say, then. Ring me when you're ready for some soup, sir."

"Thank you, Mrs. Hudson. Good evening." As she left, he turned to me and whispered, "What a delightful woman. So unlike the rest of her species. Others would do well to learn from her."

I tucked the letter into my pocket and crossed to the window. "My Mary is as perfect as anyone could possibly desire, Holmes. Takes no rubbish from me, I can tell you that. Ah! Here we are, Holmes. I think a bit of fresh air should help sort you out." I grabbed the window frame and gave it a good yank, trying to loosen the grime sealing it shut. "What the bloody deuce," I said, shaking the window so fiercely that the contents of my pockets were nearly spilling out. I shifted the letter delivered by Mrs. Hudson to my other pocket, when a vise-like grip seized on my arm. "Let go of me, Holmes. What are you doing? Go sit back down."

Holmes gripped me so firmly that I winced, holding me in place while he fished inside my pocket for the letter. "Give it to me, Watson. At once." Holmes found the letter, lifting it close to his face for inspection as he turned it end over end, then held it to his nose, inhaling deeply.

"You should not be standing, Holmes. Come, sit down," I said, taking him by the elbow. "Whatever are you carrying on about?"

"Do you not recognize this envelope, Watson? Have you not seen precisely this same paper stock once before?" His voice was shaking. Holmes cocked his head to the framed photograph hanging on the far wall.

I looked again at the letter and my eyes widened. The air whistled from my pursed lips. "Her?"

"The woman."

We both knew that for Sherlock Holmes there could only ever be one woman. In March of that year, Holmes received a visit from a client who claimed anonymity. He was the King of Bohemia. King Wilhelm required Holmes' professional assistance, and was willing to pay handsomely for both a resolution to the matter, and the utmost discretion. Holmes was not only famous for sorting out cases that baffled the Inspectors of Scotland Yard, but his was also a preferred method because he could be trusted not to reveal any of the sometimes damaging details of his findings.

The King confided to us that he was engaged to marry a woman of great standing and repute in the near future. He mentioned that the woman's lineage would link him to Scandinavian royal family, and boost both his standing in the international community, as well as his coffers. We congratulated him, but the King's face turned dark. Recently he had been contacted by a woman in possession of a photograph depicting him in a somewhat compromising position.

King Wilhelm advised us that he was being blackmailed over the photograph by a woman of iniquitous genius. The Great Detective would find himself evenly matched. My written account of the incident reflects that the King referred to his nemesis, Irene Adler, as extraordinarily "quick and resolute". In truth, it would have been more accurate to say that his words were, "She is an evil, cunning wench."

Holmes was tasked with retrieving the photograph by any means, going so far as to commit arson to create a distraction while he searched for it, but was thwarted by Adler again. One day, in the midst of it all, Adler simply vanished. She said she had grown tired of the game. Her last communication was in a letter to Holmes left in an envelope matching the one delivered by Mrs. Hudson. The envelope contained a photograph, but not the one the King sought. That one was safely tucked away, Adler wrote, as insurance in the event that she should ever need it. The new photograph was a portrait of Irene Adler, displaying a subtle, mischievous smile.

The King, satisfied that his wedding could commence without Adler's interference, offered Holmes a priceless emerald snake ring from his own finger as a reward. Holmes refused, asking only that he be allowed to keep that new portrait of Irene Adler.

At first, I suspected he meant only to have a photographic record of such a capable opponent. When it appeared on our wall several days later, I began to think that finally my best friend had found something to appreciate in the finer sex besides their ability to cook food for him and sometimes provide an efficient means to assist his investigations. We had discussed the matter only once. "When all else fails, Watson, men can be relied on to serve two masters: Greed and Need. A man can be entrusted with the most dearly-held information, sworn to keep it secret through torture and deprivation, but most cannot resist the power of a trollop."

"Must you be so cold, Holmes? Have you no compassion for our kind who are held in sway by the majesty and allure of the fairer sex?" I asked.

"None whatsoever."

"Well, perhaps you have not had the right woman then! Every sailor worth his salt will talk endlessly about French women, but I suspect they have had little experience elsewhere. Now, an olive-skinned Greek woman with long dark hair and eyes that hold the mysteries of the Ancient Gods themselves…that will turn your head quite around, I assure you. And Oriental girls, my goodness, they—"

"Enough, Watson!" Holmes cried, waving his hand in my face. "I must concentrate on my work. I insist you be quiet."

"Come on, Holmes," I prodded. "It is just us, having a gentlemanly discussion about the ways of the world. Stop being such a prig. What kind of woman do you prefer? Big-bosomed fair-haired ones, or sleek, tiny waifs?"

Holmes regarded me carefully for a moment, and his face grew still. He took a deep breath, weighing his words before finally saying, "I prefer silent ones."

I looked at the envelope in his hands, frowning. "Still, Holmes, how can you be certain that letter is from Irene Adler?" I had no wish to see his hopes stirred in this condition, and I feared having them dashed would sink him only deeper into despair.

"It has her scent." He drew a long, thin dagger from the side table and attempted to slit the envelope. His fingers shook as he tried to hold the blade steady enough so as not to damage the letter. "Look at me, Watson! You have made me an invalid. I can barely keep my eyes focused, and when I do, my stomach turns sideways and threatens to throw me into convulsions. Fetch me the bottle from my Moroccan case, please? I need it, Watson. I beg you."

I stood up, looming over Holmes, pressing my fists against my hips. "I will do no such thing. Neither will I allow you to, even it means battering you senseless. Give me the letter and blade and I will remove it."

"You are a fumbling buffoon! Your childish fingers will only damage it! You are an idiot, a bungler, a-"

"I beg your pardon, Holmes! I have removed bullets from the lungs of screaming soldiers on Afghan battlefields. I can manage this damned letter."

Holmes handed it to me with great apprehension. He lifted the blade, and for a moment I thought he was deciding whether to stick it in me. I snatched the handle and expertly slit the length of the envelope in one fluid motion. Several pieces of paper fluttered out of the folds and onto the floor.

"These two are newspaper clippings, Holmes," I said, picking them off the ground. "This one is from September First. It is about a woman, who was murdered...butchered, really, in Whitechapel."

Holmes lifted the second one. "This is from Lloyd's, dated September Ninth. There was a second murder, not far from the first. Both appear to have been quite grisly. Listen to this, Watson. On April Third, a woman in Spitalfields was assaulted and ravished. She died the next day. On August Seventh, a woman was murdered on High Street after being stabbed thirty-nine times." He looked at me and I shrugged, holding up my hands that I had no idea what he was talking about. Holmes looked back to the article, continuing, "On August Thirty-First, Mary Ann Nichols had her throat slashed and belly mutilated. She was found on Buck's Road. Then, three days ago, Eliza Annie Chapman's body was found behind a house on Hanbury Street. Her throat was cut, and although the article avoids many details, it is safe to say that her mutilations were the most extreme yet." Holmes threw down the article and gasped with exasperation. "Why wasn't I informed of these horrific murders, Watson?" he demanded.

"I've been here with you every day for weeks, Holmes!" I said. "How was I supposed to know if we did not hear it together?"

"You have been to see Mary on several occasions! You could have heard of it then,"

"Are you daft, man? Does murder seem like the proper conversation to have with my sweet Mary? I have seen so little of her that she thinks I've either died or lost interest in marrying her!" I took a deep breath, giving Holmes a moment to settle as well. "Regardless, even if I had known, you are in no state to pursue any investigations at this point."

"Has it not occurred to you that an investigation is precisely the diversion I require to spring back to life, Watson? Instead of sitting in this funeral chamber, rotting, I could be enjoying the thrill of the hunt!"

"No," I said, shaking my head firmly. "This is how it always happens. I nearly get you well, and you manage to convince me why you need to go running off on some damned adventure. Then, when it is finished, you end it with sticking a needle in your arm. This is now a matter of life or death, and I intend to see it through."

Holmes lifted the third piece of paper, containing a carefully handwritten letter. He tried to read it, clutched his eyes and handed it to me, cursing.

I took the letter, sitting back in my chair.

My Dearest Holmes,

I trust you are recovering. Obviously, the only explanation for the lack of fantastic arrests credited to Scotland Yard under seemingly impossible circumstances is this: The Great Detective is not performing his duties.

As you may be aware, there have been a series of murders in Whitechapel. I have too high of an opinion of you to suspect that the killings of such lowly subjects is not sufficient to arouse the interest of you and your Boswell. Perhaps I can propose something that will stimulate you to action.

Let us combine forces, Holmes. You and I should partner in this endeavor, chasing this villain down together.

Yours,

Irene Adler

"Perhaps her company is exactly what you need to lift your spirits, Holmes. It might help expedite the healing process," I said.

"Were you not the one who just said I was not allowed to go running off on some damned adventure?"

"I did not say go running off, Holmes. But we could find a way to participate. I mean, really, four innocent women? Butchered like that?"

"You consider them innocent, Watson?"

I thought for a moment, lighting my pipe and sitting back in the chair. "Perhaps they cannot be considered such. After all, they are indeed whores, and to make it even worse they choose to ply their trade in the filthiest, most crime-ridden part in all of England."

Holmes sighed, "That is not what I meant."

"Well then what was it?"

"No one is innocent," he said, taking Irene Adler's letter and the press clippings out of my hand and sliding them into the fire. They instantly flared and burned, breaking into tiny bits of ash that floated into the air.

Eight

Irene Adler awoke screaming.

It had happened every night since she'd casually opened the Daily Mail's September Tenth edition, and the headline "Another Murder in Whitechapel" caught her eye. She'd read the first paragraph with morbid fascination but as soon as she read the victim's name, her hands began shaking.

The dream always began the same. She was backstage, crouched in the wings of London's Royal Opera House. She pulled aside a handful of curtain and leaned out just enough to see the audience. The stagehands were gossiping excitedly that it was the largest crowd to ever attend the theater. Adler swallowed, seeing that even the standing-room only sections were crowded. A man came up behind her and said, "Isn't it bad luck to count the house before the curtain rises?"

She turned to see the seeing the sinister grin of Oscar Wilde. "Mr. Wilde, you devil. You swore you weren't coming this evening."

"The Devil himself could not keep from attending tonight," Wilde said. Irene pressed her hand against her face, pretending to blush. "You see, the French circus troupe is performing tonight. They are renowned for many things, you know."

"Such as?"

He sniffed the sunflower pinned to his lapel and looked sideways at a lithe lad with green greasepaint smeared across his bare torso. "Their physical prowess, and such. They are said to be contortionists of the highest order. Perhaps one of them might be willing to give me a demonstration later? It might be the sort of thing to cheer me up. I found a gray hair this morning, and fear that I have lost my youth."

"Well then," Irene said, looking at the male performer, "we shall have to see what we can do about finding you another one."

Wilde pulled Irene close and whispered in her ear, "If you tell anyone I am a sentimentalist, I will put a curse upon you that makes your perfect breasts droop to your knees, my darling. But I would not have missed your final performance for anything in the world."

Irene pushed Wilde back, "Who told you it was my final performance?"

"You did, with all your talk of adventuring and getting on with seeing the world," Wilde shrugged. "And how I fear for that world you are about to be unleashed upon."

"What world is that, Mr. Wilde?"

"The world of Man. All those poor, unsuspecting members of the species who will fall powerless to your gaze. Do try and send some of your forlorn conquests my way when you are through with them."

"How fortunate that you are immune to my charms," she said, putting her arm in his.

"Who knows? For you, even I might be persuaded to give it a whirl."

"You are a scoundrel, and I love you for it, Mr. Wilde. Will you be accompanying me to dinner after the show? I could introduce you to some of these performers. From what I've gathered, there are several who may be inclined to demonstrate some of that prowess to you."

Wilde smiled and pinched her cheek, "You naughty, naughty little vixen. May I bring my friend? He's the one who arranged my seat for the evening. I warn you, he is a bit of an eccentric. I fear that he will take to you like a small puppy, and that you, in your predatory nature, will swallow him up in one bite."

"Who is he?" Irene said.

"No fewer than the King of Bohemia, my dove. He's also a Grand Duke something-something. I do not really know. I just call him Wilhelm. I am cruel to him and he buys me things."

"I suppose I could stand some amusement," Irene said. "I will see you after the performance."

Wilde bowed deeply to Irene and kissed her hand, "Best of luck this evening, my little songbird. Jenny Lind herself could not hold a candle to you." As Wilde left, circus performers from the opening act began to filter into the wings. The lights dimmed, and there was a sudden explosion of light and sound as the curtain opened and the performers somersaulted onto the stage, assembling themselves into a V-shaped formation. Irene went to her dressing room and began to unbutton her wrapper, assessing the assortment of makeup carefully arranged in front of the mirror. A knock at the door threatened to steal the quiet moment of reverie from her even as she reflected on Oscar Wilde's observation that tonight was her final performance. She hadn't said a word to anyone.

"Miss Adler?" came a soft voice through the door.

Irene took a deep breath and opened it, forcing a smile. Annie Chapman, a mother of one of the child performers in the circus stood, meekly holding a luxurious dress that stood in stark contrast to the rags the woman was wearing. "Oh, hello, Annie," Irene said. "Are you finished with the stitching already?"

"Yes," Annie said, smiling nervously as she handed the dress over to Irene. She proudly displayed the torn seam she'd sewn. "I put double stitches in it. Won't trouble yeh again, Miss Adler. I swears by it."

"Excellent," Irene said, taking it from her. "It looks wonderful. I promise to wear it at the nearest opportunity."

"It would be lovely to see yeh in it, Miss Adler. Thanks for giving me the chance to do a little work for you. We certainly needed the money."

Irene hung up the dress and turned away from Annie, eyeing her wigs and makeup, hoping it was an obvious enough hint that she needed time to get ready. In truth, Irene had the finest tailors in all of London at her disposal. Men who were practically begging for the chance to create new fashions for the famous prima donna of La Scala. Certainly, they were better suited for the repairs than a common street person like Annie Chapman.

When Irene first chanced upon Annie, the woman was crying in a dark corner backstage, loudly enough that Irene could not walk past without at least inquiring if she was all right. Through thick tears, Annie blurted out the difficulties she and her family were having and asked if Irene knew of any work that was available around the theater. Irene, even as she told herself the simpler, less-involving answer would be to tell the woman no, she instead found herself mentioning that she had a few dresses in need of some light repair work. With a sigh, she asked if Annie perhaps knew how to thread a needle and sew a bit?

I certainly overpaid her for it too, Irene thought. Most of the work was sloppy, with uneven stitching and unfinished seams. That little crying jag had, in all likelihood, been a staged performance designed to catch her eye from the start, Irene reasoned. Ah well. The damn circus people were heading off for France anyway. "I seem to be all fixed up then, Annie. Which is good, I suppose, since you are all leaving us after tonight, isn't that right?"

"Yes, Miss Adler," Annie said, looking down. "It's fortunate you should bring that up, as I was wanting to speak to you about it. They leave off tonight, and you've been such a big inspiration to us all that I wanted to say thank you and bid you goodbye."

"Why thank you, Annie," Irene said. She felt compelled to reach out and touch Annie on the arm and give her bicep a slight squeeze in lieu of a full embrace. Annie was stiff, and smelled faintly of liquor. "You must promise to have a safe trip, then." Irene stepped back, ready to close the door.

"Oh, I am not going," Annie said quickly. "I can't. My little boy is a cripple, an' me eldest daughter Emily is sick as well."

"I see," Irene said slowly, ignoring Annie's hopeful, pleading stare. "Well, I am sure your other daughter appreciates the opportunity you are giving her. You must be very proud. Now I really must get ready, Annie."

Annie leaned forward, putting her body in the doorframe. "I just wish I had something to send her along with, you know? The way things are, my John works an' all, but at this point we can barely keep a roof over our heads. Medicine is so expensive."

"I am sure it is," Irene said, closing the door toward Annie.

"Yes, quite!" Annie said, standing her ground.

Irene sighed. "Is there anything else I can do for you, Annie? I am to be on stage any minute. If you need something, it would better for you to just ask for it."

"Can I borrow a pound from you to give her? Just a few, so I don't have to send her away empty handed? I will pay you back, I swear on it."

Irene shook her head, well-aware that she was doing a poor job of masking the contempt on her face. "See me after the performance and I will see what I can do, all right?"

"God bless you, Miss Adler! Bless you so much."

"All right. Run along now," Irene said, shutting the door.

The performance was spectacular. The entire audience leapt to their feet, thunderously applauding as Irene took her bows, standing knee-deep in the flowers and cards thrown at the stage. People were screaming her name. As Irene passed through the curtains, Oscar Wilde was clapping, "Oh, brava, Irene. Brava." There was a handsome and tall man standing nearby and Wilde held out his hand to say, "Allow me to introduce Wilhelm Gottsreich Sigismond von Ormstein, Grand Duke of Cassel-Felstein."

Wilhelm bowed low and kissed her hand. "I am also the King of Bohemia," he said. "Really? A King? Oscar, is this some sort of jest?"

"I assure you it is not," Wilde said with a quick smile.

"Well, then I suppose it is just us Libertines," Irene said, looping her arm through Wilhelm's.

"Pardon me, Miss Adler?" a voice creaked from behind Irene.

Christ, Irene thought, seething. Is there no one among the lower class possessed of any manners at all? She turned, "As you can plainly see, I am a little busy at present, Annie. Would you mind terribly giving us just a moment, please?"

"Yes, ma'am," Annie said, lowering her head. "Whenever you prefer."

"Who in God's name is that wretched creature?" Wilde said.

"Someone I cannot seem to escape. Would you mind distracting her while I steal His Majesty away for a little privacy? I find myself wanting to get to know him a bit better." Irene winked at Wilhelm, who was smiling stupidly. Alas, she thought. Better pretty than clever.

"Anything for you, my dove," Wilde said. He leaned in toward her ear, "Try not to break him. He's a bit fragile."

"Oh, no promises," Irene said, as Wilde moved past her to begin talking to Annie Chapman, leading her away from the stage and out the back door. "So," she said to Wilhelm, "tell me all about Bohemia."

In her dream she now turned to look at Annie, who was standing in the shadows beneath the curtain's rigging, watching her leave.

Someone came up behind Annie and pressed a knife to her throat, covering her mouth and beginning to saw the flesh with the edge of his blade. No one seemed to notice when Irene began screaming for help.

Nine

The East End of London is relatively small, composed of an area just about fifteen square miles in size. That year, over one million people were estimated to have lived there. By comparison, New York City's Manhattan is roughly twenty-three square miles, and in an 1880 census, had nearly the same number of residents.

An 1820 survey found thirty-thousand thieves operating in the East End. Police reports indicated they stole more than two million pounds of goods from local stores and residences. Like most places, immigrants sought out less-expensive, less-noticeable areas to live in their new country. Clusters of Jewish, German, and Russian ghettos were clustered throughout the East End, formed both to protect and insulate the foreigners from the natives. Outsiders were not welcome. Cliques, gangs, fraternities, or whatever other euphemism one preferred, quickly formed and those groups were often at odds with the competing interests of others who did the same. The pie is only so big. Only the most resourceful, resilient, and ruthless get to eat it.

The London Metropolitan Police Service estimated there were sixty-two licensed brothels in Whitechapel. Besides those formal establishments, another twelve hundred whores roamed the streets and alleyways. Every so often, a few were found dead. Death in general, and even murder, were common occurrences in the East End. It was no different from any city, in any part of the world, either before or since, and whatever terrible things happened there were regarded by outsiders with an air of inevitability.

   Emma Smith, Martha Tabram, Polly Nichols, and Annie Chapman changed all that. Their deaths were so gruesome, so sensational, that soon every newspaper in the world had correspondents in Whitechapel searching for headlines. The day after Annie Chapman's body was discovered, no fewer than fourteen newspapers carried precise, vivid details of her demise. These newspapers were quickly gobbled up by a terrified, gossip-hungry, morbidly obsessed populace. Journalists completely abandoned the standard non-partisan tenets of reporting, opting instead for a dogmatic, inflammatory approach to cover what was termed *"The Whitechapel Horror."* Each new article was increasingly soaked with editorial vitiation concerning the description of the killer. The character of the female victims was targeted, and even more importantly, the impotence of the police.

   The people of the East End became accustomed to seeing the names of many of their friends and neighbors in the paper. Daily, news articles quoted someone new solemnly offering their personal take on the murders and naming the party they believed responsible. Every new "revelation" was shamelessly foisted on the public as if it were fact. During all hours of the day and night, police and journalists swarmed through Whitechapel, leaping over one another like rats in the street, bucking to find just one more person to interview, one more story to fan the flames.

   George Lusk knew all of this. Gazing out at the sea of people squeezed into the meeting room of the Whitechapel Board of

Building and Design, he decided the time had come for him to convene what he intended to be a solution to the problem. "All right, let's get started, folks. Order," he said, tapping his gavel on the desk. The people in the crowd continued to shout. "I am calling the first meeting of the Mile End Committee to Protect Whitechapel to order! Everyone must settle down, please."

"This is impossible," Joseph Aarons said, taking the gavel from Lusk and banging it even harder. "Order! Order!" he shouted. Aarons and Lusk served together on the Board Committee and had been part of the decision to open their hall to the public in the event that any would want to voice their opinion to the crowd. They expected a dozen or so attendees, not the crowd so massive that they filled the hall and forced others to stand outside of the doors.

"Be silent so we can get started!" Lusk shouted.

A man stepped forward through the crowd. The men surrounding him pushed the other people back, clearing a path. A deep scar ran down the side of his face, both above and below a menacing black eye patch. "Shut up, all of you," he growled. The crowd fell silent.

"Oh God," Joseph Aarons said. He leaned close to Lusk and pointed toward the man with the eye patch and said, "What the hell is he doing here?"

"Who is it?" Lusk asked.

"Mickey Fitch. He brought the whole damned Old Nichol Gang."

"What do they want?" Lusk muttered. Regardless, the crowd was now quieted down. Lusk began, "Ahem. We would like to thank you all for coming tonight. We know that many of you have deep concerns about the recent events in our neighborhoods. We want to give you an open forum to discuss them."

"You mean how the damn cops don't give a flying frig about stopping the killer?" someone in the front yelled.

"You ain't kidding!" a man up front shouted.

Someone else yelled, "The damn police is too busy looking after the changing of bus houses in the West-end and watching over Trafalgar Square to care what becomes of poor devils like us!"

The crowd began to get loud again, and Lusk rapped his gavel futilely until Mickey Fitch held up his hand and they fell silent. When Fitch spoke, his voice was a low gravelly snarl. "There are some of us here tonight, Mr. Chairman, who feel that the people of Whitechapel can do a better job of looking after our own, on our own." The men behind Fitch grunted and nodded.

"I just bet," Aarons said out of the side of his mouth to Lusk. "His business interests have to be suffering with all the damn blue bottles around."

Lusk smiled calmly at the crowd and said, "I assure you that is the precise reason we have assembled here tonight, sir." He stood to his feet, waving his hand above the crowd, "Let us all put aside our differences to unite under one common banner of rescuing our fair city from the evil clutches of this monster. To turn our voices toward Buckingham Palace once more to announce that we, the people of the East End, will not be forgotten!"

The crowd cheered and Lusk smiled brightly, soaking in their admiration. He saw that Mickey Fitch was not cheering, but stood with his hands folded, waiting. Lusk calmed the crowd down and said, "Let us hear from Mr. Fitch. What do you propose, sir?"

Fitch licked his lips and said, "Talk is cheap, Mr. Lusk. What me and my boys had in mind was something a little more action-oriented. You see, the police trying to catch this killer are lacking one crucial thing that our lot can provide. A certain familiarity with the ways and means of Whitechapel, if you will."

"This is not what I had in mind, Mr. Fitch," Aarons said, turning in his seat. He lowered his voice and said, "George, what the hell are you doing? We were supposed to put on a nice little show and get Lord Salisbury's attention. This man is a gang leader. He will cut out throats the second we are no longer of any use to him."

Lusk was imagining the Queen putting a medal around his neck as he nodded silently while Fitch spoke.

Montague Druitt's carriage rolled to a stop in front of his old home in Dorset. He paid the carman and waited until he was alone before going up the stairs to the front door. As he went through the door, he shivered at its exact similarity to the last time he'd been in the house. Little had changed except that now thick layers of dust and cobwebs covering everything. Animals had taken up residence in the home, and he listened to them scurrying along the walls and floors as he closed the door.

Druitt checked the windows and doors on the first floor, ensuring that they were intact and none broken. He unlatched the back door and went down the steps, gazing out into the deserted fields now overgrown with weeds and grass. The spiked fence was gone, torn out by his father years ago, despite Ann's protests that her garden would be overrun by animals without it. In one of the few acts of defiance of his mother that Druitt had ever seen, William ignored her and ripped the metal posts from the earth, cursing each spike as he wept.

Druitt bent down to inspect the patch of earth his sister had been placed down on so long ago. He closed his eyes, feeling the soft breeze on his face and hearing his sister gurgle, "Monty, Monty."

He lied down on the ground, putting his face in the dirt, smelling to see if he could still find the scent of her. He dug his fingers into the dirt, and scooped a handful of it into his pocket. There was a sealed jar in his other pocket, and he'd spent the entire train ride covering it protectively as other passengers sat too close, or bumped into him.

"I am glad to take you with me, sister," Druitt whispered, patting the soil in his pocket. He walked back into the house, taking the stairs toward his father's locked bedroom, shouldering the door and shattering the wooden frame into splinters. He found William's medical bag on top of the dresser. Druitt opened the bag and inspected the surgical blades within. They were rusted. He threw them back into the bag and grabbed the handle, turning to leave. He stopped when he saw William's hatbox in the corner.

Druitt lifted the dusty lid and removed the top hat from inside. He inspected the brim and found it was still sturdy and without creases. He put the hat on his head. He shut William's bedroom door and walked to the stairs leading up to the attic bedroom. Piles of Ann's things covered every step. Druitt kicked them away, clearing the steps, scattering bottles of lotion and clothing and trinkets and faded photographs all across the hall. He looked at the top of the stairs at the closed door to Georgiana's bedroom. Light poured through the edges of the door in the places it did not meet the frame, like a portal to some other place.

Druitt opened it and went up the stairs toward Georgiana's closed bedroom door. Something was welling deep within. Too powerful to bother attempting the door handle, he reached the upper landing and kicked it in. Decades of dust covered Georgiana's mirror, and Druitt swept his hand across its surface, from top to bottom. He looked at himself in the mirror, satisfied. Druitt emptied his pockets of Georgiana's dirt and piled it on the floor in front of the mirror. He removed the jar from his left pocket and set it in front of the dirt. He opened his father's medical bag and set the sharpest looking bone-handled knife next to the jar.

He stripped naked, looking at himself in the mirror for a moment. He stepped into the dirt, feeling it between his toes. He picked up the knife, studying his palm before slicing it open, letting blood leak onto the dirt below. He unscrewed the lid of the jar and reached in, lifting the clump of Annie Chapman's wet uterus with his fingers. He squeezed it tightly with his bleeding hand, feeling its cold ichor mix into his bloodstream, stinging the wound.

Druitt closed his eyes, seeing the horror in Polly Nichols's eyes as he sliced across her throat. He saw her body crumpled on the street. He saw Georgiana on the fence. He saw his mother, naked, shrieking at him.

"I am the beast, and I will devour the world." Druitt lifting the dripping organ to his mouth and bit deeply of Annie Chapman's uterus, sucking it until the cold juices burst into his mouth. Deep within, an explosion ignited, setting fire to his insides, lighting his mind and soul aflame so that he screamed in both ecstasy and horror. A new voice spoke to Druitt, born of the inferno.

"My name," he whispered, chewing the cold flesh and swallowing, "is Jack."

Act II

COME ARMAGEDDON, COME

Ten

Mary and I arrived at the Forrester home precisely at seven o'clock. She spent the ride lamenting that she was arriving as a guest, rather than being there already, helping them to prepare for the event. "Poor Gordon never knows how to fix his hair. I bet it is a disaster. And Miss Mildred in the kitchen? God, if she forgot to get the—"

"Mary?" I said softly, "Perhaps I am not the only one who needs to adjust to the changes our life together will bring."

"You are right, darling. Tonight we begin to make our mark on society. The night the future Dr. and Mrs. John Watson reveal themselves to the world." She took my hand in hers as our cab lined up behind the others waiting to deliver their occupants to the front steps. Servants waited by the curb to assist the women from their cabs; others waited at the front doors, taking guest's coats as they entered. Smartly dressed men bowed to the arriving couples, pointing them toward their destination within. What I'd initially thought a modest stained glass window beside the doorway was now fully lit in rich crimson that swirled with cobalt, sparkling and majestic. Shapes etched into the window appeared to shift and rotate in the flickering lights. The shadows of people in the hall appeared behind the window, giving the impression that they moved within the colors of the glass itself. I held Mary's hand tightly, taking in the full view and whispered, "Something like this could be ours, if we put our minds to it. We could live like this."

Mary nodded, nestling her head in my arm as we approached the house. "We would be lucky to be half as rich as the Forrester's, John. Not by how much money they have, but how they care for one another." She pulled me toward the house, eager to make her entrance. She laughed like a little girl, excitedly racing up the steps. "I've missed being here so much. I hope you take to one another, John. They are so important to me."

"I shall be glad to know them then," I said. "I want good people to be in our lives, people who know the value of family. This home is exquisite."

"Aunt Mary!" came an excited shriek as we entered. A young man with hair standing straight up in the air came running up to Mary and threw his arms around her. "You're here!"

"Of course, Gordon," Mary said, laughing, kissing him on the cheek. She licked her palms and began flattening his hair dutifully.

"There you are!" Mrs. Forrester called out, wrapping her arms tightly around Mary's shoulders. "Dr. Watson," she said, lifting her hand toward me delicately.

I took her hand and kissed it, bowing my head. "Mrs. Forrester, thank you for inviting me to your lovely home."

She smiled, "As you know, Mary is much more than someone who just works for us. She is like a daughter, which means that I expect to be seeing quite a lot of you as well."

"I will be on my best behavior then," I said, making both women smile. "Is Mr. Forrester about? I have not had the chance to introduce myself to him yet. I suppose it was impolite of me to not have asked his permission before I proposed to Mary?"

"Of course not," Mrs. Forrester said. "Any man worthy to assist the Great Detective must be worthy of our approval."

Mary waved her hand. "John is finished running all over London with Mr. Holmes. He is now concentrating on expanding his medical practice before we marry. There will be no more chasing of basset hounds for my husband."

"Pardon me, darling, but it was not a basset-hound. It was a long fanged, phosphorous-infected devil of a-"

"Of course. Anything you say, my love." Mary smiled knowingly as she turned back toward Mrs. Forrester, "We were hoping to make some introductions this evening, to let people know that his services are available."

"I have a grand idea. The eldest son of the Sixth Duke of Gordon is here tonight. He'll inherit the title soon enough. If you impress him, he might be able to introduce you to several people. He's not yet a duke, so he can't be offended at having you sit with him." She leaned close to Mary, "Let me go make the arrangements."

Mary smiled brightly at me, clutching my hand. "An-almost-Duke! You see, John? Everything is coming together nicely!"

"I do not want to push myself on people, Mary."

"I know, and you shan't. People are curious enough about your involvement with Holmes that they will want to meet you." Mary paused for a moment, weighing her words. "I think it would be better to tell people that you worked alongside Holmes, acting as his advisor for anatomical and medical questions. It sounds better than always running around claiming to be his 'biographer,' or 'assistant.' What do you think?" She straightened my collar and fixed my jacket's lapels, looking me over in a way no one had since my mother used to prepare me for church. I half-expected her to lick her thumb and swipe it across my cheek to clean away the sticky residue of a taffy. "There. Now you look presentable." Mary diverted from her inspection when she noticed me grinning. "What is it?"

"I just wanted to look at you for a moment. No one has treated ever treated me so kindly. Thank you for taking such good care of me."

A shadow fell over us, and I turned to see an enormous man standing with an arm placed commandingly on the shoulders of two incredibly beautiful oriental females. The women, if they could be called that, for neither could have been older than nineteen years old, bowed their heads and covered their faces with ornate fans. Their hair was pulled back tight against their heads in long braids that hung below their waists. Mycroft Holmes looked down at me and smiled, "It is pleasant to see you here, Dr. Watson."

"Hello, Mycroft," I said, looking past him at the two women. Their expressions were blank and soulless. "How goes the business of nation-building? Or is it their destruction? I can never be certain."

"Never better, my dear doctor. Never better."

"Well, you certainly look content."

Mycroft laughed, patting his rotund belly. "It is called dim-sum, Watson. I swear, these two have put an extra three stone on me." Mycroft looked down at the women and spoke to them in Chinese. They nodded and shuffled off into the crowd. Mycroft watched them go, chuckling. "So," he said, turning back toward us, "who is this little beauty?"

Mary held out her hand, and Mycroft took it, kissing it delicately and bowed. "This is my fiancée, Miss Mary Morstan. Mary, this Mycroft Holmes."

"Charming," Mycroft said, eyeing the length of her. "I wish you both the utmost success in both life and love."

"Mary, please excuse Mr. Holmes and me."

Mary smiled and left us to mingle with other arrivals who she wanted to greet. I leaned close to Mycroft and whispered, "Who are the two Oriental girls?"

He smiled. "A gift of thanks from the Empress Dowager Cixi for assisting her in the Sino-French war."

"But, the Chinese lost control of North Vietnam to the French," I said. "It was a complete routing."

Mycroft smiled and nodded, "Yes, indeed it was. But the Tonkin Affair made it all worthwhile. I dare say France has seen its last Republican Government for quite awhile."

"And that was your doing?" I asked.

Mycroft patted me on the back, "Watson, my boy, there are some things at work in this world which are best left unexamined. Now, I want to ask you about my brother. What makes you so sure that he is truly ill? He's pulled this trick before, playing the sickly role while he maneuvers and cavorts about unattended."

"He is not pretending this time, Mycroft. Why not come see for yourself?"

"Things are a bit sketchy at the moment. There is some bad business to attend to out in Dufile. Damn Indians are always up to something."

"I suppose that happens when you show up in someone else's backyard and try to tell them how things should be done. Especially when you do it at point of bayonet."

Mycroft looked at me for a moment, eyes searching as thoroughly as his brother's ever had. "I can see why Sherlock keeps you close to him. You appear to be somewhat soft-brained and it lulls people into a sense of false confidence with you. That is a mistake, I suppose."

I grunted and looked around us, making sure no one else could hear. For all intents and purposes, we were just two men making polite conversation. "Perhaps I am somewhat soft-brained, Mycroft. I went into the army thinking I would be protecting the people of England from foreign threat. Then I realized we were all nothing more than cannon-fodder for a wide-array of Imperialistic schemes. In Afghanistan, I watched men I considered to be my brothers get blasted to bits at Asmai Heights because of people like you."

Mycroft removed a thick cigar from a silver case and took his time lighting it. Soon, he was drawing in large mouthfuls of smoke and blowing them toward the sky. "I envy you, Watson. I wonder what it would be like to see the world in such simplistic terms. The fact is, my boy, if you understood the true nature of how things work, you would run screaming into the ocean."

"If you say so, Mycroft."

He took out his cigar and licked his thin lips, spitting flecks of tobacco leaf from them. "I mean no offense, Watson, truly I don't. You have a heart, and it must be hard for you to understand people like my brother and me. You see, neither of us is in possession of one."

"Ladies and gentlemen, if I may have your fullest attention?" A man at the far end of the room spoke, tapping his spoon against a glass.

"Is that Mr. Forrester?" I asked Mary. She nodded, but held her finger to her lips for me to be silent.

"Can everyone hear me?" Cecil Forrester said. "All right, we have a lovely surprise for you all this evening." A man walked onto the stage behind Forrester and took his place on a stool in front of an enormous Packard organ.

"She has stood upon the finest stages in every part of the world, captivating audiences with a voice so singularly beautiful that it has been known to bring grown men to tears. Napkins are available from your servers," he said, laughing. "Without any further ado, I present, the one and only, Miss Irene Adler."

Two servants held the kitchen doors open as Irene Adler entered the ballroom in a long flowing gown, her trailing train held up from the floor by another servant. She walked up several steps to the small stage where Forrester stood waiting. Her skirt fluttered and a band of brightly shining diamonds reflected at her ankle, as if even beneath the confines of her clothing, rich gems could be found for someone willing to explore-

"Dr. Watson?" Mary said, so sharply that I turned my head.

"Yes, darling?"

"Is that the woman you told me about? I do not recall you mentioning anything about all of this."

"This?"

She turned, looking at Irene who waived to the crowd, smiling brightly. Her full, red lips puckered as she blew a kiss to all of us. "That," Mary said.

"Well, I can tell you that she looks completely different in person." I looked sideways at Mary, hoping that my lie had gone unnoticed. Even Mary could not look away from Irene now. Her long, golden hair was pulled into a tight bun that offset the high arches of her cheekbones. She lowered her arms and closed her eyes, and the whole crowd fell silent. An organist off to the side of the stage stepped on his pedals and a low-groan emitted from the pipes.

Her voice erupted over us, filling the room with sound. Her highest notes carried me upwards, spinning me delicately through the air.

"Frondi tenere e belle
del mio platano amato,
per voi risplenda il fato.
Tuoni, lampi, e procelle
non v'oltraggino mai la cara pace,
né giunga a profanarvi
austro rapace."

The organist had not finished, but as Irene stopped singing the crowd applauded wildly. Irene waited politely to acknowledge them until the pipes of the organ were silent. She then tilted her head in acknowledgement to the crowd and left the stage.

People cried out for her to return to the stage, and in a moment, the kitchen doors swung open again. Everyone leapt to their feet, shouting and applauding. The servants rushing through the doors stopped suddenly, eyeing the crowd in wonder, balancing silver food trays carefully. They then smiled and bowed dramatically, making everyone laugh and return to their seats.

I pushed Mary's seat in and nodded to everyone at our table. The food had begun to arrive, and I waited for each person to receive their plate before I stood and said, "Gentlemen, ladies, I shall return in just a moment."

"Dr. Watson?" Mary said, cocking an eyebrow at me. "Where are you going?"

"I shall be right back."

I ignored looks from the curious staff members as I entered the kitchen. Many of them were racing around, scurrying to get the massive amounts of food off of the serving trays into the hands of the hungry guests. I saw a pantry door closing ahead and Irene's angry voice from within. "Do not stand there and tell me there is nothing you can do, Charles!"

"Irene, this is a far different matter than anything you could possibly understand."

"No, it is you who does not understand. Women are being butchered right under your nose, and you will not send in the resources to deal with it."

"Why are you so angry, hmm? Come give us a kiss."

"Get off of me, Charles!"

"Stop it, Irene. Just a little reminder of when we first-"

I opened the door, meeting the crimson-faced stare of Commissioner of the Metropolitan Police, Sir Charles Warren. His hands were wrapped around Irene, who was squirming to get away.

"Watson!" Irene shouted.

"Hello, Miss Adler," I said, reaching for her. I put my hand on her shoulder and pulled her away from the Commissioner's grip as he glowered at me. "I am so sorry to interrupt, Sir Charles."

"Wait just a bloody minute," Warren barked, grabbing at Irene's hand. "This is a private conversation that—"

I saw a kitchen woman hurrying past and stepped into her path, halting her suddenly. "Excuse me," I said, "Police Commissioner Sir Charles Warren has yet to be seated and although he is too much of a gentleman to complain, I am affronted on his behalf."

"What?" the woman said nervously, "oh my."

I threw the door open and pointed at him, "Yes, this man, the Commissioner of the London Metropolitan Police Department is left standing while everyone else is being catered to. Do you know who he is? I assure you, madam, the Queen herself is familiar with Sir Charles Warren."

Other people in the kitchen were now staring at us. Irene came to my side, and together we fled the kitchen while the staff gathered around Warren, throwing accusations at one another and jockeying to be the first to offer to guide him to his seat.

Irene giggled as we made our way for the front door, down the steps toward her awaiting carriage. "My thanks to you, Watson," Irene said. "Good old Charles. Put a few whiskeys in him and he becomes Lothario."

"I do not think that was anything to joke about, Miss Adler. You were about to be ravished."

Irene laughed, wrapping her shawl around her throat. "I assure you that I was in no such danger. It takes more than any drunken policeman to corner me. Do you know Charles actually told the newspapers that it was useless to send detectives into Whitechapel? He said 'This monster will be captured by good old-fashioned patrol work.' What ignorance!"

"Well apparently he has some familiarity with you to lure you into a pantry to discuss the situation." My voice was angrier than I intended it to be. It contained a hint of jealousy that revealed itself before I could catch it. I decided it was because of my dear friend Holmes's attachment to her and that I was simply defending his honor by my hatred of seeing another man pawing Irene. "Regardless, he is one of the most powerful men in the country and could have us both arrested with a single word. It is best to use at least some caution with him."

"Did Holmes get my letter?"

"What's that? A letter, you say?"

"Did Holmes get the letter I sent him? About the killings in Whitechapel?"

"I am not certain," I said. "Holmes has been terribly ill lately and I doubt he would even have the strength to open your letter if he did receive it. It is probably lying in the large pile of letters sitting on his chair, just waiting until he has recovered sufficiently enough to get back to work."

Irene stared at me for a moment. "You have grown so used to lying on his behalf that you cannot stop yourself any longer, can you? If you were any sort of capable physician, you would have forced him off of the cocaine long before this."

"…Pardon me?"

She looked at me innocently, batting her large eyes, "What?"

"What did you just say?"

"Nothing," Irene said, looking back to the road. "I suppose I'll need to do it myself. Have a wonderful evening at your party, Watson. Hopefully not too many more women will be butchered in the street while you and your friends drink and make merry."

"You came tonight. You performed for them. If you hold these people in such low regard, why go out of your way to entertain them? I suppose the price was right, eh?"

She laughed. "I knew Warren would be here and it was the only way I could get his attention. A woman has to find her way around in certain situations, sir. It is not as simple as you men might think. Good night. And do tell Holmes I was asking for him."

When I finally sat back down next to Mary, she was intently eating her meal and avoiding making any eye contact, or taking any notice of me, whatsoever. "Hello, everyone. I hope I am not interrupting anything with my late arrival."

A man sitting in the seat across from mine waved his hand and said, "No bother at all. Miss Morstan tells us that you are the manservant for none other than Sherlock Holmes?"

"Manservant?" I said, exhaling deeply. When I looked toward Mary, she only looked away.

Eleven

Steven Morrissey weaved through the crowded floor of the London Central News Limited, waving an envelope as if it were on fire and he was trying to put it out. "Mr. Phillips! Mr. Phillips! Stop the presses! You have to see this!"

Adam Phillips looked up from his editor's desk. "What are you going on about, Morrissey?"

"It's from him! Him!"

"Him who?" Phillips asked.

"The killer!" Morrissey took a deep breath as every machine and pen in the office stopped moving. Staff members silenced one another, looking at him. "He sent us this letter. He says his name is Jack the Ripper."

Phillips looked at the front of the envelope. It read:

The Boss
Central News Office
London City

Phillips checked the postmark. The envelope had been stamped and sent by London's East Central Post that day. Phillips removed a single sheet of paper from inside the envelope, seeing it was splattered with bright red ink. At least, he hoped it was ink. "This letter is dated September Twenty-Fifth," Phillips noted. "That's two days ago, yet he mailed it today. Why would he wait to send it?"

"Read it," Morrissey said.

"It is probably just a hoax."

"Read it, sir!"

Phillips cleared his throat.

"Dear Boss,
I keep on hearing the police
have caught me but they won't fix
me just yet. I have laughed when
they look so clever and talk about
being on the right track. That joke
about Leather Apron gave me real
fits. I am down on whores and
I shant quit ripping them till I
do get buckled. Grand work the last
job was. I gave the lady no time to
squeal. How can they catch me now.
I love my work and want to start
again. You will soon hear of me
with my funny little games. I
saved some of the proper red stuff in
a ginger beer bottle over the last job
to write with but it went thick
like glue and I can't use it. Red
ink is fit enough I hope. ha. ha.
The next job I do I shall clip
the lady's ears off and send to the
police officers just for jolly wouldn't
you. Keep this letter back till I
do a bit more work then give

*it out straight. My knife's so nice
and sharp I want to get to work
right away if I get a chance.
Good luck.
Yours truly
Jack the Ripper
Don't mind me giving the trade name.*

*PS: wasn't good enough
to post this before
I got all the red
ink off my hands
curse it.
No luck yet. They
say I'm a doctor
now ha ha"*

Phillips looked up at his staff and nodded several times at them. "You see? It is just a sick joke. Anyone could tell…just a harmless prank."

None of them moved. All stared at the letter silently. Morrissey finally spoke, "What are you going to do, Mr. Phillips?"

"Do? I am going to do absolutely nothing. It is nothing but a ruse meant to get us all into a tizzy." Phillips took the letter and crammed it into the envelope, throwing it down into the rubbish pail and wiping his hands together.

"You should send for the police," Morrissey said.

"For what? They have enough on their plate with piles of mutilated bodies, I think."

"Then at least publish the damn thing! People are being killed, Mr. Phillips. We need to warn them."

Phillips glowered back at him, "Warn who? The whores? You want to warn them to stop whoring, be my guest. That is the end of the conversation. Do you not have anything else for me besides forged letters?"

Morrissey pulled several hand-written pages from his bag and handed it to Phillips. "Here's a thousand words on a man named John Fitzgerald. He walked into the police station and confessed to killing Annie Chapman."

"Really?" Phillips took the pages. "Is he under arrest?"

"Perhaps, but certainly not for the Chapman murder. Every shred of his story has proven false. He is just another one who wanted to see his name in the press."

Phillips looked at the pages and shook his head. "Let me understand. A man walks into a police station and confesses to killing Annie Chapman, lying all the while in hopes of the newspapers running a story with his name in it?"

"Correct," Morrissey nodded.

"And you are giving me a thousand word article which accomplishes precisely that?"

"Right again," Morrissey said.

"Bit of a conundrum, isn't it?"

"Not really," Morrissey explained. "You pay me to write articles that sell newspapers, sir. Unfortunately, the public wants to read every single shred of news about these killings. If people like John Fitzgerald did not exist, we would have to invent him." Morrissey bent down and picked up the Ripper letter from the trash can. "I am sure you do not mind me keeping this? I'll bet a month's salary that it is genuine."

"How can you be so certain?"

"He's given up his name, Mr. Phillips. Letting us know he's not Leather Apron or any of the other boogie men we've blamed. All artists protect their work with extreme jealousy and I would venture to guess that Jack the Ripper is no different."

On Sunday, September Thirtieth, sometime after midnight, Louis Diemschutz gently whacked his pony's rear, ordering it to keep moving. The pony's pace began to slow before they were even halfway home from the Westow Hill market, its scrawny frame struggling to pull the weight of the boxes of cheap, imitation jewelry that Diemschutz humped back and forth to the market each weekend. Few pieces had been bought that day, and the cart was still nearly full. They came to Berner Street, wheels squeaking on the uneven stones, and Diemschutz saw that the gates to the yard at the International Working Men's Educational Club were propped open for him.

"That is my Adele's doing," he said to the mount. "God blessed me on the day she agreed to marry me." It was Diemschutz's practice to talk aloud, both to fill the silence, and to trick any thieves lurking in the shadows into thinking he might not be alone. Diemschutz had been robbed before.

The pony stopped so suddenly that the boxes beneath Diemschutz shifted forward abruptly, nearly inverting the cart.

"What are you doing?" Diemschutz shouted, pushing the boxes back into place. "Damned worthless animal! Get going! Hiyaaa!" The pony would not budge. It lowered its ears, staring straight forward into the darkness, hot breath steaming from its enormous nostrils. "Move or I'll whip you until you bleed!" Diemschutz shook the leather strap in his hand fiercely, but the little horse did not move. Diemschutz cracked it across the right flank harder than he thought he had the strength left to. "Go! Hyahh! Go!" He hit the pony across the flank twice more, and the cart began to move, but slowly.

Something moved in the shadows, and the pony veered left, hooves scraping against the dirt. Diemschutz flinched, unable to see if it was anything more than a large animal. "Come out this instant!" Diemschutz looked frantically around, clutching his leather strap. "I have a weapon!"

There was no answer. Diemschutz scanned the yard, satisfied that he was alone. He cursed himself for being no better than a scared old woman. The pony grunted, scraping its hoof on the ground. Diemschutz slid slowly off the cart, lighting a match and squinting in the darkness as he moved toward the door to the club.

He saw a pair of spring-sided boots lying on the grass. The woman's dark petticoat and bonnet made it impossible for him to see the rest of her clearly. "Pardon, my lady? Are you drunk? Can you hear me?" he said, standing several feet back. The woman did not move and made no noise.

Diemschutz suddenly dropped the match and raced up the stairs to the Club screaming for Adele. He found her sitting at a table with several other members and cried out, grabbing her and kissing her repeatedly. "Whatever are you doing, Louis?" she said.

"My God, I was so afraid! There is a woman lying in the yard and I could not see her face and I thought it could have been you," he sputtered as hot tears ran down his face. "There is a woman down there and I do not know if she is drunk or…my God, she might be dead."

Diemschutz's words quickly spread throughout the club, and in moments men were swallowing the rest of their drinks and making stone-faced agreements that if his friend went down to check on the woman, he would not go alone.

A group of them grabbed lanterns, and peeled Diemschutz away from his wife, telling him to take them to where the body was lying. As they filed down the stairs, Diemschutz lifted his finger and pointed, "There she is. Next to the gutter."

No one moved.

"I think you had better go have a look, Mr. Diemschutz," a man said.

"Me? Why me? I did not even want to come back down here!"

"You're the one that found her. Here, take my lantern."

Diemschutz took the lantern, wincing at the intense heat coming from the lid, making the handle uncomfortable to hold. He went on shaky legs across the lot, holding the lantern over the woman's boots, and rumpled skirts. He moved the light over her dark overcoat, and paused, thinking he saw movement. Her head was bent forward into the crook of her arm, face turned toward the wall. Diemschutz bent, tapping the woman on the hip. "Wake up, miss. You had too much to drink. Time to get up." The woman did not move. Diemschutz grabbed the arm covering her face and as he tried to move it, his hand slipped off, covered in something wet and warm.

"Another body?" Lestrade stood up, putting both hands on his desk, his face only inches from the young constable. "You are seriously standing there telling me another body had been found? Tell me that there is another damned body out there, Constable. I dare you to. I wish to Christ you'd tell me there's another dead body lying out there on the street just so I can shove this perfectly shined shoe up your hairless little arse!"

"Y-Yes, sir. As you say sir. There is, in fact, another dead body over in Dutfield's Yard, but I told them not to touch anything until you get there. Just like you said. Sir."

Lestrade put on his hat and coat, grunting, "For Christ's sake, Constable. Why in the hell did you have to tell me that? What's your name, son?"

"Frederick Wensley, sir."

"Lead the way then, Constable Wensley," Lestrade said, following him out the door. Lestrade sighed, looking the young officer over. "What the bloody hell is making that squeaking sound."

Wensley lifted his shoes to show him the bits of tire scrap nailed to the wooden soles. "Regulation boots make an awful racket on the cobblestones, sir. I found a few scraps of rubber and nailed them to the soles of these things to be able to walk the streets a little quieter. I hope to catch the murderous bastard in the act."

"That is a bloody brilliant idea, Wensley. I'm recommending you be promoted to Chief Constable of CID."

Wensley smiled, holding his lantern higher as they approached Dutfield's Yard. "I do not know about running it, sir. I hope to join, someday."

"Compared to who we have running CID now, I reckon you'd be a vast improvement at the helm, Wensley. Keep up the good work, and you just may get there, son. Oy!" Lestrade called out. "Who the bloody hell is in charge here?"

"Constable Lamb, sir!" another constable called out, saluting Lestrade. Lamb was tall, fit and blonde. He looked like he belonged on a recruiting poster. Lestrade did not easily trust good-looking people. Too soft.

"How much did you move the body around, Lamb?" Lestrade asked.

"The body was not moved at all, sir."

Lestrade sighed. "I'll ask you this again, given that I am accustomed to being lied to first off. I give people the chance to get it out of their systems. I often tell people that I can forgive them for lying to me first off, given that I look like I am stupid, but I assure you, Constable Lamb, I am less stupid than I look."

"I am sure it is much less stupid, sir," Lamb agreed.

"Are you saying I truly do look stupid, Lamb?"

"No, sir, I was just-"

"My point is that if you did move the body, but have lied about moving it, I will make one small allowance for having lied to me, but only one. Understand me?"

"Yes, sir," Lamb said.

"Lamb. Did you move the body?"

"No, sir. We were very careful to follow your orders, sir."

"You were, eh? What exactly have you done so far, then?"

"We made a diagram of the yard, and also of the body. We ordered all of the witnesses to stand over there, but told them not to talk amongst themselves." Lamb pointed at the group of people gathered near the stairwell to the club. "And I sent someone to fetch Dr. Blackwell."

"My God," Lestrade said, looking back at Wensley and Lamb. "You two may just be the cleverest police officers I have had the pleasure of meeting in this whole sorry, sordid, nightmare of an investigation. Give us your lantern, Wensley."

Lestrade bent to examine the body. The woman was lying on her back, head tilted toward the wall of the club, resting in a carriage rut on the ground. Her legs were drawn up toward her stomach. There was a checkered scarf tied around her neck, pulled into a tight bow, just beneath the enormous gaping wound on her throat.

Blood flowed from her throat, leaking into the wheel ruts that drained into the gutter like all the other detritus of the East End. Lestrade unbuttoned the woman's coat and dress, waving the constables back. He lifted her skirt and held the lantern between her legs, peering in. "What's this?" Lestrade said. "There's no other injuries?" Lestrade checked again, still seeing nothing to indicate the woman had been cut open or had anything ripped out. Lestrade checked her shoulders, seeing that there were not organs draped over them. He checked her stomach and chest, still finding nothing. Her arms and legs were still warm. The blood was still dribbling from her neck. "Who found this woman?" Lestrade asked.

Louis Diemschutz stepped forward, "It was I, sir."

"Tell me exactly what happened."

Once Diemschutz finished recounting the events of his arrival, Lestrade looked around at the dark yard with multiple exits and cursed furiously. "You were right on top of the bastard! You could have seen him!"

"I had no idea, sir. I tried, really I did."

It's all right, man. You did well enough. You found her. More than that, you stopped him from having his evil way with her body. Do you understand what I am saying?"

"No," Diemschutz said, his voice shaking.

Lestrade leaned forward, looking Diemschutz directly in the eye. "Because of you, he did not have time to open her up. He lost tonight, and we won. We came closer to catching him than ever before, and he knows it. He is scared." Lestrade smiled, tightening his grip on Diemschutz's shoulder. "You have given us all hope," Lestrade added, taking a deep breath.

"Murder! Murder!" someone screamed, running toward them.

Lestrade looked up, annoyed. "Grab that idiot and shut him up before he sends everyone into a panic."

Constable Wensley raced into the street, grabbing the man by the collar. "Pipe down, you! We're already here! What are you still screaming for?"

"A woman!" the man cried, "cut all to pieces! Come quickly!"

"What? Where?" Lestrade snapped.

"Mitre Square!" the man shouted. "A woman's dead! Horribly mutilated."

"In the blessed name of Christ, how can this be?" Lamb muttered.

Inspector Gerard Lestrade's chest tightened to the point that he could not breathe. He bent at the waist, trying to assimilate the man's words into something logical, something he could absorb beyond the wretched horror threatening to overtake him. It's simple, a voice in the back of Lestrade's mind whispered: He beat you. You thought you'd stopped him tonight, but he just went down the street and had his little fun with someone else. Bet he got his little presents out of her, too. Bet there's bits of her hung all over Mitre Square like Christmas decorations.

Lestrade shoved past the other constables and stormed down Commercial Road. "Blessed name of Christ… Where does *that* bastard bugger off to when some bunter is getting her innards yanked out of her?"

Twelve

Catherine Eddowes looked down at the boots in John's hands. "No, John, we mustn't. These are brand new."

John Kelly smiled, wiggling his toes through the holes in his socks. He tapped his right foot against the pavement, telling her, "Go on, Katie. It's aw right. See how much Mr. Jones will give you for them."

"I can't," she pushed his hands away. "You haven't got another pair. It's not right."

John stepped back and began shuffling his feet on the sidewalk. "Look at me, love. What do I need boots for? I like being barefooted anyway. Helps me dance!" He leapt up and clicked his heels together, landing on one knee with his arms outstretched. "What, no applause?"

Catherine sighed, and clapped her hands together. "Are yeh sure, John?"

"Of course I am," he said. "Go give that Mr. Jones what for."

A few minutes later, Catherine returned, dropping several coins into John's palm. John looked at the coins and frowned. "Doesn't look like me new boots were worth much, does it?"

"No, and winter is coming soon. That old bastard would not even hear me out. He just tossed the boots over his shoulder and handed me the coins. Told me to go get drunk and try not to get gutted by Leather Apron on my way home."

"You know what, Katie?" John said. "Now that I think about it, this looks like plenty of money. Enough for us to pop on down to Cooney's kitchen for a few fresh eggs and some bacon? Maybe even a little sugar for our tea. That would do us right, I reckon."

Catherine put her arm through his and nodded, kissing his shoulder as they walked. "I think I'm going to go see me daughter," Catherine said. "Haven't seen her in a bit, an' she might have some money to lend me."

"Doesn't seem right to borrow money from your own child, Katie."

"It is if you need it," Catherine said. "An' we do. Unless you would rather me go out on the street for a few hours tonight."

John shook his head. "Absolutely not. We agreed those days are finished, Katie. I can't stand the thought of you with any of those filthy animals. Plus, now there's that maniac running around cutting everyone up. No, I will not hear another word of it."

"Then I suppose I must go see me daughter. Do you want to come?"

"That seems like a long walk for a man with no shoes," he replied, smiling. "Why don't you go, an' meet me when you get home. It is nearly two o'clock now. What time do you think you'll return?"

"I should not be any later than four."

"Aw right." John kissed her and said, "No later, then? I want you safely back before it gets dark out."

Catherine laughed, tapping John on the cheek. "You needn't fear for me, my love. I can take care of m'self."

At eight thirty that evening, Constable Robinson looked at the crowd blocking his way on Aldgate High Street and cursed. "What the bloody hell is all that racket?" Robinson made his way closer to the source of the loud screeching noise.

"Wooooooooooo! Wooooooooo!" Catherine Eddowes bellowed as she stumbled backwards and fell onto the street. "That's how they sound, tellin' you to move your fat arse!"

A crowd of onlookers laughed at her as she struggled back to her feet, standing straight at attention and clicking her heels together. "Ladies an' gents, we got a fire an' aw'! Get out of the way so we can put it out! I say, why not let ol' Katie help?" She gathered up several layers of skirt to her waist and squatted in the street, spraying urine onto the pavement.

Robinson ran forward and kicked her from behind, knocking her face forward onto the ground. Another constable heard Robinson yelling and helped him lift Catherine to her feet. "Help me get this bunter back to the station!" Robinson shouted, starting to drag Catherine away.

"No, wait!" Catherine cried, pulling her hands free. "Get off of me! I have to get home!"

"You aren't going anywhere in your condition. You can sleep it off at the station."

"Let me go!" Catherine screamed, trying to claw Robinson across the face.

Constable Robinson caught her hand and twisted her wrist so fiercely that she cried out. He drew his baton and held it up to her face. "Try that again and I'll swaddle you so hard your brains leak out. Get going."

Sgt. Byfield looked up as the station door opened. He put his newspaper down. Robinson shoved Catherine Eddowes through the door and pushed her toward the cellblock. Once she was behind the cell door, he slammed it shut and locked it. Byfield watched Robinson wipe his hands and grunt with satisfaction as he walked back toward the desk. "I thought you were patrolling for suspicious persons resembling a certain villainous murderer. That looks like a drunken woman in my holding cell, Constable," Byfield said.

"It is, sir," Robinson said. "But she's a right nasty one."

Sgt. Byfield watched Catherine slump over on the hard wooden bench and begin snoring. "You are be some kind of hero, Robinson. We've got a maniac out there butchering bunters, and you bring in a drunk woman. Where do you want to put the medal?"

"This toss pot pissed all over Aldgate, Sergeant. She gave me a bloody hard time about it, too. Can't we just keep her here until she dries out a bit?"

"What do I care?" the sergeant shrugged and returned to his newspaper. "Whole damn city's about to go up in flames. Might as well have a little company for the end of the world, no?"

Four hours later, Byfield woke up when his feet slid from the desk and slammed onto the floor. He wiped drool from the corner of his mouth and rubbed his eyes. Someone was singing. He turned toward the cellblock. The woman's back was turned to him on the bench.

"In Dublin's fair city where the girls are so pretty

I first set my eyes on sweet Molly Malone

As she wheeled her wheelbarrow, through streets broad and narrow

Crying cockles and mussels alive, alive-oh."

"Hey? Stop making all that racket," he shouted toward the cellblock.

"Alive, alive-oh. Alive, alive-oh.

Crying cockles and mussels, alive, alive-oh."

He tapped the wall with his nightstick, "Oy! You sobered up in there or what?"

Catherine turned over and smiled at Byfield. "Didn't mean to wake you, sir. You have quite a snore. Must keep your wife in shambles."

Byfield smiled. "She stuffs cotton in her ears. How you feeling?"

Catherine stretched out, yawning. "I really need to be going. Can you let me out?"

"Did you sleep it off? I'm not letting you out unless you can get home safe."

"What time is it now?" Catherine asked.

"It's nearly one in the morning."

"Christ," Catherine sighed. "I'll get a damn fine hiding when I get home thanks to you lot."

"Serves you right," Byfield said. "No one told you to go out and get drunk. You pissed all over the street like a dog. You ought to be ashamed of yourself, young lady. If I was your husband I'd strap you until you couldn't sit down."

"It's me own fault. I went to see me daughter and she gave me some money. I thought I'd stop for a drink before I went home and that's the last thing I remember until I woke up here."

"Let that be a lesson to you. All right. Out you go. What way are you going home?"

"Back toward Aldgate."

"Let me find someone to escort you."

Catherine shook her head, "I'll just get it worse if I show up with a constable. Good night, Sergeant."

"Good night, then. Mind yourself out there."

"I always do," she said, tying her bonnet and leaving the station.

From Braham Street, Montague Druitt could hear singing. It was the first noise to pierce the silence since he'd moved far enough away from the police whistles and shouting on Berner Street. Druitt cursed his wretched luck. The blasted Jew and his pony had caught him by surprise. Who the hell comes wheeling along with a cart full of trinkets at one o'clock in the morning?

"Alive, alive-oh. Alive, alive-oh.

Crying cockles and mussels, alive, alive-oh."

Druitt walked to Duke Street, peering down the block in the dark, where the singing had come from. A woman was squatting in the shadows with her skirt bunched up at the waist. Hot steam rose from the puddle beneath her. He stepped back into the shadows, waiting for her to finish, waiting until she came walking closer to him. As she was nearly upon him, Druitt stepped out of the shadows, looking in the opposite direction.

"Hello, hello," Catherine Eddowes said, waving lazily at him.

Druitt turned suddenly. "Oh! I did not see you there. You startled me."

She laughed, stumbling. "No need to be scared of me, love. I'll protect yeh." Druitt offered her his arm, and she took it, nestling against the warmth of his coat. "It has been a hell of a long night."

"I should think so, for you to be out at such an hour," Druitt said, watching Catherine clutch her side and breathe sharply. "Are you unwell, my dear?"

"I ache all over," she said, wincing. "You aren't a doctor by any chance, are yeh?"

"Of a sort," Druitt said with a gentle smile.

"They said it's something called Bright's Disease."

Druitt thought for a moment. "Is that not a disorder of the kidneys?"

"Exactly right. I needs medicine for it. You ain't got no medicine on you, do you doctor?"

"No, I am afraid I do not. Let me think for moment of what I might possess in its place." He cocked an eyebrow at her, "Does medicine require money, by any chance?"

"I believe it does," she grinned.

"Then you are in luck, for that I have."

Catherine nodded, "And would sir be willing to part with any of that money in exchange for, say, a bit of service?"

Druitt smiled and said, "That probably depends on the service."

Catherine put her arm in his, leading him toward Mitre Square. She pointed at the darkest corner of the square, at a small fenced-in supply yard filled with stacks of bricks and lumber and overturned wheelbarrows. "I am not supposed to be doing this. Hope that adds to the excitement for you. Me husband would kill me if he found out!"

"Kill you?" Druitt gasped. "How dreadful."

Catherine shrugged. "I'll need to find somewhere to doss tonight. Listen, I've a proposition for you." She leaned in close and whispered something in his ear and giggled, "Is that worth a tanner to ye?"

Druitt produced the sixpence coin and nodded. Catherine took the coin, moving into the shadows. She lifted her coat and dropped onto her hands and knees, poking her buttocks in the air. She grabbed the hems of the two skirts and petticoat she wore and pulled them up over her back. "All right," she said, wigging her naked bum. "Do it slowly, I pray you."

He wrapped his fingers around the bone-handled blade from his father's medical bag. The rust was now scraped away. He'd polished and sharpened the blade so that it shined brighter than a star in the darkness of the square. "I will," Druitt said. "I most certainly will."

Thirteen

Inspector Lestrade stormed up to the London City Police Constable blocking Church Passage, and said, "Let us through, Constable."

"You from Scotland Yard?" the constable said.

"Yes, I am, son," Lestrade said. "Now kindly piss off and let us through, all right?"

"Hang on, sir," the constable said. "I was given specific instructions to let one of the brass know if you lot showed up. Wait here, please." The constable ran toward the group of City police officers huddled in the corner of Mitre Square and they all turned and looked at Lestrade. Lestrade promptly began walking toward them.

"Wait, sir!" the constable shouted, racing toward him. "You weren't given permission to enter."

"Bollocks," Lestrade said, "stop playing games so I can see what the hell happened."

Three finely dressed men left the group and turned toward Lestrade. "Christ," he muttered under his breath, recognizing all three. Major Henry Smith, the Acting Commissioner of the London City Police, was followed by the Head of the City Detective Department, Superintendent Albert Foster. Lestrade nodded to the third, a younger man who hurried behind them. Inspector Edward Collard was a decent-enough bloke for being a City copper. "Good evening, gentlemen," Lestrade said, nodding his head. "Heard you had a murder."

"Forget the boundaries of your jurisdiction, Inspector?" Superintendent Foster replied.

"It's hard to keep track of where one little square mile begins and ends, Superintendent. An hour ago one of our residents was killed just a few blocks from here. The killer was interrupted, and did not get to finish his work. Seems that our boy came here next."

"What's the matter, Lestrade? Afraid to let us share in the glory?" Foster asked.

Lestrade laughed. "Glory? That's rich, mate. I'm up to my thomas in dead bodies and you lot think that just because you finally get to play in the sandbox, you can suddenly throw your weight around?"

"How about you get the hell off of our crime scene, Lestrade?" Foster demanded. "You are out of your jurisdiction, and this is none of your concern."

"You haven't seen anything like this before, Albert. I have worked this case since the very start. If the killer is cutting up whores down here, it is my damned concern!"

"Gentlemen! That is quite enough," Major Smith interrupted. "Mind you that we are all sworn to serve the public, and furthermore, we are representatives of Her Majesty. In keeping with that you will kindly shut both of your mouths before I have you arrested for obstructing this investigation."

"Yes, Commissioner," Superintendant Foster said.

Lestrade tipped his face down, "I apologize, sir. I only meant to come and see if I might be able to assist you."

"I think we are quite capable on our own, despite your obvious doubts, Inspector," Major Smith replied. "We have investigated a crime or two before, even in our one little square mile."

"Fair enough," Lestrade nodded. "Listen, I meant no offense, sir. It is no secret that your detective division is better staffed and equipped than mine. Still, I have a lot of experience dealing with this particular handiwork, and I should like to coordinate our investigations, to see if together we can come up with a solution."

"Very well then," Major Smith said. "Inspector Collard, take Inspector Lestrade over to the body."

Lestrade followed Collard into the supply yard. Lestrade sniffed the air, cringing. "I know that smell. He opened her up, eh?"

"Gutted her like a deer," Collard whispered. "I've never seen anything like it, Gerard. I do not think I'll ever sleep right again. I've been on the job over ten years, and this is beyond my grasp."

Lestrade put his hand on Collard's shoulder, "It's beyond all of us, mate."

"Her guts are lying up there on her shoulder. Her face is all torn up. She's split open right down the middle. There's another clump of guts between her body and arm. What kind of monster would do this?"

A doctor was bent beside the body, looking over the gruesome remains with a blank stare. Lestrade bent down to the doctor and said, "Dr. Brown? Can you tell me if she is missing anything?"

The doctor did not respond. Collard snapped his fingers in front of Brown's face. "Gordon? Oy?"

Brown blinked several times and looked at both Collard and Lestrade. "What do you two want?"

"I asked you if the body is missing any parts. Did he take anything from her?"

"What do you mean? Her money?"

"Her uterus," Lestrade said.

Doctor Brown looked at the body and his mouth opened and closed but nothing came out of it. Lestrade shook Brown by the shoulders, "Come on, chap! Fix up, look sharp. My last one was missing a uterus, and I need to know if this one is as well."

"Why?"

"Because it must mean something that the killer keeps gutting them open to take them! The sooner I figure out why is the sooner I can figure out who, you daft clump."

"Inspector, calm down," Collard said, putting his hand on Lestrade. "Dr. Brown, can you please check to see if this woman is missing any organs?"

Brown swallowed and rolled up his sleeve, reaching inside the gaping cavity of her belly, squishing her insides with his fingers as he felt around. "T-There's a stump where her uterus should be. Everything else appears to be—no… wait. She's also missing a kidney." The doctor pulled his hand out of the body and wiped it on his jacket. "How is that possible? I can barely see my hand in front of my face. How in the hell did he manage to extract her kidney? It is hard enough to do that on an operating table and next to impossible under these conditions."

"What makes it so difficult?" Lestrade said.

"There are ribs in the way, as well as membranes, bodily fluids, organs, intestines. I must take this woman to Golden Lane. If you have any questions, ask for Dr. Thomas Bond. Perhaps he can make sense of this."

A shrieking police whistle pierced the night that silenced the doctor and froze everyone in place as if they were afraid to move or speak.

Lestrade finally turned to Collard and said, "If it's another body I am going to throw him off of the Old Bailey's roof when I catch him."

City Constable Alfred Long's hands were shaking as he pointed toward the Wentworth Dwellings stairwell. "I went in here. I was checking up and down the street for any signs of the murderer and when I went past the stairwell, I looked in."

"And nobody's been in or out since you arrived?" Collard asked.

"No sir," Long answered.

Lestrade leaned in to the stairwell, holding the lantern over the length of apron crumpled on the floor. "That apron is the same exact cloth as the one your girl is wearing," Lestrade said to Collard. "I'm certain of it. Same material, same color. Except, of course, for all the blood and fecal matter on this one."

"Why did he carry it all this way just to dump it here?" Collard said.

"No idea," Lestrade shrugged. "Maybe he was carrying whatever he cut out of her in it, all bunched up? Maybe there were too many police around? Maybe he cut himself and was using it to cover up the wound?"

"Or maybe he wanted us to find it," Collard said. "Take a look at the wall."

Lestrade squinted at the words written in chalk across the stairwell's wall:

THE JUWES ARE THE MEN
THAT WILL NOT BE BLAMED FOR NOTHING.

"What the bloody hell does that mean? What is a Juwe?"

Collard shrugged. "Lots of Jews have shown up around here lately. People are not exactly welcoming them with open arms into the East End, are they now?"

"Not those Jews," Lestrade said. "He spelled it differently."

"Imagine that, a bloke who goes around cutting women open and stealing their organs in the middle of the night has the nerve to have bad spelling. I bet his mother will be quite disappointed in him, no?"

"You're a right funny bastard, Collard. What I meant was how can we be certain it has anything to do with the apron? There's police all over the place out here. Our boy was hurrying away from the crime scene and ditched a piece of evidence. Why take the time to write this? It might just be a stairwell with graffiti on it."

"Yes, but in chalk?" Collard said. "How long could that stay up?"

Lestrade handed Collard the light. "Let's play it safe, then. Make sure nobody touches that wall until we can get it photographed." Lestrade stepped out of the stairwell onto Goulston Street and came face to face with his own Commissioner, Sir Charles Warren.

Chief Inspector Brett came around behind the Commissioner. His face was red and strained when he said, "What are you doing here, Inspector Lestrade? Why aren't you at the murder scene in Dutfield's Yard?"

"I came to assist here, sir," Lestrade explained.

Sir Charles's eyes widened. "This is not our jurisdiction."

"Their murder happened an hour after ours did, sir. I came to see if I could get any information to assist our investigation."

"In what way could these people possibly assist us?" Sir Charles sneered.

"This is a serious offense, Lestrade!" Brett barked. "You are out of your jurisdiction, working on a different police department's murder while we have our own investigations to attend to! You will report to my office at seven tomorrow sharp!"

"Now listen—" Lestrade said.

Inspector Collard raised his hand, "Pardon, sirs. If I may, I asked Inspector Lestrade to see a piece of evidence in this stairwell because I did not know if it was significant or not. He only left Dutfield's to assist me for a moment. He was just heading back."

"What is the evidence?" Brett scoffed.

"There's an apron taken from one of our victims. It's covered in her filth. Right above it is some writing on the wall," Collard said.

"What does it say?" Warren said.

"Something about the Jews, sir."

"The Jews?" Warren said. "Let me see." Warren took the lantern from Collard and went into the stairwell.

"What the bloody hell is going on over there, Inspector Collard?" Major Smith said. Both Smith and Detective Superintendent Foster hurried to the stairwell, seeing several uniformed officers from the London Metropolitan Police Service. "Constables, secure this crime scene," Major Smith shouted to his own people.

The City constables shook their heads and walked over to the Metropolitan constables and asked them to move back. Both sides muttered at one another. Sir Charles stepped out of the stairwell, eyes narrowed. He pointed to one of his uniformed men, "You! Find a wet sponge and get rid of that writing at once."

"What?" Lestrade said.

"Wait just a second," Major Smith said. "You have no authority here, Sir Charles. This is a City Police investigation."

Sir Charles ignored the Major and snapped his fingers at his men, saying, "Now. Move it. Get it off that damn wall."

"The first man who lets one of these Metropolitans through is fired. This is a serious breach of etiquette, Commissioner Warren, one I will be forced to take up with the Home Office."

"The Home Office?" Warren snickered. "I am sure to lie awake at night terrified of *them*. Chief Inspector Brett?"

"Yes, Sir Charles?"

"Make sure that wall is wiped clean in the next five minutes and that no one else is allowed to see it."

"Yes, Sir Charles," Brett replied.

"Wait one second!" Lestrade said. "We have to at least photograph it first. By Christ, this is a cock-up!"

Sir Charles Warren turned to Inspector Lestrade, "If you utter one more bloody word I will plant you beneath the streets of Whitechapel, you interfering, loud mouthed, imbecile."

"I demand an explanation, Sir Charles!" Major Smith shouted.

"Damn it, Henry! I will be up to my neck in dead Jews if this gets out. Just because you have this little spot of land to concern yourself with doesn't mean that I will let you rip my entire city apart. May I remind you that you are merely an Acting Commissioner? May I remind you that I answer to the Minister's Cabinet? I will wipe my arse with your entire Home Office and send a regiment of officers to seize your police headquarters if you try and stop me from getting this wall washed."

Lestrade spat on the ground and turned on his heels and left. Collard hurried after him to catch up. "What do we do now?" Collard asked.

"What do you mean?" Lestrade laughed. "We do nothing now. We go home now because we are dead in the water now. Let the bastards have it, my friend. Let all the nasty little bastards win tonight."

Fourteen

It all started with a test tube containing a new discovery Sherlock Holmes called "haemoglobin."

In 1881, I returned to London from the Afghan front. I met up with Stamford, a friend who was helping me get acclimated to life at home. I had no place to live at that point and no funds to afford my own dwelling. Stamford suggested a man he knew who might be interested in going halves on a second-floor, two bedroom flat in the West End.

He warned me of this fellow's somewhat peculiar nature. As I recall, he described Sherlock Holmes as a man who is not "easy to draw out."

When I met Holmes, he was pricking his finger to demonstrate this "haemoglobin," a chemical he said that could verify bloodstains. In the midst of explaining how he'd achieved this considerable discovery, which anyone would rightly be busily congratulating themselves for making, Holmes took one look at me and casually remarked that I was obviously just back from fighting in Afghanistan.

No matter how astonished I appeared, or how I cajoled him to tell me how he came to know this information, he refused to explain. It bored him to bother recounting what he considered to be such a simple matter. Truthfully, when he finally revealed how he'd deduced it, it did seem rather simple. But it is the kind of simplicity that requires a unique intellect. That is my first and best answer when it comes down to why I have always been so taken with Holmes. He accepts what is seemingly impossible, and upon filtering it through the keen lens of his mind, makes it into something workable. He finds truth when there are mountains of lies. He finds hope when all is lost.

It is called The Art of Scientific Deduction, and the play on words has always amused me, though I suspect the genius of it escaped even Holmes when he termed it that. "Scientific Deduction" implies a series of mathematical calculations, or basic patterns of a problem's reduction, stripping away the entanglements and obfuscations until all that is left is the result. In Holmes's mind, that is the entire process, and all of us who are incapable of making such reductions are simply not thinking correctly.

You see, that is where it becomes an "Art." If Holmes ever attempted to create a course designed to instruct others in his methods, there would be whole volumes on his approach to investigations. How he looks for clues and what intellectual traps to avoid, and so forth. But that would not even begin to approach the depth of his abilities.

Just as Michelangelo could instruct a student how to paint, or Aristotle could give lessons on reason, the actual application of the knowledge is unique to that person. There never has been, and never will be, an artist as capable of applying his talents as Sherlock Holmes had applied his.

As unto all great artists, his apologists are willing to forgive him for his shortcomings. When Holmes is engaged in the pursuit of a criminal, all is well. He is vibrant. Alert. Alive. It is between those times, in the dark recesses of inactivity that he descends into a pit of depression and narcotics. In fairness to Holmes, he's never made any secret of his love for the needle. After we moved in at 221 B Baker Street, he celebrated by sitting in his chair by the fireplace and loading up a syringe containing a seven-percent solution of cocaine and morphine. He rolled up the sleeve of his smoking jacket, and drove the needle into his vein. I was amused, at first. "What are playing at, man?" I said. "You think that isn't dangerous?"

Holmes's eyes fluttered as he depressed the stopper, injecting himself until the syringe was empty. He sat back in his chair with a great sigh. "Narcotic stimulants are the only way to kill the stagnation weighing heavy on my heart and soul, Watson."

"So, you poison yourself intravenously because you…hate feeling bored?"

Over the years, Holmes's dependency on narcotics increased. It was no longer an activity limited to the periods of inactivity between cases. His usage grew to several times a week and then several times a day.

During the past several weeks, I have taken advantage of the lengthy amount of time he's spent sleeping by rooting out the implements of his addiction. Dozens of syringes were scattered carelessly around the apartment. They were also strewn across the mantelpiece and floor of his bedroom. I found them on his bed, uncapped, waiting to stab him while he slept. It was no wonder that he so often slept in his chair. I suppose I should have been glad to find only three syringes stuffed between the cushions there.

There were vials and vials of cocaine and morphine in his desk drawers and hidden between the pages of his books. I uncapped them and dumped them into the sewer, imagining thousands of rats were now feasting on his vicious powders and watching the gutters with greedy hopes of tasting more.

One morning, Holmes woke and came out into the parlor. The dark circles under his eyes were gone. His face was shaven and his skin had a new rosy tint, instead of its normally pale, sickly color. He smiled at me and sat in his chair, "Watson, I need to thank you. That was astoundingly kind of you to care for me while I was ill. I feel wonderful."

"It was my pleasure, Holmes. I am truly pleased to see you up and about. It has been weeks since I've seen Mary, and she is probably ready to end our engagement." I watched his eyes trail off to search the mantle. "Holmes?" I said. "Are you listening?"

He spun in his chair to look around the rest of the room. "Where is it, Watson?"

"Where is what?"

"My Moroccan case. What on earth did you do with it?"

"The case is safe, however, it is empty."

Holmes's mouth twisted in rage and I seriously thought he might strike me. "How dare you! What gave you the right to tamper with my property?"

I stood to my feet and curled my fists. Holmes was taller than me, but I was thicker. I dreaded the idea of being struck by one of his practiced boxing maneuvers, but was determined that should it come to blows, I would tackle him before he got the opportunity.

Instead, to my surprise, Holmes threw his face into his hands and began sobbing. "You cannot do this, Watson! Please! I only need a little! I beg you."

I helped him into his chair and wiped the sweaty hair from his forehead. "No."

"Please," he said, clenching his eyes and crying as he reached out to grab my arms. "I dream of it when I sleep," he hissed.

I pushed him away and sat down across from him. I folded my hands and took a deep breath. "Do you know what I think about, sometimes? I wonder what you were like as a child."

"Shut up, Watson! I want my damned cocaine!"

"My own childhood was quite simple. I was fat, lonely, and sensitive. I grew up and joined the army to prove to everyone what a man I was, intent on becoming a surgeon. I have no idea who or what you were before the first day I met you. It is as if you sprang into existence a fully formed creature capable of the most complicated deductions. For the life of me I cannot fathom you in any other way.

When I was a boy, I remember my father returning from a year long engagement in the Second Opium war. I was delighted to see him and ran to his arms the moment he came through our front door. I told him I loved him and gave him a kiss right on the lips. I was ten years old. He pushed me away and wiped his mouth off in disgust and said, 'Do not do that ever again.' I was not allowed to tell him that I loved him, because he thought it was not something gentlemen said to one another.

But in truth, I love you, Holmes. I love you very, very much, and that is why I would rather die than watch you stick another needle in your arm. You are finished with that poison, and I if I have to beat it, burn it, or cut it out of you, I will exorcise this demon from your soul whether you like it or not."

"But what if I need it, John?" he whined. "I need it...so help me God, I need it...I need it...I need it."

"Well, you cannot have it." I opened my newspaper and ignored the sounds of his pain.

There was damn little literature to be found on a method of properly extracting cocaine from a patient's system. As physicians, we barely understood the ramifications of using it for appropriate purposes. For years, medical researchers thought the Holy Grail was a mythical plant in South America rumored to cure illnesses and give its users special powers. Europeans were desperate to study the coca leaf, and speculation ran rampant in scientific journals as to what it was actually capable of, but no one could acquire an adequate enough crop to do research on it. The raw foliage could not survive the long journey back to our shores intact, always arriving as nothing more than a large batch of useless shriveled brown plant material.

Finally, a German doctor isolated the cocaine alkaloid from the leaf of a coca plant. Medical journals filled with praise for the new "Wonder Drug" and that excitement quickly spilled over into the populace. Or rather, those who could afford it.

Those who could not afford it were forced to soldier on with beer and gin, but the upperclass soon were indulging in wine, cigarettes, powders, tablets, and even toothache drops for children, all with cocaine as the main ingredient.

I've taken to reading anything I could find about treatment for addiction to the drug, but there is little interest in admitting even to the problem. I learned of a doctor in Illinois who is injecting addicts with gold chloride for treatment, and he is planning on creating franchises of treatment centers. Sadly, the only evidence of improvement seems to be that of the funds in Dr. Keeley's bank account.

Holmes stares at me when he thinks I am not watching him.

His eyes have grown dark again, shadowed. His drawn, gaunt face is motionless, but in his pupils I see hatred swirling, his rage so palpable that I can feel it coming off of him like heat from the fire. By now, the cocaine must be completely out of his system. I've spent hours calculating the rate of speed the drug would take to circulate throughout his entire body, before finally breaking down enough to no longer affect him, and there is no reason why it should not be completely gone from him. I am at a loss and can make no sense of his condition.

> *"These make six murders to the fiend's credit; all within a half-mile radius. People are terrified and are loud in their complaints of the police, who have done absolutely nothing. They confess themselves without a clue, and they devote their entire energies to preventing the press from getting at the facts."*

"Six murders? They're giving him credit for six, now?" Lestrade exclaimed in disbelief. "This bastard is going to play hell with us trying to catch up to his own myth!"

"What are the blasted Yanks thinking, writing that bollocks?" Collard said.

Lestrade shook his head. "It's written by a local correspondent. Some twiddle poop bastard without the nutmegs to write it for a paper in his own country, I reckon."

"The local papers aren't much kinder. Here's the Evening News." Collard read: *'The public cannot fail to be impressed with one fact- the apparent bravado of the assassin.'* Oh, that's just charming. Yes, I'm impressed with his bravado as he's stabbing bunters in their privates and ripping their innards out. Really quite brave of him."

"These reporters are interviewing people right after we leave. Some of the locals give better statements to the press than they do to the police. What in the hell is everybody thinking? The whole sodding world is insane." Lestrade chucked the paper across his office.

"Did you hear what they did down in Mile End?" Collard asked. "Formed a Whitechapel Vigilance Committee. Some bastard named Lusk rallied up a bunch of hooligans to 'patrol the streets' because they don't think the police are doing a good enough job."

"Well there you go," Lestrade said. "Let the public do it themselves if they think it's so easy."

"Excuse me, Inspector Lestrade?" Constable Lamb said, knocking at the door.

"What now?"

"There's a Mr. Morrissey here from the Central News Agency. He said he wants to talk to someone involved in the murder investigations. That's him in the suit."

Lestrade stormed out of his office and into the lobby. "I don't give a damn who you are or what you want, but you had better get the hell out of my police station before I throw you through the front door! You bastards have bollixed up this entire investigation from start to finish and nearly created a national hero out of this murderous scum! Get out! Now!"

Morrissey pushed his glasses up to the bridge of his nose and smiled gently at Lestrade. "I did not come to argue the merits of press coverage with you, Inspector. I came to tell you the name of your suspect."

"You and every other maniac," Lestrade said. "Half the people who come into this police station claim to have the killer living right upstairs from them. Let me guess, it's Walter Sickert. Bugger off!"

"I make no such claim, Inspector. I did not mean his legal name. I meant the one that he wants us to use. The killer has written to our newspapers twice," Morrissey handed a satchel to Lestrade. "Perhaps we can go somewhere more private and talk?"

Lestrade sat at his desk, looking over the "*Dear Boss*" letter, seeing it was received on September Twenty Seventh, three days before the double-killings of Elizabeth Stride and Catherine Eddowes. "Why wasn't this given to us immediately?"

"My editor thought it was a hoax," Morrissey said. "I believe the second victim, Miss Eddowes, had some injury to her ear?"

"Fourth victim," Collard corrected him.

Morrissey nodded, "As you say, sir."

"This says 'clip off her ears,'" Lestrade said. "Our boy only cut off a piece of Eddowes's one ear lobe."

Morrissey pulled a postcard out of the satchel and handed it to Lestrade. "We then received this, just today. I believe, in light of recent events, it is certainly worth considering these as genuine."

Lestrade inspected the card. It was written in the same red ink as the letter, but its face was stained with larger streaks of blood.

"I was not codding
dear old Boss when
I gave you the tip,
you'll hear about
Saucy Jacky's work
Tomorrow
double event this time
number one squealed
a bit couldn't
finish straight
off. Had not got time
to get ears for
police thanks for
keeping last letter
back till I got
to work again.
Jack the Ripper"

"Blimey," Lestrade said. "This was postmarked this morning. None of the papers picked up the story until the first editions hit the street today. That's not enough time for a hoaxer to write this."

"Unless he wrote it before the papers came out," Collard said.

"Right," Lestrade whispered.

Morrissey took out his pen and began scribbling on a notepad. "Inspector Lestrade, let me ask you—" Lestrade snatched the notepad and pen away from Morrissey and led him by the shoulder toward the door. "Just a few quick questions, Inspector!"

"Out! I appreciate you bringing in the letters, and so help me God, you'd better get anything else you receive to us immediately, but now is the time for you to leave while I am seeing you in a kind light and before I remember why I hate all of you reporters so much." He pushed Morrissey through the door and went back to his office.

Collard was reading the letter and post card, eyes wide. "Jack the Ripper?" he said. "What the bloody hell? This is insanity. I'm starting to think about taking my wife and girls and leaving London. This bastard can have the bloody East End for all I care. Folks like us don't have a prayer, Lestrade. There isn't a policeman in the entire world with any hope of catching this bastard." Collard fished a pipe from his jacket with shaking fingers and finally got it lit. After taking a long smoke he said, "We don't need a detective. We need a priest. Jack the Ripper is a demon and it's going to take a miracle to stop him. Unless you know any detectives who can perform miracles. Ain't got one of them lying around here, do you?"

Lestrade looked up at Collard's pipe and said, "Actually, maybe I do know one."

There was a knock on the downstairs door, coming from the Baker Street entrance to our apartment. The knock was loud and insistent and continued until Mrs. Hudson answered. "Can I help you, sir?"

"Good evening, madam. Inspector Lestrade of Scotland Yard calling for Sherlock Holmes."

"I'm terribly sorry, sir, but the--of all the outrage! How dare you!" Mrs. Hudson shouted as Lestrade stormed past her and stomped up the stairs toward our apartment.

"Suppose I'll let them in?" I said to Holmes. He only glared back at me in response. I sighed, turning the knob, and greeted Inspector Lestrade and the red-faced Mrs. Hudson.

"This-this-this ruffian pushed his way past me and forced his way up here!" Mrs. Hudson complained.

Lestrade looked at Holmes and said, "Are you sick? You look horrible."

Holmes did not respond.

"He is very sick! That is what I was trying to tell you before you barged into my home!" Mrs. Hudson said.

Lestrade looked over his shoulder at Mrs. Hudson and then back at me. "I am here on official police business. I need to speak with Holmes. Alone."

"I am afraid that is not quite possible at the moment, Inspector," I said. "But if you do not mind my staying, I think it might be good for Holmes to hear what you have to say."

Lestrade shrugged. "Just you, then. Nobody else."

I apologized to Mrs. Hudson as I shut the door. "I am sorry for that, Inspector. She takes her charge quite seriously."

Lestrade took off his coat and sat down in my chair, opposite Holmes. "Can you hear me? Your eyes aren't even open." Holmes sniffed and looked at the Inspector but did not speak. Lestrade looked at me and said, "How long has he been like this?"

"It is only temporary. He had a fever, but it has passed," I said.

"Very well. I suppose you both know of the murders in Whitechapel?"

"We have heard a little," I said. "The newspapers have certainly been paying a lot of attention to it. A little too much, I think."

Lestrade nodded. "And here I always thought Holmes was the intelligent one. Regardless, I want you to purge your thoughts of whatever you might have read in the papers. I am going to give you the information I have, which is not to be discussed with anyone outside of this room. Is that perfectly understood?"

"We are nothing if not discreet, Inspector. It is a cornerstone of our reputation," I reminded him. "Why else would so many royals and socialites come to us for help when they could just go to the police?"

Holmes chuckled slightly. I do not think that Lestrade noticed.

"There have been four killings in Whitechapel by a subject calling himself 'Jack the Ripper.' I am discounting the other murders because they do not fit in with these four. All of his victims had their throats cut. All have had some sort of injury to their abdomens. In all of the killings, except for the third, wherein The Ripper was interrupted in the middle of his deed, he is progressively mutilating them worse than he did before.

"Polly Nichols's was a forty-three year old prostitute. Jack killed her on Friday, August Thirty First, between three-fifteen a.m. and three forty-five a.m. He cut her throat, and we found several deep cuts on her abdomen.

"Annie Chapman was a forty-seven year old prostitute. Jack killed her on Saturday, September Eighth, after five thirty a.m. He cut her throat and ripped her belly completely open. He took Chapman's uterus.

"Elizabeth Stride was a forty-four year old prostitute. She was killed Sunday, September Thirtieth, around one a.m. Her throat was cut, but nothing else appeared damaged. I believe the killer was spooked and ran off before he could finish his business.

"Less than an hour later, the body of Catherine Eddowes was found only a few blocks away. Eddowes was a forty-six year old prostitute. Her throat was cut. Her belly was ripped open. Both her uterus and kidney were taken. In addition, there were many more injuries inflicted, including her face."

Lestrade looked from me to Holmes, making sure that we were following him. "Do you see? It is almost as if he is learning from each one, quite the same as you or I would, Holmes. Say, for instance, we go out on our first investigation and realize that we forgot to bring a candle in case our lantern went out. Next time we bring it. Perhaps we forget to bring a bag to put evidence into. The next time we remember. Jack the Ripper is getting better at his trade and learning as he goes on. Every killing brings him closer to something I cannot understand, but I hope that you might."

Holmes began laughing softly and murmured the word, "Monkeys."

"Pardon?" Lestrade said.

"Ignore him," I said, "he is not well, Inspector. Please continue, I am utterly fascinated."

Lestrade looked at Holmes, who was still laughing. He ignored him and said, "Those are the things that we know for certain, but because it is so little, we are awash in meaningless theories. We have detectives following up leads suspecting the Freemasons, the royal family, a prominent artist running around telling people he is the killer, and even the author of ALICE IN WONDERLAND. We have hundreds of quacks, derelicts, and publicity seekers who want to be arrested for the murders just to see their names in print."

"Jabbering, drooling monkeys!"

Lestrade stood to his feet, "Now look here, Holmes, what the hell do you mean by that? I came here as a sign of my respect for your investigative abilities to discuss this case with you. Man to man. Professional to professional."

"We cannot discuss it 'man to man' because you are not a man," Holmes shouted. "You are a monkey! All of you are. Collectively, you stand as much chance of catching this killer as a group of thick-jawed simians in a rail-yard have of assembling a steam engine. You have been given the tools, the plans, and the materials, but you do not possess the simple mental capacity. Jack the Ripper has stared you in the face and found you lacking, my dear Inspector. Can you not at least see that?"

"Holmes! That is quite enough!" I said. "I humbly apologize, Inspector Lestrade. I do not know what has come over him but we would be glad to assist you. Just give me a little while to talk it over with him. Would you mind coming to see us tomorrow?"

"Do not fill him up with false hope, Watson," Holmes said. "The Ripper is beyond you, Lestrade. He is a new thing in an old world. At least have the decency to know when you are outclassed, Inspector. When you have been made obsolete."

Lestrade was silent after that and took a deep breath and sat back down. "All right then. I am a monkey. I am outclassed. Fine. I agree to any insult you care to offer. Dispense with any ridicule you see fit, man, I only ask you to help us."

Holmes's face twisted in disgust and he said, "Get out of my sight. Go back to your masters at Scotland Yard and tell them they cannot come begging me to help after so many years of denying my superior talents. How many times have I had to sit back and watch you lot take credit for my achievements, while you publicly mocked me? While you refused to cooperate with me? Now, when the bodies are piling up, you come to my boot heel like the whimpering fools that you are, but I will not be used."

Lestrade lowered his head and whispered, "No one sent me, Holmes. I would be fired if they even knew I was here. It was my own idea, to ask you as one man to the next, to save this city. I see I was mistaken. Good night then."

After the Inspector left, I shut the door behind him and listened to him walk slowly down the steps. I turned to Holmes and tried to steady my trembling jaw. "How could you be so monstrous! That man begged you for help and you refused him!"

Holmes's eyes shined with cruelty. "Fill me up one syringe that contains a seven percent mixture of cocaine and morphine and perhaps I shall consider helping him."

"Curse you!" I shouted. I grabbed my coat and threw the door open, shouting, "Inspector! Wait!"

I found Lestrade on Baker Street but he turned away from me, taking a moment to wipe his nose and eyes. "What the hell do you want?" he sniffled. "Was he making some sort of a sick joke?"

"No," I said breathlessly. "I have no idea what he was saying. He is out of his mind."

"To hell with him then! To hell with all of you and your fancy homes and posh lives."

"I want to offer you my full and complete services!" I said.

"For what?"

"Don't you see? I have been with Holmes for years! I have seen his methods first-hand. I have worked at his side. Let me come with you and together we can stop this fiend!"

Lestrade moved close to me, leaning down to look me in the eye. "Listen to me very carefully, Doctor Watson. Just because I came and asked Holmes for help does not mean that I want any bloody fool with an opinion to interfere, do you understand? You think I am some sort of buffoon who needs the help of every amateur in London. Is that it?"

"But I only—"

"If you want to help me truly, then go back inside and convince Holmes to get off of his stinking arse and help me," Lestrade stormed down the street. "Take him to see a doctor, or something."

"But, he has one…" I stood in the street, watching him vanish into the white fumes coming up from the sewage grates. As I turned, Irene Adler was watching me from the entrance to 221 B. "What the hell are you doing here? Go away. You do not want to see him right now."

"I did not tell you the whole truth at the Forrester House, Dr. Watson," Irene said. "Annie Chapman was a former acquaintance of mine. The Ripper cut her open and left her in the dirt behind Hanbury Street."

"I am sorry to hear that, Miss Adler, but I really must be going."

She looked up the steps toward our apartment. "Did Holmes really refuse to help the Inspector?"

"Yes," I said, lowering my head.

"And the policeman refused your offer of assistance?"

"Yes. Apparently my time with Holmes has qualified me to be little more than his nursemaid, as I am not even given the respect of being his physician!"

"It would seem to me that we are left with only one solution, dear doctor."

"And what might that be, Miss Adler?"

"I think you and I should hunt that murderous bastard down together."

I stared at her for a moment. "You know, I have had quite enough with people making a fool of me tonight. Goodnight, Miss Adler."

"Why is that so hard to imagine, Doctor?"

"You and me? An opera singer and a physician out there hunting the worst murderer in the city's history? Are you daft?"

Irene shook her head, staring at me with great pity. "It is little wonder that no one respects you, Watson."

"I beg your pardon?"

"Have you become so accustomed to being Holmes's lapdog that you have forgotten what it means to stand on your own two feet? I saw you with that woman at the Forrester's. Is she your fiancé? It looked to me like she might just be tolerating you until a real man comes along."

"That is enough, Miss Adler. How dare you speak of things that you know nothing about?"

"I know that women are being killed and the two most capable men in all of London sit in their apartment, afraid to face him. I am staying at the Great Eastern on Liverpool Street. Call on me if your master changes his mind. Run along, John! That's a good dog."

I spun around to confront her, but she was already gone. I stormed back up the steps, slamming the door behind me. "Confound that woman, confound Lestrade, and confound you most of all!" I shouted. "This is all your fault, Holmes!"

Holmes's only response was to smile, close his eyes and turn toward the fire. He was soon slumbering peacefully.

Fifteen

I left Baker Street early the next morning, passing Holmes as he snored in his chair. I decided that a mug of hot coffee and a sweet roll from the corner market would suit me well. The coffee was bitter and strong, but helped to clear the fog of my thoughts left after a long night spent shifting about my bed. Over and over, I muttered the quick retort that I wish had left Irene Adler humbled and impressed; the bold statement that convinced Inspector Lestrade that I was worthy of his respect. As for Holmes, I had nothing but words that stung.

I hailed a cab and told the driver to take me to the Forrester estate. Upon arriving, I walked up the steps and knocked loudly on the door. The servant who opened it greeted me politely and asked me to wait for Mrs. Forrester. She came down the stairs and looked at me with a strange expression. "Doctor Watson…What an unexpected surprise."

"Good morning Mrs. Forrester. I would like to speak with Mary please."

"I am not certain that she wants to."

I handed my hat and coat to the servant and bowed slightly to Mrs. Forrester, "She will, and she does. I give you my word that I will not cause a scene. If she tells me to leave, I will abide by her wishes and never return. I have something important to tell her, though."

Mrs. Forrester sighed and said, "She is in the backyard walking the path." The servant led me through the house toward the rear. I looked out into the yard, where dozens of trees towered over the house, raining leaves in every hue of gold, red, and brown. I walked down the rear steps, into the woods and followed the path. "Hello Mary," I said

"Oh, so you've finally remembered me? But more importantly, how is Mr. Holmes? Feeling better? I understand there is nothing on earth quite so important as him, so let us discuss it straight away."

"Forget him. I came to talk about us." I pointed into the woods. "Can we walk along this path? I don't believe I've ever seen the foliage look so beautiful."

"So you came to admire the trees? I believe Westminster has its fair share. Perhaps you should dash back to Baker Street and ask Mr. Holmes what type of tree he prefers."

I stopped her and wrapped both my hands around hers. "I understand you are angry with me, but I must ask you to be silent for a moment and hear me out. Is that all right?"

She said that it was. I cleared my throat and said, "When I met Holmes I was fresh out of the army and recovering from a wound which I thought might put an end to my surgical career. For whatever doubts you or anyone else has about me, I have been on the battlefield and witnessed dear friends torn apart by mortar fire. I held their bodies in place, and struggled to save them even as death tried dragging their souls from my hands. Some are still here to this day because of my actions. Some are not, but at least I tried. You see, Mary, I am a doctor. I help people in need. I may never be a physician for the royal family, or be counted as a member of your high-society, but at the end of the day, I will have assisted those who needed it. I took an oath, and it is who I am.

"The reason I stayed with Holmes all this time is that it seemed to me that we were genuinely helping those who had nowhere else to turn. It is true that Holmes gets most of the credit and the world sees me as little more than his assistant. Even the woman I love regards me as his manservant."

"John, I did not mean that," Mary said.

"Let me finish, please." I looked at her carefully. "One of my decisions is that, while it does not matter what most people think, there are exceptions to that rule. It matters what I think of myself, and as of late, I have not been thinking very highly of the man that I am. Truthfully, neither have you. That is what I came to tell you. I have something I must do, Mary. One last thing that I owe to myself before I can come to you and be the man you deserve."

"But I love you as you are," she said. Tears began to well up in her eyes. "Why can you not see that?"

"I know you love me. But I need you to respect me as well. For that, I must respect myself, and there is only one way to do that."

"What are you talking about?"

"There is a man killing women in our city, Mary. The city where we live. Where my children will someday live. The police are baffled, the newspapers are stoking the fires, and our greatest chance at putting an end to the crimes is busy rotting away on Baker Street. Someone has to do something, and I suppose that leaves it up to me."

"But how can you stop him? You mustn't be foolish. How would you even find him? What if you get hurt?"

I kissed her delicately on the tip of her nose, "Relax, my love. You have nothing to fear. Do you really think I would dash off to Whitechapel without having the perfect plan?"

I entered the social room of the Great Eastern Hotel and spotted Irene Adler bent over one of a dozen newspapers scattered across her table. She was making notes on them, drawing connecting lines between multiple sections and circling them. "Miss Adler," I said, walking up to her table and setting down my hat. "I have come to join the fight. I am determined that you and I are going to find this rotter and save London. Now, please tell me you have some sort of plan."

Irene lowered her paper, "Did you know they found a woman's leg in Guildford? It had been boiled, like an Easter ham! They are bringing it to London to compare it to the torso."

"Torso?"

She paged through her notes quickly, "The torso! On October second, a torso was found in a vault inside the very building they are clearing out for New Scotland Yard! Can you imagine that? Body parts popping up all over the place, and now they find a torso at the new police headquarters?"

"Most unusual. Now, your plan?"

"It all connects!" Irene said, going back to the notated pages of circles. "Somehow there is a thread of continuity to all of this madness and if we only look hard enough, we shall find it! Almost like a grand drama playing out before us. There are twists and turns, but ultimately, they all play out in one narrative theme."

"Oh God," I groaned, lowering my head into my hand. "You have no plan whatsoever."

"Of course I do. We are going to go into Whitechapel to solve the murder!"

"Just like that, eh? Scotland Yard, the City Police, and all the journalists in London are scouring Whitechapel for Jack the Ripper, but somehow you and I are just going to march in there and sniff him out?" I stood up, "It is plain to me that this is a waste of time. Good day, Miss Adler."

"Wait, Dr. Watson," she said, grabbing my arm. "I did not mean to sound flippant about it. Perhaps it was my optimism speaking. I am relieved to have you join me in this quest."

"I would not be. I have been through complicated investigations on many occasions, and I can tell you that a majority of time was spent gathering facts, assessing all the scenarios, then ruling out the impossible. More often than not, though, our success came down to an astounding act of observation and deduction by Holmes."

Irene frowned, "The problem in this case is that no one seems to be quite sure what the facts truly are. We seem to be as awash in theories and suspects as we are in dead bodies."

"That may not be necessarily true," I said. "When Inspector Lestrade came to see us the other night he said that the only thing he is quite certain of are that four women have been killed by The Ripper. He warned us not to pay any mind to all of the other information."

"But the torso? Perhaps it is a clue," Irene said. "Perhaps the killer is trying to send a message to the police, and we should focus on that immediate vicinity for his location! After all, how far can a man carry a woman's torso around?"

"Yes, perhaps it has something to do with the murders. Or, perhaps not. Holmes would take it in as information, but not focus on it unless need be. The key is to stay focused on the facts at hand and not get distracted by all the endless possibilities. We'll be chasing Jewish slipper-makers and Freemasons for centuries if we go about it that way."

"So what do you propose, dear Doctor?"

I took a deep breath, looking up and down the street. "I can hear Holmes telling me, *'I use the unique gifts which the creator has seen fit to bestow upon me in this unique line for work, in which I alone am employed. There is a reason I am the only Consulting Detective in existence, Watson.'* Er, something like that."

"That was well done," Irene said. "You sounded rather like him."

"Now if only I could think as he does. No doubt he would use his deuced methods to conjure up the killer by midnight."

"Unique gifts," she repeated to herself, pressing her knuckle to her chin. "Holmes would use the skills with which he is uniquely possessed to solve the case. I think we should begin by doing the same!"

"We do not possess his gifts, my dear. No one does."

"But we possess our own, though, Watson. Think of it. A medical doctor with battlefield experience who's spent the better part of the past decade apprenticing to the Great Detective."

"And Holmes did say that your intellect and prowess rivaled his own."

"Really?" she said, her eyes suddenly ablaze. "When did he say that?"

"Or maybe it was something I misunderstood. Maybe it was I who said it. Regardless, I have seen much of the world's underbelly at his side. I should say I have more experience dealing with criminals than most."

"As do I," she nodded.

"A world-famous opera contralto? Experienced with the underworld?" I said.

Irene smiled, sticking her arm out for a cab. "You would be surprised what a young woman must endure while travelling that particular road, my dear Doctor."

Irene provided the cab driver with directions to Golden Lane. I leaned close to her, "Tell me again why we are going to the mortuary?"

"Picture Jack the Ripper as an artist, Watson. He is steadily progressing, moving into a new phase of his work. We are going to request a private viewing of his most mature, advanced piece to date. To that end, I am hopeful that by observing it, we gain some insight into the inner workings of his mind."

I considered her profile in the cab as the sun framed her, whispering, "There is no question as to why he finds you so remarkable." She smiled, touched my hand gently, and returned to her vigil of the passing London streets.

"At least Miss Eddowes was taken to a proper morgue," Irene said. "They took Annie Chapman to a shed in a labour yard. They treated her worse than the body of a dog would have been back in Trenton."

I had been to many of the city's mortuaries during my time with Holmes. Some were little better than barns converted into makeshift morgues with the bodies left on overturned feed crates. The Golden Lane mortuary was at least a building which appeared to be designed for its intended use. London, unlike Paris, had no central mortuary facility in which to conduct autopsies and present bodies to families for viewing.

We exited the cab and Irene handed the driver several coins. "Wait for us, all right? After this we are going directly to Whitechapel. Do not leave."

"Yes, madam," the driver agreed.

"Here we go, Watson!" she said excitedly as we walked toward the building. "This is nothing less than a gallery where Jack's most recent work is on display. From here, we'll go to the place where he selects his blank canvasses."

I eyed the imposing metal door, "Of course we shall. Tell me something, have you ever been inside a mortuary before, Miss Adler?"

"No," she shrugged. "As a classically trained performer, it is my duty to experience life in all its aspects, Watson. This experience will be just another thing that allows me to more fully envision the human condition. It is only death, Watson. I assure you that I will be all right. Try not to look so pale." She knocked politely, and when there was no answer, she knocked again. "Hello? Is anyone there?"

"Pardon my saying so, but you will never get anyone's attention that way." I pounded on the door with my fist. "Holmes always says we must knock with authority, in such a way as to let the occupant know we are here about serious business. Open up, I say! Open up this blasted door immediately or we shall break it down!"

There was a bit of shuffling behind the door. "Funeral's Monday! Go away!" a man said.

I banged on the door again, "We are not here about the funeral, man! Open the door this instant!"

Several locks were thrown and the door creaked open revealing a short, slumped man in a greasy black apron. "Good day, sir," Irene said. "We apologize for disturbing you, but we have urgent business to conduct."

"Dr. Phillips is not in. Call tomorrow if you want to see him."

"But we are not—"

"Tomorrow," the man said, pulling the door shut.

Irene thrust her foot between the door and the frame. "Now you listen to me, sir," she said, leveling a finger at him. "You will not treat such a distinguished and fine physician as the great John Watson like that. How dare you!"

The attendant stood still, eyeing me carefully. Irene grabbed the door out of his hands and held it open. "We are here on a special assignment concerning the body of the woman within. Doctor Watson is here to inspect the Eddowes woman for clues that are meant to be given directly to Mr. Sherlock Holmes himself!"

The attendant smeared the wet black surface of his apron with his slime covered hands. "Sherlock Holmes? The Great Detective?" Irene said. "Have you not heard of him?"

"Detective?" the attendant mumbled. "Like, police, yeh say?"

"Somewhat," she nodded.

The attendant nodded, stepping back from the door. Suddenly, he smiled, revealing a mouth of jagged, misplaced teeth, "Police!"

"What the hell is it, you daft clump!" A uniformed constable came storming down the hall, whacking his palm with a thick nightstick. "Better not be any more damn cookie-loos. I'll sort you bastards out with a right battering!" The constable suddenly stopped in mid-stride, staring at me. His face grew dark with rage.

"Run, Irene! I'll hold him off!"

The constable turned and struck the attendant across the side of his head with the back of his hand. "You bloody idiot! Don't you know who the hell this is? I apologize for that, Dr. Watson. Recognized you straight away. Suppose you remember me as well."

"Ah-yes. Yes of course, Constable—"

"My name is Irene Adler," Irene smiled seductively at the constable. "I am pleased to make your acquaintance, sir. Would you do me the honor of telling me your name?"

"Hawkes," he said, smiling brightly.

"Constable Hawkes," I said, "of course. How have you been, my good man?"

"It was me who helped Sherlock Holmes before on a real big case, you know. The doctor could tell you, right?" he said, looking at me.

"Ah...certainly. Let's see, it was awhile back, right? Long ago? Holmes and I were looking for that thing. It was the most unusual case. Remember?"

"Why don't you tell me?" Irene said, waving her hand. "I have to listen to him blather on all day, you know."

Constable Hawkes laughed, "I can imagine how that must be. You ever want to have some real fun, come down to the Crown and Shuttle with me when the day tour is finished. Nobody has a good time like us rozzers."

"That sounds delightful!" Irene said. "Maybe after I finish this last wee assignment with the doctor?"

"All right," he said. "What is it you need? To see the body?"

"Yes, actually!" Irene said. "That would be wonderful."

"Wait, where is Mr. Holmes?"

"Oh, he'll be along later," Irene put her arm through his and walked into the mortuary. "In the meantime, take us to see the body and tell me all about how you helped Sherlock Holmes with that case you mentioned. Was it exciting? Was it dangerous?"

Constable Hawkes laughed, telling Irene how he'd been summoned to a house in Brixton several years ago to guard some mysterious scribbling on a wall. I found myself lost in thought, watching the way Irene's hips swayed when she walked.

The lobby floor was made of wood. The walls were papered and several framed photographs hung on them, with various-sized plants stuck in all corners of the room. As we moved down the hall, the floor became firm concrete. The room ahead was brightly lit by powerful lamps. Surgical instruments lined the countertops. The stink of rotting flesh was unmistakable.

Irene suddenly gagged, covering her face with her coat. I managed to endure the stench stoically without much of a demonstration as to how utterly repulsive it was. I felt that smell of dead people crawl inside my nose, taking up residence in my hair and clothing. I felt that it would be burnt into my soul permanently.

It was there, in that room, that we came face to face with Jack the Ripper's "most advanced, most defined work to date." As I viewed the body of poor, mutilated Catherine Eddowes, I had my first glimpse into the true madness inside the mind of Jack the Ripper. It was an evil I could not fathom, and I wanted to run screaming from the room and never stop.

"He cut off her nose, Watson." The Princess Alice Pub was crowded, and Irene's voice was barely audible over the racket they made.

"Mmm hmm," I said. "You going to finish that?" She shook her head no. I took her glass and drained it.

"Her nose," Irene hissed, touching her own nose. "He peeled away the skin of her face like it was an orange rind. He slashed her eyes!"

"I know," I said, picturing the jagged, forking cut going all along the length of the woman's body. I called out to the barman, "Another round!"

"He stole things from inside her body, Watson! What the hell could he have wanted them for? The indignity of it all. It's simply inhuman."

"Be a little more discreet, Miss Adler," I said, looking around. "You have no idea who is lurking nearby. There may be people who do not appreciate us discussing this. I know it was horrible, but this is what we have tasked ourselves with."

"I keep picturing how Annie must have looked when that bastard was finished with her. I want to kill him. I want to cut things off of him and see how he likes it."

I winced and laughed, finishing the new beer after it arrived. "I suppose your grand idea of Jack the Ripper as fine artist is out the window, eh?" She did not respond to my teasing. I realized that I had not eaten all day, and the beer was beginning to lure me into that fine world of relaxation where one's face goes numb as his tongue gets sharp. I decided it was a better plan to try seriously discussing the case. "Why does he take the organs, do you think? What use could he have for them?"

Irene looked past me toward the fireplace for a long while. The flames danced in the pupils of her eyes. "He is taking trophies, Doctor Watson."

I snorted with laughter, "That is the silliest thing I have ever heard! Maybe Jack just got lost in Whitechapel when he really meant to be on safari in Africa? You really are a silly little girl, sometimes."

Irene stared at me evenly. "I have been thinking of something, Doctor. How is it that he is able to take those organs? If someone handed me a knife and said, 'Go find a uterus inside that woman' I doubt that I would be able to. Let alone find it twice. And a kidney? That seems a little trickier."

"Indeed. You want your drink? No? Mind if I have it then? The kidney is damned hard to get to as it's practically hidden by a membrane. Our boy got it out of ol' Katie Eddowes in pitch blackness from what the papers said. Most impressive."

"It implies surgical training," Irene said, staring at me.

"Could be," I shrugged, setting her empty glass down.

"And an attraction to the darker side of life? To crime, in particular."

"If you like," I said.

"Let me ask you a question, Dr. Watson. Where were you on the night of September thirtieth?"

"Pardon?" I said, swallowing.

"I asked you where you were on the night those two women were murdered."

The bar seemed to fall silent for a moment as I stared at Irene. "Miss Adler, I assure you that I do not find your insinuation very amusing."

"Dr. Watson, I assure you that I am not joking."

"I was at 221 B Baker Street caring for my ill friend. In fact, that is probably where I should be right now instead of wandering the streets of this cesspool with a damned silly girl who fancies herself a bloody detective."

Irene leaned forward and whispered, "Please settle yourself, Dr. Watson. It is a simple question. If I am having that thought, surely others will as well. I ask you so that you have an answer prepared if it ever becomes an issue."

"I'll not settle myself," I said, standing to my feet. "I have better things to do than to sit and drink with someone who does not trust me. Good luck getting home, Miss Adler. Better be on your guard, though, because I just may be skulking around the corner to gut you like a holiday turkey!"

A man stepped in front of me, barring my way toward the exit. He had a fierce looking scar underneath an eye patch, but I shoved him out of my way and slammed the door open. I paused at a lamp post to catch my breath and try to stop the street from spinning.

"There he is."

I looked up as the man from inside the bar came toward me. I let go of lamp post and lifted my fists. "C'mon! I'll teach you not to meddle!"

He just smiled, but his smile was as black and treacherous as the patch on his eye. "I just want to ask you about what you said in there, to that lady." His right hand crept behind his back. "What you said about gutting her up, and all."

I stepped back from the curb. The footsteps of several men closed in behind me, circling, cutting off any possible route of escape. "Listen, my good friends," I said, trying to collect myself. I turned to take stock of them and was greeted by six dirty faces cruelly twisted in hungry expectation. "I meant nothing by what I said in there. That woman is a friend of mine, and we were having a disagreement. I only said it in jest."

"Is that so?" A well-dressed man stepped forward from the shadows. He tipped his hat at me. "That does not seem like something one would jest about, particularly in this part of town. My name is George Lusk, and I am the Chairman of the Whitechapel Vigilance Committee. It is my solemn duty to catch the killer who is preying on the women of Whitechapel."

"Then you are to be commended, sir," I said. My legs were shaking. I attributed it to the cold and the beer. "I myself am trying to assist the police in their efforts." I gritted my teeth to stop them from chattering. I knew I was a damned coward. "Perhaps you have heard of me? Doctor John Watson, associate of the Great Detective, Sherlock Holmes?"

"The Great Detective, you say?" Lusk said.

"Exactly. Everyone in the West End knows of him. He, or rather, we, have helped people of all sorts when they are in danger, or needed our assistance!"

"Oh, the West End," the man with eye patch snorted. "That must explain it. You see, this is the East End, where most people from your part of town never sully themselves to visit. Strange, but I do not see any Great Detectives around here, Mr. Watson. Just a couple of the regular ol' blue bottles from Scotland Yard."

"That's right," one of the men said. "Ain't no justice here in Whitechapel. There's just us. Get it? If he's such a sport why ain't he here with you out catching The Ripper like we are?"

"That is precisely what we are trying to do, gentle fellows! Now, I must insist that you excuse me, I have much to do before morning. Off I go then. Back to Baker Street. Vital information to report to

Sherlock Holmes concerning these killings." I inched past them, walking quickly, trying to look determined and important. As I reached the middle of the street, I was confident that I had escaped them.

"Get him."

Let it never be said they took John Watson without a fight. I hit the closest one square in the jaw with a solid right hook, dropping him instantly. The second came around on my left, trying for a tackle and I drove a knee into his collarbone with a crack. A wooden truncheon whistled through the air into my gut, instantly folding me in half, dropping me to the street to retch on both my coat and the cobblestones.

The bastards stomped me with their boot heels. I covered my head, though my ribs and groin suffered the worse for it.

"That is enough!" Lusk shouted. "Mr. Fitch, call your men off!"

"All right, all right," Fitch said. "Hold on a second." The pounding of their heels paused for a moment. My attackers sucked air, waiting eagerly for the order to begin again.

I wept like a fool. "I am not the Ripper! You bloody bastards! I am not the Ripper!"

"You two grab some rope. Find us a lamp post or a tree branch in case we need it," Fitch said, and two of my attackers left off immediately.

Lusk bent down, prodding me with the butt of his cane. "Perhaps you are exactly who you say you are. Perhaps there really is a Great Detective whom you are assisting. Perhaps what we heard you say in the bar really was just a misunderstanding. Perhaps not. These are perilous times, Mr. Watson. It pays to be prudent." Lusk stood up. "I suggest that we search the suspect."

"No!" I gasped. My emergency surgical kit was in my coat pocket, containing a small assortment of scalpels, scissors, and knives. Exactly the tools a Ripper would need. I screamed for help as the men tore my hands away from my pocket as I tried to cover it. The body of John Watson would soon hang over Commercial Street, tried, convicted and hanged forevermore as the notorious Jack the Ripper.

Lusk suddenly shouted over the other voices, "Get back, woman! We are acting in the name of Lord Salisbury!"

A gunshot cracked the air.

Smoke poured from the barrel of Irene Alders' handgun, and the muzzle was pointed directly at a small hole in the ground between George Lusk's feet. Irene clinched one eye and lifted the gun and so that it was aimed directly between Lusk's legs. "My next shot will be placed considerably higher, sir. I doubt even Lord Salisbury could find much use for a eunuch Ripper-Hunter. I'll take Doctor Watson and I'll take him right this bloody second."

Mickey Fitch pushed Lusk out of the way, stepping in front of Irene's line of fire. "Put that barker down, girl. There's more of us than you have bullets."

Irene cocked the hammer back and trained it on Fitch's remaining eye. "I have more than enough bullets to make sure you never see what happens after you speak one more word, you little prat."

Lusk grabbed me by the arm and hefted me from the ground. "Go!" he shouted. "Get the hell out of here!"

I struggled to my feet, snatching my coat. "I am not the Ripper," I said, slamming my shoulder into Fitch as I passed. "I'm not the bloody Ripper, you bastard." I limped to Irene, eyes still fixed on the men. I held out my hand, "Give me the gun."

"Shut your mouth and keep walking." She nudged me toward the nearest alley, keeping her gun aimed at the group. "Goodnight gentlemen. Best of luck in your endeavors, sodomizing small rodents, etc." She leaned her head toward me, "Can you run?" "I refuse to run from them."

Irene's eyes flared, "Damn it, John! Are you too stupid to realize I am trying to rescue us both?"

"That's it," Fitch snarled. "Best to get going now, laddie. Run while you can. We'll be seeing each other again, though, Doctor Watson. Trust that! Nobody does this and lives! I am going to cut your bullocks off and feed them to you! Then I am going to take a machete to your whore! You wait!"

"I believe I can manage a light sprint, Miss Adler," I said.

"Good. Get going, I am right behind you."

Sixteen

"Oy, Fred, listen. Listen! Put down the damn book and look at this." Constable Lamb shook the Evening News at Wensley, pointing to an article on the cover. "Hammerton is calling us a disgrace."

Wensley looked up from the book of procedure directives and said, "Who is Hammerton?"

"A police surgeon out in Bow Street. Who gives a damn what some bloke all the way out there has to say about the job we're doing? Seen any dead bunters lately in Convent Gardens? No, we got 'em all here in Whitechapel, but that bastard wants to see his bloody name in the newspaper so he goes spouting off this load of bollocks. It's ridiculous!"

"You still haven't told me what that load of bollocks was," Wensley said. Lamb tossed the paper across the desk at him.

A DISGRACE TO OUR POLICE ORGANISATION.

Dr. Hammerton, the divisional surgeon of the Bow-street Police, stated last night to our correspondent that he considered the recent murders and their non-solution a perfect disgrace to our boasted police organisation, and there appears to be little room for doubt that the detective system in regard to murder is not at all a good one, looking at the great number of murders, mostly of women, that are continually occurring and never detected.

"Right there in tonight's Evening News. As if the public was not having a difficult enough time letting us get on with catching The

Ripper, now our own surgeons are stirring things up even worse," Lamb said.

The doors to the station slammed open and Lamb and Wensley got to their feet as a crowd of loud, angry men charged toward the gate. They came directly up to the wooden rail and began banging their fists on it, shouting. "We demand to speak to whoever is in charge!" the one in front yelled.

Wensley waved his hands and told them to be quiet. "One at a time, gentlemen. Someone start off by telling us what the problem is. We'll decide who should handle it."

One of the men stepped forward and removed his hat. "My name is George Lusk, and these men are the members of the Whitechapel Vigilance Committee. We have come forth to announce the identity of Jack the Ripper."

From inside his office, Inspector Lestrade could hear the voices of people shouting. It was nothing out of the ordinary for Whitechapel at that time of night. He looked back at Chief Inspector Brett and said, "So that is the official version, is it?"

"No, Inspector. That is the only version. Sir Charles Warren arrived on Goulston Street the night of the 'Double-Event' and immediately identified the threat to the Jewish populace from the obviously unrelated graffiti on the wall. The Commissioner took the necessary steps to prevent an incident, with which the City Police were in full compliance and appreciation. The graffiti in question was properly documented prior to being destroyed."

Lestrade smiled, shaking his head, "What a load of bollocks."

"Let us be clear about one thing, Lestrade. This version also includes that you only left a murder scene in hot pursuit of a fresh lead. It allows for you to be so caught up in pursuing the killer, you momentarily lapsed in your awareness of where our jurisdictional responsibilities are."

"Does this version put me back on the case?"

Brett handed him his old report, most of which was crossed out by a thick black pen. Brett handed him a new report which was already written, with only a place at the bottom for Lestrade to sign. "It does the moment your recollection becomes synonymous with this report."

Lestrade picked up the pen, scribbled his name on it, and handed it to Brett as if were something foul. Constable Wensley knocked on his office door, "Pardon me, sirs, but there is a crowd out front and one of the men says that he has discovered the identity of Jack the Ripper. He says he has proof."

"Let me guess," Lestrade said. "Lewis Carroll is Jack the Ripper?"

"Wasn't he the one who wrote that children's book?" Wensley replied. "That would be a good laugh. Anyway, no, sir, these gentlemen are claiming they have evidence that The Ripper is Doctor John Watson of Baker Street."

"Ridiculous," Lestrade said, jumping from his chair. He came out of his office, storming toward the gate, shouting, "What the bloody hell are you all carrying on about? You lot better have a good reason to accuse a man like…oh my God."

Mickey Fitch looked at Lestrade and sneered. "Well, well. If it ain't ol' Gerry Lestrade. Heard yeh been looking for me, copper."

Lestrade shouted, "Get them!" and dove over the gate to tackle Fitch to the ground.

Constable Wensley leapt over the counter like a deer and cracked the head of the first Fitch boy he landed near. Two of the gang members dove onto Wensley and pulled him to the ground.

Lamb leapt onto the top of the whole pile of men and started swinging and kicking in every direction.

Fitch grabbed Lestrade's face with both hands, ripping into the skin of his cheeks with his fingernails. "Get off of me, pig! I'll rip your eyes out!"

Lestrade grabbed Fitch's ears and slammed the back of his head against the floor. "You killed that girl on Brick Lane! Jammed a stick so far up her you killed her, didn't you? Rapist bastard!" Fitch's head twisted from side to side, his eye-patch coming loose in Lestrade's hands. Lestrade looked into the gaping hole and gasped.

Fitch hammered his fist straight into Lestrade's nose, instantly snapping it sideways. Lestrade's eyes swelled as blinding pain spread across the front of his face, filling his mouth with copper-tasting blood.

"Sweet Jesus! What the hell are you doing!" Brett cried.

"Stop!" Lusk shouted. "Stop!" Lusk grabbed Fitch by the back of his collar and pulled him back from Lestrade.

"You broke my nose!" Lestrade howled, pulling his hand away to see the blood. "I am going to kill you, you Irish prat."

"Come on, pig!" Fitch screamed, eye patch dangling from his ear. "Come and have at it!"

"That is enough!" Brett shrieked. "All of you stop it this instant."

Wensley and Lamb looked at Lestrade, waiting to see what he would do. Both men took a moment to fix their uniforms and check how many buttons they had lost in the fray. Lestrade groaned in pain and told Wensley to get him a towel. "Chief Inspector, I have been looking for this bastard since the Emma Smith murder. I am placing him under arrest for intense interrogation. Let's see how you hold up with that, you simpering little mandrake!"

"No, you are not, Inspector," Brett corrected.

"What?"

"No one is getting arrested until we hear what these men have to tell us about the Jack the Ripper killings. You said you have evidence?"

"Irrefutable," Lusk answered.

"Fine. Inspector Lestrade, take a statement from this gentleman. Constables, assist the Inspector by taking statements from these other ones," Brett looked around the room. "Christ, I hate Whitechapel."

"Stop the cab!" I shouted and threw the door open in time to vomit onto the street. Irene held me by the back of my coat to keep me from falling out. I wiped my mouth and looked up, thinking I heard someone shouting to me.

"Doctor Watson? Oy! That you?" I spat several times as a young boy ran toward us up the street. "Hang on!" he shouted. "I need to talk to yeh. What yeh getting sick all over the street for?"

"Hello, Wiggins," I said. Wiggins was the leader of a group of juvenile street arabs that Holmes kept in his employ for conducting searches. The pay was a shilling a day, with an extra guinea going to the finder of whatever was being sought. Apparently, I was being sought, and Wiggins was about to get an extra guinea. "Watch your step."

Wiggins looked at the sickness on the pavement beneath the cab's door and scowled, stepping carefully around it as he climbed inside to join us. "Mr. Holmes sent us out to go find you straight away."

"Why?"

Wiggins shrugged. "I suppose it has something to do with you getting arrested for being Jack the Ripper."

"What!" Irene shouted, as I vomited onto the street again.

When I threw the door open to 221 B Baker Street there were two constables waiting to seize me the moment I entered. Inspector Lestrade stood in the corner, clutching a blood-soaked cloth to his nose. Beside him, a smaller man in a fancy uniform shouted at Mrs. Hudson, who was standing on the tips of her toes screaming for everyone to get out. Sherlock Holmes sat in his chair with his legs crossed, admiring the scene around him with a smirk.

The constables grabbed me by either arm and Chief Inspector Brett cried, "Dr. John Watson, I am placing you are under arrest for the murders in Whitechapel!"

"That is preposterous!" I shouted. "I did not murder anyone!"

He waved a rolled up piece of paper at me and said, "I have a sworn statement from six men who overheard you threatening to gut a whore in a tavern. When they confronted you, you savagely attacked them and even fired a gun at them!"

"A whore?" Irene said. "How dare you!"

"Who the hell are you?" Chief Inspector Brett asked.

"Dis is insane," Lestrade said. He kept the cloth pressed against his swollen face in obvious agony but managed, "Don Wadsin is dot da Ripper. De's Dolmdes's assisdand."

"Be silent, Inspector," Brett said. "Constables, take this man away immediately!"

The two constables holding me turned me toward the door when Irene shouted, "Wait! That is not how it happened at all! I witnessed the entire incident."

"One American strumpet's word against that of six British men?" Brett laughed. "We'll see what the judge has to say about that. Off we go, boys."

"What about what I have to say about it, Chief Inspector?" Holmes said softly.

Brett stiffened, breathing sharply through his nose. "What could you possibly have to add, Holmes? Perhaps you are used to being accommodated when you go about interfering in police business, but neither I, nor the Police Commissioner, are particularly fond of interlopers who go poking their nose into official matters. The investigation of crimes in London is our responsibility, and ours alone, Holmes. I think it is time for the public and yourself to be reminded of that! If you wanted to be a police officer so badly, I suggest you file a letter of interest at Headquarters like everyone else."

Holmes regarded Brett for a moment, then shrugged. "Very well. If you choose to accuse Watson of murder, that is your right, Chief Inspector, and I will not interfere. Personally, I agree that he has been acting unusually lately, and I could not vouch for his sanity one way or the other."

"Holmes!" I cried.

"That being said, there are few things that I consider sacred in this world and your inability to pay attention to even the simplest details is something I simply cannot abide."

"My abilities are none of your concern, Holmes. They seem to have landed me your secretary quite nicely."

"At present, your abilities are my only concern, Chief Inspector," Holmes shot back. "For example, if you possessed one single shred of observational skill you would have noticed the state of Watson's clothing."

Every head turned and looked me over carefully.

"Obviously, his coat is torn at the pockets and lapels, as if from being pulled and pushed during a great struggle," Holmes said. "Further, if you had one scintilla of competency, you would see that his face is bloodied and bruised. Yet, Watson has only one small cut on the knuckles of his right hand. It seems to me that would palpably indicate he received a great many blows to the face and yet threw only one punch in return.

"Moreover, if you, in all your egregious browbeating, were instilled with the most infinitesimal speck of intuition, the minutest snippet of insight would doubtlessly make it painfully obvious to you that both the toes and insteps of Watson's shoes are scraped down past the leather. Clearly, this demonstrates, even to a brainless twit like you, that he was lying on his stomach, scrambling on the ground. Now, please enlighten all of us, Chief Inspector Brett, with all of your enviable skill, how you explain that?"

There was silence, save for the sound of Lestrade who coughed with laughter behind his towel.

Chief Inspector Brett's face turned crimson. Finally he muttered, "I will not fall for your tricks, Holmes. Watson is under arrest."

"I will make you a wager, sir," Holmes said. He stood up and reached into a jar on his mantle. "What amount of money is enough to interest you?" He pulled out a stack of two hundred pound notes wrapped in a bank seal and threw it at Brett's feet. "How many years of salary is that for you? If you go over and look at Watson's hands and see gunpowder on the sleeves of his shirt, the money is yours. If you see gunpowder on the cuffs of Miss Adler's, the money remains with me, and you will leave."

"Show me your hands," Brett snarled.

I lifted them for his inspection. Irene held up her hands beside mine and began waving them. "I think these little black spots all over my sleeves are what you are looking for, Chief Inspector," she said. "These ones that look exactly like spent gunpowder."

Brett gritted his teeth and turned to Holmes. "This changes nothing, Holmes. We are still arresting John Watson for the Ripper crimes."

Holmes sat back down and began rubbing his temples with the tips of his fingers. "I have tolerated Scotland Yard for far too long. I can see that now. Mrs. Hudson, please notify the Central News Agency that Sherlock Holmes is prepared to sit down with them and discuss the inadequacies of the London Metropolitan Police Service. I have a file containing all of the cases they have taken credit for which were only solved due to my intervention. Now I wish to express my complete and utter lack of faith in their ability to solve these killings. Let them know I recommend the people of Whitechapel rise up and form armed posses to protect themselves and their families."

"You truly are a bastard," Brett hissed.

"Better a bastard than a buffoon," Holmes said. "Take your monkeys and get out of my sight."

Chief Inspector Brett stormed past us, shoving Irene and me out of the way and charging down the steps. Lestrade was laughing so hard that tears were streaming down his face, even as he groaned in agony.

"For God's sake, this poor man needs medical attention. Unhand me at once," I said to the constables. They released me and I walked over to Lestrade, asking him to lower the towel. "I am afraid your nose is badly broken, Inspector. I can reset it for you, but it will be quite painful, and I'll need you to hold still."

Lestrade nodded, taking a deep breath and holding it, as I put my thumbs against either side of his misshapen nasal bone.

"Ready?" I asked.

Lestrade closed his swollen eyes. I pressed inwards with my thumbs and snapped the cartilage back into place, cracking the bone so loudly that everyone winced. Lestrade cried out and clutched his face but when he looked up, his nose was in its proper position. Finally, he said, "Thank you, Doctor Watson. I have to admit, Holmes. That thing you do is much funnier when I am not on the receiving end of it."

Holmes took his seat in front of the fire and turned his head away from Lestrade.

"All right," Lestrade nodded toward Irene and me. "Try to get some sleep, folks. I will talk to the Chief Inspector and see if I can make some sense of this to him. I would not worry about him again. Goodnight."

The constables followed Lestrade down the steps. Mrs. Hudson scooped up the bloody towel, letting off a string of mutterings as she left the apartment. She gave Irene a sideways look as she passed. I took a deep sigh of relief and said, "Thank God that is over with. Holmes, you have my thanks for saving me, old chap."

"I shudder to think what would have happened had you not been here," Irene added. "That was brilliant—"

"Shut up!" Holmes growled. "Would the two of you just shut up for once in your lives? Look at you both, standing there as if you'd just come back from a big adventure. The simpleton doctor and the trollop opera singer, off to catch Jack the Ripper, eh?" He turned on me, "When the Whitechapel Vigilance Committee hangs you from a lamppost I will laugh, Watson. Laugh! And you, the Opera Starlet. I bet Jack the Ripper cannot wait to get his knife into your belly. You will make a prettier picture than the other women, I confess, but after he peels the skin off of your cheeks and chin it will not make much difference now, will it? How dare the two of you go out there without someone to watch over you? You are like two foolish children who need an adult to mind you so you do not get crushed to death crossing the street! Watson, go into your room and do not come out again until you get your wits about you!"

"I am no child," I said. "Do not speak to me as such."

"Fine! I shall speak even more plainly to you then. You are an idiot! You have always been an idiot! Everyone that knows you knows that you are an idiot and they detest you for it. If you had any brains at all, you would go find that strumpet governess and marry her immediately before she catches on to exactly how stupid you really are. As for you, Miss Adler, why don't you go find another Duke, or perhaps even a Prince this time? Stop playing silly games in Whitechapel and get back to what you are really good at. Spreading your legs for men with money."

I watched Irene tremble as Holmes spoke, but when I put my hand on her I found every muscle in her arm tensed, as if she were ready to strike him. Her words were like steel when she said, "When I met you I thought I had found a man worthy of my company, Holmes. You are nothing special to look at, but the quality of your mind was so singular that I found myself wondering what it would be like to go through life at your side. There were times when I wanted to come running to you, to offer you whatever earthly delight you could dream of, anything to win you. I must be a fool. I actually wrote you that letter asking you to help me put an end to these killings thinking that if you weren't willing to give up your precious addictions to save London, perhaps you might be in order to be with me."

Holmes did not move.

"I thank God that I never came to you before finding out what you truly are," she said. She moved past me to the doorway, then stopped and looked back at me. "Are you coming, John?"

My jaw quivered as my eyes turned hot and moist. I struggled to speak, trying to steady my trembling lips.

Holmes turned on me with utter contempt. My voice shook when I finally found the strength to use it. "You are nothing more than a coward," I managed. "Perhaps I do not have the same abilities as you but at least I am not sitting up here in this damned apartment hiding. I may, in fact, be an idiot." Tears started to slide down my face as I spoke, but I did not care. "Maybe everyone truly does agree on this, but I will not sit rotting at your side one second longer while women are being slaughtered. I will not. It isn't right. If it means my life, I shall use whatever paltry means I have at my disposal to fight him. May you burn in hell for not joining us."

Holmes reached underneath his chair. He lifted his Moroccan case and opened it,

removing a new vial of cocaine and sharp syringe. He slowly began rolling up his sleeve.

I cleared my throat. "I want you to know that we are finished, Holmes. Forever."

"Good," he said. He tied off his arm and made a fist, clenching his fingers until the veins popped out along his arm.

"Forever!" I shouted.

"Are you still here?" he said.

Irene took my hand in hers and interlaced her fingers with mine. She pulled me toward the door and I followed her down the stairs. We walked through the door and away from 221 B Baker Street without looking back.

Act III

YOU ARE THE QUARRY

Seventeen

Francis Darwin looked at the broken lock on the building's front door and frowned. He stepped back from the entranceway and checked the address again. 221 B, the sign over the doorway read. He looked up and down the block. "This is definitely Baker Street," he said to himself. He checked the scrap of well-worn paper in his hand again, already knowing what it said: *221 B Baker Street—S. Holmes*

As he knocked on the door, it swung open. The wood frame surrounding the lock was splintered and cracked and shards of it lie scattered on the entryway floor. Darwin's attention was drawn to the lower apartment's doorway where he could see people milling about within. The door was marked "221 A" and was broken open. As Darwin looked closer, he saw people stretched out across the floor with their arms and legs akimbo. In the corner, a woman was spread-eagled on the floor. Open sores covered the flesh of her bare thighs. A man leaned against the corner of the wall beside her, pulling his trousers back on and fastening them.

"Fascinating," he whispered. As he spoke the stench of urine and vomit filled up his nose and he removed his handkerchief and pressed it to his face. He went up the stairs toward the door marked "221 B" and called out, "Mr. Holmes? Hello? Is anyone home?"

From the upstairs entrance he could see a man crouched on the floor, meticulously searching through the piles of the worn carpet.

He muttered busily to himself as he inspected the spaces between each minute tuft of fiber.

Darwin swept his face and neck with his handkerchief, taking inventory of the room. There were drawers that had been yanked out of desks and cabinets thrown open with their contents scattered across the floor. Books were strewn about the room and pages of notes covered more areas of the floor than the carpet did. Darwin wrinkled his nose at the distinct odor of rotting food, and as he looked down, he saw several pieces of meat near the entrance. A white cat came from around the chair, sniffed the food and looked up at Darwin with fierce green eyes. "Excuse me, sir?" Darwin said.

"Come not an inch closer!" the man said, waving his hands frantically. "If you step on any of it, I cannot be held accountable for what happens to you."

"I have not moved at all, sir. Is there any chance I could help find what you are looking for?"

"Lost?" he hissed. "You mean stolen. All of it, stolen while I was sleeping by vile bastards while I slept."

Darwin looked down the staircase at the people mulling in and out of the lower apartment. "I could ring for the police if you like."

There was no answer as the man returned to his inspection of the rug. He plucked a tiny fragment of dust from the bottom of the carpet and cried out with great joy. He popped the speck into his mouth and began rubbing the tip of his finger vigorously against his gums, only to spit into his hand. "Chalk," he moaned. "Confound it!"

Darwin nodded, mystified. "I will leave you to your mission, sir. I apologize for barging in on you like this, but I was under the impression that someone formerly lived here whom I need to meet with. Would you happen to know what became of Sherlock Holmes? It is of incredible importance to me, and I am willing to pay you for the information." When there was no response, Darwin shrugged and said, "Good day to you then, sir. If you should see Mr. Holmes, please let him know that Francis Darwin called on him. I can be reached at the Royal Society at Carlton House Terrace."

"Charles Darwin?"

"Charles was my father."

The man regarded Darwin for a moment, leaning forward and squinting. His drawn, sharp-featured face was lit momentarily by the fire. "My God," Darwin said softly. "Is that you?"

Sherlock Holmes sat back on his heels, and then lifted himself from the rug. He tied the belt of his gown around his waist and moved toward the chair in front of the fireplace. He waved for Darwin to come in and sit down. Holmes lifted the blanket to his chin and regarded Darwin carefully for a moment. "I wonder what your father would have made of your baldness, Mr. Darwin."

Darwin sat down. "He would have fretted that it was an inherited weakness passed onto me by him marrying his own cousin. He lived in eternal fear that we had inherited some sort of deficiency."

Holmes cleared his throat by coughing forcefully several times. "Forgive me, Mr. Darwin. I have not had cause to speak for nearly a week. Tell me, if you do not mind, how many people were there downstairs in Mrs. Hudson's former apartment?"

"I counted five. Where is Mrs. Hudson?"

"She left after a rather ugly incident. You would not happen to partake of cocaine by any chance, would you?" Holmes said.

"I am afraid not."

"Morphine, perhaps? Any narcotic, really."

"Never," Darwin replied.

Holmes sighed. "Very well then, what seems to be the trouble, Mr. Darwin? Are you in danger?"

"No," Darwin said. "I have a rather embarrassing situation and require someone with a good bit of reason and perhaps a tiny dash of knowledge about the elements involved. A friend recommended you as the perfect man for the job, and I thought it best to call on your expertise."

"I will make you an offer," Holmes said. "If you are able to meet my conditions, I will hear out your tale."

"You have but to name them."

"First, my assisting you must not involve me having to leave the confines of this apartment. And for payment, I want you to agree to answer a series of questions for me, no matter what they are. And you must not inquire as to why I am asking them."

"That sounds acceptable," Darwin said.

"Then you, sir, may begin."

Darwin removed several envelopes from his coat, sifting through them until he found the one he was looking for. "Here it is," he said. "In 1880, my father received this letter from Henry Faulds, a British doctor living in Japan. Dr. Faulds was working at the Tsukiji Hospital in Tokyo and, to pass the time, he began excavating for pottery around the countryside. During one of these expeditions, Dr.

Faulds found a five hundred year old fragment of a jar, and was amazed at what he saw."

"A rare relic worth millions?" Holmes inquired.

"No, the fragment was of no monetary value at all. Rather, it was something imprinted on the surface of the clay, an impression left by the artisan that crafted it so many years before. He found what he came later to call a fingerprint. Dr. Faulds became obsessed with the idea that the lines contained within this fingerprint were different from his, and that his were different from those of everyone that he encountered. As fate would have it, someone later broke into the medical supply room at the hospital where he worked, and a janitor was promptly arrested for the crime. A handprint was found on the glass inside the room, and Dr. Faulds was able to convince the Keishicho Police that the fingerprints of the accused and those found at the scene of the crime did not match. The janitor was summarily released."

"Most interesting," Holmes said.

"Dr. Faulds felt he was onto something huge and immediately flew back to London for a meeting with Sir Charles Warren, the Commissioner of the Metropolitan Police. All that he requested was the funding and support for the design of a system which could be used to classify the fingerprints of criminals and potentially change the face of criminal investigations around the world."

"Being somewhat familiar with Sir Charles, I can deduce the results of that meeting," Holmes said.

"If by that you mean it ended poorly, you are correct," Darwin said. "Sir Charles saw absolutely no merit to possessing the fingerprints of criminals. Dr. Faulds was left at a loss. He suspected the enormity of his discovery, but had little idea how to go about verifying it scientifically. He was in quite a predicament."

Holmes pondered the story carefully, and then smiled. "Naturally, he contacted the only person he could think of with experience in unraveling monumentally complicated scientific conundrums. Your father."

"Exactly," Darwin said, holding up the letter. "My father read through Dr. Faulds's letter and inspected his own fingers. I remember him saying, 'It all sounds remarkably interesting, but I have enough of my own problems.' He forwarded the letter to our cousin Francis Galton." Darwin took a deep breath, "For all that my father was in the field of science, I confess Cousin Francis to be twice that. At the time Father sent him the letter, Francis was simultaneously inventing the Quincunx Machine and formulating the basis for his eugenics philosophy. Francis Galton is a prolific intellect, Mr. Holmes. He has more proven theories, papers, inventions and awards to his name than I could ever dream."

"I sense an 'And yet' is lingering in there somewhere," Holmes said.

Darwin hung his head and closed his eyes. "And *yet*, eight years after my father sent Francis Galton this very letter from Dr. Henry Faulds regarding his discovery of the human fingerprint, Galton authored a paper proclaiming his own discovery of the same exact thing. Suffice to say, Dr. Faulds is not amused."

"Understandably so," Holmes said. "Is it a complete facsimile of Faulds's discovery, or only a strong resemblance?"

"It has both enough differences and similarities to be argued either way, Mr. Holmes."

"I do not see what it is that I can do for you, Mr. Darwin. It would seem that this is a matter best left to the courts, perhaps? I am no arbiter."

"I understand that, and certainly, it may very well come to that, but in the mean time I feel that someone must at least make an effort on behalf of the greater good. I personally believe that this science is more valuable than the name of the man who gets to lay claim to inventing it. I had hoped your unique perspective might provide some needed guidance to both parties and help them set aside their own differences in order to better serve humanity."

Holmes chuckled and looked around the room. "Perhaps I am not the person you wish to have speak on behalf of the greater good, Mr. Darwin."

"You are the only person, sir," Darwin said. "Whether it suits you or not."

"Do you have copies of both the letter and Galton's paper that you could leave for me?"

"I do," Darwin said.

"Put them on the table and I will look them both over and tell you what my thoughts are after I have had time to consider the problem. That seems to be the best I can offer you at this time."

Darwin laid both items on the table and sat back down, folding one leg over the other. "And now, you wanted to ask me some questions?"

Holmes sat up in his chair, stretching as if he had not moved in so long that his limbs would snap off if he shifted them too quickly. He tapped his finger against his chin, eyes suddenly lighting up. "Tell me something. Is this Francis Galton bald also?"

"As an egg."

Holmes smiled briefly, but his eyes remained fixed intently on Darwin, taking the man's measure as his mind collected the available information from his observations. "Most interesting. I am somewhat familiar with your father's writings. Particularly, I am fond of his ideas about the struggle all living things must endure to survive. It makes sense to me that on the surface of things, the world is completely chaotic, with millions of different species of life co-existing on the same planet simultaneously, interacting at random. But your father's idea was that beneath that layer of chaos, all is actually perfectly ordered. Each of those species is held in check by several others, so that no one is ever out of balance."

"Yes," Darwin said. "That sounds right."

"Did your father ever speculate what would happen if there was an imbalance? If one of the more aggressive species began taking hold over the others?" Holmes said.

"Can you give me an example?" Darwin said.

"Let us say that there is a large pond, and the pond is filled with a variety of fish. Some fish feed off of the scum at the surface. Some fish feed from the scum at the bottom. Other, more sinister groups feed on those fish, and likewise, there are larger ones who feed on those as well. It is all one perfectly balanced system of life where each member of the habitat understands the rules of existence. They could live that way forever." Holmes leaned forward and lowered his voice, "But, what if a new species were suddenly introduced into the pond? A wildly aggressive, intelligent, predatory creature bent only on destroying whatever stood in its path? A creature so outside of the norm that it was like nothing ever seen before. What would its effect be?"

Darwin sat back, folding his hands together. "I suppose, theoretically, if that new species upset the balance of the pond enough, it would eventually lead to complete and utter extinction."

Holmes sat back and let the air out of his chest, as if he were deflating. "Extinction," he murmured, closing his eyes. "I have nothing further to ask you, sir. Kindly show yourself out, Mr. Darwin."

"One moment, Mr. Holmes. I mean this as no offense to you, but your scenario is not plausible. It is like debating what life on our planet would be like if all of us sprouted wings and could fly."

"Explain," Holmes said.

"Nature does not allow for one singular member of a species to be suddenly introduced into any environment. There are plenty of examples of incredibly aggressive predators all over the world who regularly prey on the weaker members of their environs. None of them overrun those populations because they are held perfectly in check."

"By what?" Holmes said as he leaned forward again.

"Other members of the same species, of course. In your pond scenario, that predator would run amok for a little while, but eventually, he would encounter his equal. My father was quite explicit in his statement that the struggle for survival between members of the same species are always most severe. In all actuality, the two predators fight and one would be killed. The second would be injured enough that a lesser species would rush in and finish him off."

"A sacrifice for the benefit all else, then?"

"What pond is it that we are referring to, exactly, Mr. Holmes?"

Holmes lifted his legs onto his chair, covering them with the blanket. "Thank you, Mr. Darwin. I will review your quandary and notify you of my findings in due time. Good day."

Eighteen

There was a sound was like that of a hundred hammers clanging against sheets of metal that crashed on his skull with such impact that it jarred him. Montague Druitt clutched the sides of his head in agony.

It was time for class.

He wiped the sweat from his face and staggered down the hall, collapsing into the seat at his desk as the students began to filter in. He swept his damp hair from his forehead and sat up, ignoring the concerned looks shot toward him by several of the students.

"Today we will discuss the court of law, and those who serve it. Please get your writing implements ready," Druitt said, pressing on the desk to get to his feet. "First, we will begin with the barrister. A barrister, you see…appears before the court and presents argument. There is no…ah, no…contact with the person he is…" Druitt licked his lips nervously, gripping the sides of his desk. "There is absolutely no contact made with the accused, so that the court can trust he is impartial-"

The cacophony within him suddenly fell silent, as if a switch had been thrown cutting off their power over him. As Druitt struggled to get on with his lesson, a voice whispered clearly in his ear what he must do next.

Druitt stood frozen for a moment, terrified. The students began to whisper to one another, their voices much less coherent than the one telling him to go to Whitechapel and what he must do there. "No!"

Druitt barked. "That is too much." The clamor returned as instantly as it had vanished with so much force that it made Druitt cry out for it to stop.

"Assistant headmaster?"

"Are you all right, sir?"

"Someone fetch the nurse!"

"No!" Druitt gasped, taking a deep breath. "I am fine. Sit back down at once. I apologize, students. I am not feeling well, but we are nearly finished and must press on. Now, a solicitor, on the other hand, has to…has to…." Druitt looked up at the ceiling and blinked rapidly at the harsh bright light shining over his students heads. Everything else went dark, and Druitt collapsed to the ground where he began shaking violently and foam bubbled from his mouth.

Within the hour, Headmaster George Valentine and Will Druitt were climbing the stairs to the resident teachers' wing. "It was good of you to come on such short notice, Mr. Druitt," Valentine said.

"I appreciate the telegram, Headmaster. You said the children reported to you that my brother was yelling?"

"Yes, but apparently it was gibberish. Has he ever suffered fits before?"

"Not that I have ever been made aware of," Will said. "It is most disturbing."

They came to Druitt's door and knocked. Mark Mann, the other Assistant Headmaster opened the door and said, "Come in." Druitt was sprawled on his cot, sweating profusely. "He hasn't moved since we brought him up here."

"Monty?" Will said. "Can you hear me?"

"Blast!" Mr. Valentine said. "Of all the bad timing. We have a meeting at Blackheath on the nineteenth. If Mr. Druitt does not convince them to give us money for the new cricket stands, we will not be able to host the championships next year. We've been preparing this for over a year."

"I assure you that he will be at that meeting, Mr. Valentine," Will said. "Thank you gentlemen. I will stay with him for now."

Both Valentine and Mann left the room. Will shut the door and locked it. He sat at the bedside and reached into his coat, removing a syringe and bottle. He loaded the syringe, and leaned forward, putting his lips close to Druitt's ear. "Can you hear me, Monty?" Will flicked the top of the needle, watching the fluid ooze from the tip and drip down the thin length of steel. "Be strong, little brother. We still have work to do."

"Oh God, Will," Druitt whispered. "I am hearing voices now. You must help me. I need to be locked away. Mother's illness has got hold of me."

Will patted Druitt's damp head, smiling gently. "This is only a bad dream, Monty. None of it is real. Go back to sleep. This will calm you." He pinched the skin of Druitt's neck and stuck the needle in.

Druitt grimaced, squeezing his brother's hand. "You are so good to me, Will. We never did go to India, you know? You promised we would. You swore we would have an adventure…" Druitt's voice trailed off as his eyes fluttered.

"Oh, but we are, little brother. We already are."

Nineteen

If anything, Whitechapel is even more bleak and dismal by day. There is no clear indication that it is, in fact, day, as the sun's rays are lost in the thick yellowy cloud of mist hanging over everything. It sinks into your nose and seeps into your pores like a stinking, maculating oil. After a few hours walking these streets, my eyes begin to sting and my lungs burn from breathing it in.

Rats scurry through the streets, trying to outrace one another while dashing between the legs of disinterested pedestrians. I watch dozens of them run into the street and get crushed beneath the wheels of passing cabs.

These cabs constantly crash into one another, being jammed together from one end of Commercial Street to the other. Each of them bears a sign of some sort, advertising products such as "Nestlé's Milk" or "Pears Soap" products. All of it nonsense that no one in this neighborhood could ever afford to buy.

Some of the cabs are larger, double-decker affairs with crowds of people packed onto the upper level. These are tourists who nervously peer over the edge of the cab at the swarms of people on the sidewalks. Scary-looking immigrants and ruffians return their stares with the looks of a hungry predator watching a fat meal pass.

I looked up and down the length of Commercial Street, noting that I had not seen a police constable on patrol during the entire time I'd been standing there. Each passing man eyed me with contempt, taking measure of my clothing and manner, instantly identifying me as someone who did not belong. To them, I was from another world, a place that actively sought to oppress them, and in return, they were estimating what it would gain them to either beat me or rob me.

Many of them eyed Irene. Their eyes moved slowly down the length of her body, taking their time in measuring her generous proportions. "Why are we even out here, Miss Adler?" I said. "The Ripper will never strike in broad daylight."

"We are using our unique gifts, Dr. Watson. Just as Holmes would use his. Part of that includes me studying my character."

"What character?" I said.

Irene sighed, "Do you not understand that we must learn whatever it is that he already knows about these women. He knows why he kills them. He knows why he does what he does to them. We do not."

"Did you ever think that perhaps he killed those four women for personal reasons that cannot be known to us? What if the killer was simply their pimp and he murdered them over something as simple as a monetary dispute? There could be a relatively simple explanation for all of this and we are just not seeing it because we are too busy chasing a deuced bogeyman!"

Irene shook her head, "None of the victims lived in a close enough proximity. Why would one pimp have four different girls so spread out? That is not how they work. They keep their girls close by, never too far out of their sight, nor their grip."

"I suppose you know this, as well? In between appearances on stage at La Scalla, perhaps? To be perfectly frank with you, Miss Adler, I find it hard to believe that an opera prima donna has any knowledge whatsoever about these grimy people. It almost seems insulting for you to say so. I am no child of privilege, but even I confess that I have little ability to fathom what it must be like living in conditions like these."

"I have seen much of this world, Dr. Watson. Leave it at that."

I took a deep breath. "Perhaps what I should say is that this is completely foreign to any investigation I have ever done. Holmes and I would have been inspecting evidence, or searching for clues. The deductions he made at the end of the case were based on the observations he made during the investigation."

"Fine," Irene said. "Go and deduce to your heart's content. I will meet up with you in two hours in front of the police station." With that, she turned and crossed the street, quickly darting between carriages.

"What an exasperating woman," I sighed. Commercial Street was filled with people that all jostled about as they moved from block to block, bar to bar, squalor to squalor. Street hawkers called out from their stands, shouting as loudly and often as possible over the voices of the others, selling bent match sticks and long slimy eels snatched from the Thames.

Men stood bearing large wooden signs painted with slogans for *Salutairis Champagne* and *Royal Dutch Chocolate*, trying to divert the never ending streams of passersby into the stores they stood in front of. Drunkards were everywhere, even at this early hour. Men and women stumbled in the streets, crashing into one another, and vomiting into the gutters. Police snatched thieves by the back of the shirt and beat them to the ground with their truncheons. Several women called out to me from the alleyways, "Feeling good natured, sir?"

"I suppose so, thank you," I replied. They then stared at me curiously as I continued walking. A hurdy gurdy player plucked his instrument on the sidewalk as I left. He carefully guarded the upturned hat at his feet, which some passersby threw the odd farthing into. Beside him, a drunkard took to dancing stupidly, clapping and singing, while holding out his hat whenever someone passed by. To be fair, the drunkard seemed to be making more money than the musician.

I stopped at one of the street hawker stands who had barrels of apples stocked all around him. He had a thick stick in his hand, and he smacked it into his palm as a warning to anyone who looked like they might try and snatch one without paying. I looked into one of the barrels and grabbed an apple, then dropped it instantly when I saw it was riddled with worm holes. I turned a few more over and saw that they got worse as you went further into the barrel. "Excuse me, my good man, but these apples are all fouled."

The hawker snarled at me and told me to "Piss off!"

I saw Irene moving through a crowd of people. "Miss Adler!" I shouted, hurrying to catch up to her. "Slow down a moment, if you please. I did not mean to offend you back there. Are you still cross with me?"

Irene fixed her eyes ahead, continuing to walk. "No, Dr. Watson. I am not cross with you, but I am exceedingly disappointed."

"You are?" I said. "Why?"

"It is nothing you did, exactly. It is who you are. Who all of you are. Everyone in this damned city west of Temple Bar thinks of nothing but peerages and tea parties, but meanwhile, these people cannot feed their children."

"I would not agree that it is fair to say that of me, Miss Adler."

"Yet you are more comfortable in that world, than in this. You flinch when they walk too closely to you, Watson. You look like you want to delouse yourself every time you speak with one of them."

"Well, look at how they stare at me, Miss Adler. They watch both of us as hungrily as sharks, just waiting for the moment to pounce on us. I daresay what they do with us once they pounce upon us may be different. But I suppose they are only human, in that regard."

The corners of Irene's mouth rose and she cast her eyes sideways toward me, "Are you being saucy with me, Dr. Watson?"

"Of course not, Miss Adler. I was only trying to-"

Irene put her finger over my lips. "Be silent for a moment. I think you may be onto something, Doctor. We should try and fit into our surroundings more. I am far too clean and well-dressed and you, my dear, are much too handsome."

"I am? Really?"

Irene nodded and looked up and down the street. "A pawn shop," she said brightly. "That should do the just the trick for us."

"Handsome, you say?"

"At the very least, you are a little too well-groomed. I also think we should forego certain formalities, Doctor. From here on out, you will call me Irene, and I shall call you John. Agreed?"

"I suppose so. It seems a little improper, though."

"I trust you are made of stern enough stuff to endure it." She led me toward a store with "*PAWN HERE*" emblazoned on the front door. "This will suit us perfectly."

Within moments I was standing in my underclothes in the changing room of that pawn shop as Irene shouted, "John, try these on!" A handful of filthy, ragged clothes came flying over the door at me and as I bent to collect them, a pair of boots struck me on the back of the head.

I stared at the articles she'd collected in disbelief. "Irene, pardon my saying so, but why would I trade in my clothes for these rags?"

Irene opened the door, and I scrambled to cover myself. "Because these are the clothes a typical person in Whitechapel wears, of course. Are you serious about catching Jack the Ripper, John?"

"Yes, but—"

"Do you want to make that woman proud, and silence your critics who think you lack the faculties to be anything more than Holmes's manservant?"

"Yes," I said.

"Good," she said, smiling. "Because I see a man before me who does not seem to be lacking in any department." Her smile turned sideways, "Except, perhaps, your hair." She put her fingers against my scalp, running them through my hair and undoing the tightly slicked back style I normally wore. Irene wiped her hand against her coat, smearing it with my macassar hair oil, but nodded with satisfaction as she looked at me.

When I emerged from the changing room, pulling my stained, threadbare coat closed, I was no longer Dr. John Watson.

"You look wonderful, John." She walked to the counter where an old man sat staring at us in wonder over the rim of his thinly-rimmed glasses. "How much for these, sir?"

"Must say this is the first time anybody ever traded in clothes like yours to buy clothes like these, m'lady," he said. "Can't imagine what would possess a person to do that."

"Vengeance," Irene said flatly. The man looked at me, and I lifted my shoulders in wonder.

"Where to now, Miss Adler?" I asked as we left the store. I was wondering how long it would take for my new clothes to stop reeking of whatever booze-infested illness their previous occupant had suffered.

"Let's go find ourselves a room."

"I beg your pardon?" I said.

Irene took me firmly by the hand, pulling me along. "We need to be here, in this part of the city, John. It will help us immensely. We cannot move among them without raising suspicions unless we actually are one of them. To do that, we have to live here."

"There is not a single place in all of London that will let us room together without being married. I do not think even you are willing to go quite that far to catch the Ripper."

Irene chuckled as she led me toward a raggedy building with a sign that read *CROSSINGHAMS*. The man at the front looked up at us, "Here to doss?"

"Yes, love," Irene said, affecting the local accent perfectly. "'Ow much?"

"It's four shillings, six pence, per week. Each. You need money up front or it's back to the street with yeh. I don't take no charity cases."

Irene fished several coins from her pocket and slapped them on the table. "Here's enough for the first week. We'll see if we need the room any longer after that."

I pulled Irene toward me, "A week? Sharing one room? What about my Mary? If she learned of this, I shudder to think what would happen."

"Hush, John," Irene whispered, watching the man count the coins. Satisfied, he pulled out a ledger, opened it, and asked what name we wanted the room under. "Sybil Vane," Irene said.

"Aw right, Miss Vane. Here's your key. See me if you need anything. You lot can `ave the one up on the left. Oy," he said, grabbing Irene's arm as she passed. He put his mouth to her ear and whispered something that made her cheeks flush.

Irene smiled thinly and nodded to the man. "I will," she said. "I really must get settled first." She came to my side and hurried down the hall toward our room.

"What was that all about?" I whispered.

"He asked me when I'd be working later. He said he liked to try all the 'fresh fish' before the other boys got to it."

I turned away from her to head directly back toward the man and punch his eyeballs from his head when Irene grabbed me and dragged me up the bare wooden steps. We came to a long narrow hallway with unlined walls save for peeling wallpaper. A thin, threadbare carpet covered the floor and the room was dimly lit by several, small gas-lamps.

Irene fit the key into our door, and revealed a room that was squalid and dank and barely bigger than the bed lying in the middle of it. The bed itself consisted of a thin mattress with lice-infested sheets. "Christ," I said.

"I know," Irene sighed, "it is absolutely perfect."

Twenty

"Oy?" Constable Lamb said. "Who am I?" He puffed out his belly and sat back in the desk sergeant's chair, kicking both feet up on the desk and throwing his head back, snoring.

Constable Wensley looked up from his police manual, shook his head, and went back to reading.

"Why you always got your nose buried in some departmental book?" Lamb said. "Trying to make commissioner of police someday?"

"No," Wensley said, "just Inspector."

"You can have that," Lamb said. "I'll stay in uniform till I die. I'll take this fat bastard's job when he croaks and—"

"Who you calling fat?" Sgt. Byfield snarled from the doorway.

"Morning, sir!" Lamb said, throwing his feet to the floor and standing at attention.

"You see the bloody sign on this desk, boy? Says '*Sergeant of Police*' on it, don't it?"

"Yes, Sergeant Byfield."

"It does not say '*Place For Snot-Nosed Constables to Put Their Feet Upon,*' now does it?"

"No, Sergeant Byfield."

"Too right. Now, just to prove to me that you can read, go sort the reports from last month. Take your girlfriend with you," he said, pointing at Wensley.

"Me, sir? What did I do, Sergeant?" Wensley complained, putting his book down.

"You're a bookworm, Wensley. Hard to trust a man that enjoys reading in this line of work. Do me a favor and go prove you're no better than the rest of us, eh? Sort the blasted reports."

"Yes, Sergeant," Wensley said, glaring at Lamb.

Sgt. Byfield sat down in his chair, wiping the mud from Lamb's boot off his desk, and relaxed. Then the door opened. Two men came in, the second holding a small cardboard box with rapidly shaking hands. Byfield eyed the box suspiciously. "Dare I ask?"

"My name is Joseph Aarons," the first man said, lowering his hat. "I am secretary for the Whitechapel Vigilance Committee. This is Mr. George Lusk. I believe several of your men already know him. We need to speak to Inspector Lestrade. Immediately."

"Inspector Lestrade is busy at the moment," Sgt. Byfield looked back at the office. Chief Inspector Brett had arrived before Byfield that morning and went directly into Lestrade's office, shutting the door behind him. "Can someone else help you?"

Aarons looked at Lusk, who appeared to be close to tears. "It is really quite important, sir. We have received a letter and…something else…from Jack the Ripper."

"I want you to put Doctor Watson under twenty-four hour surveillance," Chief Inspector Brett said. "That bastard Holmes too! They are responsible for this, and I want them followed. I want them caught in the act!"

"In the act, eh?" Lestrade said. He began rubbing his cheekbones with the tips of his fingers. It still hurt to talk, and it was not made any better by having to endure the pain of speaking to an idiot. Thankfully, the swelling had gone down, but there were still large black-and-blue circles under his eyes.

"Yes, in the bloody act, so that we have irrefutable proof!"

"That's ingenious, sir. We'll wait until Dr. Watson is ripping open some poor bird apart, then just as he's digging his fingers into her uterus, we'll jump out and say, 'Drop the organ! You're under arrest!'"

"Do try not to be stupid, Lestrade."

"This whole conversation is stupid, Chief Inspector. John Watson is not the Ripper. Case closed. Get somebody else to follow him around if you want."

"I have had just about enough of your insubordination, Lestrade. You did not back me up on Baker Street, as was your obligation, and I am beginning to have serious doubts about your loyalty to this organization."

"My loyalty is with those who would make a serious effort to stop these killings, sir. And right now, there seems to be few names on that list, indeed."

Brett's eyes lowered, and he took a deep breath. "You know, I like you, Gerard. I really do. You have that fire, that 'have-at-it' attitude this division is sorely lacking. Most people see CID as just a platform for advancement. A place to catch the attention of the Department's upper echelon. Not you, though. You really give a damn about these lowlifes. I understand you perfectly, can you see that? Now, I want you to try and see it from management's perspective. These Ripper killings are making us all look bad. Especially in the highest ranks of the department, who, may I remind you, have the ear of some incredibly powerful people. Everyone wants these killings stopped, and if we do that, who knows what the reward will be? Christ, Gerard, there could be bloody knighthoods involved. Peerages, or possibly even land!"

The room was silent as Lestrade observed Brett's sweaty brow and thin, quivering lips. "Sir, I am just a simple policeman trying to catch this lunatic before he guts another bunter. I don't know about any of that other stuff."

Brett's face reddened. "You are a stupid, stubborn bastard who is going to drag this whole police station down with him if you do not smarten up, Lestrade!"

"Excuse me, sirs," Sgt. Byfield said, knocking on the office door. "I hate to interrupt such an intimate moment, but I have a man out front who says Jack the Ripper mailed him a letter and a special little present."

"Really?" Brett jumped from the desk, "I will handle this, Lestrade. Try to watch and learn how to correctly pursue a fresh lead. Excuse me, Sergeant." Byfield stood in the doorway, looking down at Brett. Finally, he moved, but just enough so that Chief Inspector was forced to squeeze by.

Lestrade and Byfield smiled at one another. "You really should not mess about with him like that, Sergeant Byfield," Lestrade said. "He just finished telling me how he is a high-ranking official with connections to the upper echelon of the Department. In fact, if things go according to his plan, he might even be knighted."

Byfield smirked, "Who, him? He's just another CID prat that ain't in my food chain. Just like you, you French bastard."

"Who are you calling high-ranking?" Lestrade said, smiling. "When this is all finished, I'll be lucky to work here scrubbing the floors."

Within moments, Chief Inspector Brett came back into Lestrade's office carrying a small cardboard box that he kept at arm's length and away from his body. He was nearly as sheet-white as the two men standing behind him. "I need you to have a look at this, Inspector," Brett said. He put the box down on the desk and coughed, putting his hand against his mouth.

Lestrade looked at George Lusk and said, "Well, well, Mr. Lusk. Where's your friend, Mickey Fitch? Bet you thought his lot would protect you once you went about sticking your nose into this sort of thing."

"I am done with them, Inspector Lestrade. This package came to my home the other day through the post. To my home, Inspector! Where my wife and children sleep! This bastard knows where I live."

"Calm down, Mr. Lusk," Joseph Aarons said. "Everything will be all right. Inspector Lestrade will make sure of it."

Lestrade cocked an eyebrow at Aarons, and moved forward to open the flaps of the box. He recoiled at the horrific odor that escaped from within, then bent to look inside.

Twenty One

Now the cat was telling him that it was time to go find more cocaine. "I am bored." The cat lazily licked its paws and scrubbed its ears. It did not move its mouth to speak, but Sherlock Holmes heard its voice as clearly as if he were saying the words himself. For a moment he was not sure that it was not, in fact, him speaking. "Let's go out and grab a few vials. There's the man down the street who will sell us as many as we like."

Holmes kicked the cat off of the chair, making it hiss and scramble across the wooden floor into the shadows. He re-read his letter to Francis Darwin by pressing it up to his face, having to squint in the dim firelight to read it.

"Mr. Francis Darwin,

I have finished my study of the findings of both Dr. Henry Faulds and the esteemed Mr. Francis Galton. It is clear that both men are of similarly astute intellects, and keen scientific minds. I would encourage you to approach them with the suggestion that, should they combine their efforts, rather than bicker about who reached whatever conclusion first, the results would be staggering.

Dr. Faulds' work clearly presents the reasoning behind his theory of the existence of unique fingerprint ridge patterns, but lacks a firm suggestion of a system to classify these patterns in a useable manner.

Mr. Galton builds significantly on those findings and begins to assign scientific terms to each of the multiple lines and shapes found within each print.

Thus, my belief is that by—"

The cat leapt into Holmes's lap. It raised a paw and batted the letter out of his hands. "You cannot ignore me any more than you can the thirst in your veins."

Holmes picked up the letter from the floor and looked into the cats viridian eyes, seeing its sharp-fanged smile curling just beneath. He leaned down so that he was face to face with it. "Listen to me very carefully. I do not want any cocaine." The words were shaky as they emerged from his mouth. "I do not want any morphine. I do not want any cocaine. I do not want any cocaine or any morphine." He continued repeating this as he sat back up and returned to the letter.

The cat leapt from his lap and into Watson's chair. It sat down and began licking itself between the legs. The sound of it purring was like the gears of an industrial machine grinding inside his head. Holmes swept his palm across his face to clear the sweat dripping from his hair. He cleared his throat.

"Thus, my belief is that by simply assigning a numerical value to each of the already scientifically termed shapes, we can accurately label a unique fingerprint in the same way that chemical elements are displayed on the periodic table.

For example, someone trained in fingerprint classification could count the number of Arches, Whorls, Loops, and the variants thereof, and write them mathematically using an agreed-upon manner of display. That way, no matter what part of the world an agent of *identification was, he could receive the coordinates of his suspect's fingerprints and be able to match them or disregard that suspect.

Obviously this is all—"*

The scabs covering his arms itched maddeningly.

Holmes studied the bruised blue flesh and small puncture marks lining his arm from the wrist to bicep. He bent over the chair and searched the piles of papers and books scattered there. "Where is it?" he asked nervously.

He found several pieces of dried-out food buried under the papers, left from when Mrs. Hudson had brought him his last meal before fleeing the house. He threw them into the fire. "Here we are!" he announced triumphantly.

He lifted the instrument case from the floor and set it in his lap. There was a thick layer of dust covering the case, and Holmes blew most of it off, feeling clouds of it go into his nose. His eyes welled up and his nose began to run as he popped the latches, but Holmes still smiled as he removed the violin and held it up to the light.

He ran his fingers along the instrument's dark, chestnut surface, stroking its deep belly and broad waist with the affection and familiarity of a lover. Holmes wrapped his fingers around her solid neck and over her fine, sturdy fingerboard, putting his ear against her as plucked one of the strings. A perfectly tuned note reverberated in response. It was the sound of peace.

Holmes put the violin against his chin and touched his bow to the strings, sliding it across the surface, but the instrument whined in complaint at his inability to form a proper note with his cramped fingers. The cat opened its mouth for a wide yawn, and Holmes threw the violin at it.

A voice boomed from below the steps, "Sherlock? Is that you up there? What in God's name has happened here? Who the bloody hell are all of you people?"

"Mycroft?" Holmes whispered, clutching his blanket. He panicked as he looked around the room, seeing the state of it. "No! Do not come up here! I forbid it!"

There were voices crying out and the sounds of things crashing against the walls below. "I'll thrash the lot of you buggers! Get the hell out of here, you filth!" Mycroft shouted. "Come back and I'll pitch you off the damn roof!"

The front door slammed shut and there were heavy footfalls on the stairs as Mycroft hurried up them. "Hang on man, I am coming!"

"It is not safe to come in here!" Holmes shouted. "You must stay outside."

"Stop being ridiculous." Mycroft Holmes opened the door to 221 B and his eyes grew wide as his voice trailed off. Mycroft's massive frame filled the doorway and it took him several moments to catch his breath. "My God…I had no idea this was what Watson meant."

"Please, Mycroft, go away," Holmes groaned. "I do not want you to see me like this."

"I was asked me to look in on you," Mycroft said softly. He looked around in wonder at the state of the apartment, then back at his brother. "Watson sent me a postcard asking me to check on you while he was away. He warned me you would not appreciate the visit, however, I had no idea it had come to this."

"Watson, eh? Leave it to him to interfere with my life, even as he trots around the East End looking to get himself killed."

Mycroft waded through the garbage littering the floor to sit in Watson's chair. "You know, I've always suspected that without Watson or Mrs. Hudson around, you would not be able to care for yourself. You are the kind of man who gets so wrapped up in his work that he would forget to bother to the minor details of existence, like eating, drinking, or apparently bathing. As usual, I was right."

"As you almost always are, is that not correct, Mycroft?"

"It is true that I am disposed of a singularly advanced intellect. Do not fret, brother. You are also gifted, in your own way. I admit to having always envied you and your position in the world."

"Do not patronize me, Mycroft," Holmes said.

"You see, my life consists of taking in all the facts as they are reported to me from every corner of the Empire, constantly calculating the tonnage and weight-ratios of the various supply lines, or the ammunition capacity of conceptualized rifles. Some petty dictator is stirring up trouble and we need a well-placed scandal to bring him down a few pegs, and it falls to me to put the events in motion that may take years to unfold. But you, little brother, you chose to come here and mingle amongst the common man. You chose to apply yourself to their petty problems and dalliances. I find it all quite charming. Quaint, even."

"Get out, Mycroft. Whatever you meant to accomplish here, it is a useless endeavor. I ask you to please leave."

Mycroft took a long look at him. Holmes instinctively covered his arms with the blanket, pulling it tight to his chest. Mycroft shook his head sadly, but did not move from his chair. "Mother would be most disappointed, Sherlock."

"Oh, shut up, Mycroft."

"She favored you, you know. You were her baby. As for our father, alas, he was of a different sort. What did Father call you? Oh, that's right. His 'Little Accident.' That is what this is all about, right? All this showing up of Scotland Yard at every turn, pissing all over the people closest to you just to prove how much you do not need them. Here you are claiming to be the greatest criminal investigator of your era but you refuse to participate in the single most desperate investigation in this country's history? You are an odd one, Sherlock. Perhaps Father was right about you."

"Get out!" Holmes shouted, beating the arms of his chair with his fists.

Mycroft leapt to his feet and roared, "That's it! Show me a little spirit! You cannot frighten me. I knew you when you shat yourself and sucked your thumb. I knew you when your schoolmates were cruel to you and when you broke your mother's heart by telling her you would never marry."

"Why are you doing this to me?" Hot tears sting Holmes's eyes like cups of rubbing alcohol. "I am sick. Can you not see that? Please, Mycroft, just leave me be. I beg you."

"And here I never thought you would ever beg from anyone. I suppose fear has broken better men than you before. I should not be surprised."

"Afraid?" Holmes said. "By all means, tell me what I am afraid of. If you honestly think I fear The Ripper, you are a fool. I would take his knife and plunge it into my own heart at the first chance. I would do it myself if I could hold the damned thing steady. I want to die, Mycroft. I cannot go on like this any longer."

Mycroft leaned forward and lowered his head until he was level with Sherlock. "For years you have hung a sign outside your door, telling the entire world that you were here for anyone who was in need. For years, you have been the one man that people could turn to when everyone else, including the police, have failed them. But that was all child's play, Sherlock. That was looking for missing race horses and fooling about with childish cryptograms. Now you finally have a worthy challenge, and what do you do? You sit in here hiding like a bloody coward."

Holmes groaned and wiped his sleeve across his nose. "What have I done, Mycroft? What the hell have I become?"

Mycroft shook his head, and sighed deeply. "I've never told you, but in my travels I encounter many people who have heard of you. It can be difficult for me to hear how they speak of you."

"Why? Is what they say so terrible? Please, tell me how they mock me because obviously I am not yet wretched enough for you."

Mycroft shook his head. "Actually, they heap praise on you as if you are some sort of hero out of an adventure story. 'The Great Detective' they call you. Balderdash, I say. He's just the small brat I used to tease and slap around until he cried. 'Oh no,' they say. 'You do not understand, sir. He found my missing little boy' or 'He deduced that my sister was slowly poisoning my old mother to get a faster inheritance.' That type of thing."

"Not the fancy international affairs you've shown such an aptitude for, I confess."

Mycroft looked Sherlock straight in the eye. "Better than that. A thousand times better than what I am, or what I do. Can you not see that? Do you not know how I admire you?"

Holmes was silent. His lower lip trembled as he tried to steady himself. Mycroft looked down, shaking his head. "There is a monster loose in the crown city of the Empire and Her Majesty's enemies are watching us closely, always plotting ways to exploit our weaknesses. Right now, I am afraid, we look quite weak. It would seem that it is the duty of those best-equipped to serve to find a way to do so. This city needs a hero, brother."

"I am not that hero," Holmes said.

"You are all that we have." Mycroft put the tip of his finger against his younger brother's heart. "Unfortunately, these times do not come when we are ready for them. They do not come when we are equipped to deal with them. They come when we are weak and frail and vulnerable. It requires something more than the rest of us can summon. It is a time for champions, little brother. It is your time."

Mycroft had left him hours ago.

Holmes sat without moving until the light of day began to fade through the windows, until darkness set completely over 221 B Baker Street. He sat sweating in his chair, feeling the urge for drugs burning within. He let it make him sick. He let the need slither throughout his body like a worm, until it was coiled around his every organ.

For hours, the cravings washed over him like waves. They rose high in the air and crashed down onto him. They tried to drown him and unseat him from his place on the earth. To swallow him into a vast, black ocean.

Holmes withstood them. He beat the urges back down inside of himself until they grew too weary to stand back up.

In time, the sun began to rise. It broke through the tattered curtains and dirt-smeared windows and shined hard into his eyes.

Sherlock Holmes struggled up from his chair and stripped off the wet, foul-smelling gown from his skin. He threw it into the fire and felt the surge of heat on his bare flesh as the fabric burst into flames. Holmes went to the window and stood bathed in the light. He looked out over the city. "A fight it is, then," he whispered.

Twenty Two

It was early evening and Irene had not yet returned from wandering Spitalfields. She insisted she needed the time to get acquainted with our new surroundings. While she journeyed into the heart of Ripper's hunting ground, I decided to purchase new bedding and some accoutrements that would help us maintain at least a modicum of civilization while we were forced to stay in such squalor. I tossed the old bug-ridden sheets out of the window and before the sheets settled onto the ground people were fighting over them on the street below.

Our bags had arrived earlier in the day and I unpacked them while listening to the people above our room stomp. Below us, they banged on the ceiling for even the slightest noise. On either side of the room, the voices of whoever was speaking came through as clearly as if they were standing at my side.

I laid Irene's skirts and petticoats out on the bed and folded them carefully. The next bag contained her undergarments. I found a chemise made of such sheer material that I could see the details of my hand through both sides of the fabric. I lifted it to my face and inhaled deeply, detecting faint traces of Irene's scent.

The door to our room burst open and Irene announced, "I have it, John! I can find my way back to Crossingham's from nearly any point in Spitalfields. How did you make out?"

I quickly stuffed the chemise underneath the folded skirts on the bed and turned. "Ah. Basically, the same as you. I did a bit of freshening up to the place as well."

"Excellent," she said, looking at the folded clothes. "You did not have to do that, John. Now, do me a favor and remove your shirt."

"Pardon me? Why?"

"You need a shave. That mustache is too well-kept. I have been studying the faces of the men here, and most of them are not nearly so well-groomed. Come on. I have what you need in my bags."

I nervously undid the buttons of my shirt, sucking in my belly as much as I could. It was hairy and jiggled from too many of Mrs. Hudson's biscuits. I stood as erect as I could and lifted my shoulders, as if I were back in the Army.

Irene did not seem to notice and handed me a pair of clippers, a razor and a bar of soap. Our room did not have a toilet, and she told me to wait there while she fetched a bowl of water from the common facility down the hall. The water she returned with was an ugly yellow color.

"There is no mirror," Irene said, looking around. "Here, let me have those. Hold still, if you please." She pressed against me, lifting my chin as she started scissoring away the ends of my mustache. Her breath was sweet and her chest crushed against me as she leaned forward. She lifted my nose and yanked on my lip.

"Ow!"

"Oh, stop being a baby, Watson," she said, smirking. She handed me one end of a leather strop and quickly sharpened the razor upon it, then wetted her hands and lathered them with the soap.

She put her warm palms against my face. "That smells lovely," I said.

"That soap costs enough money to pay for every room in this place for a month. Your skin will positively tingle when we're finished!"

"Oh good. That is precisely what I have always wanted. Tingly skin."

"Try not to move. I would hate to cut off such a perfectly formed lip. I imagine a man could get used to this. Not lifting a finger while a woman bathes you."

"Perhaps I could convince Mary to apprentice under you?"

"Only if she would enjoy it as much as I," Irene said, winking. "There you are, sir. What do you say, a thruppence ought to settle us up?"

"In Whitechapel I believe a thruppence entitles me to a much more thorough bathing." Irene looked at me with such shock that I felt my cheeks flush. "I have no idea what just came over me, Miss Adler. That comment was inappropriate and I deeply apologize."

She smiled and tapped me on the cheek, "Oh stop, John. I thought you were finally coming out of your damned shell there for a moment. All right, we need to rest up for tonight. The first girl, Polly Nichols, was killed after three in the morning. Annie was killed after five. The next two were killed closer to one. What do you make of that?"

"The Ripper is a creature of the night?"

Irene stared at me for a moment. "Sometimes I really think you are playing with me, Dr. Watson. Anyway, I would venture to guess that he killed the first girl in the middle of the night but found that too many people were out and about. Many were probably still stumbling home drunk at that hour. He killed Annie closer to the morning thinking there would be fewer people. For some reason, he then switched to a much earlier time. Why would he do that?"

"Transportation, perhaps? Depending on where the Ripper lives, he may have needed to find a cab to get home and had trouble finding one before."

"An interesting theory. And here, I had been thinking that the killer lived relatively close to Whitechapel."

"When he killed Annie Chapman at five in the morning, he would have found many more people on the street than he expected," I said. "People who live here that can find work must have to travel, for I have seen no factories or plants in Whitechapel. They must go out of the area, and that would mean getting up quite early. I would expect one o'clock was a much better time to kill his victims, because the people who work were asleep already and those who are unemployed were probably still inside a tavern."

Irene nodded, "I believe that is a rather brilliant deduction, John. Has Holmes been pulling the wool over all of our eyes all this time, while it was really you doing all the detective work?" We both laughed, and Irene checked her pocket watch. "It is nearly six now. We should try to get some sleep."

"All right," I said. I watched Irene cross to the other side of the bed and begin undoing her clothing. I lowered myself to the floor and unlaced my boots. I stretched out on the cold wooden floor, listening to the whisper of Irene's clothing sliding off of her body. I turned over on my side. "If it is not too much trouble, Miss Adler, would you mind throwing me down a pillow when you have a chance?"

"What are you talking about?" Irene asked.

"A pillow maybe? Or, even a blanket? It is rather uncomfortable on the floor without one."

"Stop being silly and come up on the bed this instant, John." Irene patted the mattress, "Really, I will not bite."

I laughed sharply, "I could not begin to imagine how inappropriate that would be."

"John, there is not one thing in this whole damned world that is as appropriate as you imagine it. I have been with royals and nobles all over the world; the exact people we fall all over ourselves to impress with good manners and etiquette, and let me be the one to tell you, they engage in more depravity than the worst whore in Whitechapel. It is a gigantic ruse that people like you and me scurry around trying to be appropriate, while every other Lord is busy buggering his own sisters. Get in the damned bed."

I started to stand up, saying, "If my Mary ever found out about this, I should be in..."

"What? What is it?"

It was the sheer chemise, and she wore it lying on the bed, turned toward me. Her hand was beneath her head, so that her hair spilled down onto the pillow. The soft pale skin of her neck and the tops of her breasts were revealed by the gown's low-cut neck and her nipples poked through the fabric. Two long, shapely legs stretched out toward me, with Irene rubbing one bare foot slowly over the other.

"Why are you just standing there? Surely you've seen a woman without her petticoat before."

"Of course I have," I said, sliding into the bed beside her. Irene closed her eyes and in moments, her breathing became slow and rhythmic. In that instant, she eclipsed all that I knew, casting my remaining days into a cold and empty night. Like the bright star sailors set their course both to and from, I would be doomed forever to follow her distant glittering light.

"Wake up, John."

"Mmm. What? Something wrong?"

"Yes, you snore like a grizzly bear and I weep for your intended bride. We have to get going." Irene was already dressed in a dark frockcoat and a wide black bonnet. "How do I look?"

I regarded her costume. It was the same attire as that of every other woman in Whitechapel. She wore several skirts and a thick coat. Her bonnet was tightly wrapped under her chin, and two long black ribbons hung down over her chest. Only her throat was exposed. I thought for a moment, then said, "Undo your bonnet. I have an idea. Hand me your leather strop. I may have to get you a new one, but if this works, you will thank me for it."

From my medical bag I retrieved a sharp knife, suture and thread. I measured Irene's neck with the strop and began cutting the leather at either end. "When I was in the army, we were travelling on the Arabian Sea and had to be escorted by an American naval vessel. The ship was protected by a group of US Marines."

I cut several holes in the leather and began stitching. "The Marines all had tightly fitting leather collars that were designed to protect their necks from sword strikes. 'Leathernecks', I think they called themselves." I held up the length of leather strap to measure it around Irene's neck. "All of the Ripper victims' throats were cut first. It is the killing blow that incapacitates them enough so that he can do his business." I wrapped the leather around her throat. "It will fit you snugly like a belt around your neck. Can you still breathe? Good."

I tied the ends with thick suture cord as Irene held her hair up, pressing back against me. Irene tied a black scarf around her neck over the leather, and I smiled. "There you are," I said.

Irene touched her neck, feeling the leather. She drew a finger across her neck like the blade of the Ripper would and nodded satisfactorily. "I'm ready."

The local tavern was crowded, but we managed to find a table in the corner where we could hear one another without shouting. "The way that I see it, we have several options. We can pick a likely location and wait in the shadows in hopes of seeing him in the act. Or, we can pick a likely victim and follow her in hopes of him attacking her while we are close by. Or, we can do this properly and lure him into a trap he cannot hope to escape."

I gently sipped my beer, looking around the ale house. No one paid either of us any attention. I barely recognized my own face in the mirror. "What does luring the Ripper entail, exactly?"

"The right bait, obviously," she said. "We will give him a victim standing in exactly the right place, at exactly the right time. A woman he cannot resist, in a place so dark that he can easily use that blade of his to open her up and play with her innards. But in that darkness, he will find something altogether different. For the first time, Jack the Ripper will know what it is to fear."

I rubbed my bare lip, feeling the stubble with the tips of my fingers. "I am not quite sure what he will fear about us, my dear. What I am sure of is that he will try his damndest to kill you."

"Let him," Irene said, eyes flashing, "I want him to fight, John. Before this hunt is ended, more blood will run in the streets of Whitechapel. If some of mine must be spilled in order to put an end to this monster, I'll gladly give it."

"Do not say that," I said. In that moment I pictured Irene sprawled out on the mortuary table at the London City morgue, her belly cut open and devoid of all its contents. Her eyes stared up at me dim and cloudy.

Irene patted my hand. "You are a good man, John Watson. I wish I knew more like you."

We set out into the night, as Irene listed the murder sites one by one, "Polly Nichols was killed on Bucks Row, at the northeast corner. Annie Chapman was killed on Hanbury, in the northwest. Liz Stride was killed in the southeast, and Katie Eddowes was killed in the southwest."

"All of the victims were killed in a geometrical square, then?"

"Somewhat," she said. "What if we bisect that square? Wentworth and Montague Street run somewhat through the middle. They seem as good a place as any." We travelled Commercial Street, passing Flower and Dean, then Thrawl, and I noticed that the neighborhood was becoming more decrepit and menacing with every step. Buildings at either end of the streets were abandoned and dark, but in the shadows I could see eyes peering out at us. A small group of men gathered down on Thrall Street, watching us. "Stay calm, John," Irene whispered. "Do not make eye contact with them and keep walking."

I checked my waist. The gun Irene had given me was secured in my waist band. As the men came to Commercial Street and began following us, I put my hand on the handle, ready to draw. "Turn left," I said, leading her down Wentworth Street. More men emerged from George's Yard. "Isn't that where that woman was killed? Emma Smith?"

"Yes," Irene said, beginning to walk faster. "Keep your head down and keep moving." The men followed us, matching our pace.

"Out for a stroll, eh, love?" one of them called out to Irene.

I turned, seeing the men were getting closer and cursed. "Bloody hell, I recognize him. He was one of the bastards that attacked me."

"I doubt they can recognize us now, John," she said, pulling her bonnet tight. "We look too different. Remain calm."

"Oy, slow down, bunter. Did you pay your tax, old girl?"

"What tax is that, love?" Irene said, continuing to walk.

Several men stepped out of the shadows ahead of us, blocking our passage. Irene and I froze in place. "The tax that allows you to whore in this area without us doing you like that other bunter. The one that got the broom. She refused to pay her tax, you see."

"I can pay," Irene said quickly. "Just tell me how much it is, and be on your way."

"A half crown."

Irene shuffled in her bag and pulled out the coin, showing it to him. "Here, take it and leave us be. This gentleman does not have all night-"

"Bring it over here," he said.

Irene walked over to them and put the coin in the man's outstretched hand. He snatched her by the wrist, "You are a fine right one, I reckon. I think we might need to charge you a bit more than a half crown."

"Now see here," I said, starting forward.

"Have no fear, friend," he said, holding Irene tight. "We'll not use her too hard. You can have your go with her when we're done."

The other men began grabbing at Irene, reaching between her legs and pulling on the buttons of her coat. "Unhand her at once!" I shouted.

"Piss off, mate," the man said to me. "What do you care, anyway? Surely we ain't the first to fill her sockets tonight."

The one holding Irene reached under her skirt, and she cursed at him, kicking him and slapping his hands. I reached into my waistband for the handle of the gun and was about to pull it when the sharp, piercing sound of a whistle erupted from the far end of the alley. Four constables came running toward us.

"You Nichol bastards had better learn to lie low when we're about," the first constable said. He stopped directly in front of me and grunted. "Is that you, Dr. Watson? What the bloody hell are you doing out here?"

I recognized Constable Lamb as one of the ones who had come to arrest me at Baker Street and lowered my head, "Yes, constable."

"Watson? Dr. Watson?" the Nichol boy said. "Wait till Mickey hears about this. Tried to disguise yourself, eh?"

Constable Lamb turned and cracked the man across the face with his nightstick, dropping him to the ground instantly. Lamb wiped blood from his nightstick and smiled, "There you go, Dr. Watson. Reckon this bastard will not be giving you any more trouble tonight."

I grabbed Irene by the arm and we walked directly back to Crossingham's. She was shaking as we entered our room. I untied her bonnet and undid the leather strap and scarf from her neck. She tried undoing the buttons of her coat but her fingers were trembling too much. I undid them for her, then I turned my head aside and undid her bodice.

As I laid her clothing on the table, I saw she had not moved. She was holding herself, shivering. "Come here," I said, putting my arms around her. "I would not have let them hurt you. My gun was ready the entire time. If the police had not come, I would have started putting bullet holes in the lot of them."

"Thank you, John," she said, looking up at me. I had never seen her look vulnerable before. She was always in command, always so strong, and now she looked like nothing more than a nervous child.

"I would do anything for you," I said.

Irene unbuttoned my coat and took the gun from my waist. Her hands slid across my pelvis as she removed it, stirring me. She removed my coat from my shoulders and let it fall onto the ground. "What are you doing?" I said.

"I need to feel alive, John." She kissed my fingers, then the inside of my wrist. "Before it is too late." She kissed my chin, my neck, and my lips. Her nipples swayed against my bare chest through the thin cloth of her gown. I caressed her, opening my mouth to intertwine our tongues. She turned us toward the bed. She pushed me onto it and undid my trousers.

Twenty Three

"Wake her up, mate. She's had it."

"She ain't movin'. She look all right to you?"

"'Cept for the extra half pint o' mettle."

"Well, wake her up and get her out of here. I think her little girl is sitting out in the bar somewhere."

"Her what? Oy, what a dirty little puzzle! She's been back here all evening, getting knocked by every tickle tale in Whitechapel while her daughter is sitting at the bar? With the bastards around here, it's lucky the little girl weren't put to task as well."

Louise's eyes flickered open as the two men grabbed her by the ankles and began dragging her across the floor toward the storeroom's door. The shelves of flour and salt spun wickedly, and bile spilled out of her mouth. "Get off of me," she shouted.

One of the men raised a fist to her face, "You got spit up on my shoe, slag! I'll crush your skull in!"

The other one held up his hand, "Leave it. Richie said we could have a go at her, but that he did not want her tussled up."

"Mummy?" Abigail was standing at the doorway, staring at the men.

Louise groaned, rolling over. "Abbie, me love? Come here." She steadied herself on the ground and wiped her mouth, spitting a mouthful of foul regurgitated liquor onto the floor. Abbie came through the door, racing to her mother and clinging to her.

"Abbie? Where'd you go, me love?" Richie, the owner of the Blue Comet Boy, came around the corner. He looked at the two men standing over Louise and Abigail, then wiped his hands across his apron. "You two are all finished, then? So sod off," he said, cocking his head toward the door. As the men left, Richie helped Louise get to her feet and held her steady. "The little one ran off on me, Louise. Were you all done back here?"

Louise straightened herself. "All finished. You have me money?"

"Yes," Richie said, reaching into his pocket. He dropped five coins in Louise's palm, counting them as he did.

"You're joking, right?" Louise said.

"Sorry?"

"What is this, Richie, some sort of an effin joke?"

"Oy, shut your bone box or I'll pop you one across the lip, get me?" He looked down at Abigail's innocent eyes and sighed. "You know I got a soft spot for little ones, Louise. She ate four plates of food and I only charged you for one. She guzzled down enough bread and meat to stuff a longshoreman. Poor thing was starving."

"Why did you let her?" Louise cried. "You let a child's greedy stomach swindle you out of my money, you twit!"

"She was starving when you brought her here! And like I said, I only charged her for one meal. You drank the rest of it away."

"I only had a little brandy, Richard. How much could that have cost?"

Richie snorted, "A little? You only drank a little? You can barely stand up straight. Look at yourself, Louise. For God's sake, you used to be so pretty. Tell you what? Get yourself cleaned up and I will make you something to eat."

"You think I need pity?" Louise growled, pushing him out of her way. She dragged Abigail through the door. As they left the bar, the cool November air cleared her senses as she breathed it in deeply.

"I want to go to sleep, mummy," Abbie said, tugging on her mother's hand. "Carry me."

"Mummy can't carry you." Louise looked up and down Dorset Street for the police, knowing that if she got nibbed for being too drunk to walk, they'd put Abbie in some god awful orphanage and it would be hell trying to get her out again. "Can you walk just a bit more, my love?"

"I want to go home," Abbie whined.

"I know. And we can go home, right after Mummy makes one last stop. A friend of mine is waiting for us at the Oxford. He wants to give us a present if we hurry."

"A present?" Abbie said, lighting up. "What kind?"

"Something to make Mummy feel better and a piece of sweet treacle for you for being such a big girl. I love you, Abigail. No matter what, always remember that."

Montague Druitt sat in the darkness of his room for an hour after the hallways of the Valentine's Boarding School went quiet. Druitt walked to the door, stopping to listen for anyone who might be lurking outside. He looked through his instruments and chose several of his sharpest knives and a long, thin, saw. He placed the tools inside of his medical bag except for one knife, which he placed inside his coat pocket.

Druitt folded a pair of trousers into a tight square and laid it inside the bag over the instruments. He then did the same with a fresh, clean shirt.

The fourth killing had left his clothing covered completely in blood and Druitt had barely managed to hide it from the prying eyes of the carman who drove him back to the school.

He checked the lids of his specimen jars and made sure they would seal tight enough to contain the intended contents. His salivary glands ached dully in the way one anticipated a much-needed meal. He relished the memory of his previous victim's organs. Druitt put on a dark overcoat and his father's top hat.

The boards creaked from down the hall just as Druitt emerged from his room. He leaned back into the shadows and watched Mark Mann exit from the bathroom. Mann scratched his belly for a moment and looked down in Druitt's direction. Druitt lowered his head to keep the broad brim of his hat down so that it cast his face in shadows. His coat covered the rest of him, allowing him to blend perfectly into the shadows. It was a technique perfected by standing in the alleyways of Whitechapel, watching people walk past without noticing.

Mann yawned and went into his room, shutting the door. Druitt made his way down the stairs silently, heading out through the hall and front door to Eliot Place. He breathed in the crisp November air, glad to be out in the night to roam, to hunt. Dark swirls of fog surrounded the gas lamps above him and he resisted the urge to throw back his head and howl.

People crowded the street corner near the entrance to the Brittania. Inspector Lestrade tried saying "Excuse me" several times, but finally began pushing people out of his way when no one moved. New Court sat halfway down the block on Dorsett Street, and it was a sea of people from where he stood to the small, dismal courtyard. Everyone felt the excitement and panic that came with being at the center of the country's most important event. Another body. Another victim.

"Good evening, Inspector," Constable Wensley said. "Looks like it's just a false alarm after all."

Lestrade peered at the woman lying face-down in the middle of the weeds. "What, she ain't dead?"

"She's dead all right," Lamb said. "Just not murdered. Poor bunter looks like she drank herself stiff."

"No use for me then?"

"Unless you want to help find her missing little girl. You know that bunter that always walks around with the kid? Well, that's the bunter there," Lamb pointed at the body, "and her kid ain't nowhere to be found. People around here are nervous that somebody might have snatched her up and put her to bad use."

"Louise?" Lestrade said, feeling the breath go out of his chest all at once.

"I think that was her name. You know her?"

Lestrade slid past Lamb, standing over the woman's body. Louise's eyes were open, staring in wide-eyed wonder. Her clothes were filthy and torn, and her legs were set apart at odd angles, with one bare foot turned inwards toward the other. "No," he said softly. "No, of course not, I mean, other than to have seen her wandering town with the little one in tow. What happened?"

"People said she staggered in here and dropped. Some bastard stole her shoes and went into the Brittania bragging about it. He said she wasn't moving, and when a few others came out here to see if there was anything else to steal, they realized she was dead."

Lestrade nodded, feeling the muscles in his jaw tighten. "And the little girl?"

"Nobody's seen her," Lamb said. "Vanished. Just more fodder for Whitechapel, I suppose."

Lestrade sucked in air between his clenched teeth. He left the courtyard and waded through the crowd, going back toward the Brittania. People now steered clear of him, bumping into one another to clear his path. He opened the doors and walked to the barman, who was busy filling a mug of beer and laughing. Lestrade grabbed him by the collar, yanking him forward. "Good evening, mate. Who came in with the dead woman's shoes?"

"Who the bloody hell do you-"

Lestrade grabbed the back of the barman's head and slammed his face against the bar. He looked up at the other patrons, who were muttering among themselves and beginning to close in on him. "Who brought in the dead woman's shoes?" he said loudly.

"You came in the wrong place alone, copper," one of the men said. "We got more here `an you got."

"Yes," Lestrade said. "Except I'll have all the doors locked and burn this place to the ground with all of you inside it if one of you so much as speaks another bloody word other than to say who took the dead woman's shoes."

No one spoke, but enough people turned to look at the man sitting in the corner of the bar behind a tall glass of beer. He looked at Lestrade and scowled, "Aw, screw all o' you disloyal bastards."

Lestrade let go of the barman and began walking toward him. "Look, I didn't know the bunter was stiff, I swear it," he said, pulling the shoes out of his jacket and putting them on the bar. "You can have them back. Look, here they are. Safe an' sound, sir."

"Safe and sound?" Lestrade said. He picked up one of the shoes and inspected it. They were men's shoes, with the soles worn through so that he could stick his finger through them and touch the other side. Worthless. Probably something Louise found in the street, or worse yet, made a trade for. "You see her daughter?"

"No, I swear it," the man shook his head quickly. He tried sliding a half-finished glass of beer behind his back, out of Lestrade's sight. "Just the bunter."

"You sure?"

"Positive."

"All right," Lestrade nodded. "What were you going to do with the shoes?"

"Sell 'em to get some money for food. I got two kids an' they ain't eaten in days. I was desperate."

"But you had enough money for that beer you're hiding behind your back?"

The man turned and looked at the glass, eyes widening. "That isn't mine, sir. I just sat down, and it was already here."

Lestrade picked up the glass, "You should finish it."

"I don't want it, sir. It ain't mine."

Lestrade leaned so close that his spittle landed on the man's quivering lips. "You must be thirsty though. Coming in here, after a hard night of stealing the shoes off a dead woman. Two kids at home who ain't eaten. Seeing all these people making merry. Bet that does one in, right?"

"No, sir. I was just leaving in fact."

The man stood up and Lestrade slammed him back down into the stool. He shuffled in his pocket for a few coins, and slapped them on the bar. "Barman, give us a full pitcher!"

The barman came quickly over with a pitcher. As he set it down, he said, "Listen, Inspector. We don't want no trouble here, we're a quiet little neighborhood place. Would you mind—"

Lestrade picked up the pitcher by the handle, "My friend here is going to have his drink and then I'll leave. Open your mouth, mate."

"No, I don't—"

Lestrade snatched him by his hair and yanked his head backwards. The man's mouth opened as he cried out. Lestrade tipped the pitcher into his mouth, filling it with beer. It bubbled past his lips and spilled across his face. "Drink up, mate. Drink up," Lestrade said, making sure the beer went into the man's nostrils and tearing eyes. "Better start swallowing faster or you'll drown."

"Leave him alone!" one of the women cried. Others in the crowd began to cry out as Lestrade continued pouring. The man gagged and choked, splashing Lestrade with his disgorge.

"Almost finished, lad. Don't stop now. Don't waste it," Lestrade growled, struggling to hold the man in place as until the last of the beer was down his throat. Finally, it was done. He tapped the bottom of the pitcher, watching the last of the foam trickle down its sides into the man's vomit-caked face. Lestrade slammed the empty pitcher down on the bar and wiped his hands. "There you go. Now you've had your drink."

Twenty Four

The Christ Church of Spitalfields was now a rundown respite for wandering drunks and bunters looking to get out of the bad weather, but it had not always been so. In 1850 some bastard named Ewan Christian gutted the interior of the once-beautiful church and blocked up all the windows.

Kind of like the East End itself, Lestrade thought. "Used to be a pretty nice place till some nutter came in and started gutting everything in sight," he muttered. From a distance, the church still looked impressive. Its tall, towering steeple and Tuscan columns set it high above any other building in that part of the city. From far away, Christ Church looked like a beacon of light to all weary travelers. A House of God that stood tall and proud even in a place as awful as Whitechapel.

"Here is the church…and here is the steeple," Lestrade said. "Open the doors…Jack's killed all the people…heh…heh…." He put his hand against the entryway and waited for the ground to steady. Six pints at the Princess Alice had gone down easily, but the rum he'd chased it with was threatening to make a sizzling reappearance on the church threshold. Lestrade sucked in gulps of air and righted himself. He headed stiltedly down the aisle toward the altar, trying to get past the rows of shifting pews before dizziness overtook him.

Some local tramp was dutifully sweeping the aisles. The Church probably paid him a penny to each night to clean up the place and keep an eye on it so nobody defiled the altar. He nodded at Lestrade as he staggered down the aisle, but Lestrade waved at him and said, "Piss off. Mind yer own business 'if'n yeh knows what's good for yeh."

Lestrade collapsed into the pew with a grunt. He was just about to lie down on its hard wood surface when he realized there was a group of four women seated across the aisle from him.

Each of them was dressed in black veils and mourning cloaks. Lestrade could see the imprint of their faces beneath the thin black fabric, but they did not move or speak. "Pardon me interrupting, ladies. Real sorry," Lestrade said. He grabbed the back of the pew and leaned forward, trying not to vomit.

The women sat with their hands folded, looking toward the statue of Christ harnessed above the altar. There was a stained glass portrait behind the statue that showed Christ hunched over, bearing an enormous crucifix on his shoulder. Lestrade squinted in the dim candlelight to see the portrait, but the tramp came to stand in front of him, looking concerned. "Sorry mate," Lestrade said. "I did not know there were mourners in here. Didn't mean to make a fuss."

The tramp shrugged and came around the side of the pew to sit beside him. "Long night? Came to seek a little solace in the presence of the Lord?"

"The only solace in Whitechapel is for the dead, friend."

"Perhaps not even then, eh?"

Lestrade regarded the man carefully. His vision was blurry, but he blinked, trying to focus on him. "I've had a bit to drink tonight, but if you don't mind me saying, you look familiar to me. Do I know you?"

The tramp shrugged and wiped a dirty hand across his sweaty forehead. "I been spending quite a bit of time around here lately, though I keep to myself, mostly. I might know yeh, but yeh might not know me, right?" He held out a filthy hand, nail-bitten fingers wiggling in front of Lestrade's face, "It's a pleasure."

"Inspector Lestrade of Scotland Yard," Lestrade took the man's hand firmly in his. "Pleased to meet you."

"A police officer? That sounds exciting. Mind if I sit here with yeh for a bit? "

Lestrade shrugged and the tramp let his broom rest on his shoulder. There was an unusually strong smell about the man but it was not the stale booze and vomit that most vagrants reeked of. Lestrade finally recognized it as the incense the priests used for consecration during Mass. He chuckled, imagining Joseph probably had found a pot of the stuff in a storage closet behind the altar and filled his pockets with it. Screw it, Lestrade thought. Let him have a little bit of this place to carry around with him.

The women still had not moved. Lestrade frowned as he watched them, trying to clear his mind enough to make sense of why four women dressed in funeral garb were sitting in the Spitalfields Church in the middle of the night. "What are they doing here?" Lestrade whispered.

The tramp looked at the women sadly. "They're waitin' for their sister. Sad story, really. One a' the worst I ever did hear."

"I'm all spent on sad stories for now, mate," Lestrade said. "Not to be rude or anything, but I've had enough of dead people for one evening."

The lights dimmed inside the church. Everything went dark except for five flickering candles lit across the lowest step leading up to the altar. The women mourners all lowered their head.

"The bloody hell?" Lestrade whispered, sitting up in his seat and looking around.

The tramp shook his head sadly. "Their sister is nearly arrived and they are afraid for her. It is a time of great darkness in the world."

"I can understand that. I certainly wouldn't want my sister wandering around this cesspool at this hour. Tell you what. I'll go find her and escort her here, all right? I should be out looking for a lost little girl anyway, instead of sitting in here."

"There is hope for you yet, Inspector Lestrade. I think yeh are a good man who's just lost his way, lad."

Lestrade laughed at that. "Is that right? You know all that from a five minute conversation? Tell you what, mate. You go back to your job and I'll go back to mine."

The tramp smiled gently. "I am sure the torment and cruelty yeh deal with every day has seeped into yer being. Don't let it steal your faith."

"Faith?" Lestrade said. "Faith is for children. The sort of thing you tell them so they don't piss themselves at night for fear of growing up in a world where nothing matters and God is either dead or oblivious."

"Do yeh truly mean that?"

"Did faith do Annie Chapman any good when her guts were lying across the sides of her belly? "Should I have had faith when I was trying to find poor Catherine Eddowes' nose in the shadows of Mitre Square? Some lunatic is racing around chopping women to bits and stealing their organs. And the sad fact is that nobody cares. Nobody really gives a damn when all is said and done. Little Abigail might be dead by morning, and all anyone will say is there goes another life wasted in Whitechapel. Who can possibly have faith in a God that lets a beast like Jack the Ripper come into creation? Here's how I see it. If there is a God, and it's him that lets all this madness happen, he's a right sadist. I hate him. I hate him and I'd spit in his face if he ever had the nutmegs to show it to me. Goodbye, sir, and stay clear of me the next time our paths cross."

As Lestrade turned to leave, he heard the man say, "You were the one who abandoned your family, Gerard. You are the one who gave up path of righteousness. Do not blame anyone else for that."

"What did you say? Who the hell do you think you are?"

"His word says that he comes with a sword in hand to strike down the wicked. What if you are that sword, Gerard? What if, when it came time for him to take you up against evil, you were nowhere to be found?"

"Stop it. Stop looking at me like that."

"Believe me, my son, I know your burden and it is indeed a heavy one. But it is no heavier than theirs." The man turned and held out his hand toward the altar.

Another woman, shrouded like the others, emerged from behind the statue of Christ. She moved awkwardly across the altar, descending the steps on wobbling legs to sit beside her sisters in the pew. Lestrade's eyes twitched, and his knees began to shake. He looked back at the tramp and suddenly had to shield his eyes from the burst of light coming from the man.

"There are dark forces at work in this world, my son. I forgive you, Gerard Lestrade. Be a good man. Your family needs you. I need you."

Lestrade collapsed between the pews where he cowered and shivered like a beaten dog. At last he struggled to his feet to see that the church was quiet and empty.

He looked at the large statue staring down at him from over the altar and her heart began hammering inside of his chest. Lestrade hurried up the aisle toward the church doors and threw them open as he ran, tumbling and rolling into the street. He scrambled to his feet and kept running into the streets of Whitechapel, screaming the whole way.

Act IV

NOVEMBER SPAWNED A MONSTER

Twenty Five

Constable Wensley pointed down Thrall Street at the shoe sticking out of an alleyway. "Let's have a look down there."

"It's probably just another blasted vagrant," Constable Lamb sighed.

Wensley squinted to look closer, then took off down the street. "It's him! Here he is."

"Christ, he's a mess," Lamb said. "Oy, Inspector? You all right?"

Gerard Lestrade tucked his knees beneath his chin, muttering to himself and refusing to acknowledge they were there. "Help him up," Lamb said, grabbing Lestrade under the arm. "There's a good chap. Christ, he's stink like a brewery."

"Better snap to, Inspector," Wensley said. He brushed the dirt off of Lestrade's coat. "Chief Inspector Brett is losing his mind trying to find you."

When Lestrade did not answer, Lamb said, "Another girl's been murdered, sir. It's a bad one. Not even like the others."

"...The fifth sister," Lestrade whispered.

Lamb cocked an eye at Wensley. "Whatever you want to call it. It's another victim. Just worse, this time."

Lestrade stared at them for a moment. "What do you mean?"

"This one was found in her room, Inspector. The Ripper really went to town on this one, sir. Enjoyed himself quite a bit," Wensley said.

Lamb put his arm around Lestrade to keep him steady. "Listen, Inspector. You are in no shape to go over there. Tell you what, I don't live too far off. Go to my flat and get washed up, catch a little slumber, and come find us in a few hours. We'll hold Brett off until then. The dead bird certainly is not going anywhere. She'll just smell a bit worse by the time you get in."

Lestrade blinked, trying to focus. There was a look of concern etched on Lamb's face that was far beyond the young man's experience on the job. Wensley only looked afraid. The boy had come to rely on Lestrade to provide a lead the rest of them could follow and now he was clearly worried Lestrade was lost to them. Lestrade took a deep breath and swept his hand through his hair. "Boys, when we took up our oaths to be policemen, we swore to serve and protect. Not serve and protect when it was convenient. Now stop standing about and help me get over there."

"Yes, sir!" Wensley said.

"Too right," Lamb said. "The walk to Miller's Court will do us some good. Best to enjoy all the fresh air while we can. You'll miss it quite soon, I reckon."

Whatever Lestrade expected to see inside Thirteen Miller's Court, it did not come close. At first, he tried peering through front window but gagged on the foulness coming through the broken glass in the lower corner. Once he opened the door, a wave of nausea broiled in his stomach, making his belly twist and turn until he dry heaved. He wished there was still something in his stomach left to vomit up. Lestrade turned back toward the open door and took several deep breaths before returning to look at the splattered body spread out on the bed.

The woman's organs were carefully arranged on either side of her. It seemed impossible to believe that there was that much blood, intestine, organ and tissue inside of one body. It was ludicrous that one person had so much material stuffed inside of them. He laughed sharply at the sight of it in complete shock.

"I'll give you a hand in there, Inspector," Wensley said. The young constable opened the door as he said, "That old ninny Lamb said it was bad, but I can handle it—" Wensley froze in the doorway and all the color drained from his face. He lurched forward just as Lestrade spun him around and shoved him back through the door. He held Wensley by the collar until the sound of vomit splashing the pavement ended.

Lestrade patted Wensley gently on the back. "You are going to stay out here, my boy. You'll be fine."

"But…but, I can…holy Christ….that's inhuman. Just give me a moment, Inspector. I swear, I'll be fine." There were tears in the boys eyes but he blinked them away and wiped them with his sleeve.

"I said for you to wait out here, Fred. Someday I do not doubt that it will be up to you to go into rooms like that. But right now, at this moment in time, the responsibility falls to me and lately I haven't been doing my part. You stay outside. Do you understand?"

"Yes, sir. What can I do to help you, then?"

"Let no one enter this room without my permission." Lestrade shut the door marked Number Thirteen and turned to take in the room. It was small and cluttered. The front door could not open fully without banging against a small bedside table, and the bed, while not particularly large, nearly took up the whole room.

The woman on the bed was…no, Lestrade said to himself, looking away. Don't look at her. Not yet.

The fumes of decomposition coming out of the body began to sting his eyes. Mucus running down the back of his throat already tasted of it. Lestrade coughed and gagged. He felt his legs trembling to the point that he could no longer stand steadily. He leaned back against the bed and sank to the floor. "Can't do it," he said, wiping his sleeve across his nose and eyes. "I simply cannot do it."

He stood back up, ready to call out to Wensley to open the door. It was time to go fetch the doctor. There was nothing left to be accomplished by standing in the room except becoming more nauseous. He turned to the body, "I'm sorry, love. I just do not have it in me to do this anymore." Her face was gone, nothing more than bone and muscle. Just stripped flesh, Lestrade thought. Could be any woman, really. Could be Carrie. Could be me mum. Could even be my little girl in a few years, he thought.

His teeth were grinding together at the thought of the viciousness needed to strip away the flesh of a woman's face. "What kind of an animal does this? What kind of beast are you?"

Lestrade lowered his head and reached out to touch the tip of the woman's bare left foot. It was the only thing left that was recognizably human. He put both his hands around her toes and pressed them between his palms. He bent at the knee and closed his eyes, and for the first time since he'd become a policeman, he prayed.

A knock at the door interrupted him. "Inspector?" Wensley said, without opening the door.

"What!" Lestrade barked.

"There is a man out here asking to come in. He is quite insistent that he can assist you," the constable said.

"Tell him to piss off! We do not need any amateurs and lookie-loos snooping around, Wensley."

"Actually, I think it might be-"

"Pardon me, Constable." The door creaked open and a man said, "Good morning, Inspector Lestrade."

"Look, just bugger off, all right?" Lestrade lifted his hand to block out the bright sun pouring through the door that silhouetted a tall, thin man in a flop-eared travelling cap. "It's you. You came."

Sherlock Holmes nodded solemnly. "I apologize for being late, Inspector. Might I have permission to enter the scene of the crime? I believe I may be able to lend you some assistance." He surveyed the room. "By the looks of things, you are in great need."

Lestrade leapt to his feet. "Yes, yes, come in. Of course!"

"Then the time for niceties has passed, Inspector, and we must get to work," Holmes said as he took off his coat. He rolled up his sleeves and looked about the room. "Have you touched anything in the room? Anything at all?"

"No one has touched a damn thing in here, except for the front door handle when we forced it open."

"Excellent," Holmes nodded. He walked around the outer edges of the room, checking the table where the flaps of her skin were stacked, but ignoring them as he bent close to examine the empty space on the table's top.

"What are you looking for?"

Holmes covered his hand with his shirt sleeve and shut the door, staring at the handle. It was smeared with blood. "Something that the suspect would have to have touched." Holmes inspected the door so closely that the tip of his hat nearly touched the wood. He checked the lock and surface of the door. Holmes looked down at the broken pieces of glass on the ground and his eyebrows began to twitch. "Yes, yes, that's it," Holmes muttered, looking from the bits of glass to the window.

"Yes, what, man? Tell me!"

"There is a new type of investigative tool I have been recently made aware of, Inspector, but at present, I have little more than a theory. Still, we need more. Come with me." Holmes opened the door, seeing the sea of people pushing toward them, trying to get past the two Constables.

"Keep every one of these people back," Lestrade shouted.

"Yes, sir!" Lamb yelled over his shoulder.

"It is imperative that no one goes into this room before we return. All will be lost!" Holmes said.

More policemen began to arrive, swinging their batons at random, knocking people away. Lestrade put his hand on Wensley's shoulder, shouting, "Not one person goes into this room. Not one!"

"But Chief Inspector Brett is bringing Dr-"

"I do not care if the Commissioner himself shows up and wants to go in that room!" Lestrade said.

"Yes, sir!" Wensley shouted, whipping his baton at the crowd.

Holmes pulled on Lestrade's sleeve, pointing into the distance at a red knit shawl lying on the ground. As they approached the shawl, a woman came out of the alley near it. Her face was red and blotchy from crying. "That was hers," the woman sniffled.

"Whose?" Holmes said.

"Mary Jane Kelly's. The woman that's dead in Number Thirteen. I saw her wearing that shawl last night."

"What time did you see her? Was she with anyone?" Lestrade snapped.

"Why are you yelling at me?" the woman said, inching back into the alley.

"One moment, madam," Holmes stepped forward. "My name is Sherlock Holmes and this is Inspector Lestrade of Scotland Yard. We are investigating this woman's murder and can only hope that something you saw might be of great use to us. What is your name?"

"Mary Cox. I live in Number Five, Miller's Court. I knew Mary Jane."

"We are both dreadfully sorry for what happened to your friend," Holmes said. "You saw her last night?"

"Yes," Cox lowered her head. "She was a good woman. Give you the shirt right off her back. She was wearing this shawl as she walked with a man back toward her place. I didn't get much of a look at him, but when I called out 'Good night,' to her, she could barely answer me."

"Why is that, Miss Cox?"

Cox shrugged, "I suspect she was too drunk. Just a few seconds later, I heard someone cry out, 'Oh, Murder!' from the darkness. There was nothing after that."

"But she was wearing this shawl when you saw her? Where did you see her, exactly?" Holmes said.

Cox pointed, "Down there, coming from the courtyard. This wasn't supposed to happen. Mary Jane only worked close to home because she knew the area."

"Thank you, Miss Cox. You have been invaluable to us." Holmes bent down to the shawl, inspecting it carefully. He found a piece of it that had been stretched so thin that Holmes could see his fingers through the fabric. He stuffed the shawl in his pocket and checked the walkway.

"What are you looking for," Lestrade said.

"These," Holmes said, showing him the light black scuff marks along the concrete. A new series of shouting arose from down the street, and Holmes frowned. "We'd better get back to Number Thirteen before it is too late."

Chief Inspector Brett stood screaming in Constable Lamb's face. "I am giving you a direct order, Lamb! Move or you are going to be standing in the soup lines with the rest of these miscreants!"

"Who you calling a miscreant?" someone shouted from the crowd.

"You police are useless!" cried another. "How many people have to die before you bastards catch the killer?"

The crowd pushed closer to Brett, who turned, looking at them nervously. "I'd be a little more polite to these nice Whitechapel folk, Chief Inspector," Lamb said grimly. "These blokes do not recognize how important you are by the fanciness of your uniform."

"Let me in that room at once, Lamb."

Lamb shook his head, "Inspector Lestrade ordered us not to let a single person in here, and that includes you until he tells me otherwise. We shall defend this room by force, if necessary."

"What about you, Wensley? You going to throw your career away like this simpleton? I can get you into CID, lad. We can use a smart boy like yourself. Do not bollix that up."

"I'm sorry Chief Inspector, but I cannot," Wensley said as thick beads of sweat streamed down his forehead.

"I am giving you an order, Wensley!"

"I am deeply sorry, sir, but your order is unlawful. Regulation One One Three states that the lead investigator at any crime scene is responsible for its security and integrity, regardless of rank or privilege. Inspector Gerard Lestrade is the lead investigator in this case, and he ordered us to not let anyone in."

"Regulation One One Three, you say?" Brett growled fiercely. There was enough uncertainty in his eyes that Wensley did not faint dead on the spot. "God help you if it does not say exactly what you think it does." Brett forced his way back through the crowd, screeching at everyone to get back from him.

Lamb watched Brett vanish and clapped Wensley on the back. "I knew all that reading would come in handy, mate. I'm tired of seeing us all play toad eater for that bastard Brett. Good for you!"

"I'll be pushing a merchant cart on Commercial Road this time next week," Wensley moaned, wiping his hand across his head. "I'm finished!"

"Why's that? Regulation One One Three--"

"There is no Regulation One One Three, you dolt!" Wensley said. "I am finished, and it's all because of you and Lestrade!"

"Well…it sounded good, if it makes you feel better," Lamb said. "Really should be a regulation if you ask me."

"Oh, shut up, Lamb!"

Lestrade opened the door to Number Thirteen again and began coughing, trying to breathe into his shirt. "It is getting worse in here, Holmes. Let's move this along. What's your big theory?"

Holmes refused to be fazed by the stifling fumes. "At this point, I believe it is safe to speculate that the Ripper did not intend to kill Mary Jane Kelly in her home. From Mrs. Cox's account, I surmise that they were walking together when Miss Kelly became afraid. She bolted from the Ripper in an attempt to escape and ran here for safety. He snatched a handful of her shawl as she ran and ripped if off of her shoulders. She must have made it back inside and locked the door, but the murdered was already onto her. He simply smashed the window and let himself in."

"Wonderful, Holmes, really," Lestrade said. "But what the hell do we do now to catch the bastard?"

Holmes bent to one of the broken pieces of window glass lying on the ground. He lifted a shard into the light, holding it only by the edges. He inspected the piece and threw it away. He picked up a second piece and placed it directly in the rays of sunlight coming through the window so that it formed a prism on his face. Holmes waved Lestrade over and showed him the perfectly preserved fingerprint sitting in the center of the glass. "Allow me to introduce you to Jack the Ripper."

Twenty Six

The police station bustled with activity as journalists shouted questions at every passing person and civilians slammed their fists against the railing, demanding to see whoever was in charge. Inspector Collard of the London City Police was holed up in Lestrade's office, peeking out through the curtains. "This place is a bloody madhouse," he whispered.

Sherlock Holmes removed a silk handkerchief from his pocket and unfolded it on Lestrade's desk, revealing the small shard of glass inside. He picked up a pen and tapped the shard's edge, rubbing his chin as he concentrated.

"What exactly is that, sir?" Wensley asked.

"That, my dear fellow, is a finger-mark left by the man who killed the woman on Thirteen Miller's Court last evening. It shows us the unique fingerprint pattern that can only be found on…I believe…the right index finger of the killer."

"And how does that help us, sir?" Wensley said.

"It doesn't," Holmes replied. "At least, not yet. We are gathered here, gentlemen, to put all of the facts at our disposal on the table and develop a plan of attack. Who wants to go first?"

"The killer is a man," Lestrade said.

"Is that a deduction or a guess, Inspector?" Holmes said. Lestrade scowled and looked down at the ground. "Forgive me, Inspector. What I mean to say was, please give us more details so that we can determine if it is a sound enough theory for us to continue."

"Well, there's about twenty-eight feet of intestines in the human body," Lestrade said. "Our boy scoops them right out of the bodies and dumps them onto his victim's upper torso. Then he still has strength enough left to start cutting out the organs he wants. I imagine there's a good deal of pulling and yanking involved. This leads me to believe the Ripper is male."

Holmes nodded, "That is a very good supposition. I think we are safe in assuming it to be true. Further, he has the physical strength to keep them from escaping once he is in the midst of his deeds, and the swiftness to escape from the scene of the crime before being detected. And now, we have an eyewitness account from Mrs. Cox that Mary Jane Kelly was seen walking with a man, toward the scene of the crime last night. So we are confident that the Ripper is a man, and that he possesses some stamina and strength. I would suggest that limits our suspects to males who are likely younger and athletic. What else do we know?"

"He hates the Jews," Inspector Collard said. "We saw it for ourselves in the stairwell."

Holmes frowned. "Unfortunately, I must disagree with you on that point, Inspector. As far as I understand, the graffiti you are referring to was found in the same stairwell as the bloody apron after Miss Eddowes was killed, correct?"

"Yes," Collard said. "But it was spelled funny. We saw it before it got wiped away. It said '*THE JUWES ARE THE MEN THAT WILL NOT BE BLAMED FOR NOTHING.*'"

"But that is a common stairwell, is it not? And certainly, it would not be unreasonable to find graffiti in that area? It is my understanding that the neighborhood in question is not particularly fond of outsiders." Holmes waited as Collard considered this, as everyone else nodded in agreement. "Further, none of the victims are Jewish, or connected in any way to Jewish society. There is also always the possibility that the graffiti was left by the killer, but as a subterfuge designed to create confusion. Regardless, it gives us much less that is of value than the precious time it consumes. We should move on. What else?"

"He's good with a blade," Lamb said.

"And he knows anatomy, as a doctor would," Wensley added. "He knows where to find what he wants inside each body and how to get it out quickly and efficiently."

"Excellent," Holmes said. "I agree that there is a strong possibility our killer has some manner of medical training."

"He hates the whores of Whitechapel," Lestrade muttered.

"Mmmm," Holmes said.

Lestrade's eyebrows raised and his voice rose, "You can't have seen what I saw at Miller's Court and not believe that he utterly hates those women."

Holmes's eyes brightened, "Yes! Yes, that's it exactly, Inspector. He hates women. He is killing the prostitutes of Whitechapel because they are easily accessible at the times when he is free to do his bidding. Let's face it, one could not lure a wholesome nursemaid into an alleyway in the dead of night. I believe he is killing them because they are targets of opportunity."

"Why Whitechapel, then?" Collard asked.

"Obviously, he lives nearby," Lestrade said.

"In Whitechapel?"

"Doubtful," Holmes said. "Whitechapel consists mainly of dwelling houses that are busy all day and night. To get to one's room, you have to pass the doorman, and whoever else happens to be roaming around the house. I would imagine that people would notice someone soaked in blood returning to their room."

Everyone in the room fell silent, waiting for someone else to speak. "Is that all we know?" Lestrade said. "After four months? How can this be?"

"It is regrettably little," Holmes said.

"What about the letters to the press? The torso?" Collard said.

"We've got no way to tie him directly to any of it," Lestrade said. "Bloody useless."

"Perhaps not useless," Holmes said. "Let's stick it to the back of our minds, but not become overly focused on it. Gentlemen, what we desperately need are hard facts. And we need them quite fast, I might add."

"So what do you propose, Holmes?" Lestrade asked.

Holmes bowed his head for a moment in thought as the mechanisms in his mind began to assemble and re-orient the information into something new and workable. "If you are all in agreement, I would like to assign each of you to a task." Holmes looked around at the men, all proud, capable police officers who now stood with their arms folded, looking at the ground. These were men who were not accustomed to taking orders from civilians. Lamb whispered something to Wensley that made him chuckle.

"Gentlemen," Holmes said. "I know that you have all been at this much longer than I, and it is somewhat presumptuous of me to show up now and try to stir you into action. I assure you, that is not my intention. This is an evil that none of us can fight alone. We must work together if we are to defeat it."

"We'll do whatever you require, Holmes, isn't that right, boys?" Lestrade said, looking around at the others, who nodded. "Give us your assignments."

"I would like Inspector Collard to make an inquiry of all the medical schools in London and see if they are aware of a young man who was too unstable to continue in his training. Pay particular attention to any mention of a student who only showed interest in anatomy and cutting open cadavers but not in healing the sick. Also, check all of the persons arrested for grave robbing within the past several years. It simply makes sense to me that our killer would familiarize himself with working in an anatomical environment before setting out to perform his deeds."

"All right," Collard said.

"Inspector Lestrade, you should remain in Whitechapel as a central hub of our intelligence. Everyone else is to report any and all new findings to Inspector Lestrade immediately, whether in person or by telegraph." I will go to all of the asylums in the area and see if they have recently released anyone who fits our limited portrait of the Ripper."

"What do you want me and Fred to do, sir?" Lamb said.

Holmes removed a letter from inside his jacket and handed it to Lamb. "I'd like for you to go find Francis Darwin at the Royal Academy and give him this letter and this piece of glass, Constable. Tell him that the time for pontificating is past. His countrymen are relying on his ability to persuade Dr. Henry Faulds and Francis Galton to stop their bickering and find a way to analyze that print." Holmes turned to Wensley, "And I need you to handle a particularly important missing person investigation. Finding this person is of vital importance to our success."

Lestrade spoke up, "The two of you take off those stupid uniforms. Change into your street clothes."

"Yes, sir," both men said.

As the men began to clear out, Holmes put his hand on Wensley's arm. "Just a moment, Constable. I want you to know I consider this a personal favor. It is of vital importance to me, and nothing less than the necessity of the task at hand could keep me from it."

"Anything, sir," Wensley said.

"I have lost my Watson and I need him found."

Lestrade watched the other men leave. "Why am I being held back, Holmes? Are you not quite finished with our old rivalry yet?"

Holmes looked at him and said, "Actually, the reason is that you smell. You smell foul, and by my estimation you have not slept properly for days. You will be of little use in the field until you go home and collect yourself enough to assist us properly in this investigation."

"Be of use? Who the bloody hell do you think-"

"Inspector, this is hardly the time for our little charade of who is outdoing whom. Go home, get a few hours of sleep, and meet us back here so that we can begin coordinating our efforts."

"A few weeks ago you were so undone by whatever poison you'd been shooting into your arm that you could barely lift your head, and now you think you can stand in my own office and bark orders at me?" Lestrade said.

"Yes, I confess that it was my frailties that let The Ripper get away with this for so long, Inspector. I shall not allow yours to prevent me from finding some sort of redemption."

"Redemption, eh?" After a moment, Lestrade he looked down at his filthy clothes, thinking of the man in the church. "I suppose I could do with a bath."

Lestrade tapped the carman on the shoulder and pointed to where he wanted to be dropped off. It was still a half-block down from his front door. Walking toward that door, the words would not come to him. He had no excuses to offer and knew of no lies big enough to cover his disgrace. He felt as if someone had beaten him with a heavy stick on the legs, so that they dragged and cramped the closer he got to his home. He used the hand-rail to support himself as he trudged up the steps and knocked on the front door.

"Poppa!" Little Gerard yelled out. "You're home!"

Lestrade dropped to his knees and hugged the boy tightly. Juliette let out a cry of delight as she saw her father and raced toward him as quickly as her tiny legs could take her. Lestrade scooped her up into his arms and squeezed her. He kissed both children repeatedly, going back and forth from one to the other, over and over. They giggled and squealed as his rough beard tickled their faces. Lestrade stopped and said, "Give me a moment now. I have to go talk to your mother."

Carrie was in the kitchen chopping vegetables, keeping her back turned to him. "Good evening, love. How are you?"

"I was not expecting you for dinner," Carrie said firmly. "It will take a few minutes to make extra. That is, if you intend on staying."

"Yes," Lestrade said. "I would like that, if you allow me to."

"If it suits you, what say do I have?" she said, chopping forcefully.

He moved to touch her shoulder and she flinched. "I would like to stay and eat with you. After that, I have to return to the police station, but I promise you that I will be home once this investigation is finished. I swear to it."

"I do not believe you, Gerard. But the children will be happy to have you here, even for a little while," Carrie said. "You smell positively dreadful. Your clothes are all still where you left them. I kept your favorite shirt and trousers pressed and ready, should you ever have decided to come home. Go bathe and get changed."

"I am changed."

Twenty Seven

Will Druitt yelled, "Stop! Carman, stop the carriage!" He tried elbowing past those blocking his way down the carriage steps, but found himself forcefully wedged between a side-rail and the bosom of an excited overweight woman who rushed toward the edge, pointing.

"Look, darling! A whore!" the woman cried out happily.

"Yes, I believe it is."

"Do you think she might be the next to go?"

"I doubt it, my lovely. That haggard little thing has scabs around her mouth. I heard that Jack the Ripper only selects the loveliest ones to be his dark brides."

"Monty!" Will cried out. "Carman, stop the bloody cab!" He pushed the woman off of him and made his way down the rickety steps to street level. "Monty!" he called out. "Carman, stop the cab this instant!"

"I can't just get over to the side like that, sir," the carman said. "There are too many other cabs."

"Slow down then, I'll jump off."

"You serious?"

"Monty! Wait!" Will called out, holding the hand rail. Carriages whizzed past only inches from the bottom stair. "Yes, I'm serious! Slow the horses down."

"Be bloody careful you don't get run over!"

Will leapt into the street, scrambling as he landed to get out of the way of the hooves and wheels charging toward him. Montague Druitt was hunched over against the wall of an alleyway, glaring at his brother like a feral animal. He saw Will and snarled, "Get away from me!"

Will dashed through the carriages and made it onto the sidewalk. "Monty! I've been looking for you all over! Where the hell have you been?" There was dried blood caked around Druitt's mouth and streaking his throat in dark red-crusted lines. Druitt collapsed to the ground.

"It has all gone wrong, Will," Druitt said, as tears swelled in his eyes. "Everything! Nothing is happening the way it was supposed to. I tried, Will. I tried and tried, but it was not enough."

"Everything will be fine, Monty. We just need to get you cleaned up and back to Blackheath. I promised Mr. Valentine that I would have you at that big cricket meeting. Can you walk?"

Druitt ignored Will, staring at his hands. "What have I done, Will? Why did this happen to me?"

Will grabbed Druitt and began lifting him to his feet. "I see that I have let you down, little brother. I put too much upon you at once. It is my fault, and I am sorry. Starting now, I am going to do better, but first I am going to get you to that blasted meeting so we can get this all sorted out. All right? On your feet."

"I cannot be this thing any longer, Will. Please save me."

"Of course, Monty. Just as soon as we get on the train back to Blackheath, all right?"

"All right, Will."

They made it to the train station in time to board one leaving for Blackheath. Will managed to scrub Monty's clean face enough that no one stared at them on the train. As the whistle on the towering steam engine's stack blew and the wheels began to turn, Druitt put his arm on the cabin window and watched flakes of ash scatter past just as they had so many years ago when he first went to Portsmouth. He looked at Will sitting next to him, whose beard and face resembled their father's so much. Druitt put his head against Will's shoulder and closed his eyes, imagining that he had never come to Whitechapel at all.

The board members of the Blackheath Cricket, Gottball, and Lawn Tennis Company were sitting and talking quietly as they smoked cigars and sipped tea. George Valentine stood before them and said, "Thank you so much for coming today, gentlemen. I appreciate the Special Finance Committee scheduling this session to discuss something that is so near and dear to all of us." From the corner of his eye, Valentine saw Montague Druitt coming up the steps toward the room. Druitt was neatly dressed, but his eyes were red and darted about the hallway nervously.

"I would like to present a most extraordinary young man. In just one year in Blackheath he has served our community in ways that many of us would do well to emulate. He is an Assistant Headmaster at my school, a barrister for the court, and a valued member of this very club. There is nothing closer to this man's heart than encouraging the young men of Blackheath in the sport and etiquette of cricket, and today he will explain how you can help him do that very thing. Mr. Montague Druitt," Valentine said and began to clap.

Druitt walked toward Mr. Valentine, who put his arm around Druitt, waiting for the applause to die down. Valentine glanced suspiciously at him, but returned to his seat.

Druitt straightened his collar and checked his tie, feeling that the knot was too big. He fussed over it for moment, then took his notes out of coat pocket and cleared his throat. "Gentlemen and fellow members, thank you for attending today. We have an order of business to discuss that pertains to Mr. George Valentine's school for young men. The school is asking for this committee's assistance in obtaining an extra acre of land to erect a grandstand. You see, we would like to host the cricket championships here in Blackheath next year…" Druitt's voice trailed off as he stared at the back of the room.

Some of the members shifted in their seats, turning around to see what had stolen Druitt's attention, but seeing only a wood-paneled wall with a few paintings hung on it. Druitt did not move, did not even blink. Fat droplets of sweat streamed down his forehead, balancing for a moment on the tip of his nose before dropping to the floor.

Five women, clothed in gowns as fine and white as wedding dresses stood at the rear of the room, watching Druitt silently.

Blood drained from Mr. Valentine's face as everyone in the audience began to murmur. Valentine jumped to his feet, "Gentlemen, I apologize. Mr. Druitt has been quite ill and only recently returned to us. Allow me have a moment with him-"

"Be gone from here, you filthy whores," Druitt growled. "You are as unfit to walk the earth in death as you were in life." Druitt threw down his speaker notes and stormed toward the back of the room, knocking chairs from his path as the members of the committee dove out of his way. "How dare you return to mock me from the grave! I sent you to hell!"

"Monty!"

Druitt looked back at the man standing in the doorway and froze for a moment. He was dressed in a familiar top-hat and carried a black leather medical bag. "Father?"

"Yes, Monty. Come here, son. It is time for us to go."

"I want to go home," Druitt whined, turning away from the awful looking women who would not stop staring at him. He had stolen their faces and still they stared. He had un-sexed them and removed their organs of regeneration, even consuming them to make their power his own, and still they mocked him. "Take me away from this place, father. Away from all of you!" he shrieked, flailing wildly at the members of the committee who lifted their arms in self-defense and fled, yelling that Druitt was mad.

Mr. Valentine turned at the doorway and shouted, "Do not return to my school ever again!"

William Druitt closed the door on George Valentine and turned to Monty, smiling gently. "It is time to take our leave of this place, and these people. Your work is finished my son."

"At last," Monty said, gasping in relief. He felt his chest seize as he staggered toward his father, about to embrace him, when he stopped. Druitt blinked rapidly, realizing it was only his older brother. "Will? Why did you try and trick me?"

"What are you talking about, Monty?" Will said, lifting the brim of his hat.

Druitt snatched the medical bag from his brother and began cracking the latches. "How dare you play games with me, Will! I am not the little boy you knew in Dorset."

"Of course I know that, Monty." He watched Druitt shuffling things around inside the bag. "You must try and calm yourself, there is still much work we can do."

Druitt whipped a blade from the bag and held it at Will's throat, forcing him back against the wall. "Look at me, brother. What do you see?"

Will looked down at the knife. "Put the knife down, little brother. There is much that you do not understand. Let us find a quiet place to talk, and I shall make everything clear to you. Put the knife down at once, before you hurt someone."

Druitt put his face close to Will's. "I asked you a question. Answer me or I'll chop your precious wife's bosoms and feed her bits to your children. What do you see?"

"I see a beast."

Twenty Eight

Nearly all of the knowledge available to the known world was housed on Piccadilly Street at The Burlington House; an enormous mansion with steep archways and high-reaching spires, housing no fewer than seven of Her Majesty's royal institutions of learning.

The Royal Academy, Geological Society, Royal Astronomical Society, Society of Antiquaries, Chemical Society, and Linnean Society, were all set within the enormous confines of Lord Burlington's former residence. Deep within, located beneath a brass sign inscribed with the words: Nullius in Verba (*"On The Words Of No One"*), sat the entrance to the Royal Society of London for the Improvement of Natural Knowledge.

The Royal Society was founded in 1660, and since its inception had worked toward its goal of building an empire of learning that stretched across continents. One could only become a Fellow of the Royal Society by election, and elections were held on one day a year. Of all the eligible candidates, only forty-four fellows could be entered into their esteemed ranks. Charles Darwin had been a member of the Royal Society, and after him, his son Francis, and their half-cousin, Francis Galton.

Dr. Henry Faulds was not a member. In fact, he was never even nominated.

As Constable Lamb led the old man toward the "Nullius in Verba" sign, the old man grumbled, "This is an insult! Those bastards are making me come here so they you can lord their status over me. Well, it will not work! I will sod off back to Stoke-on-Trent if they even try it!"

"I'm sure no one is going to insult you, Dr. Faulds. Everyone appreciates you making the long journey here," Lamb said as he knocked on the door.

Francis Darwin opened the door and thrust his hand out toward Dr. Faulds. "It is the Royal Society's great privilege to have you visit us, sir."

"Piss off!" Faulds said. "And don't try lording any of this Society bollocks over me either."

"No one is lording anything over anyone, Henry," a second man reassured as he came up to stand behind Darwin. "Just come in and sit down."

"Galton…" Faulds whispered. "I did not think you'd have the courage to show up."

"It is my understanding that Sherlock Holmes has requested our aid in catching this monster loose in Whitechapel. I think it is our obligation as men of science to assist as we can."

"You look like your father, Mr. Darwin. How I used to admire him," Faulds said. "Tell me, was the Theory of Evolution his or was it simply the result of reading a letter some other scientist happened to send him?"

"Gentlemen," Constable Lamb tapped the table with his finger. "That's quite enough of this, now. I have no clue what exactly you are all on about, but time is of the essence, right? All of Scotland Yard is—"

"Screw Scotland Yard! When I tried to explain all of this to that bastard Warren, he stared at me like I had three heads and a forked tongue."

"Commissioner Warren resigned several weeks ago," Galton sighed. "Perhaps news of it did not reach you all the way down in Fenton where you practice now, hmm? Bustling hub of activity that it is."

"You dirty bastard!" Faulds hissed, reaching over the table for Galton.

Constable Lamb grabbed Faulds and yanked him back into his chair. "That is quite enough out of both of you. One more word and I'm going to start opening up some skulls, get me?" Lamb reached into his pocket and pulled out the silk handkerchief with the piece of glass inside, showing it to them. "Sherlock Holmes said this little piece of glass has a finger mark left by the man killing all the bunters in Whitechapel and he believes that you bunch of squeeze crabs are the only lot who can figure it out. Now sit down and start bloody figuring it out!"

Only one asylum for the criminally insane existed in all of England, and it was located a little more than thirty miles away from London. Sherlock Holmes entered the Broadmoor Asylum and felt stale air escape as he pulled on the cold iron handle, prying open the massive wooden door. The air carried the scent of sickness.

Broadmoor opened in 1863, intended only to house the ninety-five female lunatics then under the forced care of Her Majesty. One year later, an additional wing was added onto the building for two hundred male inmates. The asylum sat on two hundred and ninety square acres in the village of Crowthorne at the edge of the Berkshire moors, surrounded by enormous stone walls and a thick iron gate.

Many of the most famous maniacs in England called it home. There was Roderick Maclean, who fired a gun at Queen Victoria at Windsor Station in 1882. Richard Dadd had been a famous painter prior to murdering his father, and continued to paint prolifically during his many years in captivity. Dr. William Chester Minor, an American who relocated to London and wound up killing a furnace-stoker, achieved a minor bit of celebrity upon taking up the duties of acquiring quotations and citations for the much-anticipated First Oxford English Dictionary from the confines of the Asylum.

An older man in a clean white laboratory coat approached Holmes. "Good day, Mr. Holmes."

"Thank you for meeting with me, Dr. Orange."

"I admit that your telegram intrigued me. Of course, the series of crimes you mentioned are none other than the Ripper killings, correct?"

"Indeed they are, Dr. Orange."

"And you think the Ripper may be an escapee or former patient, hmm? Ever since those dreadful killings began, I have been waiting for some policeman to come sniffing around Broadmoor."

"You sound skeptical, doctor. Surely you see the logic in that theory."

"Surely I do not, Mr. Holmes. The men and women confined to Broadmoor are ill, sir. They are capable of horrific crimes of the most violent nature, and to that I make no argument, but they have always been localized incidents brought on by a specific series of emotional events. The Ripper killings appear to be something else altogether."

"And what are the Ripper killings in your opinion, sir?"

"A cultural phenomenon, Mr. Holmes. A new type of evil that has been visited upon us all and will not go away any time soon."

Holmes paused for a moment, weighing his words. "Dr. Orange, I am not quite certain that I follow you. The Ripper is just a man. Just another criminal."

"Whoever is doing these killings is not the only one responsible for the true horror taking place in Whitechapel. After you arrest him and throw him into Broadmoor, he'll be just another of the babbling lunatics roaming these halls. But others will follow him. Pandora's Box has been opened, Mr. Holmes, and The Ripper is only the beginning."

"I would love to stand here and debate this with you, Dr. Orange, I truly would, but I am afraid it will have to wait. For now, please indulge me with a list of all the prisoners who have been released from your facility in the past two years."

Dr. Orange shook his head, "I am afraid I cannot help you, Mr. Holmes. All of our lunatics are confined to Broadmoor by the court because they are not capable of understanding the ramifications of their actions. We go strictly by the McNaughton Rules. If anyone were ever found to be competent, they would be returned to a traditional prison to serve whatever sentence was seen fit. And, between you and me, that has yet to ever happen."

"What of escapees?" Holmes said.

"There has only been one this year, a man named James Kelly. Sad soul, really. Murdered his wife five years ago and spent every night here crying himself to sleep, begging her to forgive him," Dr. Orange said. "It is most certainly not Mr. Kelly."

Holmes took a deep breath. "Doctor, I am not implying that someone under your charge could be responsible for the murders in Whitechapel. I am simply trying to stop the person responsible. Is there any other suggestion you might provide?"

Dr. Orange thought for a moment. "A relative, perhaps? There is some research that insanity can be passed on through heredity. I have heard of a young, ambitious doctor named Steward at the Brook Asylum in Clapton. You may want to pay him a visit."

"Thank you Dr. Orange."

Orange watched Holmes go to the large doors and press them open. "Close them tightly when you leave, Mr. Holmes. It has come to the point where I am more afraid of the world outside those doors than of the few lunatics confined within."

Twenty Nine

"Almost at Shoreditch Mortuary, Inspector," the carman said.

Lestrade pulled the cloth away from his neck, frowning at the blood on it. The cuts left by his razor had finally stopped bleeding. He stuffed the rag into his pocket and rubbed the raw skin on his chin and throat. He smelled the cuffs of his shirt several times, reveling in the familiar scent of Carrie's favorite washing soap. She'd put on a good show in front of the children, Lestrade thought.

"Why do you have to leave?" Little Gerard said as he was told them goodbye.

"Your father is going to put an end to someone very evil," Carrie said. "All of us should be very proud of him."

"Be careful, Father," Julliette said.

Lestrade kissed his daughter on the nose, "I will, princess."

"Are you going to kill the bad man?" Little Gerard asked.

"No, of course not," Lestrade replied. "We are going to bring him to justice. It is not our job to go around killing people, son."

Unless they really deserve it, Lestrade thought now, thinking of Mary Jane Kelly's body as he'd found it. A team of journalists surrounded the front door to the mortuary. As the carman brought the carriage to a stop, he barked at them all to back off and let Lestrade through. It was Mary Jane Kelly's last few hours above the earth, and the press wanted to capture in every detail the events of her body being driven to Walthamstow Catholic Cemetery. Several journalists recognized Lestrade and cried out his name, peppering him with questions about the investigation. He ignored the men and their queries and signaled to the constables guarding the front door to push everyone back enough to let him in.

The mortuary's greeting room was silent and dark. The visiting room was empty save for the open coffin of Mary Jane Kelly and a well-dressed man sitting in the pew closest to it. Lestrade took off his hat and walked up to the coffin. He was nervous about what he would see there, but Kelly's entire face and neck were covered in white bandages. Someone had paid for her to be buried in an expensive gown. Somehow, the undertaker had managed to fill the voids of her body's empty cavities so that her corpse appeared whole. Lestrade could not help picturing her on her bed at Thirteen Miller's Court and his hands started to shake. He turned to the man sitting near him, offered his hand and said, "Gerard Lestrade."

The man looked at him for a moment, and clasped his hand tightly, "Bond. Thomas Bond."

"The Division A police surgeon?" Lestrade asked. "You did the post-mortem on her. I read your report."

Bond just stared at the coffin. "I keep seeing it over and over again, Inspector. I've been a police surgeon for twenty years and I served in the military before that. I have seen death and destruction in many forms, but this was something completely different. The man that killed her… I'd studied the medical notes from his previous murders, and then the torso they found out in Whitehall. I fancied myself some sort of expert. Can you imagine that? When I went to Thirteen Miller's Court, I realized how little I knew."

"Not quite the same, seeing them in person," Lestrade said.

"No, not quite the same. He wanted us to find her like that, I think. He wants us to know just how much of a monster he is, if only to terrify us."

"You are probably right. Who paid for the coffin and the dress? Was it you?" Lestrade said.

"I thought she deserved at least that little bit of dignity." Bond unscrewed the cap from a silver flask and took a long drink from it. He wiped his mouth and held the bottle out toward Lestrade. "Bit of Gordon's, Inspector?"

"No thank you, Dr. Bond. I must be going. It really is a lovely dress. That was most kind of you."

"What are you doing here, anyway? Still looking for clues?"

"No. I just wanted to see her and let her know that I did not forget my promise. We will hunt this bastard across the earth if needed. He will not kill again."

"God help you, Inspector," Dr. Bond said, lifting his flask to his lips. "God bless you, but God help you."

Sherlock Holmes entered the Brooke Asylum, walking toward the desk nurse. "Good afternoon, madam. Is there a Dr. Steward present in this facility?"

The nurse checked her chart. "He is down the hall to the right with patients in the east wing. Just follow the sound of screaming."

"Thank you, I think," Holmes said, tipping his hat at her. He travelled the corridor quickly, hearing a great din of screaming and yelling from the room ahead. He entered a large community room crammed with patients and staff members. Some of the patients wore restraints, and some sat quietly playing card games. Others fought with the staff, trying to rip the chairs and tables from the floor to fling them, but they were bolted firmly to the ground. A few of them copulated in a corner together, taking turns climbing on one another's backs like animals. Holmes saw a man in a white coat peering at notes on a clipboard and approached him. "Are you Dr. Steward?"

"Yes I am. May I help you?"

"My name is Sherlock Holmes. Dr. Orange of Broadmoor recommended I meet with you. It is about the killings in Whitechapel."

"Really? Fascinating!" Dr. Steward said. "What would you like to know?"

Holmes explained his understanding of "Inherited Insanity" and how it might pertain to the research Dr. Steward was conducting, but before he finished, the doctor was frowning and shaking his head. "All of our patients are accounted for, and I have never seen one who fits your criteria, Mr. Holmes. That being said, I do think it is highly possible that your suspect would be related to one of our inmates."

"What makes you say that, Doctor?"

"I have been doing a fair amount of research into the heredity of mental aberration. Several of my patients exhibit the same symptoms of their ancestors, and I am convinced that they inherit these traits in the same way that we do others. Are you familiar with the writings of Charles Darwin, by any chance?"

Holmes nodded, following Dr. Steward as he looked over his patients, making notes on his charts. He checked off a series of blocks for each, then pointed ahead to an older woman sitting by herself at a table, staring blankly. "Darwin teaches us that everything comes from heredity. The youngest of the species is taught by its parents, over and over, until the behavior is ingrained in us biologically. If someone possessed a homicidal impulse, there is a strong chance that it could be passed on to one of their children."

"Indeed?" Holmes said. "So, have you had any inmates who might be capable of a particularly gruesome murder?"

"No."

"Of course not." Holmes checked his pocket watch. "Thank you for your time, Doctor. I must be going. There is much to be done. Good day—"

"You!" an old woman hissed at Holmes from across the room. "I know you," she said. She lifted a crooked finger at Holmes's face. "I know you, for I saw you in my dreams. You are coming for him, but you will be struck down by his blade!"

"What now?" Dr. Steward said, looking over his shoulder. "Calm down, Mrs. Druitt."

Ann Druitt moved slowly, dragging her slippers on the tile floor. She laughed, "You cannot stop us. Not you, not the simpleton, and not his little trollop. The streets will be washed clean by your blood."

Dr. Steward lifted his arm to keep Ann from advancing any further. "Just days ago she was a complete invalid, but as of late she's been babbling nonstop about the killings."

"He grows stronger than ever feasting on each little piggy's chitterlings," she hissed, digging her fingernails into Steward's arm, trying to pry his fingers away.

"Who does?" Holmes said. Ann spat directly into Holmes's face. A gob of it ran down his cheek and he wiped it away and said calmly, "Who is growing stronger?"

"You will not live to see the dawn, Sherlock Holmes." Her voice was no longer that of an old woman but now twisted into something strange and sinister. "He will destroy you."

"You know my name," Holmes said. "How peculiar. Perhaps you are right as well about my imminent demise, but if this person is expecting me, it would be most rude of me not to arrive in a prompt fashion. Who is it?"

Ann Druitt collapsed to the ground in seizure. Foam spilled out of her mouth as she wracked back and forth. Dr. Steward told one of the aides to get a few more doctors. Holmes looked down at her in silence, waiting for the seizure to end. Once Ann ceased flopping around, he tapped Dr. Steward on the shoulder. "I require the name of every male member of her family."

Dr. Steward shrugged his hand away, "It will have to wait, sir. This woman is in immediate need of medical attention."

Holmes's grip on his shoulder tightened. "She will not be the only one if I do not get what I require immediately, Dr. Steward."

Thirty

Inspector Lestrade looked at Collard and Wensley with disbelief. "What do you mean, 'nothing!'"

Collard shrugged, "I mean there is nothing in any of the medical school records I checked that show anything close to what Holmes suspected."

"What about grave robbers? Surely you found something there."

"About four hundred incidents over the past ten years, mate. People are stealing corpses all over this entire country. It has its own black market and it would take a team of researchers a year to go through every suspect."

"I guarantee you that Holmes is out there hot on the trail of the Ripper while we lot sit here with our John Thomas's in our hands. So help me God, I refuse to play the weak sister on this investigation. Christ, we need to get our acts together. What about you?" he said to Wensley.

"No John Watson's or Irene Adler's are registered at any of the doss-houses, Inspector. I figured they might be using fake names, so I gave their description to all house deputies as well, but no one recognized them."

"Well, get back out there and roam the streets until you find them, Wensley. I'll tell you this much, Lamb had better have some good news for us from those Royal Academy blokes. I'll go sort out that Darwin fellow out personally if I have to. To hell with him and his blasted monkeys!"

"Why don't we pull every report of people claiming to have information about The Ripper?" Collard said. "Maybe one who was written off as a lunatic actually had good information."

"I have a few of the reports lying around here somewhere," Lestrade said, shuffling his papers. He picked one up, "Here's a man named Stowell who claims the killer is none other than Prince Albert Victor. Ah, here's one from scrap dealer in Liverpool who claims to have found Jack the Ripper's diary. He's willing to sell it to us for a reasonable fee."

"How thoughtful of him to keep a personal journal of all his whore-killings," Collard said, laughing bitterly. "It'll take a century to untangle this."

"Let's go see if Sergeant Byfield has anything better to offer." Lestrade leaned out of his office and called to Byfield, "You got anything that isn't complete bollocks in your file of walk-ins for people with information about The Ripper?"

Byfield pointed down at a waste basket next to his feet, "You mean this file?" The basket was piled high with crumpled pieces of paper. "You want to take a Ripper walk-in, you can start with that bloke over there," the sergeant said. "He says his brother's the man we're looking for. Cheers."

Lestrade looked at the man sitting on the wooden bench in the lobby. His face was smeared with tears. "Fine. I think I will. Excuse me, sir. You have information for us?"

"Yes. My brother Montague Druitt is the killer."

"Come on into my office, sir," Lestrade said, holding open the wooden gate.

"His brother and every other loony in Whitechapel," Sgt. Byfield muttered under his breath.

"Right this way, sir," Lestrade put his arm on Will's shoulder. "What's all this about your brother, now?"

"He said he would hurt my wife if I told anyone," Will groaned, covering his face. "Oh God, little Monty. How can this be?"

"What makes you so certain he's the Ripper, Mr. Druitt? We get lots of people who think their relatives are up to no good, but it normally turns out to be nothing."

"He has not been himself lately," Will said. "He went missing from his teaching job in Blackheath a few weeks ago, and I found him in Whitechapel, living on the streets. He was covered in blood. I thought he had been attacked, you see?"

"All right," Lestrade said. He looked at Collard, who held up his hands. "What then?"

"I took him home, and cleaned him up for an important meeting. I thought everything was going to be fine. We went to the meeting, and all of a sudden he starts having some sort of delusion. When I tried to keep him from leaving, he put a knife to my throat and told me."

"He told you he was Jack the Ripper?" Collard said.

"I could see it in his face!"

Collard frowned and gave the thumbs down sign to Lestrade. Lestrade took a deep breath and sat back in his chair, defeated. Will began talking faster and louder, "He threatened to hurt my wife. You have to believe me!"

"I am sure he only meant to upset you, Mr. Druitt," Collard said.

"He said he would cut off her breasts!"

Lestrade shot up. "What did you say?"

"Her breasts, Inspector. Who the hell would think of such a thing?"

"Get your coats on, both of you," Lestrade said. "Move, move, move."

"What the hell are you getting so excited for?" Collard whispered.

"The bird on Miller's Court had both her breasts lopped off. We never gave the press that information. I want you to take us to your brother's apartment immediately, Mr. Druitt." Lestrade winked at Collard and said, "We are going to beat that bastard Holmes to the killer. I can't wait to see the look on his face when he sees us!"

Lestrade and Collard raced one another to the front door of the George Valentine Boarding School. Lestrade grabbed the handle and yanked it open triumphantly. "We've done it, Collard, we've beaten that bastard Holmes to the punch!"

A tall man with a pronouncedly bent nose stood in the lobby, and turned toward them as they entered. "Good evening, Inspectors," Sherlock Holmes said. "Welcome to the Valentine Boarding School. I confess that you arrived sooner than I thought you would." Holmes looked at the man with them and said, "William Druitt, I presume?"

Collard let out a soft whistle and said, "By God, he really is good."

"What are you…how did you…Aw, bloody hell!" Lestrade shouted and stomped his foot on the ground.

"Language, sir!" A small man stood up from behind the desk and wagged his finger at Lestrade. "I have been through quite enough today, and I refuse to have to stand for it in my own school!"

"I was just explaining to Mr. Valentine that I intend to search Montague Druitt's apartment. He was just refusing to allow me entrance," Holmes said.

"You know the way to your brother's room, Druitt?" Lestrade said.

"Yes, sir. I do," Will said, looking nervously at Valentine. "But I would really prefer-"

"Don't start," Lestrade said. "Get up those stairs right now before I become seriously irritated with the entire lot of you."

"This is an outrage!" Valentine cried, chasing after them.

"It is an outrageous world, sir," Lestrade said, turning toward the smaller man. "I suggest you stay out of our way before I show you just how strange and dangerous it really has become."

The men followed Will Druitt up the stairs. Lestrade leaned close to Holmes, "Just had to do it, right, Holmes? Just had to get here first."

"I assure you I have no idea what you are talking about, Inspector."

"Yes you do, you smug bastard. Somebody open this door before I kick it in."

George Valentine called down the hall for Mark Mann to come open up Druitt's room. "Has anyone been in this room since Montague Druitt left it last?" Holmes said.

"I was in it once to look for him," Valentine said.

"Perfectly understandable, sir." Once Mann opened the door, Holmes said, "I would like everyone to please put their hands inside their pockets. Under no circumstances is anyone to touch anything. Is that clear?" All the men nodded and stuffed their hands either into their coats or trousers. "Mr. Valentine? Does this room appear as it was the last time you saw Druitt inside it?"

"Yes, sir. It looks just as it did before."

"Did you see him touch anything before you left?"

"No, sir," Valentine said, confused by the question. Suddenly he looked at a half-full glass of water sitting on the table next to Druitt's bed and said, "Well, he was drinking from that glass before I left."

Holmes walked over to the table and inspected the glass without touching it, moving around the table to see the glass from every angle. "Are you certain this is the same one?"

"I watched him drink out of it myself, sir," Mark Mann said. "Why?"

Holmes saw the faint impression of several finger-marks on the outside of the glass. He put his fingers inside the rim and pressed outwards with his fingernails to lift it into a better light. "This will have to do, I suppose."

Inspector Collard pointed to a stack of cut-out newspaper articles about the killings on the table. "Looks like our boy has been reading his own press clippings."

"We need two things, gentlemen," Holmes announced. "First, a photograph of Montague Druitt, and then something to put this in so that it does not get disturbed on the way back to Whitechapel." Holmes poured the water inside the glass into an empty vase.

Collard looked around the shelves of books, and came upon the photograph of a slender man in a buttoned-up suit, his right arm bent in pensive thought over a stack of large books. The man was soft-featured, with a kind expression. "This isn't him, is it?"

"Why, yes, in fact, it is," Valentine said.

"Monty," Will said, taking the photograph and running his thumb along the surface. "God, it stabs me in the heart to think of the monster I last saw."

"Hmm," Lestrade said, looking at the photograph. "Not what I expected," he said to Holmes. "Looks too normal to be out there ripping women apart."

Holmes looked down at the photograph for a very long time, studying the details of Montague Druitt's face. "Anyone is capable of anything, Inspector. All that is required is the proper motivation."

Will Druitt turned and looked at Holmes for a moment, and their eyes locked on one another. Will handed Holmes the photograph and left the room.

Lestrade jiggled a desk drawer handle and heard rattling within. Upon opening the drawer, he saw several rows medical preservation jars. "Come have a look, Holmes. What do you suppose he needs all these for? The bigger ones look to be the right size to hold a uterus, do they not? And the lids seal so tightly on these that they wouldn't spill while he made his escape."

Holmes peered in at the rows and rows of specimen jars. He selected the largest jar of the group and placed the drinking glass inside it, screwing the lid tight. "I am beginning to suspect that matching these fingerprints is a only small formality. We are hot on his trail, Inspector."

"How does that one saying go? The one that you like, Holmes," Lestrade said. "Something about a game?"

"I believe the expression you are referring to is, 'The game is afoot'."

"That's the one," Lestrade said, looking down at the jars. "The game is now afoot."

Thirty One

Frederick Wensley walked into the Ten Bells bar and searched the faces of the men and women crowded inside. Not one of them resembled Dr. Watson. There were drunken sailors looking to purchase pleasures from the wide variety of whores lurking around the bar, and just as many whores looking to take advantage of the sailors in return. Off to the side of the bar sat a different group of men who kept to themselves. They all sat around a one-eyed man who Wensley recognized and quickly turned away from.

Wensley could feel Mickey Fitch's eye fix on him, but no alarm was raised amongst the other gang members. Wensley turned to try to slide back out of the bar and just before he reached the door, five more members of the Old Nichol gang walked in. Two of them were men Wensley had fought face-to-face with at the police station.

Wensley spun toward the bar and thrust his head down between his arms, slapping his hand on the wooden surface. "Beer!" he shouted at the barman. He tapped a coin urgently against the counter until his glass arrived, then focused intently on the warm, sudsy ale. He tried to filter all of the laughing and shouting going on around him to listen to what the others were saying to Mickey Fitch.

"I saw 'em just down the street! Hurry before they get away."

"Settle down, and shut it," Fitch growled. He called everyone to come closer, and as they formed a huddle around him, Wensley could no longer hear them. He checked his coat pockets for his sap and police whistle, reassuring himself that he'd brought both.

The Old Nichol gang started putting on their coats and moving toward the door. Mickey Fitch passed near Wensley and looked directly at him, but Wensley lifted his glass and started chugging it so quickly that foam spilled down the sides of his mouth. He let out a large belch and slammed the empty mug down, calling to the barman, "Another beer, man! Be quick about it!"

A cool autumn wind whispered against the back of his neck as the front door opened. The barman set another beer in front of Wensley and Wensley pulled out another coin from his pocket and put it next to the glass. As he turned, the last of the Old Nichol gang went through the door. One of them said, "I'll take the bird. You can have Watson."

Sgt. Byfield watched Lestrade open the station door and stomped his foot on the ground, shaking his head urgently. Lestrade froze in place at the entrance, blocking Holmes and Collard from coming in behind him.

"What is it?" Lestrade mouthed.

Byfield cocked his head at Lestrade's office as he drew a menacing line across his throat with his finger. Lestrade leaned forward so that he could see around the corner. Chief Inspector Brett was screaming at Constable Lamb. Lamb was seated with his hands folded, looking down at the ground. "Out of uniform and out of your jurisdiction!" Brett roared. "Acting under the authority of an unauthorized person! And if you think I've forgotten that little stunt you and your friend pulled on Miller's Court about Regulation One

One Three, you are mistaken. I will have your arse for this if you do not tell me where Inspector Lestrade and Constable Wensley are!"

Lamb did not look up when he spoke. "I told you I do not know where they are, Chief Inspector. I was in Piccadilly on my own, nobody else knew. I wasn't following anyone else's orders."

"You are a liar! I swear that by the time I am finished with you, you will not be able to find a job selling fruit in this city. I will ask you one last time, you blubbering little simpleton. What is this piece of glass being used for?" Lestrade watched Brett lift the shard with the fingerprint on it from the desk.

Lestrade looked back at Holmes and Collard. "You two need to leave."

"Forget it," Collard said. "You'll need all the help you can get in there."

"I will handle this," Lestrade said. "Go. Do what you can in the meantime."

Lestrade watched Holmes and Collard vanish into the night. He took a deep breath and walked through the door toward the sergeant's desk. Byfield shook his head sadly and said, "You know, there is nothing in the rules that says you need to go in there, mate. Lamb is still a young bloke. Even if they sack him, he'll find other work. He ain't got no wife or kids like you do. You could just go home and pretend you never knew anything about it."

"Is that what you would do?"

"That is what most people in your position would do, m'boy."

"When I worked for you in uniform, you never did that to me."

"No, I never did," Byfield sighed. "But then again, my balls were never in quite the sling yours are."

Lestrade pushed the front gate open and went into his office. He put his hand on Lamb's shoulder and said, "Run along now, son. I'll take it from here."

"Do not move an inch, Constable Lamb," Brett commanded. "Well, well, well, Inspector. You have done it this time. By the time I am finished with you, you will beg for mercy."

Lestrade shook his head. "Not to offend, but you do not intimidate me, all right? Stop it before you embarrass us both. If you have something to say, just say it and be done with it. Otherwise, I have police work to do and am sorely lacking in time to stand around bantering with the sorry likes of you. Wait. I meant to say, sorry likes of you, sir."

"You are going to lick the soles of my shoes before I get finished with you, Lestrade."

"I doubt that."

"What is this piece of glass that you had one of my constables traipsing all over the country with?" Brett held up the handkerchief with the glass inside it. "What is this unauthorized train ticket doing in his pocket for all the way out to Piccadilly? What was it exactly that you had this constable doing?"

"Give me that piece of glass before you hurt yourself, Chief Inspector. It's too sharp for you to play with."

"Do not toy with me, Lestrade! What is the significance of it?"

"It's just a piece of glass, Chief Inspector. Give it to me before I accidentally hurt you when I take it from you."

Brett set his jaw and let the glass drop out of the handkerchief onto the table. "Just a piece of glass, eh? Not important?"

"Not in the slightest," Lestrade said. He moved to snatch it from the table but just missed as Brett grabbed it again. "Give it to me."

Brett dropped the glass on the ground and smashed it with his foot, shattering it into fragments.

Both Lestrade and Lamb stared down, speechless, at the glass. Brett held his arms out wide and said, "Just a piece of glass, right? You both had better take a good look at it because I am going to do the same thing to both of your careers!"

Brett slammed Lestrade's office door shut and walked over to the front desk, shouting, "Neither of those two men are to leave under any circumstances tonight, do I make myself clear?"

"Yes, Chief Inspector!" Sgt. Byfield said, snapping a salute at him.

"I will be back first thing in the morning to deal with them and anyone else who was involved in this debacle!"

Lamb watched Brett leave and turned to Lestrade with tears in his eyes, "He searched me as soon as I got into the station. He found the print, and the ticket. I am so sorry, sir."

Lestrade looked at the shattered pieces of glass. There was no way to fix it. Each shard was cracked all the way through and broken into too many fragments. "How did you make out anyway? Did those Royal Academy blokes give you a hard time?"

Lamb shrugged, pointing at the crumpled up piece of paper on the desk. "See those numbers written across the bottom of the train schedule? Took 'em long enough, but they finally came up with a system they could agree on and told me that's the scientific way to write out the fingerprint on the glass."

Lestrade looked down at the broken pieces. "This print, you mean?"

"Yes."

"All right," Lestrade said, "we might not be sunk after all. Do you remember how to figure this gibberish out?"

"I think so," Lamb said. "It is really, really complicated."

"How the hell did you get them to agree to help?"

"It wasn't easy. That Dr. Faulds did not want to help the other two do anything else that would give them any more recognition. He'd only agree to assist them if everyone agreed to leave their names off of the formula."

"So whose name is going on it?"

"My cousin Ed Henry is with the Bengal Police out in India. He's a bit of a prankster, and would get a kick out having something like that named after him. I gave them his name, and they agreed to it," Lamb said.

Sgt. Byfield knocked on Lestrade's door. "Well now. It is my understanding that one of my boys is still out in that festering dung heap. Is that correct, Inspector Lestrade?"

"Yes, Sergeant," Lestrade said. "Young Frederick Wensley is out there on his own."

"According to the Chief Inspector, you two are under strict orders to sit in this office until tomorrow morning. Is that clear? Now, I am going to go sit at my desk and take a nice long nap, and when I wake up, I had better see young Mr. Wensley back in this police station safe and sound. I do not care how he gets here. Just make sure he is. We clear, gents?"

"As crystal, Sergeant," Lestrade nodded.

Thirty Two

I tightened the bonnet under Irene's chin and checked the leather harness to make sure it was snug to her neck. "Is everything all right?" I said.

She took up the gun from the table and ejected the cylinder to inspect that six bullets were within its chamber. She spun the cylinder and flicked it shut with a jerk of her wrist, then tucked it into her coat. "I am fine, John. Stop asking me that."

"Are you sure you do not want me to carry the gun?"

"Not after last time. Get your own," she said, smiling thinly.

I carried nothing with me but a few coins. I had nothing that identified me as a doctor, nor even my name. I was no one but another faceless citizen of Whitechapel. My medical bag had not left our room in Crossingham's since it first arrived.

On the night before, I was on the streets with Irene, and we were watching a man whom we thought looked suspicious. He had a way of eyeing the bunters, taking their measure as if he might snatch them and drag them off into the darkness. Without any warning, another man came up behind him and smashed a brick across the back of his skull. "Cheat me at cards now, yeh bleedin' clove!"

The man collapsed to his knees with his head split open. His hands instinctively tried to clutch the wound as dark blood pumped through his fingers and spilled onto the street below.

There were a dozen people with me who saw it happen, and none of us moved to help. Irene looked to me, and I turned to lead her away. As we neared the top of the street, I looked back. The man had stopped moving. Somewhere in the distance, a police whistle sounded.

I now found myself adept at locating weapons anywhere. I looked for bottles that could be smashed against a wall and give me a weapon of jagged glass that was ready to slash an attacker's gullet open. I made note of loose stones that would be big enough to smash someone in the face if I needed to. Whenever my boots struck a loose nail on the pavement, I watched where it went, just in the event that I needed to grab it and jab it into an aggressor's eye.

Luckily, the only attackers I had to dispatch were the hissing, teeth-baring rodents that lurked in the shadows. The sight of a foot-long rat would have sent me yelping in disgust only weeks before, but now I stomped on their heads at the first sight of them as they tried to race out and bite me in the ankle.

"Irene," I said. "Before we go out tonight, there is something I need to say to you."

She looked at me for a moment as she buttoned her coat. "Does whatever you are about to say have something to do with the task at hand, John? We need to concentrate."

"I believe I would be able to concentrate better if I tell you what I am feeling."

"Well then, I guess you had better get it off your chest. What is it?"

I looked at her face and saw nothing but a firm commitment to the task at hand. There was no kindness in it for me. "I just want you to know that I have come to care for you deeply, and I want you to exercise the utmost caution. We must be ever-vigilant."

She smiled and kissed me on the cheek. "You are a good man, John Watson. Miss Morstan is a lucky woman indeed."

I looked up and down Commercial Street. "We're staying in Spitalfields tonight? May I ask why?"

"He's killed twice in this immediate area," Irene said. "The other three murders were spread out all over Whitechapel. It makes sense to me that the Ripper is more familiar with Spitalfields than any other location. He is comfortable here, and I would think that it is his preferred hunting grounds. He probably only ventures outside of it when necessary. Did you play hide-and-seek as a child, Watson?"

"Yes."

"I was the best at it," Irene said. "When the other children were supposed to be seeking, they ran around shouting for people, expecting to stumble upon them. When it was my turn to hunt them, I hid." Her eyes sparkled with excitement as she spoke. "I waited for them to emerge, thinking it was safe, and I then took them. Tonight is our night, John. I can feel it. You stay back from me, keep to the shadows. I shall go further up Brick Lane, and survey the area. Are you listening to me?"

"Yes, of course."

"You looked for a moment as if you weren't paying attention."

"I was," I said. "Be careful, please."

"You do not understand, John. It is not we who need to be afraid of the Ripper. It is he who needs to fear us." With that, she disappeared into the shadows and began to move silently up Brick Lane. I squinted and tried to follow her yellow scarf as best as I could in the thick fog. When she was so far ahead that I could not see her, I moved to follow her up the alleyway just as an arm clasped me and a hand clapped over my mouth.

"It's Constable Wensley, Doctor Watson," he whispered in my ear. "I implore you to not make a sound. The Old Nichol boys are right around the corner and they are looking for you and the woman."

As he took his hand away from my mouth, I turned and realized that he looked little more than a boy without his uniform on. Wensley was crouched low in the shadows, peering down the alley. I bent with him, feeling my heart thumping against my breast. I searched for Irene, but she was already gone. I leaned over to Wensley and whispered, "We have to go warn Miss Adler."

"There! I heard something," a voice called out from the street and my blood turned to ice.

Another man answered him, "You only heard yourself huffing and puffing yeh fat bastard."

"Shut up, I'm serious. I heard something. Over there."

They were coming closer. Constable Wensley crouched, keeping his thick wooden police truncheon at the ready. "When they get close enough, we'll jump out and take them by surprise."

I searched the ground for a weapon but saw nothing. I swallowed hard and said, "All right. On your go."

"I'm telling you I heard a voice," the man repeated, now close enough that I could see his outline through the smog.

"Go look then, yeh tommy dodd!"

"Bugger off! Oy, where you going! Come back!"

Their voices trailed off as they left and I let out a long breath. I clapped Constable Wensley on the shoulder, "We are safe. Now quickly. Let's go find Miss Adler."

At my first step I was frozen by a bright light that illuminated the entire alleyway, cast from behind us and trapping us in its glare. There was a harsh laugh and I heard Mickey Fitch say, "Well, well, well. You just never know what you'll find slinking around the alleyways of Whitechapel, now do you, boys?"

I turned to see Fitch's one dark eye fixed on me above his bullseye lantern. A dozen members of the Old Nichol Gang stood to his side with a variety of weapons in their hands.

Men came running into the alley behind Wensley and me, sealing off our exit. "What the hell do you want with us, Fitch?" I said.

"Me an' you got unfinished business, mate." Fitch reached behind his back and removed a large Bowie knife that he held up to the light.

Thirty Three

There was a man was standing on Hanbury Street with his hands in the pockets of a long dark coat that flapped lightly in the breeze. He did not move from the place where he stood staring at the rear Twenty Nine Hanbury. The house's rear wall was where Annie Chapman had braced herself as the Ripper's blade severed her throat.

Irene moved quietly toward him, carefully avoiding stepping on any trash or loose stones scattered on the street as she came closer to him. He was still too far away to see in the soggy, stinking mist, and the brim of his tall top-hat cast his face in shadows.

She turned to look back down Brick Lane and waved her arm in the air to signal for Watson to hurry forward. There was no response. Irene's chest tightened and she had to force herself to breathe steadily. She put her hand inside her coat and felt the revolver's warm wooden handle, keeping it at the ready as she emerged from the shadows. She waved her hand and said, "Hello guvnah! Yeh feelin' good natured this evening? I bet you are, on such a fine night."

Irene came around the man's side and looked at his thin face and narrowly set eyes. They were red-rimmed and shining like those of a creature that lived in caves and had not been exposed to the light. "Go away. Please," he said. "I just want to be left alone."

"Now, now, me lovely. Why yeh lookin' down that alleyway, anyway? Yeh see something' yeh like down there, do yeh?

Somewhere yeh wanna go, maybe?" Irene peeked over the man's shoulder, hoping to see Watson emerge.

He squeezed his eyes tightly as if he were in pain and pressed his palms against his temple. "I-I am trying to remember. It all seems so blurry to me now."

"What's that, handsome? What seems blurry? Somethin' about this house here?"

"Something happened back there in that yard. Something terrible."

"That's right," Irene said. "A woman was killed there by the fence."

"I knew her," he said.

"Is that so?"

The man looked up into the starless sky and took a deep breath. "Have you ever been to India?"

Irene paused and said, "Er, yes. Once. Is that where you are from?"

"No." He wiped his sleeve across his nose and looked back at her. "When I was a boy, my older brother promised to take me there. Whenever I become afraid, I imagine myself there. Can you tell me what it was like?"

"Some places are very beautiful. In other places there is tremendous poverty, and the people suffer. Somewhat like the East End."

He nodded and cleared his throat, looking back at the rear yard. "I am so tired. So very tired. I think I am finally finished." The man smiled with relief as he said the words. "That means I can stop now.

I have just enough left for one more bite, and once that is gone, I will finally be finished and free of this thing forever. Do you know what that means?"

"No," Irene said. "Please tell me. What can be finished?" She leaned over again, still looking for Watson, but saw nothing.

The man reached into his pocket and pulled out a glass jar. As he unscrewed the lid, he said, "After this, I will be free."

Irene recoiled at the horrific odor as the lid came off. He lifted the jar and poured the liquid into his mouth, catching a small brown object as it tumbled down and chewing it pleasantly. He wiped the liquid from his face with his hand and smeared his hand down the front of his coat. He looked at Irene and said, "Oh, no. I am afraid I am still hungry."

They rushed us in swarms from every direction. Two grabbed me from behind by my hair and my coat and yanked me backwards, throwing me to the pavement. I watched Wensley swing out with his truncheon in a wide, whistling arc that smashed as many of them as he could reach. I swung and I kicked, I scratched and I bit, I tried tearing their skin from their very faces. It was not enough.

A boot kicked me in the mouth and loosened my teeth. I struggled to scream "Irene! Run for your life and save yourself!" between my broken lips as blood gushed into my mouth.

"Dr. Watson!" Wensley cried as he tried valiantly to fight his way toward me. I watched one of them crack him across the back of the head with an axe-handle and drop him on the spot. They beat him savagely.

"Get off of him, you bloody cowards!" I screamed. "You motherless dogs, have you no honor! Help! Help us! Someone save us!"

In that moment I thought of the man I'd watched collapse to the ground after the brick smashed open his head and I knew that no one was coming. Nobody cared.

"Stop all that yelling now, Dr. Watson," Mickey Fitch said. He kicked me over onto my back and showed me his knife. "You're going to need to save your voice."

Fitch looked over his shoulder toward Hanbury and then back at me. "We'll find that saucy bird of yours once I've finished with you. But it would be un-gentlemanly of me to show up without a present, wouldn't it? I think I should bring her something she might like. A small token of my appreciation for all that she's done for us good citizens of Whitechapel."

"Go to hell!" I shouted.

Fitch called for several of the others to hold me down. They grabbed my arms and legs and pinned me to the ground. Fitch reached for the buckle of my belt and undid it. He pressed the tip of his blade against my trousers' buttons and began slicing them off one at a time.

I squirmed against them. "What are you doing? Let go of me!"

"Stop struggling, doctor," Fitch chuckled. "I am about to perform a very complicated surgery, and I can't have you thrashing about. I told you what I was going to do when I found you. Mickey Fitch always makes good on his promises, mate."

I shrieked into the starless sky as he touched the cold steel of his knife against the skin of my scrotum.

Irene raised the barrel of her gun at Montague Druitt's face. "If you so much as flinch I will pull this trigger and blast you to hell."

Druitt continued to chew the last-remaining piece of Mary Jane Kelly's heart. He ran his tongue over his teeth and said, "Mmm…she was delicious."

"You monster." Irene squeezed the handle of the gun so hard her she could no longer feel it.

Druitt's eyes were now wide enough to show white on all sides as his irises shrunk to small black dots. "Fear fills you. It is pumping through your heart, the same way it did all the others. It will flavor your organs so that when I rip you open and the lights explode behind your eyes, your screams will ring in my ears each time I take a bite."

"Why don't you bite this instead?" Irene Adler cocked the hammer and pulled the trigger. The hammer slammed against the gun's frame and sparked as it struck the bullet's firing pin. Flame shot from mouth of the barrel and the bullet flew across the surface of Montague Druitt's face. His hair ignited in flames and black smoke poured from his ruined eyes. The ruined flesh of his face hung dangling from his cheeks, revealing the pearl white skin beneath in the seconds before blood began filling in the gaps.

Irene stared, mystified, at the sight of his exposed skull. She was unable to move as flailed, clutching his face. She saw the knife in his hand and that it was covered in blood. Something warm and wet was running down the front of her chest.

Irene coughed and it was a gurgle. She reached up to touch her throat and felt the hot, sticky blood pumping through the severed leather strap tied there.

Druitt howled in fury, his blade slashing in every direction. Irene staggered backwards as dark bubbles popped in and out of existence in her vision. She started to panic as the blood began gushing from her neck and tried to scream, but all that came out were high-pitched wheezes.

Druitt turned toward her. He followed her by the sound of voice, hunting even as smoke still rose from his face. He lifted his knife with its tip aimed directly at her. Irene watched as Druitt stood over her, his face now a grinning, bloody skull.

Irene closed her eyes.

Feet were scuffling across the stones, moving toward them both quickly. Irene saw someone leap over her and tackle Montague Druitt to the ground.

There was the sound of a struggle and two men fighting. Irene tried to get up from the ground but collapsed. She was cold and tired and wanted nothing more than to lie back down and surrender.

Someone was calling her name. "Irene? Irene? Come back to me. Can you hear me?"

Her eyes fluttered and she realized that Sherlock Holmes was shaking her. She looked at him and nodded and he gasped with relief. "Thank God you are alive."

"Where is he?" Irene whispered. "Is he not dead? Go after him!"

Holmes shook his head and said, "Be calm. He will not get far. He is critically injured. By your own hand, I might add." Holmes lifted her chin and inspected the damage to her throat as he untied the leather strap around her neck.

Irene noticed that Holmes was even paler than the night she'd last seen him. "What is wrong with you? You don't look well."

Holmes said, "Just give me a moment. I am nearly finished." He methodically removed the scarf that secured her bonnet and began wrapping it around her throat, keeping it pressed against the open wound to stop the bleeding.

Irene looked down and realized there was a knife handle sticking out of the center of Holmes's chest. She gasped and struggled with him to try and pull the knife free. Holmes calmly held her hands steady so that he could continue to tend to her. "Leave it. I must stop your bleeding."

"No," she rasped. "Go and find Watson. Save yourself. Please!"

"Hush now, my love," Holmes said. He tied the scarf tight around her neck and secured her wound. He reached down for the severed, blood-soaked leather strap that had been wrapped around her neck and said, "It must have been this that saved your life tonight. Did my Watson make this? It is quite…ingenious." With that, his eyes rolled into the back of his head and he collapsed beside her on the street.

Mickey Fitch grabbed the skin of my privates and pulled it flat, preparing to saw with the edge of his knife. I begged him not to, and the bastard just grinned. "I'm going to feed these to your woman when I find her," he hissed. He held up the knife, "Say goodbye to your nutmegs!"

A hand grabbed the top of Fitch's head and yanked him back by the hair. Inspector Gerard Lestrade stood looming over Fitch with a nightstick in his hand, pointed directly down at Mickey Fitch's widened eye. "I think it's about time you saw the light, Mickey." Lestrade drove the tip of the nightstick down as far as it would go into Fitch's skull through his eyeball. Vitreous fluid and blood exploded across Fitch's face as Lestrade ratcheted his nightstick deeper and deeper into his skull.

Fitch shrieked and flopped around on the pavement. His screams were so loud and horrific that everyone stopped fighting to stare gaping at the yellow and red streams of thick fluid spilling down his face and into his wide, wailing mouth.

A sea of constables flooded into the alleyway, their truncheons cracking the head of every Old Nichol boy they could reach. Constable Lamb charged through the crowd, "Where's Wensley? Fred! Fred!"

I pulled up my pants and crawled over to where Wensley was lying unconscious, but still breathing. Lamb and I shook him by the shoulders until his eyes opened. I asked if he could see how many fingers I was holding up. "How many fingers are you holding up?" he whispered.

"Yes, lad. How many do you see?"

He pushed my hand out of his face and sat up to look at the melee surrounding him. "What I see is a few bastards that aren't bleeding yet. Give me your sap!" he barked at Lamb.

It was then that I heard the gunshot ring out from Irene's direction. I sprung to my feet and raced down Brick Lane, calling for her through the thick white mist. The alleyway ended at Hanbury Street where I saw her huddled over a man lying on the street.

Irene looked up at me, weeping profusely. I saw blood stained around her neck through a makeshift bandage and gasped, "My God! What the hell happened?"

She grabbed handfuls of my coat and yanked me down to look at the man. I first saw the knife buried in his breastbone and then finally realized it was Holmes. "Oh no," I whispered. "No, no, no." I leapt over his chest, tapping his face frantically, "Holmes! Holmes! Answer me! Holmes!'

His eyes opened to narrow slits. "Watson?" he said. The corners of his mouth curled into a tiny smile. "Is that you?"

"Shhh," I said, wiping his forehead. "Try not to talk. I have to get you into surgery." I leaned my head toward the alley and shouted, "Lestrade! Help! Come quickly! Lestrade!"

"Watson, listen to me," Holmes said, but then began coughing violently. There was blood on his teeth, coming up through his throat. "I do not have much time and I need to tell you…need to tell you…" He took me by the hand firmly and placed it over his heart. "I am so, so very sorry. I beg you to forgive me."

"No! No, I do not forgive you because if I forgive you, you will think it is safe to die, and it is not safe to die, Holmes. I do not forgive you so you have to fight to stay alive long enough to make me forgive you." My words began to ramble together through thick sobs.

"I am at the end, my friend. I am going to die."

"You are not!" I screamed.

There was a gurgling sound from the wound in his chest and Holmes's voice was little more than a whisper. "You can see this wound as well as I can. It is a fatal blow and I will soon pass on. It is a fact. It is….it is…elementary," he said, and his eyes closed.

Thirty Four

A carriage awaited Montague Druitt on Baker's Row with a hooded driver standing by the side door holding the horse's tether. "Over here, Monty! Quickly!"

"Will?" Druitt shouted, spinning in the darkness. "Is that you?"

"Follow my voice. We have to go!"

"I cannot see, Will! Where are you?"

"Just over here. Hurry, Monty, or I shall be forced to leave you. Just a little further. This way!" Once Druitt came near enough, Will grabbed him and pushed him toward the carriage. "My God, Monty. What the hell happened to you?"

"That woman shot me!" Druitt moaned, touching his face. "How bad is it?"

Will looked closely at the injury, seeing the scored bone between shreds of dangling flesh. "Not as bad as you might think, Monty. Get in the back and do not make a sound. We have to leave and there are swarms of police everywhere."

"Will," Druitt said, bracing himself against the cab's door. "I did not mean what I said earlier."

Will patted him on the shoulder and helped him up into the carriage. "Do not fret. Your older brother has everything under control. I shall take you to get help."

"I mean it, Will," Druitt said. "I love you. I would never hurt you or your family. I have no idea what comes over me sometimes."

"I know, Monty." Will quickly reached into his pocket and unscrewed the cap of a vial that he then poured it into a syringe. He loaded the needle's barrel and flicked the tip so that fluid spilled out of it.

Druitt was touching the exposed bones of his face in wonder when Will lifted him by the chin and said, "Let me just take a look for a moment." Once Druitt's head was tilted back, Will stuck the needle into his neck and pushed on the stopper.

Druitt recoiled and grabbed his neck. "What are you doing?"

"That is just to help you rest, little brother," Will said. He watched Druitt slump over in his seat and then climbed into the front of the cab and snapped the horse's reins.

The launching dock for the Torpedo Workshop of Sir John Isaac Thornycroft was located in Chiswick, only a few blocks from the Brooke Asylum. At that early hour, the shop was dark and silent save for the waters of the Thames softly lapping against the dock. Will drove past the workshop, to go toward the stony field in the rear. When they came to stop he turned back to see Monty sprawled across the carriage's floor. Will pulled Monty's coat off of him and said, "We're here, Monty. You must wake up."

"We are?" Monty said, feeling around the back of the cab. "Is this India?"

"What? What do you mean? Why on earth would we be in India?"

"You said you would take me there, Will. You promised."

"Oh, yes," Will said softly. "Now I remember. Did you still want to go? In fact, I think that is a capital idea and we should go there immediately after everything we've been through."

Monty tried to smile but grimaced at the pain in his face. "She really did me in. I suppose I deserved it. Is she dead?"

"I do not know," Will said. "I was not there, remember?"

"She called me a monster, Will. I killed all those women. I ate the things I found inside of them. Why did I do that? Am I like mother? Is something wrong with my mind?"

"Nothing is wrong with you, Monty. You were perfect! You were a complete revelation! In fact, you made my paltry work look childish by comparison." Will bent to the ground and selected several of the heaviest stones he could find. He dropped them into the pockets of Monty's coat.

Monty's head lolled forward from the narcotic in the syringe. "What work is that, Will?"

"Well, after I killed the first two, I knew I could never keep going. The first one survived even after I jammed a broom stick so far up into her I thought it would pop out of her mouth. I couldn't even finish her off properly. Good thing she was too afraid to tell the police what happened, or I might have been nibbed. Such a bungler."

"That was you?"

"Of course it was me, Monty. Who do you think put those newspapers under your door? I was so inept that my own wife nearly caught me after I killed Martha Tabram. She found the bloody clothes and became immediately suspicious. I am just not cut out for this type of work, Monty. But you…my God, you were genius."

"You did this to me? But why?"

Will came around to Monty's side with the coat and draped it over his shoulders. Monty grunted under the weight of it as Will fastened the buttons all the way up to Monty's neck. He cinched the belt tightly around Monty's waist and tied it in a complex knot. "Now, to be fair, I cannot take full credit for what you accomplished. All I did was point you in the right direction. I gave you the means, maybe even the push you needed, but it is you who achieved greatness, Monty."

"Is that water?" Monty whispered. "It sounds as if we are standing on a dock."

"Yes. We're getting on a boat. We are going to India, Monty. Just like you wanted, and just like I said." Will led Monty to the edge of the pier. "I have had all of this planned out from the very beginning so have no fear. I will guide you." He brought Monty to the edge of the dock and looked down into the black shimmering water. He put his arm around Monty and said, "Just remember how much I love you."

"I love you too, Will," Monty said, but his words were cut short by the sharp intrusion of Will jamming a second needle into his neck. Will held him steady so that he could not break free and squeezed the syringe's stopper in so quickly that a bubble formed in Monty's skin that leaked pus around the needle. Monty gasped and his knees buckled. He clutched Will's arm and said, "No more, Will. Please."

"I agree," Will said. "That is quite enough." Will removed the needle and tossed it into the water. He found a thick steel docking chain coiled on the ground nearby and hefted the chain over his shoulder and carried it over to Monty.

"What did you put inside of me?" Monty said, clutching his neck. He staggered around the dock, but could not see and could not find anything to hold.

"Be careful, Monty. You don't want to fall in," Will said. "I gave you a mix of opium and a very special fungus called amanita muscaria. They believe it is what made the Vikings go into those berserker rages, you know. Based on your response to it, I would think they are correct."

Will draped the chain around Monty's neck and held him steady. He looked once more into his little brother's ruined face and said, "It is time to go."

Monty smiled weakly at him, and Will pushed his brother off of the edge of the dock and sent him crashing into the Thames with an enormous splash.

Frigid, polluted water filled Montague Druitt's nose and mouth as he spun down and down and down. His ears roared, popping, bursting. His lungs filled with mud and water. The heavy chain and rocks in his coat dragged him toward the muddy bottom, toward the silt and dirt and centuries of trash that the people of England had thrown into the river.

Toward India.

Act V

A LIGHT THAT NEVER GOES OUT

Thirty Five

Irene wrapped her hands around the knife's handle and tried wrenching it from Holmes's chest. "No!" I shouted and shoved her hands out of the way. "We must leave it in, it is plugging his wound!" She fought with me and tried getting free of my grip, but I pinned her arms to her sides to keep her from killing Holmes by trying to save him.

Lestrade was commanding Lamb to whip the donkey harder over the sound of the carriage's clanking wheels. "That way, you daft bastard!" he barked. "Turn right, the doctor's office is on Bishopsgate."

"Listen to me, Irene," I said. "That knife is the only thing keeping Holmes alive right now. If we remove it, we'll kill him instantly."

She looked down at Holmes and slumped forward as if someone had undone her at the waist. I put my arm around her. "I need you to sit back and keep your head and knees up above your heart. You are not out of the woods yet, either, my dear," I said. The makeshift bandage around her throat was saturated, and the wound needed to be sutured or it risked becoming septic.

"There it is!" Lestrade shouted. Lamb stopped the cart and both men raced around the back to undo the gate and lift Holmes.

There were no lights on within the office. I ran straight at the front door with my shoulder and the frame shattered. I toppled onto the floor near two surgical chairs and cabinets of chemicals and instruments. "Come on, come on," I shouted. "Bring him in." They carried Holmes past me and placed him into one of the chairs, while I returned to the cart to fetch Irene.

Holmes was now trembling. His pulse slowed to a crawl and his skin was cold to the touch. I told Lestrade to cut off Holmes's shirt while I rifled the cabinets, tossing things over my shoulder in my haste. "Where the hell is it?"

Finally, I came upon a large brown bottle and syringe. I told Lestrade to stretch out Holmes's arm while I prepared the injection. There were no track marks on his skin. The veins were solid and bright blue. He'd done it. He'd managed to wean himself from the poison that I was now injecting into him. I worked at it quickly, begging his forgiveness.

I administered several more injections, and his pulse returned. I covered him with a blanket and turned to Irene. Her throat needed twenty stitches. I could see the quivering ends of several vocal chords within the wound that no surgeon's hand could repair. While I was sure she would survive, I doubted her arias would ever ring out over an audience again.

I tied Irene's last suture and returned to Holmes. "You both have to hold him down," I said to Lestrade and Lamb. I climbed onto the operating chair and straddled Holmes's chest. Whatever demon possessed The Ripper to the last, it gave him enough strength to drive his blade through Holmes's breastbone. "Hold him down so I can wrench this thing out of him," I grunted. "I'll have to rock it back and forth until it comes loose." I grabbed the handle and started rocking it back and forth.

"Christ, he's bleeding like a fountain, Watson," Lestrade hissed.

"Hold him tightly, damn it! I am almost there!" Finally, the blade came loose with a pop and I tossed it across the room, lifting my hand to shield my face from the sudden crimson spray.

The next morning, Chief Inspector Brett stood on the street waiting anxiously for the carriage to arrive at the Whitechapel Division Police Station. His entire future was aboard that carriage, he thought. Brett adjusted his tied and straightened his hair as it pulled up to the sidewalk and he moved to open the door. "Welcome home, sir," Brett said, snapping a salute at the tiny, bearded man in back. "How was France?"

"Far away from all this mess, is how it was," Sir Robert Anderson grumbled, ignoring Brett's attempt to help him out of the carriage. "I was hoping this would blow over while I was away, but it seems as if you people have done nothing but stoke the fires, hmm? Becoming a bit fond of seeing your names in the papers, I suppose?"

"Only those of us who care more about our own popularity than the integrity of this organization," Brett said grimly. "That was why I sent you such an urgent telegram. This Inspector, in particular, has made quite a spectacle of things, and I am glad to have him finally removed from my division."

"My division, you mean," Anderson said.

"Of course, sir." Technically, this was true, Brett thought, as he nodded politely to the Assistant Commissioner in Charge of CID. Anderson had been promoted to that rank in just August of that year, but only one month into the Ripper investigation, he'd unexpectedly announced he was going on extended vacation in France. He left with the implicit orders that he not be bothered until the damn thing was sorted out. Well, it wasn't sorted, Brett thought, and so sorry to ruin your little jaunt, but if you don't have the decency to retire and free up one of the higher ranks, I suppose I should make you earn your salary. "Inspector Gerard Lestrade was already in clear violation of a multitude of our ordinances when I sent you that telegram, Assistant Commissioner, but I fear it has only gotten worse. Just last night I was forced to confine him to his office. It is providence at work that you arrived this morning. I was also forced to confine one of the young uniformed constables that Lestrade managed to pollute with his wickedness."

"Just open the door, Brett," Anderson said.

"Yes, *sir*." Brett pushed the door open to reveal a dozen prisoners scattered across the lobby floor. Some had thick white bandages wrapped around their heads with blood stains seeping through. Others had badly swollen eyes, or mouths of shattered teeth. All of them were shackled together, and several constables walked between their ranks with nightsticks slapping against their palms menacingly.

Constable Wensley was seated at the sergeant's desk clutching what appeared to be a pound of raw steak to his face. Sergeant Byfield and City Police Inspector Collard glared at Brett as he came into the station.

"What is all this?" Brett said. "What happened here?"

"What happened, despite your every attempt to forestall it, was the culmination of a months-long joint investigation between the London City Police and Scotland Yard, Chief Inspector," Collard said. "No disrespect, sir, but I must confess it is a highly unusual way to do business, and I will be forced to report it to my superiors."

"What on earth are you talking about?" Brett hissed. "Who the hell are all these men?"

"It's the entire Old Nichol Gang!" Sergeant Byfield said. "Inspector Lestrade has been hot on the trail of these bastards since Emma Smith was killed. Who knows if they might have been responsible for some of the other so-called Ripper killings too? And then, just as Inspector Lestrade was about to put an arrest plan together to collar the whole buggering lot, you had the brilliant idea to confine him to his office."

Sir Robert Anderson grunted, and Brett looking around the room nervously. "Why wasn't I informed? Nobody told me about this. H-how could I have—"

"They tried to kill a civilian last night!" Byfield said. "Caught him all alone in an alleyway and were trying to do unspeakable things to him when our boy Wensley intervened. Fought the whole gang by himself single-handedly until the rest of my men got there."

"Well, er, good show, Wensley!" Brett said, waving meekly at the Constable.

"Good show my arse!" Byfield said. "Your orders to put Watson under constant surveillance almost got the lad killed! We'd all be down at Spitalfields Church saying 'Hail Mary' for him right now if it weren't for such a fine investigation done by Inspectors Lestrade and Collard. They knew right where to go. Now I have to put nearly every person in the station in for a damn medal! You know how much bleeding paperwork that is going to create?"

"Just so I am clear, you arrested an entire criminal street gang last night?" Sir Robert Anderson said.

"All except for that one-eyed bastard Mickey Fitch," Collard said.

"So," Brett sniffed. "Despite all this, you still failed to capture the leader?"

"Well, we'd have him by now," Byfield said. "Trouble is, the only copper that knows how to get him was ordered to sit in his office until you got back."

Brett and Anderson both leaned forward to see Gerard Lestrade sitting in his office with his arms folded. Anderson turned to Brett and said, "Am I correct in understanding that you confined the lead investigator to his office right in the middle of a full-scale joint operation that you never even bothered to become informed of?"

"No, not exactly," Brett said. "I can explain, sir."

"The Metropolitan Police's reputation is in desperate need of a boost, Chief Inspector. I would suggest that firing the men responsible for cleaning up our filthiest streets is not a wise idea in these times." Sir Robert Anderson turned and went back toward the door, carefully stepping around the arms and legs of the Old Nichol Gang as left. Brett turned, glaring murderously at Lestrade, who folded his hands above his head and smiled widely back at him.

Thirty Six

When the morning sun came through the windows of the doctor's office and Holmes was still breathing, I began to feel as if he might survive.

Irene followed behind as I carried him to the carriage and set him in the back. She climbed up onto the gate and kneeled down beside him as I went to the front and began to drive. At one point I turned back to check on them and saw that Irene had laid Holmes's head on her lap and she was gently stroking his face.

The front door to 221 Baker Street was boarded shut. I thought of the soft, weeping man I'd been when last crossing that threshold how he would recoil in shock as I pried off the wooden slats with my bare hands. Shards and jagged nails gouged my flesh, but I tore and yanked each plank until they came loose from the frame. I carried Holmes from the carriage and up the staircase to our old apartment to lay him in his bed.

I wiped his face with a damp cloth and said, "Rest, my friend. I will give you something to assist you." I rolled up his sleeve and retrieved the bottle and syringe from my pocket. I put the needle into the vial and began to draw it into the chamber, about to inject him when his eyes suddenly flew open and he covered his arm.

"Give me no more of that, Watson," he wheezed. "I will manage."

"This is a special circumstance, Holmes. I promise it will not-"

"I said no. Please. Take it away." He folded his hands on his stomach, just below the sutures and winced as he breathed. "I have not survived this night just to succumb again to the very things that nearly cost me everything. I will never again surrender my faculties."

"If that is what you wish, Holmes. I will stay close in case the pain becomes too much."

"You saved me, Watson," he said, turning to look at me. "I always knew you were a good friend, but who could have guessed you were such a remarkable doctor?"

I laughed, for the first time in what felt like forever.

Irene came into the room and sat next to him on the bed. She laid down beside him and nestled into the crook of his arm. I realized I did not belong there. I left the bedroom and shut the door to sit in my old chair and stoke the fireplace.

He was certainly a handsome bastard, I had to admit. Well dressed, with a long, spotless coat and black leather shoes decorated with bright silver buckles. I had given up such a pair at the pawn shop in Whitechapel and traded them for the dirty brown boots I was still wearing while I spiked on Mary. I peeked around the corner to watch this gentlemanly fellow escort Mary to her door.

"Good evening then, Miss Morstan," he said. He tipped his hat at her as she ascended the steps to her house.

"Good evening, Edmund."

He paused, and by his shy smile I knew he was only a breath away from asking for some further token of her affection. I was not confident enough that she would say no, so I came around the corner and said, "Well, well, hello."

The man flinched at the sight of me. "Oh God," he muttered and stuffed his hand inside of his pocket. "Run inside, Mary!" he said. "Do not harm us, you scoundrel. Here! Take the money and be gone from here." He thrust a handful of coins toward me, rattling them like seeds you would feed to an animal in a zoo.

I laughed at him and turned toward Mary. "May I speak with you?"

She folded her arms and looked at me sternly. "I do not see why I should, John Watson."

"Wait. You know this person?" he said, scowling.

"I am her fiancé," I said. "She is my intended bride."

"Is that so? You really have the nerve to still think so?" she said.

"You're engaged to this…this…ruffian?"

"That she is, mate," I said. "Madly in love we are."

"Now see here," he said, lifting his cane defensively. "You have no business just barging up on us like that. I have been in Miss Morstan's acquaintance for several weeks now and she has not mentioned you once!" He tapped me on the chest with its thick brass end and said, "Slink back to whatever part of the East End you crawled forth from and leave us alone! I should warn you that I am trained in *baritsu*!"

I looked up the stairs at Mary. "Is that what you want?" She did not answer.

"Of course that's what she wants!" He poked me in the chest with the cane again and I snatched it out of his hands. I grabbed him by the neck and threw him against the wall.

He bleated and squirmed when I lifted the cane to his face. "If she weren't here I'd stick this thing inside of you and break the tip off. You get me? Now piss off before I lose my temper, fancy boy."

"Both of you stop it!" Mary shouted. "Everything is all right, Edmund. Please just go home."

He looked at her in bewilderment. I handed him his cane back and said, "Sorry, mate. Have a good evening."

Mary waited for him to go and turned on me with blazing eyes, "I have never been so ashamed in all of my life, John Watson."

"You have every right to be angry," I said. "I did not mean to just come barging back into your life like this. I would have written you a letter first if I thought you'd have read it."

"I wouldn't have," she said. "You are a cruel, cruel man to vanish like that without a single word. If I did love you, which I do not, how do you think I felt after not hearing from you for so long?"

I went up the stairs and put my hands on hers. "I do not know how to tell you all of the things that happened to me in Whitechapel. I just needed to say that there was a moment when my life was ending and you were the thing I thought about. My single regret about dying was that I'd never get the chance to see you again. You can send me away if you wish. I just wanted you to know that."

She waited a moment without speaking. "So is it finished, then?"

"No," I said. "There is still much left to do, but if you will have me, it is nothing that will ever take me from your side again. I promise."

"No more racing off into the night after the evil-doers of London?"

"No more."

"What else is there then? I do not see us making a return to high-society and surviving long around people like Edmund."

I frowned and said, "Would you want that?"

She smiled slightly and said, "No. My God but he was a bore."

"I was thinking about starting a practice that affords me the chance to heal those in need. All I need is a home and a woman. A wonderful, wonderful woman who I hold tightly every night, as if it were my last."

Mary reached out and touched my face, running her finger gently across my lip. "You know, I never did like you with that mustache," she said.

Thirty Seven

"I ain't got the money to pay yeh, Dr. Watson," the woman said. Her little boy bent forward and coughed forcefully into his hand. I kneeled to him and touched his forehead.

Mary looked down at their chart. "They live next to the lodging house on Dorset that's been quarantined with the fever."

"Thank you, Mrs. Watson," I said. "Stick out your tongue, lad." The boy did as I asked, and I saw green spots covering the surface of his mouth. "He needs a rather expensive medicine and he needs it quickly, I'm afraid. Are you working?"

She looked down at the ground for a moment and shuffled her foot back and forth. "Here and there, sir. Whatever it takes to make the doss, if yeh catch me meaning."

I looked at Mary, who nodded and pointed to a stack of boxes in the corner. "Do you read?" The woman nodded. "Good. Do you see those boxes of patient files? We need someone to organize them and put them into alphabetical order while Dr. Watson examines your son. Start with that and then I will have more work for you."

"Thank yeh. So, so much. Everything they say is true," she said, hurrying over to the boxes. I led the boy to my examination chair and lifted him up, mussing his hair and smiling before I went to the cabinet and found the proper medicine.

At five o'clock the church bells of Spitalfields rang and I closed the door to my office and locked it. As Mary and I walked arm-in-arm to the train station, I tipped my hat to those who greeted me by name along the way. When I went to purchase our tickets, the conductor shook his head and smiled. "You don't ever pay on my train, Dr. Watson. It's an honor to have you on board. Please enjoy your ride."

That night I travelled to Baker Street where Mrs. Hudson answered the front door and smiled at me warmly. "Good evening, sir. How have you been?"

"Excellent, Mrs. Hudson, thank you." I went up the stairs and when I entered 221 B, I had to walk between stacks of carefully arranged papers on the floor. Every available surface was covered in carefully arranged papers.

Holmes was sitting on the floor in front of the fireplace, writing quietly. He did not look up as I greeted him, but continued staring intently at the page when he said, "What the deuce is the name of that fellow from New York who wrote to me? The one with questions about how to reform their police department?"

I squeezed my eyes, trying to remember the name on a letter that had arrived what seems like a lifetime ago. "Was it Roosevelt?"

"Yes!" Holmes said, writing the name "*Theodore Roosevelt*" on his paper. "He is making a bid to be Commissioner of Police there, and I think he may find some of the things I am working on quite useful." As Holmes looked over what he wrote, I noticed him absent-mindedly stroking the long vertical scar on his chest through the opening in his robe. After two years, it was still a deep purple line of raised flesh. Holmes nodded in satisfaction as he finished reading and lowered his pen. "There we are. So, how goes the crusade?"

"It goes, I suppose. Some weeks we can actually afford to leave the lights on and heat the place."

"I am certain you could improve your situation if you ever chose to move your office to a location that had citizens who could actually afford your services," he said. "But then what would the people of Whitechapel do without their dear Saint John?"

I laughed. "Perhaps someday, my friend. Just not today." I looked at the stacks of papers and said, "So what is all this, then?"

"This is the bare beginnings of the Apiary Society, Watson. The most ambitious thing I have ever attempted. Now, if only I can somehow manage to extract every thought pent up inside my brain fast enough to set it down on paper before I perish, I will succeed."

"Is Irene helping you?" I asked. As I walked further into the apartment, I noticed it had been redecorated since my last visit. No, that was not quite accurate. It had been un-decorated. The fancy curtains, lace doilies, flower vases, and everything else that Irene Adler had brought to 221 B were gone. And then I realized that so was she. "Good God, man. Are you all right?"

He ignored me. "So how is Mrs. Watson? Still helping you at the clinic?"

"Only for a short while longer, I'm afraid."

He put down the paper with a look of concern. "Is she ill?"

"No," I said. "She's pregnant."

Perhaps you have heard of Sherlock Holmes, before all this.

I certainly did my share to inform the world about the existence of a man I considered the keenest investigative mind of our era. Any era, really. Over the years, I published fifty-six short stories and four novels featuring the adventures he and I shared. Some of them were even true.

During the course of my publishing career, I encountered numerous legal difficulties in accurately depicting our investigations, and protecting myself from lawsuits brought about by the parties involved in them. It became so tricky, in terms of last minute changes forced by attorneys, that when I look back over my writings as they appeared in print, I am horrified by some of the mistakes.

One incident stands out in my mind, when the printer referred to my wife by her middle name and my loyal readership assumed my first wife had died and I'd remarried. I subsequently began receiving condolence cards from people who wished to apologize for not attending the funeral.

Not all of the problems were caused by editors or lawyers.

There was simply not enough money to keep the clinic open and continue to afford a roof over our heads. I spread the ledger across the kitchen table, recalculating the numbers grimly. I already knew the answer would be the same as the other times I'd done it. I lifted the book and shook it, looking to see if I'd misplaced anything that might be of use. There was nothing.

"John!" Mary cried from the living room.

I leapt from my seat, racing to her side. Her stomach looked ready to burst, and she sat on the couch, taking short, sharp breaths. "Is it time? Are you contracting?"

"No," she said, grimacing. "The baby is walloping my ribs though. Someone is at the door. Would you mind?"

"At this time of night?" I said. There was the enormous shape of a man filling the door's window. I told Mary that I would only be a few moments.

"Good evening, Watson," Mycroft Holmes said. "We need to talk."

Mary stroked her belly worryingly, looking at me from the couch. I nodded to her and went out onto the porch and closed the door behind me. Mycroft waved for me to follow him away from the steps. As we walked I said, "I'd invite you in for tea, Mycroft, but Mary does not feel well."

"I did not come for tea, Watson. Your publisher's office caught fire this evening. He managed to barely escape with his life."

"That's horrible!"

"Mmm," he said. "Seems that someone put the idea into his head that your latest manuscript is to blame. He's opted not to publish it after all."

"What? My manuscript? But that's preposterous. He cannot do that," I said. "We have a contract and I was relying on that money. I'll need to find another publisher straight away."

Mycroft fixed his tiny black eyes on me, "His was the example the others will go by, Watson. No one will publish *WHITECHAPEL* from here to across the pond. Do you understand?"

"It was you, wasn't it?" I said, balling my fists. "Damn you, Mycroft! Why? I left you out of the other stories. You do little more than sit in your damned Diogenes Club in any of them. Why are you so threatened by this story?"

"It wasn't me," Mycroft said sadly. "And there is nothing I can do to stop them. This time it was your publisher's office." His eyes glanced back at the doorway to my home where Mary stood in the window watching us. "Who knows what it might be next time?"

I lowered my head. "At times I feel like there is something deeply wrong in the world, Mycroft."

"That is because there is, my friend." He put a massive hand across my shoulder and said, "It may come as only a small comfort, but I do have some good news. Her Majesty allowed me to add an item into my budget for an intelligence office in the East End. I'll need a good front for the operation. I was thinking a medical clinic that caters to the poor and unfortunate would be perfect. What do you say, Watson? All the medicine and equipment you could ever need, courtesy of Queen Victoria?" He reached into his pocket and produced a cheque from the Bank of London. It was issued by a company called, "Universal Export."

I looked at the cheque and the enormous amount written on it for a long time. "Is this the price of keeping secrets, Mycroft? Is this how much it costs to keep people from ever knowing the truth about Jack the Ripper?"

"One gets used to keeping secrets, Watson," he said. "If there is anything I've learned after all these years, it is that you have to choose your battles. Some things are much more important than the truth."

Mycroft raised his hand and waved to Mary before turning to walk up the street.

Thirty Eight

On the day John Watson II was born, I sat kneeling on the floor beside the delivery bed and watched him suckle Mary's breast. I put my finger inside his hand, and as he held it, I knew for the first time what it truly meant to be afraid. In all of the times I had faced danger, or even death, the fear had been momentary and was quickly replaced by a laughing satisfaction at having overcome it once again.

This small, fragile creature clutching to his mother's breast was more vulnerable and more valuable than anything in existence, and at any moment the cruel hand of fate could reach out and try to snatch him away. As I stroked his head, feeling the soft spot at the center of his skull and the fine, silken hair there, I made private promises to God, Mary, the baby and myself. The midwife knocked on our door and asked if we were taking visitors. "Who could that be?" Mary said, covering herself.

The door opened and I turned to see our visitor. His tall, slender form was now slightly stooped and he did not come any closer than the doorway or take off his hat or coat. "I only wanted to offer you any assistance if you required it," Sherlock Holmes said. "Everyone is all right, I trust?"

"Yes, yes, of course," I said. I got to my feet and waved him in. "Come inside, Holmes, do not be afraid. Have a look, man. We had a boy! This is my son!"

Holmes hesitated but did finally come in. He got close enough to the bed to look down at John and say, "I see he looks much more like his mother. Which is quite lucky for him, I should think." He flashed me a mischievous smile and I laughed.

"Do you want to hold him?" Mary said.

"Me? No, no, of course I couldn't. I just wanted to—"

"Nonsense," she said, sitting up. "You are to be the boy's godfather after all."

"I am?" Holmes said, looking at me.

"I hadn't had time to ask you officially, but there is no one else we would think of asking."

He did not move as I lifted the baby and instructed him how to hold out his arms. I laid John on them and let go as Holmes nervously adjusted his hands to better hold him. "So innocent. So soft," Holmes said quietly.

"Do not look so nervous, man," I said. "Has it been that long since you held a baby?"

"I've never done so," he said. "I've never cared to until now."

In all my years with Sherlock Holmes, I'd never known him to laugh unless it was at something he found foolish. Imagine my amusement at watching him cackle like a schoolboy every time John stuck his slobbery fingers into his mouth. Holmes would shake his head in mock disgust and John would shriek with delight and do it again. Holmes kissed the boy on the forehead and hugged him in a tight embrace. "You are very, very fortunate, Watson. I wish I'd found the time to start a family."

"You still could, my good man," I said. "Mary and I could arrange to introduce you to a few of the women she knows. You could make me a godfather as well."

Holmes wrinkled his nose at the thought, shaking his head. "What woman would suit me, Watson? Who would put up with me? In all my life, there has only ever been one, and I sent her away."

It was the most he'd ever spoken about Irene since she'd left. I was stunned. "It was you who sent her away? I always thought…"

He looked at me for a moment and his keen eyes pierced me. I realized that the tone of my voice had told the Great Detective more than I ever had about my own feelings for her. "Yes, Watson. Someone like her would not be content to stay huddled up in an upstairs apartment on Baker Street. But we have remained in contact. She has contributed greatly to the creation of the Apiary Society."

"What the bloody deuce is this 'Apiary Society,' Holmes? You mention it but never explain what it is, or what it does. Are you creating a secret society of bee keepers, or something?"

"In due time, Watson," he said, bouncing John on his knee. "Do you want to be a beekeeper, John?" he said to the boy while they both laughed. "Oh, yes, you do. A fine one you will make at that. A fine one, indeed."

That was nearly twenty years ago.

Now, my life is filled with simple things and simple pleasures. I enjoy daily walks from our country cottage to the nearby market while watching the sun rise over wheat fields that stand taller than I. Along the way I take long, deep breaths of air that is blessedly free of the fumes and damp stench of London.

At the market, I tip my hat at the young woman who runs a fruit stand. "Good morning, Mrs. Carter. How are you?"

"Call me Abbie, Dr. Watson. Yeh needs not be so formal at this early hour," she laughs. The basket she hands me is filled to the brim with fresh fruit. When no one else is around, she reverts to her natural cockney accent. Last summer, while speaking to her, I detected a trace of it and asked if she'd ever been a resident of London's East End.

She eyed me suspiciously for a moment, then said, "Yes, back when I was a girl, sir. What makes you ask?"

I eventually told her a few things about my time in Whitechapel. Not nearly all of it. Just enough.

"Made sure yeh got the best of 'a the bunch," she says. Abbie then leans close to me and whispers, "Just promise to bring tha' handsome son of yours around. I likes to look at him."

"I promise to do so tomorrow," I said, smiling. "Good day, Abbie."

Twenty years, I muse. At times, things that happened then seem more in the present to me than anything that has happened recently. I find myself reminiscing in full detail about conversations or events long since passed, yet I am unable to recall the complete list of items Mary sent me out to pick up just an hour ago.

Not everyone has made it this far on the journey with me.

At times it seems as my dreams are more real to me than anything that happens when I am awake.

I am sitting in my old chair at 221 B Baker Street.

The fireplace is lit, but I am shivering with cold. Holmes sits across from me with a look of deep concern etched across his face. "You do not belong here, Watson," he says. "Not yet."

"I only came to tell you about John. He did the most remarkable thing yesterday," I say quickly. It is always a good tactic to win his sympathy and get him to allow me just a few more moments there, at his side.

Holmes sighs, "All right. You know I cannot resist hearing about my godson."

But then I cannot remember anything to tell him. "I lied, Holmes. The truth is, I only wanted to see you again."

He smiles gently and shakes his head. "You cannot stay here, Watson, for I am dead."

I remember how John wept at the funeral. Such a strong and virile lad, but there he stood, crying like a child. "Where is his violin? He should have his violin," John said. "It should be in the casket with him."

"No, it should not," I said. "I was going to wait until the will was read to tell you, but he wanted you to have it. He always said you were twice the violinist he was."

John lowered his head into Mary's waiting arms. As she patted him on the back she pointed over my shoulder at the front door and said, "People are arriving, dear. You should attend to them."

A group of men came in, the first of whom used a cane, and was somewhat bulkier than he'd been when I last saw him. However, the solemn face of Gerard Lestrade was unmistakable. I extended my hand and said, "Welcome to Sussex Downs, Detective Superintendent."

"It's just Gerard now, Watson. I retired several years ago. Thought I'd leave crime-fighting up to these young lads." Lestrade cocked his head at the men following behind him.

"So what do you do to occupy yourself now?"

He shrugged and said, "My three grandchildren keep me busy. The littlest one says he wants to join Scotland Yard someday. Over my dead body, I say."

I patted him on the shoulder and pointed him toward the casket. I shook hands with the next man and said, "I feel as if I should be saluting you. What exactly is your rank now, Fred?"

Lamb leaned around Wensley's side and said, "He's the bloody Chief of the entire Criminal Investigative Division. A posh big shot out in headquarters now. One of the most decorated members ever in the whole history of the damned force."

I shook hands with Lamb. "And surely, you must be Chief Inspector by now?"

Wensley sighed and said, "I keep trying to steal him over to headquarters with me but he refuses to be promoted."

"I am quite happy to be a sergeant, thank you very much," Lamb said. "Nothing would suit me better than going out like Old Byfield did. Boots up on the desk, snoozing, and never wake up. It's too much work to be an Inspector."

Wensley shook his head. "That's what he tells everyone, but the real truth is that he is the finest mentor of young constables we have. He won't even let me take him out of Whitechapel."

"And who is this gentleman?" I asked, indicating the man standing behind Lamb. He looked familiar to me but I could not place him. I racked my brain trying to remember where I'd seen him before, when suddenly it dawned on me that he was Police Commissioner of the London Metropolitan Police. "My word, Sir Henry! It is a pleasure to meet you."

Henry shook my hand pleasantly. "Hello, Doctor Watson, my cousin Lamb has told me much about you and your little adventures together. In a way, I have all of you to thank for my success. If not for that, I'd still be stuck with the Bengal Police."

I looked at him in confusion for a moment. "I cannot agree with that, sir. Everyone knows you created an entire fingerprint classification system while working as nothing more than an Assistant Tax Collector in India. Your system has single-handedly changed the face of criminal investigations the world over."

The three of them laughed as they followed Lestrade toward the casket to pay their respects. More people had begun filtering in and I was quickly greeting so many that I lost track of new arrivals. Even through the throng of people, the enormous shape of Mycroft Holmes stood out. My eyes widened when I saw that he had his arm around my son, and the two were huddled in the corner. "John!" I called out. "John! Come here at once. Your mother needs you."

John looked at me from across the room and said something to Mycroft. The two of them shook hands and I heard John say, "I will." Whatever he'd just agreed to made Mycroft smile broadly.

I pointed John toward Mary and turned to Mycroft. "He will what?" I said. "What have you been telling my son?"

Mycroft looked bored by my attempt to stare him down. "I was simply discussing the boy's opportunities with him for when he graduates Oxford."

"I will discuss them with him, thank you," I said sharply. "Do not try to lure that boy into your world. I'm warning you. Stay away from my son."

"Settle down, Watson. It was not for service to Her Majesty, but rather to my deceased brother. Sherlock told me there is much potential to be found in the boy as a member of the Apiary Society. He will need the right guidance though."

"I have had just about enough of this mysterious 'Apiary Society!' Now my son is being recruited into it, and I still have no idea what they are or what they do! Holmes said I would find out someday but apparently I'll have to wait until I am standing next to Saint Peter now to ask him."

"He never told you because he did not want to tempt you into running off on another adventure with him, Watson. He knew that your heart lies in being with your family, but he was afraid you might feel compelled to take off with him out of loyalty. You are not only a member of the Apiary Society, you are one of its founders."

"So what is it, Mycroft?"

He put his massive arm around me and hugged me tightly. "That is another story, my friend. Another story, for another time."

We were near enough to the front door that I felt a chill wind blow across the back of my neck when it opened. I saw Mycroft's wide face grow flush as he whispered, "My word, age has not diminished her at all, has it?"

I did not need to ask, because I already knew.

I turned toward the front door, and there she was. There was a thick scarf wrapped around her neck and tossed over her shoulder casually, as if it were nothing but a fashionable affectation. I knew its true intent was to conceal the jagged scar across her throat. The rest of her was draped in black. It was the kind of outfit a widow would wear to her husband's funeral.

Irene looked older. Her once perfect features were now lined, but above the sagging skin of her cheeks, her eyes gleamed fiercely as she and I looked at one another.

I felt my heart pound, cursing the way my legs weakened at seeing her. "Hello, Irene," I said.

"Hello, John."

We were about to politely embrace one another when I saw a young woman coming through the door to stand behind Irene. This girl had dark, chestnut brown hair that curled down to her shoulders. Her face was exquisite, so reminiscent of Irene's younger self that I gasped. And that is when I saw the girl's pronouncedly bent nose.

She was taller than Irene, more slender. She had a keen, piercing stare that I had not seen since the man in the coffin had last closed his eyes, and I opened my mouth to speak, but no words came out.

Mary came up beside me and Irene said, "Hello, Mrs. Watson. It is lovely to finally meet you. I have heard so much about you."

Mary cocked an eyebrow at her and said, "You have? And what is your name, dear?"

"Irene," she said. "Irene Adler."

Mary looked at her blankly. "Were you an acquaintance of Mr. Holmes and my husband's?"

Irene did not speak for a moment. I cleared my throat and Irene finally said, "Yes. Yes, from back when they lived on Baker Street. They helped me once. This is my daughter Johanna."

Mary smiled at the girl and said, "My goodness, what a ravishing beauty! I have someone to introduce to you."

Irene and I watched Mary escort Johanna by the hand through the crowd to find my son. I felt her staring at me without needing to turn my head. "You never told your wife about me?" Irene said. "Not a single word?"

I turned on her and said, "Did you ever tell Holmes he had a daughter?"

Both of us turned to see Mary lead Johanna Adler up to John and introduce the two of them. He looked at her, and I watched the boy's reaction as she lifted her hand and he lowered his lips to kiss it. Johanna smiled at him delicately when he looked back up at her. "Christ. The poor boy is doomed," I whispered.

Irene laughed and very casually put her hand against my elbow. It was the lightest of touches but it scored me hotter than all hell's flames. "Could you imagine the possibilities, John?" Irene said.

I looked at the young couple standing across the room and said, "I suppose stranger things have happened."

Thirty Nine

On December Thirty-First in 1888, a man's body was fished from the dark waters of the River Thames. At the time, that was all anyone knew of the bloated, blackened corpse found snagged on vegetation around the pillars of the pier at Thorneycroft's Warf.

The authorities estimated the man had been in the Thames for several weeks, but after being exposed that long to the pollution and river wildlife, the body barely resembled anything human. Several heavy stones were found inside the pockets of his clothing. It was assumed to be a suicide.

At the coroner's inquest, a man named Will Druitt appeared before the board to identify the victim as his missing brother, Montague. The newspapers reported that Mr. Druitt swore out a statement that his brother was "sexually insane" and that "Monty" had been dismissed from his position at George Valentine's School just prior for a "serious transgression."

By the sheer timing of his death and his body's proximity to Whitechapel, Montague Druitt was cast Montague Druitt headfirst into the Ripper mystery. Sport has been made of speculating why Druitt was fired from his job at the school. It normally ends with the implication that he was caught having an unhealthy relationship with one of the young male students.

Will Druitt produced a letter he claimed was written by Montague which read: *"Since Friday I felt that I was going to be like mother, and the best thing was for me to die."*

No attempts were ever made to authenticate the letter. No one saw a need to.

All that the world truly knows is that this quiet, lonely man named Montague Druitt lived until the age of thirty one. They know he died under mysterious circumstances. And they think he might have been Jack the Ripper. But Druitt is not alone in this. In fact, a whole cast of suspects has been paraded in front of a never-weary audience that regularly gathers to celebrate their elegant, romantic anti-hero.

Montague Druitt was not Jack the Ripper.

Many experts will tell you that. There are those who will authoritatively tell you why the killer was actually Lewis Carroll, or Walter Sickert, or William Gull. There are hundreds of experts with thousands of theories. Some even spice it up with a little Royal Family conspiracy, or suspicions implicating the Freemasons.

A variety of flavors is readily available for the discerning Ripper connoisseur.

All that is said for certain is that in 1888, from Friday, the thirty-first of August, to Friday, the ninth of November, five women were killed. Some were disemboweled. Some were harvested for specific organs significant to no one but the killer himself.

That is it. Officially.

Officially, the Jack the Ripper killings ended with the death of Mary Jane Kelly at Thirteen Miller's Court, with no hope of ever definitively solving the crimes. But you and I know better. And nothing ended.

On the fourth day of June in 1889, three young boys were bathing in the Thames near Battersea Park when a severed limb went floating past them. Other remains were soon discovered in Horselydown. Police became inundated with reports of an armless, hollowed out torso found near Covington's Wharf and a lower right leg washed up on the shore near Wandsworth Bridge. Arms, hands, buttocks, a pelvis, a liver and other organs all began popping up on the surface of the Thames all along the countryside. The victim was eventually identified as a missing homeless woman named Elizabeth Jackson. The killing remains unsolved.

On the sixteenth of July 1889, a Whitechapel prostitute named Alice McKenzie was killed by having her belly slit open. There were several stab marks to her genitalia. The killer was believed to have some degree of anatomical knowledge but not the skill of Jack the Ripper. The killing remains unsolved.

On the tenth of September 1889, a new torso was discovered under a railway arch on Pinchin Street. Its abdomen was heavily mutilated and the remains were never identified. The killing also remains unsolved.

And then, finally, on the twenty-fourth of April 1891, the body of an American prostitute named Carrie Brown was found mutilated in a room at the East River Hotel in Manhattan. The autopsy documented how her killer tried to gut her completely. Much to everyone's relief, the American police proved much more adept at arresting suspects than their English counterparts. New York City Police Detectives swiftly arrested an Algerian named Ameer Ben Ali in a nearby hotel room.

Bloodstains were found in Ben Ali's hotel room that matched the ones at the murder scene. Ben Ali was tried and convicted of the murder and promptly sent off to prison for what was thought to be the remainder of his life.

Eleven years later, an investigation into the murder investigation revealed that the bloody footprints found in Ben Ali's hotel room were brought there by the detectives who had just left the body. Ameer Bal Ali was released from prison and vanished into history. The real killer of Carrie Brown remains at large.

Sometimes I wonder, what is Jack the Ripper?

Crazed killer preying on the downtrodden or progenitor of an entire cultural movement? I might suggest he is both. If Jack had been famous for painting, rather than killing, we would refer to those who picked up his mantle and continued his work as the students and successors of a genre-defining grandmaster.

"Jack," you see, was neither Druitt, or Gull, or Sickert, or any of the usual suspects. Not any more than he is you, or me. I was there. I saw the results first-hand of Druitt's madness, and there is no doubt that the Ripper was birthed by Druitt's actions during that horrible autumn.

I'd argue that his true self manifested in the countless newspapers scurrying to cover every detail as if it were the most sensational event in all of history.

He festered in the mischievous minds of those who wrote fake "Ripper" letters for nothing but the thrill of partaking in the events surrounding the case. Jack the Ripper was formed in the consciousness of the gossip-hungry citizens of the world who fed on each prurient detail and harvested the body of evidence more hungrily than Jack ever did on his victims.

Long, stringing innards of fact were removed well after they'd grown cold and gray. Any tendons attaching those facts to reality were severed under the sharp knife of speculation. The tastiest organs were plucked out, and we savored each delicious bite. Dishes of this particular fare are still served, so many years later.

You are eating some right now.

These will be the last words written by Dr. John H. Watson. I will finish this manuscript while sitting in my rocking chair on the porch of the country cottage I share with my beloved wife of these many years. Mary is inside the house right now, making tea. When she finishes it, she will bring it out and sit in the chair beside me. We will not speak, but we will hold hands, and look out together over the fields of amber grain.

It has been a good life.

From my chair, I watch John walking to the far end of our property while arm-in-arm with Johanna Adler. Her beautiful features remind me at once of two people I have loved and lost.

They look happy. They look like they are sharing things that young people only tell one another when they are truly in love. John leans forward to whisper in Johanna's ear, and she wraps her arms around him in a passionate embrace.

Could it be that some strange twist of fate winds up intertwining all of us?

For a moment, I imagine that particular future, and am astonished at the possibilities it reveals. I chide myself for being foolish to even consider it.

"How often have I said to you that when you have eliminated the impossible, whatever remains, however improbable, must be the truth, Watson?"

I turn in my chair to see Holmes sitting beside me. He looks young. Vibrant. Alive.

There is a soft rustle of wind that crosses the porch, carrying the scent of lilacs. "Am I dreaming again, Holmes?" I say.

"No, Watson." he says. "Not this time, I'm afraid."

"Is it time, then?" I say.

He stands up and buttons his long houndstooth coat. "Indeed it is, my dear fellow. What do you say? Once more unto the breach?"

"Of course," I say. I look down at someone lying crumpled on the porch beneath my feet, and suddenly our little cottage is far below us and far away. The fields surrounding it glow in hues of both red and gold that across the countryside. I see London, with her tall buildings casting shadows on the people below.

There are people lurking in those shadows who make sport of the weak and vulnerable, preying on them for sport. And there are those who make it their business to seek out those who would harm the innocent and bring them to task.

The sun has nearly set now, and it is time for me to go.

Author's Dedication

For the victims of Whitechapel,

both then and since.

You are not forgotten.